Praise for *Hannah's Choice*

"*Hannah's Choice* is a compelling story of family and place that demonstrates how choices in life can be both difficult and exciting. Jan Drexler's Amish family is so engaging that we're right there with them, sitting down at their supper table, sharing their joys and sorrows as they embrace the adventure of life. A great read for anyone who enjoys a page-turning mix of appealing characters, exciting story action, sweet romance, and interesting history."

—**Ann H. Gabhart**, bestselling author of *The Innocent*

"A new historical romance with family dysfunction and well-written characters who are caring and strong-willed, both in body and mind. The story will leave fans wanting more. Drexler weaves a beautiful storyline, and her research makes it shine."

—*RT Book Reviews*

"This is a compelling story that speaks on depression and family ties, as well as looks into the historical and Amish setting. The story is a definite page-turner."

—*Parkersburg News & Sentinel*

MATTIE'S
PLEDGE

Other books in the
Journey to Pleasant Prairie series

Hannah's Choice
Naomi's Hope

MATTIE'S PLEDGE

A NOVEL

Jan Drexler

Revell

a division of Baker Publishing Group
Grand Rapids, Michigan

© 2016 by Jan Drexler

Published by Revell
a division of Baker Publishing Group
P.O. Box 6287, Grand Rapids, MI 49516-6287
www.revellbooks.com

Printed in the United States of America

Library of Congress Cataloging-in-Publication Data
Names: Drexler, Jan, author.
Title: Mattie's pledge : a novel / Jan Drexler.
Description: Grand Rapids, MI : Revell, a division of Baker Publishing Group,
    [2016] | Series: Journey to Pleasant Prairie ; 2
Identifiers: LCCN 2016020553 | ISBN 9780800726577 (pbk.)
Subjects: | GSAFD: Christian fiction. | Love stories.
Classification: LCC PS3604.R496 M38 2016 | DDC 813/.6—dc23
LC record available at https://lccn.loc.gov/2016020553

Author is represented by WordServe Literary Group.

Baker Publishing Group publications use paper produced from sustainable forestry practices and post-consumer waste whenever possible.

To my great-grandmother,
Bessie Ellen Schrock Sherck,
in whose eyes I saw Mattie's dreams.
Thank you for your faithfulness to God
and our family.

Soli Deo Gloria

Shepherd your people with your staff,
    the flock of your inheritance,
who dwell alone in a forest
    in the midst of a garden land;
let them graze in Bashan and Gilead
    as in the days of old.
As in the days when you came out of the land
      of Egypt,
    I will show them marvelous things.

                              Micah 7:14–15

1

"Mattie."

Mattie Schrock ignored her sister, intent on the flutter of wings she spied through the branches of the tree, pulling her attention from wringing the water out of *Daed*'s shirt. She leaned as far toward the edge of the covered porch as she could, her toes clinging to the worn wooden planks. The bird wouldn't hold still. What kind was it?

"It's your turn to hang the laundry. I have to help *Mamm* get dinner ready." Naomi shoved the basket of wet clothes toward the porch steps with her foot.

Mattie gave up on identifying the bird. Hanging laundry wasn't her favorite chore, even though it meant she was able to be in the yard instead of in the hot kitchen. She picked up the heavy basket and rested it on her hip as she took the bag of clothes pegs from the hook next to the porch steps. "It's your turn next time, then."

Naomi pulled the stopper from the washtub and let the

water drain onto the flower bed in the yard below the porch. "I'd rather hang clothes than work inside today. The weather is so lovely and warm after the days of rain we've had."

Mattie stopped with one foot on the bottom step. "Why did you insist I take my turn, then? You can hang the laundry if you want to."

"*Ne.*" Naomi shook her head and wiped out the empty tub with a rag. "Fair is fair. It's your turn." She gave Mattie a smile. "I know how much you like to be outside."

She hung the washtub on the wall and turned to the rinse tub. Naomi was tall and slender, the opposite of Mattie's own short stockiness. Her hair, which had turned to a soft brown during the winter months, was beginning to lighten to its summer blond where it peeked out from under her *kapp*. Naomi worked with a spare efficiency that wasted no motions. She hung the rinse tub on the wall next to its mate, draped the rag over its hook, and started toward the back door, but stopped when she saw Mattie.

"You haven't even begun yet. What are you doing, standing there? Daydreaming again?"

"You'll be a wonderful wife someday."

Naomi turned her face away. "Are you sure God's plan isn't for me to remain single? A *maidle* caring for Mamm and Daed in their old age?"

Mattie pulled her bottom lip between her teeth. She shouldn't have said anything. "There is someone for you. Someone wonderful."

"You're kind to say so. But don't worry about me." Naomi fingered the door latch. "I'll be content, no matter what happens." She slipped inside the house.

Mattie shifted the heavy basket on her hip and crossed the

yard to the line strung between the porch roof and the big oak tree. Naomi had never had a beau. The boys who vied for Mattie's attention never noticed Naomi except to enjoy her pies. They never teased her to join their games or asked her to go for a buggy ride on a spring evening. She didn't mention it, but Mattie knew the slights bothered her. She had heard her sister crying in the middle of the night when Naomi thought no one would hear, especially after Mattie had been for a buggy ride with Andrew Bontrager. There must be someone for Naomi.

Lowering the basket to the ground, Mattie picked up the first shirt, shook it to release the wrinkles, then pegged it to the line.

If the boys ignored her, she wouldn't be as calm as Naomi. At eighteen years old, Naomi should be planning her wedding. She should be filling her wedding chest with quilts and bedding, but Naomi kept herself busy helping Mamm or their sister Annie, or one of their sisters-in-law. She never took time to plan for her own future. She never made anything for herself.

Mattie stopped, a peg halfway onto the line, an apron forgotten in her hands. Why not make something for Naomi's wedding chest herself? She pushed the peg onto the line with a firm shove. Because she could never sit still enough to finish any needlework. Her own quilt was barely started.

As she finished hanging the apron and reached for a dress wadded in the basket, an idea swirled through her mind. She could finish that quilt for Naomi. That would show her sister she had faith that there would be a husband for her, that she wouldn't remain a maidle forever.

As she hung the last few items of laundry, Mattie tried

to remember where the pieces for her quilt might be. Not in her own chest. She had packed it yesterday for their coming move to Indiana.

At that thought, she looked toward the west. Even though the surrounding hills blocked her view, she could see the western mountains in her imagination. Any day now the folks from the Conestoga in Lancaster County would arrive in Brothers Valley, and then they would leave on their journey.

Now she remembered. The quilt had been packed. It was in the barrel, the one with the blue lid, where she had packed her winter shawl and heavy comforter. Daed had already taken it to the barn, but if she looked for it now, she could start working on it this afternoon. Naomi needn't know it was for her, she would think Mattie was continuing to sew her own neglected quilt.

Mattie took the basket and bag of clothes pegs back to the porch and hung them in their places. If only she could slip away to the barn before Mamm saw her. With her sister Annie, her husband, and their family coming to share dinner, Mamm would want Mattie's help. But she could find her quilt and be back before she was needed.

Running across the yard to the barn, Mattie stopped inside the big open door, catching her breath while she waited for her eyes to adjust to the dim interior. Daed stood on the far side of the center bay, silhouetted against the open door on the other end. Christopher, Annie's husband, stood facing him. Neither of them noticed Mattie.

"We're staying here."

Daed moved to the workbench and dropped a hammer on the wooden surface with a thump. When Mattie saw the expression on his face as he turned back to Christopher, she knew she should make herself scarce. She slid behind some boards standing against the wall next to the door.

"You can't stay here. Our family is going west in a few days. You and my daughter are coming with us."

Mattie peeked out between two of the boards. Eavesdropping was almost as great a sin as . . . as . . . Well, bad enough. She should leave or make her presence known. But she had to find out what was going on. Christopher held himself stiffly, his entire five and a half feet quivered as Daed stepped toward him, a frown on his face as he looked down on his son-in-law.

"We're staying." Christopher squared his shoulders. "I'm not taking my family to the wilderness. It's too dangerous."

"That isn't your only reason though, is it? I saw you talking with Peter Blank last Sunday. You're still in favor of building the meetinghouse."

"I am. I think it's time we let go of the past and move on toward the future. We no longer need to live like our ancestors, afraid of being arrested every time we meet. And hosting the church is too hard for some of the folks. A meetinghouse is the best solution."

"And the Mennonites have meetinghouses." Daed's sarcastic words cut the air.

"I'm not talking about becoming Mennonite. I'm Amish, and that won't change. My family will stay Amish, but we don't need to move to Indiana to do it."

Daed bowed his head, his shoulders sagging. "Annie agrees to this?"

"Of course. I wouldn't make a decision like this unless my wife agreed." Christopher scuffed his foot in the dust on the barn floor. "It isn't easy for either Annie or me, this separation. But we both know you and I would come to an impasse sooner or later. I believe with all my heart that we as Amish need to progress or die. Change is coming, Eli. You need to face that, not run away from it."

Daed's head shot up, his dark eyes lit with fire. "I'm not running. Indiana holds new opportunities for us. For all of us." His expression softened as his voice dropped. "Christopher, come with us. We want you and Annie close. We want to watch your Levi and little Katie grow up."

"Our minds are made up and talking won't change them." Christopher took a step back. "I'll help you load the wagons tomorrow."

"Send us on our way?" Daed turned back to the harness he had been mending, his voice again holding a bitter edge. "We don't need your help. You've made your choice."

Mattie wiped her eyes with the hem of her apron. Christopher hesitated for a few seconds, but when Daed didn't turn from his work, he left the barn.

Wiping her eyes again, Mattie started to follow him, but a sound from the workbench made her turn back. Daed leaned on his elbows, his face buried in his hands, his shoulders shaking as a quiet, sobbing groan escaped. Mattie slipped out the door.

She ran for the swimming hole, a spot where the willows and sycamores grew thick at a bend in the creek. The water in the wide elbow was deep and shaded. Cool on hot summer days, and secluded on this spring morning. She climbed her favorite sycamore, the one leaning toward the opposite bank, to a large branch hanging over the water. The old rope swing, dark brown and fraying, swayed in the gentle breeze.

Mattie settled herself on the wide branch and looked up

through the new spring leaves, just beginning to reach toward their length, but still a soft green. The leaves fluttered in the intermittent zephyrs, pale green alternating with the perfect blue sky. She wiped her eyes again.

She had seen this coming. Had wondered if Annie would ever be able to leave her home and her friends. But now that the time was here . . . why would Annie give up the chance to go west? The family had been talking about this move for months, with Christopher and Annie part of every discussion. Nearly every Sunday afternoon through the entire winter, the families had gathered together. Her older brothers, Isaac and Noah, with their wives and children, had stayed far into the evening many times as they talked over the best routes to Indiana, deciding what tools and furnishings they should take with them, what to leave behind, and how many wagons were needed for the four families. They had all listened as Daed told and retold the tale of his trip to Iowa and Indiana last summer. Christopher and Annie had been part of that planning . . . until the last few weeks.

Mattie leaned against the tree's trunk. The last few weeks, Christopher had sat silent while Daed and her brothers talked. Annie had volunteered to care for the little ones while Mamm and the rest of them had planned how much food to take and how to store it. Mattie blinked her eyes, vainly trying to keep the tears back. They must have decided they weren't going west weeks ago but hadn't told anyone.

A burning sensation rose in Mattie's breast, constricting her throat. If Annie hadn't married Christopher, this wouldn't be happening. If it wasn't for him, Annie would come west with them. She would walk behind the wagon with her sisters just as they had done when they came to

Brothers Valley from the Conestoga seven years ago. They would play games as they walked, and make up stories—

Mattie drove the thoughts away. She couldn't change Christopher's mind, and it was no use blaming him for making a decision he thought was best for his family.

But, oh! If only he had decided to come with them. What did Amish have to do with new ways and meetinghouses anyway?

Swinging one foot, Mattie stroked the sycamore's smooth trunk. When summer came, the branches of the surrounding willows would brush the ground, mingling with the meadow grass or catching in the creek's current, streaming green ribbons in the shaded water. Annie would be here to see it, but by then Mattie and Naomi would be in Indiana. In the wilderness without their sister.

"Hey, Mattie!" Henry, her fourteen-year-old brother, scrambled up the tree and straddled the limb next to her. "What are you doing up here?"

"I'm thinking."

Henry stood up and walked along the limb, holding on to the fragile twigs over his head for balance.

"You thinking about going west? When do you think the Lancaster folks will get here?"

"Any day now, Daed said. He expected them last week."

Henry started bouncing on the limb, making it sway up and down.

"If you fall in the water, Mamm will skin you, for sure. You know she doesn't want to do any more laundry before we leave."

"*Ja, ja, ja*, I know." He walked toward her again and lay down along the branch, his chin in his hands. Mattie looked

16

toward the sky so she wouldn't have to watch him try to keep his balance on the still swaying branch.

Henry sat up. "Are there willow trees in Indiana? Do you think we'll have a swimming hole like this one?"

"Of course there are willow trees. We'll have to wait and see about the swimming hole, though."

He picked at the bark. "Mamm doesn't want to go, does she?"

"She agrees with Daed that we should." But when she heard about Christopher and Annie's decision, that might change. "You want to go, don't you?"

Henry looked at her then, his bright blue eyes shining beneath his hat brim. "Ja, I do. I know you do too. I've seen you staring out to the west as if you could see Indiana from here."

"Not only Indiana." She leaned back and closed her eyes. "I can see beyond the big river to the mountains."

"Of course you can. They're right there." The branch swayed as he gestured.

"Ne, not those mountains. The ones farther west." She leaned over to catch Henry's gaze. "I've heard they have snow on the tops all year around."

"You're not joking? Do you think you'll ever see them?"

She shrugged. "Why not? All we have to do is keep moving west."

He grinned at her and she matched his expression. They would always keep moving west.

Mamm's voice floated through the air from the direction of the house.

"Ach, Mattie, I forgot. I was to come fetch you. Mamm wants your help."

Mattie started down the tree. "You forgot, but I'll be the one in trouble." She reached the ground and headed toward the house. "And you had better go to the barn to see if Daed needs your help. There is a lot to do before we leave."

She left him still sitting in the tree.

Mamm was at the table with her back to the door when Mattie walked in. Annie sat on the opposite side, holding little Katie, her baby. Two-year-old Levi was in Mamm's lap. Naomi, sitting next to Annie, looked up as Mattie came near, her eyes red from crying.

Annie had told them the news.

Without a word, Mattie slid onto the bench next to Mamm and handed her a clean handkerchief from the waistband of her apron. Levi looked from Mamm to Annie and back again.

Mattie took a cookie from the jar on the table and handed it to her nephew. "Here, Levi. Have a cookie."

She set him on her own lap as Mamm sniffed back her tears.

Annie reached across the table toward her mother. "I'm sorry. If there was any way for us to go with you, you know I would. But this is our home."

Mamm nodded, controlling her tears. "I know. But we will miss you." She looked at her oldest daughter then. "Perhaps sometime you might follow us?"

Annie watched their hands, entwined in the table's center. "Who knows what the future holds? Perhaps God will call us to go west someday."

The front door opened. Christopher took one step into the room, his normally pleasant face grim. "Annie, we must go home."

Mamm hiccupped. "You were going to stay . . . it's dinner-time."

Christopher shook his head. "We won't eat here today." He held out one hand. "Levi, come home with Daed."

Mattie lowered the little boy to the floor and he ran to Christopher. Annie slowly let go of Mamm's hand and rose. She didn't look back as Christopher closed the door behind them.

Naomi rose from the table, motioning for Mattie to follow her out the back door.

When they reached the porch, Mattie whispered, "We can't leave Mamm alone, can we?"

Her sister took her hand. "Right now Mamm needs to cry. When she's done, she'll be back to her usual self, but she won't let herself cry while we're in there."

Naomi was right. "How do you know things like that? You always know what someone needs and I never do. I wouldn't have thought that she wants to be alone."

"I saw it on her face. She didn't want to cry in front of us."

She sat on the top step and Mattie sat beside her, leaning her elbows on her knees and resting her chin in her hands. "How long should we wait?"

"For a while. Dinner is in the oven and will be done soon. Mamm should feel better by then."

"I never really thought Annie wouldn't go west with us."

"She needs to stay with her husband."

"Is that what it's like when you get married? Whatever your husband decides, you have to do?"

Naomi brushed some flour off her apron. "Annie said she agreed with Christopher."

"But you saw how miserable she is. And Mamm doesn't

19

want to go west. She agreed because Daed wants to. If she had her way, she would never leave Brothers Valley."

Naomi scooted down to the next step and leaned back with her elbows propped behind her. "The Good Book says that when two people marry, they become one flesh. I suppose married people have to agree on things, or else they'd be torn apart."

"But would you agree with some man if he wanted to do something awful like take you away from your family?"

"First of all, I wouldn't marry 'some man.' If I ever get married, it will be to the man who loves me." Naomi crossed her legs at the knee and bounced one foot in the air. "And second, he would be my family, not you." She bounced her foot again.

Mattie felt a little sick. "You would choose him over me?"

Naomi looked up at her, smiling. "Of course, even though I would hope I will never have to make that choice. But you will do the same thing when you marry Ephraim or Andrew, or whoever wins your heart."

"Never." Mattie shook her head. "If he doesn't do what I want, then I'll head west to Oregon or somewhere without him."

Naomi grinned. "You just wait until you fall in love, like Annie did. Nothing will be as important as being with your husband."

Mattie didn't answer, but watched a male robin chase another away from the oak tree. Andrew Bontrager would never win her heart. Only one boy had ever come close to doing that, but when he arrived from the Conestoga, he probably wouldn't even remember her.

2

The good weather held through the end of the week and into the next, the spring sunshine causing flowers to burst from their buds and garden soil to become warm, soft beds for the carefully preserved seeds from last year's bounty. Mattie closed her eyes and lifted her face to catch the sun's rays. Fresh odors assailed her senses, carried on the warm southwest breeze. She sifted through the spring's scents. Apple blossoms and lilacs from Annie's front yard, freshly turned garden soil between her toes, and beneath it all the constant reek of manure piles. Every farmer along the Glades Pike had opened his barn and cleaned out the winter bedding from stalls and cow pens this week, and the ammonia-laced pungence was a balm to her winter-sick soul.

But Mamm had sent her to plant peas in Annie's garden, not daydream in the sunshine. Mattie poked a hole in the dirt with her stick and tossed a pea in. She pushed dirt over the seed with her toe, and moved half a step to her right. Another hole. Another pea. She felt the bag tied to her waist.

Much more than a handful. She sighed and turned her face to the late-morning sun again.

They would come down from the mountains that filled the eastern horizon. Three families, Daed had said. One older couple from the Ephrata settlement and two from the Conestoga.

She wasn't the little girl of ten who had left the Conestoga, but surely they would remember her. Hannah and Liesbet, Johanna, Annie, Naomi and Mattie . . . as girls they had played together for hours while their mothers quilted or spun.

Mattie stared at the distant mountains, rolling a dry pea between her fingers, her chore forgotten.

On butchering day, the autumn before her family had moved to Brothers Valley, the girls had all put their fingers in their ears and stared at each other with solemn faces until the pigs stopped squealing, and then burst out laughing at each other's expressions. Hannah and Liesbet's brother, Jacob, had roasted the pig's tail that day. He had skewered it with a stick and held it in the fire until it was crackling hot and dripping grease, and then shared it with her. They had taken turns biting off the crunchy bits until he laughed at the grease dripping from her chin.

The eastern mountains were the past, and she knew them. She had traveled down from those ridges when she had been a little girl. But the western mountains . . .

Mattie turned around. From Annie's garden she could see the distant ridges rising in blue-green piles. Soon, very soon, she would follow the Glades Pike west and cross those mountains. Soon she would see what wonderful things were on the other side, and Jacob Yoder would be with her.

Mattie sighed, the garden forgotten. The dream had come

again last night. She had often had the dream of the tall cliff standing between her and something wonderful, but last night had been different. This time she had searched all along the base of the cliff, looking for the passage that would take her to the other side. But when she awakened, she still hadn't found it. Maybe, just maybe, the answer was on the other side of those mountains.

The pea dropped from between her fingers, bringing her back to her task. She bent to retrieve it, then planted it along the willow trellis Annie had built last week, after Christopher broke the news that they wouldn't be coming west with the rest of the family. The peas would grow to cover the trellis, but by then Mattie would be over the mountains, leaving Annie behind with her husband and the little ones.

As she reached the end of the first row, a horse's whinny sounded through the air from the direction of the road. Mattie shaded her eyes against the spring sun. A bright blue wagon appeared over the rise, pulled by a team of four Conestoga horses. Behind them came another, smaller wagon. A young woman walking next to the second wagon waved to her. Mattie almost jumped in the air with a squeal. They were here! The waiting was finally over.

She stuck her hand into the bag of seeds, impatient to be done with her chore. If she hadn't been daydreaming, she might have been done already and could go to greet the Conestoga folks. She jabbed at the soil with her stick and tossed peas into the holes.

"Baa-aa-aa."

Mattie turned to see a sheep standing behind her. It fixed its unblinking eye on her, and then reached out to grab a willow twig from the trellis.

Mattie dropped the stick and flapped her apron. "Shoo, sheep. Shoo!"

The sheep skittered sideways, but only moved a couple of steps before it grabbed at the willow twigs again. This time it tugged with a toss of its head and the woven branches pulled away from the ground, falling over in a heap.

"Rosie!" A girl's voice sounded from the other side of the blueberry hedge. "Rosie, where are you?"

Mattie grabbed the sheep with one hand around her neck and the other around her middle. "I have her here," she called.

A young girl appeared around the end of the bushes. "That sheep. She's always running off somewhere."

Rosie saw the girl and started bucking, but Mattie held on. "Why don't you tie a rope to her?" Mattie's words came out in grunts as the sheep struggled.

"Jacob says she needs to browse as we walk, but she never stays with the rest of the flock."

As a man walked around the blueberry bushes, Mattie's stomach churned and she gripped the sheep tighter. Jacob Yoder. Older, taller, and with broad shoulders, but it had to be Jacob. He stopped when he saw Mattie. He looked from her to the demolished pea trellis and back to the sheep. He thumbed his hat brim up on his forehead and grinned at her. "What did you do to the trellis?"

"I didn't do anything to it. This sheep started eating it." Mattie pulled the sheep toward her, but it bucked again at the same time and pushed her over. She landed on her bottom in the damp garden soil with the sheep lying on her lap. Off its feet and helpless, the sheep lay still. Mattie narrowed her eyes as she looked back at Jacob, daring him to laugh.

He rubbed his chin, and then beckoned to the little girl.

"Margli, take Rosie off with the others. Daed will know where we can pen them for the night."

Mattie pushed the sheep off her lap, and Margli left, pulling the sheep by the wool around her neck until they were out of the garden and then sending her toward the road with a poke from her rod. Jacob planted one end of his shepherd's crook in the ground and reached a hand down to help Mattie stand. His brown eyes still held a twinkle as he pulled her toward him.

"You're one of Eli Schrock's daughters, aren't you?"

Mattie reached behind her to brush the dirt off her skirt. "I'm Mattie." She looked at him again. His eyes hadn't changed at all. He was still the finest-looking boy she had ever seen. "You're Jacob. Jacob Yoder."

His grin widened and the dimple appeared on his left cheek. The dimple that had appealed to her even as a little girl. "You remember me?"

How could she not remember him? Not a day went by that she didn't think of him. He had been the kindest boy on the Conestoga and had kept the other big boys from teasing the girls with snakes and frogs. She stood straighter. She could feel the blush rising in her cheeks. Now, seven years later, he wasn't a boy anymore. "Of course I remember you. You and your sisters always played with us. I remember . . ." Her voice lost its strength. He would think she was a silly little girl for remembering him the way she did.

"I remember how you used to hate fishing." His voice was deeper, without the straining squeaks of the fourteen-year-old he had been when she last saw him. "You hated baiting the hook."

"No matter what you said, I know it hurt those poor worms."

25

"They were going to be eaten when we caught the fish."
Jacob shrugged his shoulders and grinned again. "And you
hated taking the fish off the hook too."

Mattie shuddered, in spite of herself. "And you always
laughed at me."

His brown eyes looked deep into hers. "Because you were
always so much fun to tease. And now we're moving west
together."

A warm feeling spread through Mattie that had nothing
to do with the spring sunshine. He continued to watch her,
the grin on his face.

"Ja, we are." She smoothed her wrinkled apron and her
hand bumped the sack of seeds. "Ach, Annie's trellis."

She turned to the tangled mess and Jacob joined her, sticking the ends of the willow branches into the soft earth and
reweaving the tips together.

"Your daed told us your whole family is moving to Indiana."

"Everyone except my sister Annie and her family." Mattie
felt the ache rising again. If only Annie's Christopher would
agree to go west with them. The decision had created a gulf
between Daed and his son-in-law that may never be healed.

Jacob gave the trellis a last firm push into the ground and
stood back. "That should hold up as long as our sheep leave
it be."

"Denki." Mattie took her stick and a handful of peas.
She poked another hole, starting again where she had left off
before she had been interrupted, and dropped a seed into it.
Jacob would need to see to his sheep, and she mustn't delay
him, but he still lingered.

"Hannah is looking forward to getting to know you again."

"I always had so much fun playing with Hannah and Liesbet." Mattie dropped another pea. "And Fanny too." She glanced at Jacob. His face had grown hard.

"Liesbet died in February."

Mattie clutched the next pea before it could drop. "Ach, ne." The Yoders had lost another child? First Fanny, Hansli, and baby Catherine that awful winter when she was seven, and now Liesbet. She remembered Liesbet after the diphtheria had struck. She was always pale, never playing with the other children. She had been too weak to walk far, and her daed had always carried her to the Sunday meeting.

"I will miss her." Mattie had always wished her own brown hair had curled the way Liesbet's did. That's what she remembered most, Liesbet's golden curls flying in the breeze as they played tag around the apple trees at the Yoders' farm.

Jacob shifted his feet. "I thought you should know."

Mattie dropped the pea she had been holding into the hole and covered it.

Jacob shifted his crook, but didn't leave. He watched her drop another pea. She glanced at him again. His face was stony, his eyes focused on the hole she poked for the next seed.

"Margli has grown up since the last time I saw her," she said. "She was only a baby when we came west to Brothers Valley."

He looked at her, and then shook himself a little. His mood shifted. "Has it been that long? We have two more brothers, also. Peter and William."

"It's a fine thing for you to have brothers."

He shrugged. "They're all right. Too little to do anything with, though."

It must be because he was a man. If she had little brothers, she would dote on them. Henry was fourteen already, and had grown from a little boy into a friend. "Maybe when they're older and can be a help to you, you'll like them better."

"Maybe." He tapped the ground with his shepherd's staff. "I have to go help Margli and Peter with the sheep."

He moved off toward the road, walking with an easy stride, as if he hadn't just gotten to the end of a long journey.

Mattie dropped another pea into a hole and turned toward the western mountains. Jacob Yoder. She would see those far-off lands with Jacob Yoder. She hugged herself and grinned. All of her dreams were coming true.

The sheep, after moving slow as molasses over the mountains from the time they left home a month ago, now charged down the narrow road between farms as if they knew a few days of rest were ahead of them. Jacob jogged past Peter and Margli, one on each side of the road with their staffs, and caught up with Bitte, the lead sheep. She slowed her pace as he came alongside, her bell's clanking finally silent as she fell in behind him. The dozen ewes and one ram followed, baaing questions back and forth as they bunched together behind Bitte.

"Here, Jacob." Daed waved to him from the gate of a fenced pasture ahead. Eli Schrock stood with him next to the road, alongside the new wagon that had brought their family from the Conestoga Valley and across the mountains.

Jacob led the sheep into the pasture, green with spring grass. Bitte fell to grazing and the rest of the flock followed. Daed walked among them, patting a woolly side here, lifting a leg there.

"You've done a good job, son. Even after that last dash for the pasture, they show no signs of stress."

Nodding his thanks, Jacob fastened the gate and sent Margli and Peter off with a wave to help set up the camp. They had been good help on the trip, even as young as they were. He dipped a cup of water from the barrel hanging on the side of the wagon and listened to the men's conversation as he drank.

"Two days' rest, I think." Daed stood with his hands clasped behind his back, watching the sheep.

"Will that be enough?" Eli stood at an angle to Daed, his stance identical.

"The animals are all doing well, and I don't see any reason to wait longer than that, do you, Jacob?"

Jacob straightened his shoulders. He still hadn't gotten accustomed to Daed asking for his opinion on matters. "Ja, two days."

"We'll be ready to go by then." Eli stroked his beard and looked toward the farmhouse beyond the sheep. "My wife isn't too happy about leaving, since our daughter Annie and her family are staying here in Brothers Valley. But she'll need to say farewell, and better sooner than later, in my thinking. Long goodbyes just make it harder to break away at the end."

"Where should we set up our camp?"

Eli waved his hand beyond the sheep, to a field near the house. "There in the hay meadow. There is good grass for your animals, and plenty of room. Lydia says not to bother with cooking fires. She'll fix meals for us all in the house."

Daed nodded. "My Annalise will be happy to see her again. She has missed the friendship since you came to Somerset."

Jacob waited while Daed drove the big blue wagon into

the field. Hannah's new husband, Josef Bender, drove the green wagon with the older couple from Ephrata, Daniel and Mary Nafsinger, riding with him. Behind them came the Hertzlers' wagon, the final one in the group from the Conestoga Valley.

Mamm had chosen to ride with Magdalena Hertzler and the little children this afternoon, talking with her friend and sharing the care of Magdalena's little ones. Mamm was suffering during this trip. She was showing the same signs of stress Jacob had been keeping watch for in the flock of pregnant ewes. Daed worried about her, but they couldn't stop their journey if they were to arrive in Indiana before the ewes were ready to drop their lambs.

They had taken longer to travel from Lancaster County to Brothers Valley in Somerset than Daed had planned, and it was mid-April already. They could expect the lambs to come late in May. Jacob turned to watch the ewes in the small pasture, spreading across the grass as they ate. He had no idea when Mamm expected the new baby to come, but he couldn't see arriving in Indiana until the middle of May, or even early June at this pace. Daed felt the pressure of fleeting time also. Jacob could see it in the deep vertical line between his eyebrows.

The three wagons filed into the meadow and formed a rough half circle, facing the Schrocks' limestone house. Jacob helped the men unhitch the teams of horses and turn them into the field behind the house where a stream ran in a winding line through the midst of the spring grass. The horses rolled in the lush growth, ridding their backs of the feel of the harness, before they stepped to the stream for long drinks. Twelve horses pulled the three wagons, and when they left

Brothers Valley, more wagons would be joining them, and more horses to care for along the way.

Jacob pulled a flower from a wild carrot plant as he watched the little children run in the soft grass of the meadow, playing tag around and between the wagons. William chased after Johanna's brothers, four-year-old John and three-year-old Lias. The three little boys had been inseparable ever since they left home, just as he had been with his friends when he was little.

He hadn't forgotten how cute Mattie Schrock had been back then. He remembered her pug nose with the sprinkling of freckles that appeared every summer, and he remembered how she liked to follow the boys around as they played, no matter how much the others teased her. He remembered her earnest brown eyes watching his every move as he taught her to fish. And he remembered the day their family had left the Conestoga Valley. Mattie had waited impatiently as everyone said their goodbyes, anxious to start on their way.

The little girl Mattie had been a wren. Never still for a minute. Always sticking her nose into everything and interested in anything that came her way. The grown-up Mattie? Jacob rubbed his chin, scratching the growing whiskers. The little wren had turned into a beautiful woman.

"Did the sheep get into their pasture all right?"

He turned to see Johanna Hertzler at his elbow. "They're doing fine."

She rubbed her nose before she spoke again. "I'm glad they are." She shifted her feet in the grass. "We haven't seen much of each other on the trip here, have we? You've been with the sheep the whole time."

"I'm their shepherd." Jacob shrugged. "I need to be with them."

Johanna twisted her kapp string around her finger and chewed on her lower lip. Jacob kept himself from sighing aloud. Johanna was his sister's best friend, and he tried to be friendly to her for Hannah's sake. She was a pesky thing, though, especially since Hannah had married Josef. But she should feel better now that they had met up with the Schrocks. She would renew those old friendships and leave him alone, for sure.

As if she read his mind, she looked toward the Schrocks' house. "Do you think they remember us? Annie, Naomi, and Mattie? And the boys? It's been seven years since we've seen them."

"You don't have to worry. I saw Mattie a few minutes ago, and she remembered me. The others will too. You'll have plenty of friends."

She shot a look at him, her eyebrows raised. "You saw Mattie? Where?"

He gestured to the house across the road. "In the garden over there. She was planting peas."

"I should go say hello." Johanna shifted from one foot to the other, as if she was reluctant to leave him.

"You should do that." He stepped away from her. "I have to get to work."

She took the hint and started toward the road, looking behind her shoulder once, as if to see if he really was working. He shook his head as he walked back toward the wagons. That Johanna needed someone to take her mind off Hannah's marriage. She should get married herself, and then she and Hannah would be closer than ever.

3

Jacob pulled planks out from under the wagon where they were stored for traveling and laid them out to make benches for folks to sit on. Setting up camp was becoming routine after four weeks of travel. Four weeks, when the trip should have taken no more than two. Heavy rain had delayed their passage through the mountains between Lancaster and Somerset Counties. Jacob had become as short-tempered as any of them during the four days that their wagons had been stuck in heavy mud up to their axles. After they had dug them out, they had waited another week for a flooded river to subside enough that they could cross at the ford. They had nearly lost one of the ewes on that crossing as it was.

Mamm's strained face peered around the edge of the canvas cover of the Hertzlers' wagon as he pulled out the last plank.

"Jacob, help me down, please."

"For sure." He held Mamm's hand so she could balance as she reached with one foot for the spokes of the front wagon wheel. He averted his eyes from her stomach, grown so much larger during this trip.

When she reached the ground, Mamm squeezed his hand before releasing it. "Denki, Jacob. The climb down is getting harder every day."

"Are you . . ." Jacob faltered. It wasn't proper to mention Mamm's condition, but she didn't look well with her swollen and flushed face. "Are you feeling all right?"

"Ja, ja, ja." She waved off his question with her hand. "Riding in the wagon is tiring, and the prospect of a couple days' rest is welcome." She smiled at him, but her eyes betrayed her exhaustion. "I'll be fine. Don't worry."

After he retrieved Mamm's stool from the wagon and set it on the ground for her, he looked for Hannah. She was helping the Nafsingers climb out of the old green wagon. The older couple spent part of their days resting in the wagon but walked alongside the others during most of the mornings. From their slow movements, the two days' rest would do them good, also.

As soon as she could, Hannah hurried over to Jacob. She leaned close and spoke in a low voice. "How is she?"

"I'm not hard of hearing yet." Mamm smiled at them. "I'm doing fine. A little tired perhaps, but I know when I need to rest."

Hannah met Jacob's gaze and he shrugged. If Mamm said she was all right, it wasn't his place to argue with her. But if she was a cow or a ewe and tired this easily, he would have shut her in the barn with good food and plenty of water until it was time for the calf or lamb to be born.

Daed had unloaded some small kegs from the wagon. Jacob joined him, setting the kegs at the right distance to make a bench with the planks. When they were out of Mamm's hearing, Jacob asked, "Will two days' rest be enough?"

"For the ewes? Ja, for sure. The lambs shouldn't start coming for more than a month, and they're in good shape."

"I meant for Mamm. She looks awfully tired."

Daed paused, a keg balanced on the rear wagon gate. "I know. She insists everything is normal, but it isn't." He pulled the keg down and set it on the ground. "You know she expects the little one to come in the summer?"

Jacob nodded. Daed must be very worried to mention the subject.

"I hope the rest of our journey is easier than this first month has been. She needs to be settled and rested before her time comes."

"But won't traveling at a faster pace be worse?"

Daed's shoulders slumped. "Ja, for sure. If I had known how hard this trip would be for her, I wouldn't have insisted that we come. But I thought . . . after Liesbet . . . and she wanted to make the journey . . ." He rubbed the back of his neck. "When you marry, you'll feel the burden. Being responsible for a family is a great joy, but also a weariness at times."

Jacob didn't answer. He pushed down his concerns about Mamm. Daed would take care of things. Borrowing trouble never did anyone any good.

He picked up the box of brushes and curry combs and started toward the back pasture.

What if something happened to Mamm? Jacob pushed harder to keep that thought from surfacing again. Ever since Liesbet's death, it was as if he was standing at the edge of a cliff. He could keep a distance between the little ones and himself. If something happened to Margli or Peter, he might survive it. Even William, who looked so much like Hansli. But Mamm . . . He teetered on that cliff. At the bottom lay something dark and brooding. He couldn't let himself risk going over the edge.

Jacob pushed again. Until last winter, Mamm had been caught in a trap of her own grief and despair. Since Liesbet's death, he thought perhaps he understood the demons that had plagued her then. He glanced back to the wagon, to Mamm and Hannah setting up their camp with Margli's help. She must feel that helpless pull into the darkness, but somehow, so far, she had fought against it. He would fight too. He wouldn't let himself lose this battle.

As long as he had someone to hold on to. Mamm, or a bright little wren of a girl. That Mattie. He could face anything with someone like Mattie beside him. Meanwhile, he just wouldn't think about it. Mamm would be all right.

When he got to the pasture, he reached out his hand to open the gate.

"Ha, Jacob!"

He turned just in time to catch Peter as he barreled down the hill, running at full speed.

"Watch it, there. You run into that fence and you'll break it or yourself."

Peter's face was bright red from playing with the other children. "Come with me, Jacob. We're playing tag, and some of the other men are playing too. You'll beat them all, I know you will. You're the fastest runner in the world."

Jacob looked at his brother's grinning face, like looking into a mirror. Peter was a smaller version of himself. A brother he could love, if he let himself.

"I'm too busy." He went into the pasture, closing the gate behind him. "You go on and play with the others."

Peter didn't say anything. He never did when Jacob pushed

36

him away, but only ran off to join in the game again. Peter's yell came to him over the fields, carrying above the shouts of the other children. Jacob gripped a fence post, letting the rough wood bite into his skin.

Mattie hurried to finish planting the peas, turning her thoughts away from Jacob Yoder. If Jacob remembered her from all those years ago, perhaps his sister, Hannah, would too. And Johanna Hertzler. One thing that made this move west so exciting was to have friends along. If they could resume the friendship they had as girls, it would be such fun.

Of course, back then Hannah and Johanna had been Naomi's friends, being the same age. Mattie had been the same age as Liesbet. She pushed the last pea into the ground and rocked back on her heels. But they were grown up now, and there was no reason for them all not to be friends. She counted on her fingers. Hannah, Naomi, Johanna, and herself.

Mattie stood, straightening her skirts and apron with a brush of her hand. They would have such fun on the trip. Unless the girls from the Conestoga were married. Mattie sighed. That would leave just her and Naomi the only spinsters again.

"Mattie! Mattie Schrock!" A young woman peered over the pea trellis. "You're Mattie, aren't you? I'm Johanna. Jacob said you were over here."

A stab of jealousy surprised Mattie, but she ignored it. "Johanna! I would have recognized you anywhere." She circled the pea trellis and Johanna caught her in a hug, and then Mattie held her friend at arm's length. "You look like your mamm."

Johanna's nose turned pink. "Do you think so?"

"For sure you do."

"Do you remember when she used to chase us out of the kitchen when we snitched pinches of her bread dough?"

Mattie laughed. "She would chase us out of the house, flapping her apron just like when she was chasing the hens off the porch." She took Johanna's hand. "I hope I didn't make you sad by mentioning her."

Johanna smiled and squeezed her hand. "I like to remember her. I don't miss her as much then."

"Did I hear your daed remarried?"

"Her name is Magdalena. You'll love her when you meet her. She isn't that much older than I am, but she's a wonderful mamm for the little ones. And we have little brothers and a baby sister now." Johanna looked at her, a grin on her face. "It's so good to see you, Mattie! I've been so lonely on this trip so far, and I'm glad you and Naomi will be traveling with us the rest of the way."

"What about Hannah?"

"Jacob didn't tell you? Hannah is married. Her wedding was the day before we left the Conestoga."

"Hannah has abandoned us, then. She'll be so busy with her new husband, we'll never get her to go berry picking or help with the babies."

Johanna laughed. "She'll help us, all right. But she'll talk about Josef the whole time."

"That must be what it's like to be in love."

Johanna's face grew serious and she looked away across the road, toward the busy camp of wagons. "It must be." The mood passed quickly and she turned back. "Let's go find Hannah, and you can meet the others."

Mattie followed Johanna to the three wagons set in a shallow arc in the back field. Children ran everywhere, playing and calling to each other. It would take the entire trip just to learn all of their names.

When they reached the smaller wagon, a green Conestoga, Mattie saw the young woman who had waved to her from the road making a bench out of two kegs and a plank.

"Hannah, look who I found."

Hannah straightened up from her task. "Mattie Schrock?" She took Mattie's hands in her own. "It's so good to see you! How is your family? I haven't seen Naomi yet, or your brothers. Is it true that Annie is married?"

Johanna stiffened before Mattie could reply. She followed her friend's gaze to the next field, where Jacob was grooming the horses. So that's the way it was. She should expect that Jacob would have a girl, or even be married after seven years. The hero of her childhood was someone else's hero now. Maybe Johanna's.

She forced herself to smile as she turned her attention back to Hannah. "Ja, it's true. Annie and her family are staying here in Brothers Valley, though."

Hannah sat on the bench, motioning for Mattie to join her. "That's too bad. Your family will be divided, then."

Mattie nodded. The family was divided already, with Annie's husband following the change-minded deacon in his plan to build a meetinghouse. Once the families left for Indiana, they would probably never see Annie or her babies again. But, as Mamm said, that was in God's hands.

"Look," Hannah said. "The men are setting up tables outside the house. Supper must be close to being ready."

"Is it that late already?" Mattie glanced at the sun, lowering toward the western mountains. "I need to do the milking.

But you two go ahead and join the others. Naomi is inside the house, helping Mamm with supper. I know she'll love to see you."

She watched her friends make their way across the field toward the house. This trip was going to be just like old times as they learned about each other again. She would miss Jacob, though. She had been looking forward to renewing their friendship too, but she would never try to take Johanna's place in his life.

Mattie went to the next meadow where their cow was grazing. Pet was the only one of their milk cows they would be taking to Indiana. She was young and strong, with plenty of years left to provide them with calves and milk. Millie and Boss were continuing their comfortable life in Brothers Valley, so they would never know the adventurous life their sister would live.

Pet raised her head from the soft rich grass of the meadow and watched Mattie approach. Her long lashes blinked once, then twice, and she switched her long tail over her flank. The young Kerry often led Mattie on a chase when it was time to go to the barn, but not tonight. Whether it was because Mattie was late, or because of the strange horses and cows in her meadow, Pet stood quietly as Mattie came close and let her scratch around her white, lyre-shaped horns and stroke her neck.

As she patted the sleek brown shoulder, Mattie saw Jacob heading into the barn with the two cows from Lancaster County. It looked like he had milking duty too. Now she had the opportunity to find out how he really felt about Johanna. Did he like Johanna as much as her friend hoped he did? She gave Pet one last rub.

"Come on, Pet. It's milking time." Pet took one step and then another toward the barn. Mattie let the cow walk ahead of her. She looked past the meadow where the sun was dipping toward the horizon, its lower rim resting on the crest of the blue mountains. Soon. Soon she would see what was beyond those hills.

∞

Evening came quickly, with the sun sinking toward the crests of the western mountains between one breath and the next.

With the camp set up and while the women were preparing supper, Jacob headed back to the pasture to find the black milk cow that had followed behind the wagon all the way from Lancaster. Even with the daily travel, she still had a good supply of milk. The Hertzlers' cow was grazing nearby, and he took both to the barn.

He led the cows into the cellar, to the milking house. Eli Schrock had told him to use the stanchion there, and to feed the cows from the supply of grain in the bin. He wouldn't be taking it west, he had said, so it might as well be used for a good purpose.

Jacob tied the Hertzlers' cow to a post and put Schwartz into the stanchion. When he poured some feed into the trough at her head, the Hertzlers' red-and-white cow mooed in protest.

"Wait your turn, Bess. You'll be fed soon enough."

A stool was nearby and clean pails stood on a bench along with a bar of soap. He went to the well for a bucket of water, shaved some soap into it, and stirred it with his hand until the flakes had melted. Taking a cloth, he washed the udders and then grabbed a clean pail.

Jacob sat on the stool and pressed his forehead against Schwartz's flank, letting his hands work in the even rhythm that filled the milk pail without thought. Most nights each family milked their own cows, and he, Daed, and Elias Hertzler would discuss the day's travel as they worked. But tonight Jacob had volunteered to milk both cows so the men could visit with the families of Brothers Valley.

The bumping and clopping sound of another cow entering the milking house interrupted his thoughts, and he looked around Schwartz's tail to see a brown Kerry enter the neighboring stanchion. Mattie followed her but stopped when she saw Jacob watching her.

"You're the milkmaid in your family, I see." Jacob smiled at her, then went back to his milking before Schwartz got restless.

"We only have the one cow left, so the milking has fallen to me."

Jacob leaned around the cow's tail again to watch Mattie settle on her milking stool with her back to him. She washed her cow's udder and soon the rhythm of milk drumming into the tin pail matched his own. Crouched on the stool, bent into her work, she reminded him again of the little girl she had been.

"Do you still get freckles on your nose in the summer?" The question was spoken before he even thought. What kind of thing was that to say to a girl?

But she only laughed. "Ja, for sure. Mamm says I'll outgrow them, but I don't mind. They don't bother me." She paused in her milking and turned to look at him. "And does your hair still turn the color of straw?"

He grinned at her and ducked back behind the cow. "Ja, for sure. Not as light as it once did, though."

The sounds of her milking resumed as Jacob finished with his cow and switched the cows around, pouring a measure of grain for Bess. The first streams of milk rang in the empty tin pail.

Mattie's voice rose above the sound. "I saw Hannah a little while ago, and Johanna. You didn't tell me Hannah was married."

"I never thought about it."

The sound of her milking stopped. He looked to see her turned toward him. "You never thought about it? Getting married is the most important thing in a girl's life."

He shrugged, ready to tease her. "Maybe to you it is. It isn't such a big deal to a man."

He ducked as she sent a stream of milk his way. "That's what you think, Jacob Yoder. My brothers were just as nervous as their brides were on their wedding days. When you and Johanna marry, you'll see."

"Johanna?" Jacob felt his face heating, and it wasn't from the exertion of milking. "What did Johanna say to make you think we are getting married?"

"She didn't have to say anything." Mattie finished milking and stood, holding the full pail in her hand. "I could tell by the way her eyes have been following you ever since you got here."

Jacob thrust his head against the cow's flank. If Johanna Hertzler thought he was going to marry her, she was going to be disappointed. She might be Hannah's best friend, but marriage? He'd rather stay single.

He heard Mattie leave the barn as he finished milking Bess and turned the cows back into the pasture. She looked at him over her shoulder. "I'll show you where the springhouse is.

43

The milk keeps plenty cool there," and she left him to follow her around the corner of the barn.

He could follow Mattie anywhere. She was fun to be with, unlike Johanna, who looked like she was about to cry every time he glanced her way. Was that what Mattie had meant? If Johanna thought she was in love with him, she had a strange way of showing it.

The springhouse was built over the creek, upstream from where it entered the meadow. The thick limestone walls made the little room quiet and dark. Mattie showed him where he could set the pails in the shallow, flowing water of a limestone trough, and they covered them with clean squares of cloth. As Jacob's eyes grew used to the dim light, he took in the shelves built into the walls and bins along the floor.

"Did your daed build this springhouse?"

Mattie shook her head. "Daed bought the house and farm from a family that was moving to Ohio. The springhouse is Mamm's favorite thing about this farm. She isn't happy about leaving it, but Daed said he could build one in Indiana."

"Your daed likes to move around, doesn't he? Didn't you used to live in Chester County?"

"The folks did, but that was before they moved to Lancaster County. I was born a couple years after they moved to the farm along the Conestoga Creek."

"And you moved here seven years ago."

Mattie nodded and grinned at him. "And in a couple days we'll be moving on, across those western mountains." She stepped past Jacob to look out the open door toward the west, where light still lingered behind the hills in pink and gold clouds.

"I wouldn't want to move that often. Once I get to Indiana

and buy my land, I'll never leave it. My children's children will live on that land for years to come."

She turned to him. "But what if you find something better? What if you want to see something new?"

He shook his head. "I'll make my farm the best there is. I'll work to make it a place to last. Why would I ever want to leave it?" Mattie looked out the door again and he touched her arm to bring her attention back to him. "When I have my farm, it will be my home. Mine and my family's. Don't you feel unsettled when you change your home so often?"

She shook her head. "Home is where you make it. So whether it's here on this farm in Brothers Valley or somewhere like—" she waved her hand vaguely toward the west—"like Oregon, it is still home. I could never be content living in one place all my life, not when there are open prairies and vast mountains that I've never been to."

"There will always be more. You can't see everything in the world." Jacob kept his voice low. Mattie spoke of a life with no stability, no community. A life he couldn't imagine living. "What about your church? A husband someday? Children?"

She didn't answer, but turned her gaze toward the west again.

He studied her profile. Her chin tilted up, a smile spreading as she drifted into her thoughts. Years ago, she had wormed her way into his life, and the time between hadn't lessened that bond. Even when they were children, she had been more than his little sister's playmate, more than one of the girls among many at Sunday meeting.

Jacob smiled at a sudden memory. Mattie's brothers had gone fishing, and she had tagged along without them knowing. She started across a log spanning the creek, but lost her balance halfway and slipped into the stream. When he came by a few minutes later, she was clinging to the log, the flowing water dragging at her dress. Silent, her eyes sought his, pleading for help. From the moment he pulled her out of the creek and took her home, shivering in her soaked clothes, she had been his responsibility. She must have been only five years old, and he her eight-year-old protector. Ever since that day she had been his shadow, and he had never minded her presence. She was part of his life.

With a jolt, Jacob reined in his thoughts. All the months of planning his farm, he had assumed he would have a family like Daed and every other man he knew. But to have a family, he would need a wife. A wife who would need his protection and his love. He closed his eyes, shutting out the sight of Mattie's profile, so soft and vulnerable. The soft lap of that dark, brooding sea in his mind lessened as he leaned toward her. His Mattie.

4

Two nights later, Johanna Hertzler kept herself from looking toward the barn as she and Hannah walked arm in arm toward the big limestone house. For the third night in a row, Jacob was milking the cows and had declined her offer to help. He had avoided her more than usual during the last two days as the families had rested at the Schrock farm. Of course, she had been busy herself, helping Mamm keep the little boys, John and Lias, out of mischief. And she and the other girls had spent hours together, catching up on the years since they had last seen each other.

But Jacob had remained aloof. He could milk every cow in the world, for all she cared. She had hoped he would notice her on the trip from the Conestoga Creek to Brothers Valley, but he had ignored her during the entire journey. He could have stayed home and nothing would have been different.

"There's Naomi!" Hannah dropped Johanna's arm and ran toward her friend, who was laying a basket of bread on one of the long tables set up in front of the house.

Johanna hurried after her. "What can we do to help?"

All of the traveling families were eating one last supper together in Brothers Valley, here in the yard of the Schrocks' home. The men had set up tables under the trees, and now most of them were gathered around a fire near the well, where the younger boys took turns rotating a sizzling pig on a spit.

Naomi smiled, her right eye meeting Johanna's. "There are dishes in the house ready to be brought out. Mamm just took the last of the bread from the oven."

Johanna smiled back. In spite of Naomi's cast eye, an affliction that caused only one of her eyes to focus at a time, Naomi had never let the condition bother her. When they were children, Johanna hadn't noticed it. Even now, it was only when her focus switched from her right to her left eye that Johanna remembered.

Naomi's gaze shifted, both eyes looking at something over Johanna's shoulder. Her face reddened and her grasp on Johanna's hands tightened.

"You haven't met the Bontragers yet, have you? They and their son and daughter are coming with us to Indiana. Their daughter, Sarah, is married to Thomas Fisher, and they have five little ones. There will be a lot of children on this journey."

"What about their son? Is he married?"

Naomi only directed her gaze over Johanna's shoulder. Turning to look, she saw a tall young man join the circle with Josef and Naomi's brothers. The newcomer slapped Noah's shoulder and shook hands with Josef Bender, Hannah's husband, but even as he greeted them, his gaze scanned the rest of the group in the yard. When his eyes met Johanna's, he stopped. His handsome face settled into an easy smile as he stared at her. Johanna felt her face heating. Jacob Yoder never looked at her with such open interest.

"Who is that?" She turned to see Naomi watching her closely. Her friend didn't even look to see who Johanna was referring to.

"That's Andrew, the Bontragers' youngest. Everyone wonders why he's still unmarried, even though he's twenty-four."

Naomi turned toward the house, but Johanna caught her arm. "What's wrong, Naomi?"

Naomi shook her head, not looking at Johanna or the group of young men. "Nothing is wrong. Mamm needs my help to get supper ready."

Johanna didn't let her go. "Something is wrong. Is it Andrew?"

Naomi took a step back.

"Are you sweet on him?"

Her friend bit her lip. "Don't tell anyone, especially him." Her voice dropped to a whisper and Johanna had to lean close to hear her.

"How could I tell him?" Johanna whispered in return. "I'll probably never speak to him."

"Ja, you will. He's right behind you."

As Naomi hurried into the house, Johanna froze. Someone behind her cleared his throat. She put a welcoming smile on her face and turned around. He was even taller than she thought when she had first seen him. He looked down at her with his wide mouth stretched in a grin. His blond hair swayed under his hat brim like a field of wheat blown by the wind, and his eyes were the color of a summer morning sky. Johanna forced herself to breathe. No wonder Naomi was sweet on him.

"Hallo."

Even his voice was perfect. Low pitched and as smooth

as October honey. Johanna's tongue stuck to the roof of her mouth.

His smile grew wider. "I'm Andrew." He leaned toward her, dipping his head to look into her eyes. "Andrew Bontrager."

"Jo-Johanna Hertzler." Her face was on fire. He had to notice. She had never been tongue-tied around Jacob.

Andrew straightened to his full height and scanned the activity around them. "You're traveling west with us? You and your family?"

She nodded. "Ja."

He brought those blue eyes back to her. "I wasn't sure I wanted to go west . . . until now."

Johanna's heart raced. "Until now?"

He grinned. "Now that I see what kind of friends I have to keep me company."

"What about Naomi, and Mattie? Aren't they your friends?"

He shrugged. "I've known them so long that they're more like sisters. But you . . ." He winked at her. "You're a mystery to be solved, and I love a mystery."

Johanna took a step backward. "I . . . I need to help with supper."

"We can talk later. We'll have plenty of time."

She backed away a few more steps, his eyes on every move, until she turned and fled into the house. She grabbed the first dish she saw and took it outside to the tables. The men were taking their seats, and she could hear Andrew's voice rising above the others.

"Johanna?"

She blinked. Hannah stood in front of her.

"Do you want to sit with us for supper, or will Magdalena need your help with the little ones?"

"Ne. Ja. I'll sit with you."

"Are you all right? You're all flushed."

Johanna put her hands to her burning cheeks. "Am I? It must be from meeting all these new people."

"New people like Andrew Bontrager?" Hannah laughed. "I saw you talking with him. Naomi says every girl likes him."

Johanna let herself look in Andrew's direction. Jacob joined the group of young men, but she didn't let her gaze linger on him. Next to Andrew, he was nothing special. Jacob was solid, comfortable, and boring. Andrew was . . . completely different. She had never met anyone like him.

"He's always smiling, did you notice that? People like someone who is friendly. I'm sure that's what Naomi meant."

Hannah watched her face for a moment as Johanna hoped the redness was disappearing. "Probably."

Johanna went to join Mattie and Naomi at one of the makeshift tables set up in the Schrocks' yard, sure that Hannah would follow. So all the girls liked Andrew Bontrager? She could see why.

Mattie savored each bite of her meal, chewing slowly. Daed had killed a hog for tonight's supper. Since there were so many people to feed, the pig had been saved for their last evening meal in Brothers Valley. It had been butchered and set over the fire early in the morning, and all day long the aroma of roasting hog had tantalized Mattie's hunger. She remembered the trip from Conestoga Creek years ago. Daed hadn't wanted to hunt while they traveled since it would only slow down their journey, so they lived on salt pork, beans, and the sourdough biscuits Mamm made each morning. Mattie shuddered and took another bite of the savory pork. If she had to eat salted meat for the next month, she was going to enjoy the fresh roast tonight.

"I hope we have good weather for the rest of the trip." Johanna cut a potato in two. Mamm had cleaned out the root cellar for tonight's supper too. "Those three days of rain last week were miserable. I never want to be that cold and wet again."

"The first night wasn't as bad. Josef got our fire going, but after that the wood was too wet to burn well." Hannah smiled, in spite of her words.

Johanna nudged Mattie with her elbow. "That's Hannah. Her Josef can do anything, she thinks. Even as awful as the rain was, Hannah still kept a smile on her face."

"Perhaps that is what love does to a person." Naomi kept glancing at the table where the young men sat with their heads together. Mattie looked over there too. Jacob Yoder's hat looked just like all the others, but she had noticed that his had a different curl on the left side of the brim. It was only one of the things she had noticed as they had milked the cows together morning and evening for the past two days.

A movement near the road caught her attention. Beyond the group of young men, three strangers on horseback watched the crowded tables in the yard. Daed saw them the same time Mattie did and stood to greet them.

"Good evening," he called to the strangers in English. All conversation among the Amish families stopped.

One of the strangers, a young man who looked to be less than thirty years old, nudged his horse forward. The other two, one a younger man and the other barely older than a boy, hung back.

"Hello. Your supper smells good. Do you have enough to share with hungry travelers?"

Daed glanced at the other men sitting near him. "You're welcome to come join us."

The three tied their horses to the fence along the road and jumped over, not bothering to go to the gate. The older one moved with the assurance of a puma, looking from table to table as he approached Daed. When he saw Mattie's table, he stopped. Mattie blushed and he grinned at her, holding her gaze until she lowered her eyes. His companions circled around the edges of the yard.

"We thank you kindly for your invitation. We're plumb starved to death. Haven't eaten a bite since the tavern in Bedford this morning."

Daed caught Mattie's eye and she rose from her seat. "Let's take the children to play in the meadow." She kept her voice low and spoke in Deitsch to the other girls.

While Mattie and the others started gathering the children, Naomi told Mamm their plans. Mattie paused at the path leading to the barns and looked back. Mamm and the other women set up tubs and pans to wash dishes while the strangers sat at the table with the men, eating the last of the delicious pork. From their grasping ways, it looked like there would be no leftover meat for breakfast in the morning. She followed the others into the meadow where Naomi was already helping the children form a circle to play ring-around-the-rosy in the soft twilight.

Hearing footsteps behind her, she turned to see Jacob.

"You feel like playing too?" She smiled, but Jacob didn't return it.

"I don't like the thought of you girls alone with the young ones."

She stopped at the gate to the lower meadow. "Because of our visitors?"

"Because they might not be alone."

"What do you mean?"

Jacob's gaze took in the meadows before he leveled it on her. "Strangers can't always be trusted. Those three may be a distraction so that their companions can ransack our wagons, or . . ." He stopped, rubbing the back of his neck. "I suppose you think I'm too suspicious."

"Strangers have come by our farm before, and even eaten with us and camped in our fields. Daed often provides hospitality to travelers."

"Don't these men seem different to you?"

Mattie shrugged. "They're the same as other outsiders, aren't they?"

Jacob shook his head. "I'm not sure what it is, but something about them doesn't seem right. Why does only the oldest one do the talking? He seems like he's the leader and the other two are his soldiers." He looked back at the house, and then glanced over the meadows again. "It will be dark soon. Don't let any of the children wander off. I'm going to check on the horses."

As he made his way along the fence toward the creek where the horses grazed, Mattie ran back to the house. She hadn't seen anything suspicious about the strangers, other than their obvious hunger. She peeked around the corner of the house. The women chatted quietly as they cleaned up from supper, and the men sat or stood around the table where the strangers leaned on their elbows, finishing their meals. The oldest one, the leader according to Jacob, was speaking. Mattie couldn't hear him clearly, but whatever tale he was telling was keeping the men laughing.

She could see the speaker's face from where she stood. Someone had lit a lamp and set it on the table in their midst, and the light shone on him. His mouth was broad and his teeth gleamed in the light. He wore a mustache with his short beard, and his dark eyes were black jewels that flashed as he watched his listeners. Mattie found herself taking a step forward, but retreated. Something about him drew her—was that the same thing that Jacob had seen and had made him suspicious? But she saw and felt nothing dangerous. She even laughed when the men did, even though she hadn't heard the joke.

With reluctant steps, she turned to go back to the meadow to help with the children. Perhaps Daed would invite the strangers to travel with them in the morning. There must be a way for her to meet him.

Jacob checked the horses, counting them as they grazed or rested, scattered over the grass. All was quiet. None of the animals even flicked an ear.

He circled them and approached the wagons from behind the camp. He heard no sound other than the birds in the hedges and the children's game in the distance. He continued on to the small walled-in pen near the road.

The ewes were lying in the grass with their legs tucked under, chewing their cuds. The ram, young and energetic, paced along the far wall, his nose lifted up, and his half-grown horns reflecting the light from the lanterns in the farmyard. Three-year-old William had called him "Bam" when the ram first arrived on the farm back along the Conestoga Creek, and the name had stuck. Bam would settle down with the ewes as the sky grew darker. The rest of the sheep were so used to Jacob's presence they didn't lift their heads to take notice of him.

When he reached the house again, the group was breaking up. The families moved toward their houses or the campsite. Tomorrow morning would start early, with the last-minute packing and hitching up of the wagons taking place in the early hours just after dawn.

Jacob fell in step next to Daed as they followed the other Conestoga men toward their camp. The Bates brothers—Cole, Hiram and Darrell—led their saddle horses as they walked at the head of the group with Eli Schrock.

"What are they doing?" Jacob leaned toward Daed with his question.

Daed grunted. "Eli has given them permission to camp near us tonight. They insisted."

Jacob pulled Daed to the side, letting the others pass by. "I'm not sure that is a wise thing to do. They're strangers."

Daed laid his hand on Jacob's shoulder. "I know, but Eli and I thought it best to have them camp near, where we can see them, rather than trust them too much."

"So you aren't sure of them, either?"

"Ne, son." Daed looked after the group as they turned toward the circle of wagons. "Something doesn't seem right about those young men, in spite of how friendly they seem. I hate to be so suspicious, but there are evil people in the world."

"I'll take the first turn standing watch tonight. I'll wake Josef at midnight, and he can take over then."

As they reached the camp, Mattie and the others brought

the children from the meadow where they had been playing and everyone prepared to turn in for the night. The Bates brothers tethered their horses to stakes in the space between the wagons and the road, then rolled out their bedrolls near the middle of the circled wagons. Jacob normally slept near the campfire, keeping it burning by adding wood as he woke now and then through the night, but tonight, with no fire, he made his bed close to the green wagon, where Daniel and Mary Nafsinger, the older couple going only as far as Ohio, slept. There he would be able to keep watch on their visitors.

Josef stopped on his way to the canvas tent where he and Hannah slept. "If you need my help, don't wait to call."

"For sure."

Jacob looked around the camp, his eyes accustomed to the growing darkness. Mamm shooed Margli, Peter, and William into the big wagon where they would sleep on pallets on top of the crates, while the Hertzlers, at the far end of the circle, gathered their family together. Johanna often slept in a lean-to attached to their wagon with her sisters, thirteen-year-old Susanna and seven-year-old Barbli, but tonight they stayed inside the wagon with the rest of the family. It seemed that Elias Hertzler agreed with Daed when it came to trusting their guests.

The quiet voices throughout the campsite drifted off as families soon settled into sleep. Jacob pulled a blanket around his shoulders and nestled into the soft grass. Mary Nafsinger had given him a bundle to use as a pillow, and he put it against a wagon wheel where he could lie with his head propped up.

He watched the Bates trio. Jacob had never seen brothers that looked less alike than those three. Cole was handsome

enough, but the other two reminded Jacob of a couple wea-
sels looking for a hole in the chicken yard fence.

The three sat in the dark opposite the wagons, talking in
low tones that barely carried across the short space to Jacob's
blanket. He could recognize Cole's voice. The words were
indistinct, but the tone was calm. Assured. The other two
seemed to be arguing with him, their voices cajoling.

One of the brothers raised his voice in a whine. "We're
going to lose our chance."

Cole hushed him. Jacob saw the starlight gleam in his
eyes as he looked toward the wagons. His voice continued
for a few more minutes, and then all three of them lay down
where they were. Jacob waited until they were still, and then
glanced around the rest of the camp. All was quiet.

He scooted further into his blankets. The night air was cool
and damp. A yawn overtook him and he shifted again. If he
let himself get too comfortable, he wouldn't be able to stay
awake until his watch was over. He searched the stars, locat-
ing the Big Dipper. He'd be able to tell it was midnight when
the handle was directly over the barn roof across the road.

Glancing over at the Bates brothers, Jacob blinked, and
then sat up. There were only two dark mounds. He stood
up, looking all around the camp. He could see no movement
at all. Keeping an eye on the still forms in the grass, Jacob
stepped around the wagon to the starlit space between the
camp and a woodlot. He circled from one end of the camp to
the other, but there was no sign of the missing Bates brother.

Jacob stopped at the far end of the camp, in the shadow of
the Hertzlers' big wagon. Which brother was missing? The
whine he had overheard echoed in his head. What chance
were they going to lose?

A short neigh from the pasture where the horses were bedded down for the night pulled Jacob in that direction, following the slope of the meadow toward the creek. As he slipped over the split rail fence, he saw the horses standing in the starlight, their heads all pointing toward the gate at the far side. A figure stood there. Jacob watched as it walked slowly into the pasture. The horse closest to it stepped forward, stopped, and then tossed its head.

If Jacob moved, whoever was on the far side of the pasture would notice him, so he waited. It had to be the missing Bates brother, but what was he doing?

The figure reached for the closest horse, then circled its neck with his arm. He stood at the horse's head, then moved back toward the gate. The horse followed him.

A cold hand twisted in Jacob's gut. The horse was following because the man had tied a rope around its neck. It was being stolen, right in front of Jacob's eyes. The dark figure walked out of the gate and toward the road.

Jacob took a deep breath. "Thief!" He yelled as loudly as he could. He needed to rouse the camp. "Horse thief! Stop!"

He ran to the gate. The horse reared, silhouetted against the starry sky, and the man bolted, leaving the horse behind. Jacob ran toward the wagons. He had to stop them before they could escape, but by the time Jacob reached the camp again, all three of the Bates brothers and their horses had disappeared.

Lights gleamed in the house behind him and lanterns were lit near the wagons. Jacob looked around, frantic. Cole and his brothers couldn't be far away.

"What is it?" Daed stopped Jacob from going past them toward the road.

Jacob panted, trying to get his breath back. "They were stealing a horse. I saw them."

Elias Hertzler held his lantern high in the air. "You saw them? But they aren't here."

"One of them was in the horse pasture. He had a rope on one of the horses and was leading it out."

"Maybe it was one of their horses?" Old Daniel Nafsinger's voice was calm and persuasive. "Could you have been mistaken?"

Jacob shook his head, but the rest of the men nodded in agreement with Daniel.

"Perhaps it was his own horse," Daed said, stroking his beard. "Either way, they are gone now and the horses are safe. There is nothing more to do, so we'll go back to bed."

Josef Bender stepped close to Jacob as the older men went back to their families. "Are you all right? Will you be able to get some sleep?"

Jacob took a deep breath and whooshed it out. "The Bates brothers are gone, but they'll be back. I don't trust them. I know what I saw, but no one believes me."

His brother-in-law cupped his hand around the chimney of his lantern and blew out the flame. "I believe you, Jacob, and I think the others do also. But they believe the danger has passed. Perhaps it has."

"I'm going to keep watch in the horse pasture anyway. I don't trust those three."

As Josef made his way back to his tent, Jacob gathered his blanket and went to catch the horse Bates had tried to steal. It hadn't gone farther than the well near the house and willingly followed Jacob back through the gate. It was Daed's wheel horse, Beppli, and he would have been sorely missed if he had been stolen. Jacob untied the rope from the gelding's neck and the horse greeted his teammates before reaching down to crop a few bites of grass.

Jacob fingered the short length of rope, scanning the edges of the pasture. If the Bates brothers tried again tonight, he'd make sure they didn't succeed.

F riday morning was chaos. Every time Mattie started one task, Mamm called her away to do another. Since Naomi was watching their young nephews and nieces so that Isaac and Noah could get their families loaded and on the road west, every chore fell to Mattie. She carried piles of blankets to the tables still set up in front of the house and rolled several of them into a bundle.

The wagons were lined up on Glades Pike, the road that ran between their house and Annie's and then west toward the final mountain range before the prairies. Six Conestoga wagons loomed over the low fences on either side of the pike, and two spring wagons followed behind. Daed had suggested using them for the families with little ones, since walking all the way to Indiana would be too hard for them.

Footsteps approached her from behind.

"Henry, can you help me?" She had seen her brother run past a moment ago, and she needed an extra pair of hands to tie the rolls of blankets.

"I'll help." A pair of strong hands grasped the bundle for

her so that she could pull the rope tight. As she tied the last knot, she looked up into Jacob's brown eyes.

"I couldn't have done that without your help, but I thought you had already left with the sheep."

"The sheep do best following behind. We'll come last and let the sheep browse as they go."

"Being last doesn't sound like much fun." Mattie rolled another pile of blankets into a bundle and Jacob held them again as she tied the rope. "I always like to see where we're going."

"And be the first one there?" Jacob's voice held a teasing note.

"Don't you want to see what is over those mountains?" She looked past Jacob's shoulder toward the western hills. Today or tomorrow she would finally see the other side.

Jacob shrugged. "Whatever is there won't disappear between the front wagon and the sheep following behind."

Daed walked by with Mamm's rocking chair. "This is the last, Mattie. Bring the blankets, and we'll be ready to go."

Jacob lifted the bundles. "Your daed is as anxious to leave as you are. Will he be driving the lead wagon today?"

"I hope so."

"I thought you might want to help me herd the sheep, if you don't mind following along behind."

Mattie looked at his face, hopeful and waiting. Follow with the sheep? Mamm came out of the house, hurrying to Annie's to say goodbye one last time. Mattie had said farewell to her sister last night, but this morning Mamm was beside herself with grief. All day long Mamm would ride in the spring wagon with her daughters-in-law Miriam and Emma and their little ones. Mattie imagined the long day of all of them fighting tears, and Naomi holding Mamm's hand, grieving every mile of the way. Their sadness would ruin her anticipation.

"Perhaps I will help you. Riding in the wagons won't be very much fun."

Jacob grinned at her. "I'm not sure the sheep will be fun, but it will be interesting. Meet me at the sheep pen. We'll start after all the wagons are gone."

He left, heading down the road to where the Lancaster County folks were preparing their wagons. Mattie could see the men adjusting harnesses and making a final check of the wheels and running gear. Daed's team stood quietly, already hitched to their old Conestoga wagon and ready to go. It was the same wagon that had brought their family west to Brothers Valley so long ago. That had been a happy time, with all of them anticipating their new home. But this move had Mamm in tears from the day Daed first mentioned it. Leaving Annie and her family behind was the worst part, but Mamm had loved the house and farm like they were part of the family.

"It's only a building and some land," Daed had said. "Our future, and our children's future is more important."

And so he had gotten Mamm to agree to the move, even though it pained her.

Mattie went to the flower bed by the front door and pulled a few weeds that had sprung up between the spring lilies. The violets were growing, but no buds had appeared yet. Her throat tightened. If she had thought about them last fall, she could have dug up some of the plants to take to Indiana. The violets that grew in this protected corner near the house were light blue, almost white, and she would never see them bloom again. Perhaps she could understand Mamm's feelings after all. She touched the limestone wall of the house. There were memories here. They would take the memories with them, for sure, but without these reminders, would they stay fresh?

She opened the door and walked in. The rooms were empty and silent. Only the table and some chairs remained. The inglenook bench where she had warmed herself on so many cold nights faced an empty fireplace. Mamm had even asked her to sweep out the cold ashes before her cousins moved into the house.

She climbed the stairway to the bedroom she shared with Naomi on the west end of the house. She sat on the window seat and gazed out at the familiar scene. The fields, the creek, the woodlot . . . and rising behind them all, the western hills. Her melancholy dropped away at the sight. Today. Today she would go there. She jumped up, ran down the steps and out into the front yard. Enough saying farewell to the old. She was ready for adventure.

Daed called her over to the wagon. "You'll ride with your mamm today?"

"Can Naomi do that? Jacob said I could help him with the sheep."

Daed smiled. "You would like that. But don't ignore Mamm. This is a hard day for her."

"I know. I'll check on her when we stop at noon."

Daed's team and wagon were ready to go, and the other wagons waited in line behind him. After Daed came the Bontragers, with Andrew riding the wheel horse, then the Yoders, and then the small, green wagon driven by Hannah's husband, Josef. Following him were Isaac and Noah, with their families, and then the two spring wagons. Everyone gathered together next to the line of wagons, and Daniel Nafsinger prayed for their journey. Finally Daed started his team down the road, and they were on their way.

The wild desire to run past the wagons rushed through Mattie. If only she could be ahead of all of them, even Daed's team, and be the first to step on the distant reaches of Glades Pike, where only Daed had been before. The blue crests of the mountains beckoned her, but she knew Daed wouldn't let her go ahead. Instead, she closed the gate behind her with a final look at the empty house under the spreading oak trees, and ran down the road to the sheep pen.

Jacob was in the pen with the ewes and one ram, petting each of them in turn, his crook resting in his elbow. He looked like the shepherd boy, David, from the Good Book.

Mattie climbed onto the top of the stone wall and walked along the top, balancing with her arms out at her sides just as she had done every day when Daed had kept the pigs in this field. "When will you leave to follow the wagons?"

"As soon as the last one reaches the top of that rise." Jacob pointed with the curved end of his crook. "You can walk ahead of the sheep with me. Margli and Peter will follow behind to make sure none of them straggle."

"Will I need a crook?"

"Ne." Jacob reached out with the end of the long stick to guide a ewe into line with the rest of the flock. "They follow me pretty well. You won't need to use one."

She jumped down from the wall and met him at the gate. "Then why am I walking with you?"

"To keep me company, of course." His smile started in his eyes and crept to his mouth.

A flush heated Mattie's face. He only wanted her company? She could have stayed with her family after all. But the memory of Mamm's tears stopped her. Naomi was better at helping Mamm than she was. She could ride with her family tomorrow, and the day after. Nothing she could say today would help Mamm.

She opened the gate while Jacob led the ram out, the ewes following. He called them all by name, and they bleated in answer. Each one looked like the others to her, but he had no trouble telling them apart.

Margli and Peter guided the rest of the sheep through the gate, pushing them with the side of a long, thin willow rod whenever one of them balked. As she joined Jacob at the front of the flock, she glanced behind. The lead ewe followed Jacob and the rest of the sheep followed her. If this was the way they traveled, herding the flock should be a simple task. She waved at Margli at the back of the line, and then turned her attention to the road ahead. The way was easy, and with the picket fences dividing the farm yards from the byway, the sheep followed their shepherd willingly.

They traveled for a few miles and then crested a rise. Glades Pike continued straight through the rolling fields, but they had left Brothers Valley. Soon they would pass through the town of Somerset, and then they would be farther west than Mattie had ever gone before.

"What will happen when we get to Somerset town? Won't the sheep run off?"

Jacob glanced at the sheep following behind. "They might. But we'll keep them together as much as we can. That's when we'll need your help. With three behind the flock instead of two, they'll stay in line better."

"Do you like herding the sheep? Wouldn't you rather drive one of the wagons?"

He didn't answer her question right away. They reached the ford through a little stream, and he waited until all the sheep were safely through before looking at her. "When we first left home, I thought Daed had given me the worst job of all when he said the sheep were my responsibility." He stepped to the side of the road. "We'll let them browse a little here by the water before we move on."

Mattie joined Margli as she sat down on the grass along the road, but Peter waded into the little stream again, his hat in his hand. "Help me, Margli. We can catch some crayfish for dinner."

Margli shuddered. "Not me. You can catch all of them that you want. I'm going to rest while I can."

"I'll help you." Jacob followed his brother into the stream. As he turned rocks over, Peter grabbed the creatures and dropped them into his hat.

Margli picked some dandelions and twisted the stems together, one by one. "I'd rather make flower necklaces, wouldn't you, Mattie?"

Mattie picked some flowers and braided the stems to make her own chain. "What will you do with yours when it's finished?"

"I like to put them on the sheep. They look pretty like that, don't you think?"

Mattie lifted her dandelions out of a ewe's reach. "Don't they eat them?"

"Ja, they do." Margli sighed. "But they're still fun to make."

Jacob waited until all the sheep had finished eating from

the bushes along the stream, then led them to a quiet eddy where they drank. Soon they were back on the road, a few of the sheep decorated with flower garlands. Peter ran ahead to catch up with the wagons, carrying his hat full of crayfish.

Mattie watched Jacob. He had said he thought taking care of the sheep was the worst job his daed could give him, but he walked with a swinging step, enjoying himself.

"What changed your mind?"

He glanced at her. "About what?"

"The sheep. You said you didn't want to take care of them."

"When I learned to know them, I found out I was wrong." He turned to watch the flock following him, with Margli bringing up the rear. "I thought they were stupid animals, and I never liked the smell, or the work of shearing them. I was afraid they would take off in all directions once they were away from the sheepfold at home." He reached down and scratched the head of the lead ewe. "But they grew on me. They need me, and as long as I take care of them, they'll follow me anywhere."

"Doesn't it get tiresome? Wouldn't it be more exciting to drive one of the wagons?"

Jacob shrugged. "This is peaceful. As we walk I can let my mind wander and think about all kinds of things."

"Like what?"

"Like the farm I'll have when we reach Indiana."

"You mentioned your farm before. Having your own place is a lot of responsibility and work, isn't it?"

"It's time for me to have my own place and my own family. To have a home that I'll never have to leave again."

They came to the top of another rise and the town of Somerset nestled in the valley below. Mattie let her eyes drift past it to the hills beyond. "Not me."

"You want to keep traveling."

"What could be more exciting? I want to go farther on. I never want the road to end." Mattie waved to the distant hills beyond the town and the fields rising to the western mountains. "Do you see the road going up through the hills? I want to see what's on the other side." She faced Jacob. "I want to see the open spaces of Iowa. I want to see the mountains. I've heard there's an ocean to the west, beyond Oregon." She looked to the mountains again. If she was a bird, she could fly to those far lands and never have to stop in one place.

"And I can't think of anything worse than not having a home." Jacob's voice was so quiet, she almost missed his comment.

Ahead, on the road, Peter came running toward them, his hat firmly on his head.

"They're stopping in Somerset," he called as he came close. "Some are buying supplies. Daed said to take the sheep through to the other side of town and find a place to stop for dinner."

Jacob glanced at the sun. "By the time we find a place to stop, the noon hour will be upon us."

As they drew closer to the town, Mattie dropped back with Margli and Peter to help get the flock safely through the streets. Peter had cut a willow branch for her and trimmed the end to give her a strong but light rod for the sheep.

"You don't poke at them," he said. "You guide them like this." He thrust his rod along the left side of one ewe and she turned to the right. "If they don't obey, you can hit them a little. Their wool is thick, so you won't hurt them."

Mattie practiced with her rod, helping to bunch the flock

closer together as they reached the outskirts of Somerset. An inn by the side of the road had its doors and windows open to the spring sunshine. Some men sat on a bench set between the front of the inn and the road. She stared. Cole Bates and his brothers. So this is where they ended up after they had disappeared during the night. Jacob had chased them off, claiming he had caught one stealing a horse, but Mattie couldn't believe it. No one would accept a family's hospitality and then steal from them.

One of the ewes ducked past Mattie's feet to grab at some dusty grass growing along the fence in front of the inn. Mattie went after her, her willow pole extended to drive the sheep back into the road, but the hungry ewe ignored her. It planted its feet in the dried mud and nibbled at the grass and weeds.

Mattie buried her fingers in the thick fleece. "Come on, now. Get going."

A shadow fell over the sheep's back.

"Having a bit of trouble, are we?" The voice was silky smooth. The words were English.

Mattie released the sheep and stepped back. The night before, he had been dark and mysterious. In the sunlight he was no different from any other man.

Except that he wasn't Amish.

Mattie's tongue clung to the roof of her mouth. Cole leaned over and scratched the sheep's ears.

"It's easy for a sheep to get separated from the flock, isn't it?" His wide smile pulled an answering smile from her.

"I don't know. I've never herded sheep before."

"You looked like you knew what you were doing, until this one decided it was hungry." Cole leaned closer to her.

"If I didn't know better, I'd think it came over here just so we could get acquainted."

"I . . . I already know who you are. You're Cole Bates. You and your brothers were at our farm last night."

The smile grew even wider. "Yeah, that's right. I remember seeing you there." His eyes never left hers, pulling her in. "What's your name?"

"Mattie Schrock."

She heard someone running toward them.

"Mattie," Peter called. "We need to keep the sheep together."

Mattie grasped the ewe's wooly neck and tugged. "I need to go."

"It was nice meeting you." Cole grasped one of her hands and brought it to his mouth. His lips were soft, barely touching the skin on the back of her hand as he gave it a kiss. "I'll see you again soon."

Mattie finally got the ewe walking down the street toward the rest of the flock. She dared to look back at the inn. Cole stood at the fence along the roadway, watching her.

Andrew Bontrager shifted in his saddle as they passed through the outskirts of Somerset and into farmland again. He'd gladly give this job up to Papa this afternoon. Walking sounded good after five hours in the saddle. Up ahead, Eli Schrock turned his wagon off to the side of the road where a stand of trees gave some shade. Andrew's stomach growled. Dinnertime couldn't come soon enough.

He drove the team onto the shady grass just beyond the Schrocks, where Papa took the lead horse's bridle. Andrew eased up, putting his weight on his left foot, then slowly lifted his stiff right leg over the saddle and slid to the ground. His brother-in-law, Thomas Fisher, had advised him to ride often through the last few weeks to prepare for all the time he would spend on horseback during this trip, but something more appealing had always come up.

Late-night rides in Papa's spring wagon with Mattie Schrock, for one. He felt a grin starting at the thought of Mattie. She was a feisty girl who loved to match wits with him. So many of the girls around were moony-eyed cows who would do anything to get him to look in their direction. But he had tired of that kind of thing by the time he was twenty-two. Of course, he'd miss Fronie Mast with her giggling kisses, and Heddy Cable with her sly, teasing looks in his direction during the church meeting, but Mattie's verbal sparring was fun. An evening with her made him feel like maybe he could settle down with one girl.

With both feet on the ground, Andrew flexed his knees, trying to keep them from trembling. He should have listened to Thomas.

Lydia Schrock, Annalise Yoder, and his mamm took charge of the communal meal, and soon pots were hanging over the fire and the fragrance of stewing meat drifted over the clearing.

The men gathered in groups of three or four, and Andrew walked over to where the younger men were standing around one of the Hertzlers' horses. Josef Bender had the horse's left front hoof between his knees in the traditional farrier's pose.

"Ja, ja, ja. A loose nail is all." He straightened up, letting the horse's hoof drop to the ground. "I haf my toolbox, and quickly it will be fixed."

"She hasn't gone lame, then?" Elias Hertzler stroked the mare's neck.

"Lame she is not. There is no harm done."

As Josef turned to go, Andrew let loose with the laugh he had been holding in. He turned to Jacob Yoder, standing next to him. "He has the funniest accent. Where did he come from?"

Jacob raised his eyebrows and Andrew grinned before his face could turn bright red. Josef was Jacob's brother-in-law, and he remembered it too late. He had spoken before thinking and put his foot in his mouth again.

He slapped Jacob on the back. "I was just making a joke. He's a good guy, and it's a real bonus to have a farrier along on the trip."

Jacob's face relaxed into a grin. "He is a good guy. He came over from Europe alone when he was fourteen, and that's why he has the accent. But he knows his horses."

As the men separated, Jacob started walking toward the Yoders' wagon, and Andrew followed him, grinning at the group of girls gathered there.

"We haven't gotten a chance to talk much yet." Andrew shortened his stride to match Jacob's. "I heard that you know the Schrocks from back when they lived along the Conestoga."

Jacob looked up at him. "Our families were neighbors, so we spent plenty of time together as children. Isaac and Noah were a lot older than me, but the girls were good friends with my sisters."

Andrew laughed. "They're still a lot older than you. But a six- or eight-year difference is greater when you're a kid than when you're grown up." He glanced ahead of them to

74

the girls. Mattie was there, watching the two of them, along with her sister, Naomi. Next to them was the Hertzler girl, Johanna. She might be a lot of fun, and he for sure wouldn't get tired of looking at her. She had a sweet look about her.

He glanced at Jacob and saw the other man's eyes were on the girls too. Jacob seemed to be the type who would choose one girl and marry her without any thought that there might be more than one that could catch his eye, and from the look on his face, Jacob had already made his choice. But which one?

Soft giggles came from the girls as they drew closer.

"It looks like all the pretty girls survived our first morning on the road." Andrew sidled close to Mattie, making sure his hand brushed her arm.

Mattie stepped just far enough away from him to avoid his touch. She always played hard to get. He glanced past Naomi's red face to Johanna. She smiled at him, then ducked her head, her hand over her mouth. He left Mattie's side and stepped close to the Conestoga girl. He bent toward her.

"Did you have fun this morning, Jo?" He kept his voice low and she had to lean closer to him to hear his question. That nickname had appeared on his tongue without thought, but he liked the way it sounded, pronouncing the *J* like an Englisher would.

She giggled and glanced at the others. "It is a fine day for a ride. How about you?"

He straightened, giving an exaggerated stretch and yawn that made all the girls laugh. "Driving the wagon is like sitting in a rocking chair. I slept all the way here."

Naomi left the group and walked toward her family's wagon. Just as well. With her cast eye, she always made him uncomfortable. She was nice enough, and a good cook. She would make someone a fine wife, but it wouldn't be him.

Mattie grabbed Jo's hand. "We need to help get dinner ready. You boys should get some rest while we're stopped."

The girls caught up with Naomi, their skirts swinging in the breeze as they ran across the grass.

Andrew plucked a dandelion blossom and brushed the furry center with his thumb. "She's a nice girl."

Jacob turned toward him. "Which one?"

"Does it matter?" Andrew looked at his new friend and grinned. "When they're that pretty, why not enjoy them all?"

Jacob raised those eyebrows again, but Andrew kept on grinning. This trip might turn out to be fun after all.

6

Mattie didn't help Jacob with the sheep in the afternoon. Instead, she chose to walk behind the spring wagons with Naomi and Johanna. Jacob worked to keep his disappointment from showing. As it was, he was making Bitte skittish, and her agitation transferred to the rest of the flock. In his mind all he could see was the girls having a grand time with Andrew Bontrager while he slogged back here on the dusty road with the sheep.

Jacob kicked at a rock in the road. No matter how he wanted to dislike Andrew, he couldn't. He was just too likable. But when it came to Mattie . . . Jacob kicked at another rock, making Bitte jump sideways.

How could one man be attractive to so many girls?

Or was it Mattie who was attractive to so many boys?

He hadn't missed the exchange between Mattie and Cole Bates back in Somerset. The man reminded Jacob too much of George McIvey, the Englisher who had stolen Liesbet away last year. His sister would still be alive if it hadn't been for that man. And he didn't have to spend too much time wondering to know that Cole Bates probably wanted the same thing from Mattie. To steal her away from her family. All these Englishers were like that. Rough, coarse, selfish, and dangerous. If the Bates boys showed up again, he'd be sure to send them on their way.

Bitte bleated and Jacob slowed his walk. Being a shepherd meant putting his flock ahead of everything, and he was letting his feelings put the flock in jeopardy. Jacob patted the ewe and scratched her ears. She butted her head against his leg, then moved to the side of the road to crop some grass. He stopped then, letting all the sheep move to the side of the road for a rest.

"How far are we going today?" Peter asked when he caught up to Jacob.

"I don't know, but I'm sure we'll walk for a few more hours before we stop for the night."

"You're right." The boy sighed.

Just seven years old, Peter was more like Jacob than he was like Hansli. Jacob pushed at the memories of his brother with the straight blond hair. So light it had almost been white. Ten years ago, he and Hansli had been as close as brothers could be. Jacob had taught him to fish and to swing on the rope in the barn loft. They had hunted mushrooms and greens together in the spring and played in the haystacks in the summer. They had made plans to build a bobsled that winter. Jacob was going to teach him how to use the saw.

Jacob cleared his throat as he pulled his thoughts back from the edge of the darkness. Hansli was gone and no one would ever replace him. This little brother, this Peter, he was too young. He wasn't really a brother. Not like Hansli had been. Besides, Peter had William. At twenty years old, Jacob had no time for little boys.

Margli came up to them slowly, braiding another garland for the sheep. She had made dozens of them today. But they kept her busy. Girls always seemed to find silly things like that to do.

The sheep started moving on down the road as they grazed and Jacob followed. He'd let them graze until they reached a stream, then he'd let them drink and rest for a while.

"Peter, go catch up with the wagons. Tell Daed that we're going to rest the sheep and we'll catch up later."

When Peter came back, Mattie was with him, along with Johanna, Naomi, and Hannah. They giggled as they came toward him, hiding their mouths in their hands as they whispered to each other.

"What are you girls up to?" Jacob kept his eyes on Mattie. She seemed to be the ringleader among them.

"Nothing," Johanna said. "Mattie told us how much fun it was to herd the sheep, so we thought we'd come help you."

"There isn't enough work to keep all four of you busy this afternoon."

"Who says we want to be busy?"

Johanna's smile was different from her usual look. Jacob took another glance at her. The sad eyes and the worry lines on her forehead had disappeared. She almost looked pretty.

The sheep took no notice of them, but grazed in the soft grass along the road. The rich spring grazing would do them and their coming lambs good. Even with the traveling, they should all have healthy lambs. Mamm was a different worry.

Mattie and Naomi sat with Margli in the grass, weaving even more dandelion garlands. Jacob wandered over to where

Hannah and Johanna were perched on some boulders. He sat in the grass near their feet, facing the flock.

"Hannah, I don't know how to ask this . . ."

"I'm not taking care of the sheep for you, Jacob."

His face grew hot. "That's not what I meant." He laid his crook down. "It's about Mamm. Is she all right?"

Hannah stilled. "You've seen it too?"

"She is tired all the time, and short of breath."

"I'm afraid this trip is too hard for her, even riding in the wagon." Hannah drew circles on her knee with her finger.

Johanna looked from one of them to the other. "She's only having a baby, isn't she? There's nothing to worry about."

Hannah sighed. "Ja, and Liesbet was only having a baby."

Jacob kept his eyes on the grass stems bent under Hannah's toes. She moved her feet, and the blades sprang back up, one by one.

"Liesbet was ill." Johanna leaned toward them. "You don't have to worry about your mamm."

Hannah shook her head. "But she wasn't like this with William. We didn't even know she was expecting a little one until just before he was born. But this time, she's so . . . so . . ."

"Big." Jacob finished her sentence. "And awkward. She has trouble keeping her balance. I've never seen her like this before." He plucked a grass blade. "Should we say something to Daed?"

"I have already," Hannah said. "He's worried too. But he'll think of something to do. He knows best when it comes to taking care of Mamm." She straightened with a sigh. "And we have the other women to help. Mary Nafsinger is a midwife, and Mamm talks to her nearly every day. I don't know what else we can do."

"We'll watch her and take care of her." Jacob looked up

at Hannah. The corners of her mouth trembled as she met his eyes. "She'll be all right. She has to be."

On the second evening, the group stopped for the night near a stream at the foot of the small range of mountains on the western edge of Somerset County. Jacob joined the men as they surveyed the road stretching in front of them, disappearing behind the soft mound of a tree-covered slope.

"The grade is gentle enough," said Yost Bontrager. "We should have no trouble on Monday morning, with the horses fresh after a rest over the Sabbath."

"We've climbed quite a ways already." Eli Schrock gestured behind them, where the rolling hills fell away toward Somerset and Brothers Valley beyond. "The rise has been so gradual that we've scarcely noticed." He turned to look at the mountains looming above them to the west. "Monday's road will be different, though."

"Ja, ja, ja." Daed ran his thumbs up and down his suspenders. "Take it one step after the next. But worry about tomorrow just wastes today's time."

Jacob gathered the sheep together in a grassy spot near the road. While they settled into their grazing, Jacob took a seat on a fallen log and watched the families set up camp. After even this short time on the road, the folks from the scattered valleys had become one community. Andrew, Josef, and the other young men unharnessed the horses and put them on picket pins away from the wagons, while the older men made a community campfire for cooking. Mattie and Johanna helped the children find ways to help, while the women started the supper preparation.

Mattie's brother, Henry, had been given the responsibility of the four milk cows the families were taking to Indiana. Tethered to the back of the wagons as they traveled, the cows walked along easily. And then Henry was the one who cared for them during the noon hour and at night, making sure they had water and plenty of grass for grazing. He also milked the cows morning and night, a job that Mattie or one of the other women shared with him as they had time.

Jacob pulled a grass stem and twirled it between his fingers, watching the boy. He remembered Henry from years ago when the Schrocks lived on the Conestoga. Henry and Hansli had been playmates. The two of them had looked so much alike, with their bowl-cut straight blond hair and blue eyes. If he closed his eyes, he could see the two little boys playing in the creek, chasing frogs, and sometimes catching them.

But then Hansli had died.

The diphtheria hadn't touched the Schrock family, or the Hertzlers or Bontragers. Out of the Amish families living along the Conestoga, only the Yoders had contracted the illness when the epidemic traveled from one home to another in random leaps from Mennonite families to Dunkard to Lutheran. Only the Yoders had lost so many of their little ones. Jacob wrenched the grass stem into two pieces and threw it aside.

Maybe it had been a good thing that the Schrocks had moved to Somerset County when they did, because Jacob had found himself hating the sight of Henry. Every church Sunday, the little boy would seek him out for some reason, but Jacob couldn't stand to be around him. He didn't need that constant reminder of his brother.

Even now, watching Henry as he picketed the cows in the

lush grass, he only saw the kind of boy Hansli would have grown into. Would he be as tall as Henry? As quick to laugh? Jacob turned back to the sheep, his eyes blurred. What would his life have been like if Hansli hadn't died?

By the time supper was ready, the sheep had eaten their fill and settled down in the shaded spot between the wagons and the stream. Jacob left them and stepped into the circle just as the community joined together in prayer for the meal. After filling his plate with chicken broiled over the open fire and dried apples, Jacob sat on one of the benches that had been placed around the fire, positioning himself so he had a view of the sheep between two of the wagons. Mattie and Naomi came to sit with him, followed by Henry.

"You look lonely over here, Jacob." Mattie sat next to him, leaving room beside her for Naomi. Henry sat on Jacob's other side.

"Not really lonely, but company is always welcome."

"Do you remember Henry?" Naomi leaned forward to see around Mattie as she spoke. "He was so little when we moved to Brothers Valley, but he says he remembers you."

Jacob turned to the young man next to him, nearly as tall as he was, but thin and long legged as a colt. His hair had darkened over the years, but it was still straight as corn silk. "For sure, I remember you." He stopped as his throat grew tight. Swallowing, he went on. "You were good friends with my brother."

Henry looked down at his plate. "That's right. I still miss Hansli." He looked up into Jacob's eyes. "I would imagine you do too, even though it's been a long time." Henry's face was tight with caution.

"Do you remember very much from those days?"

Henry grinned. "I remember that you always chased us away from the hen house when we tried to play there."

It was Jacob's turn to grin. "You were a couple of rascals."

"I remember, too, that you and Hansli planned to build a bobsled in the winter. I remember we talked about it in the barn one day." Henry stopped and ducked his head. "Sorry. I didn't mean to bring up that day."

The day before Hannah got sick. The last day he and Hansli played together. "It's all right, Henry. It was a good day to remember."

"Do you think . . . ?" Henry rubbed at his chin. "Do you think if Hansli was here now, we'd still be friends?"

Jacob squeezed the boy's shoulder. Henry was the only boy his age in the party, and he must be lonely at times. "I'm sure you would be." He looked sideways at the young hands tearing crumbs off a piece of bread. "I think the three of us would have been good friends, don't you?"

Henry looked at him. "I think so." He grinned. "Maybe I could help you with the sheep sometimes."

"And leave the cows?"

"I only need to take care of them a few times a day. Other than that, I don't have much to do."

Jacob nodded. "You're welcome to help with the sheep whenever you like. Do you know much about them?"

Henry shook his head. "Only what I've seen you do. We've never had sheep on our farm. They need to browse as they walk, right?"

"I need them to walk steadily, but not strain them. The ewes are all due to drop their lambs soon."

"Are they a special kind? I've never seen ones that look like them."

84

Jacob glanced at Mattie and Naomi, afraid they might feel ignored, but they were holding their own conversation. "They're a breed called Leicester Longwools. My grandfather bought the first pair for our farm, and we've been raising them ever since. Their wool has longer fibers than other sheep, and that makes the cloth Mamm weaves softer than other wool cloth."

They continued discussing the sheep and their care until the younger children were called to their beds and Naomi left the group to help with her nephews and nieces. Then Andrew, Johanna, Hannah, and Josef came to join them and the talk turned to the road ahead. Jacob watched Mattie as they talked. Her eyes continually went to the mountains above them. She had said something about crossing those mountains, hadn't she? Whatever it was, she looked like she could hardly wait to get to the top. She would have to, though. Tomorrow was the Sabbath, and they would be resting in this campsite all day.

After the talk slowed to a comment here and there, and the fire died down to coals, Andrew started singing a song from the Ausbund and the rest of them joined in. The song spoke of sacrifice, dedication, and God's care. As they sang, Jacob felt Mattie lean toward him and he drank in her profile. If the rest of the journey continued on as well as the first two days had, he couldn't ask for anything better.

7

The first Sabbath morning on the road dawned clear and cool, with drops of dew clinging to the leaves on the huckleberry bushes at the edge of the campsite. Mattie brushed through them on the way to the stream with Naomi, soaking her skirts.

"Too bad it isn't June," Naomi said, tugging at a branch resplendent with blossoms. "We could have huckleberry pie for supper."

"By June we'll be in Indiana and we can pick berries there." She grinned at Naomi. "Pie, and blueberry buckle, and dried berries for the winter. I can taste them already!"

Naomi pulled at her dragging skirts. "If we ever get there. My skirts are so wet from the dew that I might just melt into the ground."

"Why are you so grouchy this morning?" Mattie reached for Naomi's hand, pulling her along. "Your dress will dry in no time."

"Am I grouchy? I guess I just didn't sleep well."

"You should have stayed with us around the fire last night.

We had so much fun talking, and then Andrew started the singing."

"I know. I heard you."

Mattie glanced at her sister. Naomi's face was as stormy as the sky was clear. Something was bothering her, for sure.

They reached the stream and Mattie dipped her pails in the clear water, then waited for Naomi to fill hers. She lifted her face up to the sunbeams dancing between the branches of the trees overhead. On a day like today, she could climb the highest mountains. When they left this campsite tomorrow, they would follow the well-worn road to the top of the western mountains. After all the years of wondering what the other side was like, she would finally find out. But not today, on the Sabbath. No traveling on this beautiful day. That joy would have to wait.

By the time they returned to the campsite, the fire was burning well and the older women had the big cast-iron skillet on its tripod, filled with sausages. Mattie put one pail of water on a bench with Naomi's and poured the other one into the big coffeepot. She reached for the bail to hang it over the fire, but a strong hand took it from her.

"I'll get that for you."

She looked into Jacob's face, freshly shaved and scrubbed, his hair still dripping from his morning wash, and let him hoist the heavy pot to the hook over the hottest part of the fire.

"Denki."

He smiled at her. The sun behind his head turned the wet curls around his ears into a ring of sparkling light. "I'm going to help Henry milk the cows while breakfast is cooking. Will you be helping too?"

Mattie flushed as she remembered how close she had felt to Jacob that first evening as they milked the cows together in the barn back in Brothers Valley. It was less than a week ago, and yet it seemed so far away.

"I'm needed here, helping with the little ones."

Jacob took a step away. "Ja, well, I thought . . ." He stopped and rubbed the back of his neck. "I thought we could keep each other company while we worked."

Beyond him, Mattie caught sight of Andrew filling the feedbags for the Bontrager team. "Henry will be there. I have too much to do."

He took another step away. "Then I'll see you later."

He turned toward the meadow where the cows had been picketed, catching his foot in the long grass and nearly falling as he went. Mattie couldn't help a giggle escaping before she covered her mouth. Jacob didn't turn back, but continued on his way, the back of his neck as red as if it was sunburned.

Johanna stepped up next to her. "You're so mean to him."

"What do you mean?"

"He just wanted to spend some time with you. If he had asked me to milk the cows with him, I would have jumped at the chance."

Mattie eyed her friend. Johanna still watched Jacob as he made his way toward the milk cows. "Are you sweet on him?"

Johanna blushed and ducked her head. "I was once, but I'm not so sure now."

"Why?"

"All the way to Somerset County from home, he didn't pay any more attention to me than he did before we left. I've always thought we were made for each other, since our mothers were best friends, and his sister and I have always

88

been friends too. But I might as well not exist, as far as he's concerned."

"I'm sure he knows you exist."

Johanna sighed, crossing her arms at her waist. "He knows I exist, but he doesn't think I'm anything special. Just one of Hannah's friends." She turned toward Mattie. "But you—he looks at you the way I've always wanted him to look at me."

Mattie bit her lower lip. "He doesn't look at me in any different way than anyone else."

"You don't see it, do you?" Johanna rubbed her upper arms against a chilly breeze from the north. "He looks at you like he has known you since he was born and wants to know you for the rest of his life."

"You're such a romantic." Mattie squeezed her friend's shoulders. "But if you want him to notice you, I'll stay out of the way." Even as she said the words, her stomach gave a small flip. She would hate to ignore Jacob for the rest of the trip.

"Don't worry about it." Johanna smiled as she looked toward the field on the other side of the wagons where the horses grazed. "There is more than one good-looking boy on this trip."

"You're talking about Andrew Bontrager."

"For sure. You probably haven't noticed him since you've grown up with him, but I think he's pretty special."

Mattie laid her hand on Johanna's arm. "I need to tell you something about Andrew. He isn't exactly . . . well, I'm not sure he's ever going to get married and settle down."

"Why not?"

"You've seen how all the girls like him."

Johanna nodded.

"He likes all the girls too."

"Has he ever taken you out?"

Mattie laughed. "Too often. I've gone riding with him in the spring wagon all around Brothers Valley. He knows the best quiet, secluded spots to rest the horses." When a frown crossed Johanna's face, Mattie squeezed her friend's arm. "And I'm not the only girl he's taken to those places. He isn't one to get serious about a girl. Do you know what I mean?"

"I think I do. But maybe he'll meet someone who will change his mind someday."

Mattie gave Johanna's arm another squeeze as she turned to find Mamm. "Maybe he will."

Annalise shifted on her pallet, making the wagon sway. She stared at the canvas cover, bright white in the afternoon sunshine. She sighed, the deep breath bringing the now familiar scents of sun-warmed cloth and still-fresh lumber and paint from this new wagon Christian had made last winter.

He had worked so hard on it, wanting her to be comfortable on the trip west. He had made it large enough to carry her loom, the pieces bundled together along one side of the wagon bed. And he had created this pallet for her out of packing cases and quilts so she would have a comfortable place to sleep. Her husband was a loving and caring man. He always had been, since the first time she met him.

Soft murmurs of conversation drifted through the canvas wall from the camp outside. This Sunday afternoon rest was a blessing, but for some reason she couldn't remain still. She was tired to the point of exhaustion, but couldn't relax.

She pushed herself to a sitting position, straightened her apron as well as she could, and climbed out of the wagon. She left the circle of the camp and headed in the direction Hannah had gone that morning to fetch water. Perhaps watching the stream would help her relax.

Picking her way through the tall grass, she skirted a patch of brambles and followed the trail of bent grass to the water's edge. It was a small stream, only a couple feet wide. She could step across it. Or she could have before this babe had grown so large.

Annalise rubbed at the taut side of her stomach, pressing at the tiny feet that pushed against her hand.

"Annalise?"

She turned toward Christian's voice. He had followed her, always watching out for her. "I'm here, by the stream."

He came around the edge of the brambles, smiling as he caught sight of her. "I saw you leave the camp, but when you didn't return right away, I grew concerned."

"I couldn't sleep," she said, taking his hand as he reached her. "I thought a walk might do me some good."

"The babe keeps you awake during the day as well as at night?"

She leaned her head against his shoulder. "I can't find a comfortable way to rest."

"I saw you talking with Mary yesterday. Is all well?"

"She seems to think so. But she also thinks the babe will come sooner than I have been expecting. Perhaps as soon as May."

"But you told me it wouldn't be until July." Christian ran his hand up and down her arm, his touch familiar and comforting. "We won't be settled in Indiana by May."

She looked into his face, at the worry lines that had grown deeper in the last minute. "We rest in God's hands, Christian."

"Ja, ja, ja. But he gives wisdom to act when necessary."
He shifted, took a step away, and clasped his hands behind
his back, staring at the stream.

Annalise watched him as he stood there, this man of hers.
So patient. And at times, so wise. They had survived much
pain together, with the loss of their three little ones years
ago, and Liesbet so recently. She lowered herself onto a log,
sighing from the ease of the pain in her back. She rubbed her
swollen stomach. Poor Liesbet. She could only pray that this
wee babe of hers would live to see the light of day. She turned
away from the dark thought that she might be destined for
the same end as her daughter, in pain and suffering, with
only death for both her and the baby at the end.

The baby inside kicked at her hand again, and she smiled.
This babe was strong, for sure. She needn't fear for his safety.
Or hers. The baby kicked again, sharply. This baby could
very well be a girl.

Christian sat on the log beside her, dropping heavily and
rubbing his beard. "Perhaps we shouldn't go all the way to
Indiana. We could settle in Ohio."

"But won't the land be too expensive there? Jacob was planning to buy a farm, and he was expecting to pay Indiana prices."

"You're right, the prices in Ohio are higher. We wouldn't
be able to buy as large a farm as I had hoped. And Jacob . . ."
He sighed, keeping his eyes on the little stream. "Jacob would
probably choose to continue on to Indiana. Josef and Hannah, also."

"We can't let them go on to Indiana without us. I couldn't
bear to be parted from them." Annalise's eyes filled, as they
did so often lately. How could she say goodbye to Jacob and
Hannah so soon after losing Liesbet?

"We needn't worry about it now." Christian took her hand, rubbing the rough, red skin. "But please, speak with Mary again, and often. She has much experience with these things, and we will rely on her advice."

Annalise squeezed Christian's hand. "I will talk to Mary every day, if you wish. But I'm not sure what she could tell us, other than when she might think the babe will be coming, and I'll be able to tell that."

"I know. After giving birth so many times, you know what to expect. But this time is different, isn't it?"

Annalise nodded, even as the overactive baby kicked again, this time on the other side of her stomach. *This time is very different.*

Sunday supper was a cold meal of sliced souse on pieces of brown bread. Mattie was thankful for the pot of mustard Josef and Hannah shared with the group. Souse wasn't her favorite meal, but the mustard made it easier to swallow.

By sunset, the young children had been taken to their beds and settled in for the night. Mattie lingered near the dying fire with Naomi and Johanna. Once the evening chores were done, they were joined by Jacob, Henry, and Andrew.

Andrew pushed himself between Mattie and Naomi, making them move aside for him. Her sister's face glowed in the firelight, but Mattie sighed. Andrew didn't realize he was only leading Naomi on by this kind of attention.

"You girls have been off by yourselves all day," he said. "What have you been doing?"

Naomi giggled and Johanna stared into the fire. Mattie was ready to box Andrew's ears. If he was trying to cause trouble between the girls, he was succeeding. She stood, threw another stick on the fire, and moved around to sit on the other side of Johanna. Let him try to play favorites. She wasn't going along.

"We took the children on a walk so their mothers could rest," Naomi said. "We found all kinds of wildflowers."

Andrew reached across Naomi's lap and poked Johanna's shoulder. "What about you, Jo? Did you go with them?"

She glanced at him, and then back at the fire. "You know I did. You watched us leave."

The breeze shifted, blowing the smoke in Mattie's face. She scooted closer to Jacob.

"That was a good thing you did." Jacob's voice was quiet, his words intended only for her. "I know it was your idea, to keep the children occupied this afternoon."

Mattie felt her face heat at his words. She hadn't thought he was paying attention earlier when she had suggested the idea to Johanna and Naomi. "There are so many children in our group, and when left to their own games, they can get quite noisy."

"Which is fine for a Thursday evening, but not so much for the Sabbath."

She looked into his face. His smile gave a warmth to his eyes she hadn't seen since they were young children back along the Conestoga.

"Hello the camp."

The English voice from behind her made Mattie jump. Jacob's smile turned to a frown.

"Those Bates brothers again. What do they want with us?"

Daed and Christian Yoder came forward as Cole Bates stepped into the firelight, leading his horse by the reins, his brothers still mounted behind him. Mattie and the others stood.

"Good evening. What brings you to our camp?" Daed's voice was welcoming, but Mattie heard the note of cautious reserve.

"We're passing through, and thought we might share supper." Cole answered Daed, but his black eyes drifted to Mattie, making her stomach flip. His gaze held her as if she was a sparrow and he the hawk who hunted her. Mattie shook off the notion as quickly as it came.

"Sorry, we had a cold supper tonight, and it's all gone. We're settling in for the night," Daed said. "You're welcome to use our fire, though."

Beside her, Mattie felt Jacob stiffen at those words.

"We thank you kindly for your invitation." Cole smiled, that black gaze moving from one of them to another. "But with the bright moon tonight, we'll keep traveling on." He turned and mounted his horse, then pierced Mattie with that look again. "Since we seem to be traveling the same road, I'm sure we'll run into each other again."

He reined his horse around, and then the three men were shadows on the moonlit road.

Once they were out of sight, Jacob said, "I don't trust them."

"They're gone now." Daed stepped out of the firelight in the direction of their wagon. "It's time for bed, Mattie. Naomi."

Before following Daed and Naomi, Mattie turned to Jacob. "You don't trust them because you don't know them. They're different from us, but that doesn't make them evil, does it?"

"It isn't just that they're English. I don't like the way that

Cole looks at the camp, and at you. As if he's trying to see how much he can steal before we stop him."

Mattie laughed. "You should hear yourself, Jacob Yoder. I never knew you were so suspicious."

He fixed his brown eyes on her. "I wasn't when we were younger, but I am now. I don't trust him."

Jacob walked toward the edge of the camp where the horses were picketed, and Mattie turned to follow Daed and Naomi. She held on to the image of Cole Bates standing in the firelight, and a shiver went through her. She had never seen anyone like him, with his sharp features and striking black hair and eyes, and his mustache a thin black line on his upper lip. There was no one like him among the Amish.

When Mattie reached their wagon, Mamm was standing near the wagon tongue with a bucket in her hand, peering into the darkness in the direction of the stream.

"Mattie, take this and catch up to Henry. He only took one bucket when he left to get water, and we need both pails filled."

Mattie grabbed the pail and headed toward the stream. After a day of use, the deer trail she and Naomi had taken this morning had become wider and easier to follow, even in the moonlight. Up ahead she saw a dark figure in the path and hurried toward him.

"Henry, Mamm wanted you to take both pails. Here's the other one."

"You can stop with that Dutch talk, little girl."

Mattie stopped short on the path. Cole Bates stood in front of her.

"I hoped you'd come this way tonight. Maybe we can get better acquainted." Cole stepped closer, reaching toward her with one hand. "Let's talk for a while." His voice lowered to a whisper as he drew her off the path.

A thrill went down Mattie's spine. She took another step, then looked back. The path was only a few feet away. "What do you want to talk about?"

His teeth flashed as he took her hand. "Every time I run into you folks, I see you watching me. Why is that?"

She felt her face heat in the cool night air. "I don't look at you more than any of the others."

He chuckled low in his throat. "Now, now. You don't want to lie to me, do you? I see those brown eyes of yours watching me." He turned her hand over and stroked her palm with his thumb. "You're different from the rest of those Amish, you know."

"No, I'm not." Mattie tugged her hand out of his grasp. "I'm the same as any Amish girl you meet."

"You want something . . ." His voice drifted off as he cocked his head. "I'll figure out what it is eventually."

She shook her head. "I need to look for my brother." She took a step back toward the path.

"I'll be watching you, Mattie-girl. I'll find out what it is you want."

Henry came up the path from the stream. "Mattie?"

Cole glanced in Henry's direction, then squeezed Mattie's elbow and melted into the underbrush.

Henry caught up to her as she tried to control her quivering knees. "Mattie? Who was that?"

"It was . . . it was . . ." She took a deep breath and felt the shivering stop. That Cole Bates was dangerous. Exciting, but dangerous.

"It was Andrew, wasn't it?" Henry pushed past her with his full pail. "He's sweet on you, I know he is."

"Henry, wait." Mattie ran to catch up with him. "I'll take the water back to the wagon. Mamm wants you to fill both buckets."

She traded the empty pail for Henry's full one, then watched him go back down the trail toward the stream. Cole might be along the path, waiting to find her alone again, away from the safety of the wagons, but Mamm was waiting for the water. She turned toward the camp, then glanced back again. She would give anything to know if he was watching her like he said.

8

When Jacob reached the edge of the camp, he turned back to watch Mattie. Once she had reached the wagon safely, he turned his attention to the horses.

Mattie's brothers, Isaac and Noah, had stretched a length of rope around some trees when they made camp yesterday evening, enclosing a grassy area for the horses to rest. Jacob walked around the circle, counting the twenty-six horses and checking their halter ropes, tied to the encircling main rope so they wouldn't wander during the night. If the Bates brothers tried to steal a horse again, they'd find the task to be easy. They could just cut the makeshift corral and lead the string of horses away.

Jacob pushed his hat back and then settled it on his head again. They were too trusting, these Amish from Brothers Valley. If they knew what he knew about these English thieves, they would have secured the horses differently, or set a watch, or something. But they hadn't watched their sister stolen away by a smooth-talking rascal.

He had watched Cole Bates leave with his silent brothers, but Jacob wasn't fooled. They weren't going to just travel on down the road when they had already tried once to steal a horse.

He turned as someone approached from the direction of the camp. He relaxed when he saw Andrew.

"I saw you head in this direction. Is something wrong with the horses?"

"I don't like the thought of Cole Bates hanging around."

Andrew peered into the dark underbrush. "I don't see anyone."

When he turned back, Jacob expected to see the moonlight flashing on the mocking smile Andrew always seemed to have ready. But his face was solemn.

"I believe you, you know. Those Bates brothers tried to steal one of the horses before we left Brothers Valley."

"I thought no one took me seriously."

Andrew shrugged. "What good would it have done to go after them, once they left? The horses were safe."

"Maybe they wouldn't have tried to come back."

"If they did steal a horse or two, would that really hurt us? The church teaches us not to resist when an enemy tries to harm us. Why not just let them take a horse?"

Andrew reached toward the nearest horse, one of his father's, and stroked its long nose.

Jacob clenched his fists, then let them loosen again. "Because thieves like that don't stop at one horse. They always want more. Didn't you see the way Cole looked at Mattie and the other girls?"

Andrew's hand on the horse's nose paused, and then moved around to the neck as the animal took a step closer to him. "I hadn't noticed, but they wouldn't think of trying to woo one of our girls, would they? Not with all the fathers and brothers around."

Jacob moved closer to Andrew, lowering his voice. "That's what I thought too, until a man just like them stole my sister from our home."

Andrew's head turned toward him. "Is that what happened to your other sister? I heard that she died."

"She did. Trying to give birth to the Englisher's child."

Andrew stroked the horse. "I'm sorry. I didn't know."

"I don't want the same thing to happen to one of the other girls."

"Then here's what we'll do. I'll organize the men, and the girls will always have someone keeping watch over them."

Jacob's fists clenched again at Andrew's assumption of authority. "I'm not sure keeping watch over them will be enough." It hadn't been enough for Liesbet. She had been safe, at home with her family, and had still fallen prey to George McIvey's plans.

Andrew straightened to his full height, a good six inches taller than Jacob. "Don't worry about it. Our girls know a scoundrel when they see one. They'll be fine." He glanced around the circle of horses. "The horses, on the other hand . . . It would be a hardship to lose even one of them, wouldn't it? I wouldn't fight one of the Bates brothers to keep them from stealing them, but it wouldn't do any harm to try to keep them away."

"You'll help me keep watch tonight?"

"I'll get my blankets and meet you back here."

Jacob walked around the string of horses as Andrew headed back to his wagon. Andrew was a welcome help, but he didn't seem to take Jacob seriously. He didn't take anything seriously. The girls all liked him, that was obvious. It must be his fun-loving attitude.

He stopped on the far side of the horses from the camp. Out here, all was dark and still. The only sound was an owl hooting in the distance. The light breeze from earlier in the day had died down, and the horses stood quietly, heads down and relaxed.

Was he too suspicious? Too serious? He looked across the circle of horses toward the camp. The fire was burning down and the wagons were quiet. Perhaps he should be more like Andrew, ready to forgive and forget, trusting people unless they gave him a reason not to. He glanced into the darkness behind him and tried to ignore the shiver creeping up his back, as if someone was watching him.

Cole Bates had given him enough reasons to distrust him.

Andrew passed between the fire and the horses, carrying his blankets, and Jacob met him at the edge of the camp.

"If you watch here, I'll settle in on the far side," Jacob said.

"Why don't we keep each other company? The horses will alert us if a stranger comes near."

Jacob shifted. The woods on the far side had been quiet, that creeping feeling just his imagination. Perhaps Andrew was right. He went to the wagon to fetch his blankets and told Daed what they planned, then went back to the makeshift campsite Andrew had set up. He had even started a small fire.

The firelight showed his grin as he greeted Jacob. "I thought we'd want to be cozy tonight. It has gotten chilly since the sun went down."

Jacob didn't answer, but spread his blanket on the other side of the fire from Andrew. The bright light from the flames would make it impossible to see into the darkness around the horses.

Andrew plopped onto his blanket, kicking his feet out as he leaned back on his elbows. "Now this is the life."

Jacob gave up on trying to see into the woods. He would have to rely on the horses to alert them to any danger. "What do you mean?"

"Out here, away from parents and responsibilities. Nobody telling us what to do."

Jacob put another small stick on the fire. As long as it was burning, he might as well keep it fed. "That doesn't bother me. When Daed gives me work to do, it's the best way to learn. When I buy my farm in Indiana, I want to know everything about how to take care of it."

Andrew pulled at a stem of grass and stuck it in his mouth. "It doesn't bother you that you still have to take orders from him?"

"It never has." Jacob shrugged. "I guess I never thought about it much."

The other man sat up. "Have you joined church yet?"

"Of course I did, when I was eighteen." Jacob calculated Andrew's age. At twenty-four, Andrew should have been baptized and joined church long ago. "You have, haven't you?"

"Not yet."

"What are you waiting for?"

Andrew's teeth gleamed in the firelight as he grinned. "I like to have my fun. There will be time enough to make my pledge to the church when I'm ready to get married and settle down."

Jacob stared into the flames. "Do you have anyone in mind? I mean, when you're ready to get married."

"That Jo is a lot of fun, and pretty too." Andrew sat up and hooked his elbows around his knees. "But Mattie has always been my favorite. With a girl like her, a man would never be bored."

∞

Cole Bates crouched behind a tree, watching Mattie as she walked up the trail to the Amish camp. He wasn't mistaken. She was interested. He had first seen it when the Amish movers passed through Somerset the other day, and then again tonight, at the campfire when the old man turned them away. The old grouch. But Mattie couldn't keep her eyes off him.

"Cole." Hiram's whispered call echoed through the underbrush.

"Hush, you."

Cole rose from his position and waited until Mattie's form disappeared into the darkness. He turned to find Hiram and Darrell close behind him. Too close. Darrell fidgeted with his suspender while Hiram waited for his orders, his bulky body a darker form in the shadows under the trees.

"Let's get back to the road. We'll wait until things are quiet before we make our move."

He followed the game trail the short distance to the road where they had left their horses in Darrell's care. But like usual, Darrell couldn't stick to the task. He had to follow behind, getting in the way. Both those boys were as stupid as their cow of a mother had been. Why Pa had ever married up with her, Cole would never know. But then she had died after one of Pa's binges, and they had been stuck with her whelps.

Or at least he had been stuck with them. Pa had told him

that day that he was to take care of Hiram and Darrell because they were his brothers.

Less than brothers, but still, they came in handy. Sometimes he needed an extra pair of eyes or someone who would take orders without a fight. And at least Hiram would do what he was told, so far. Darrell was as dumb as a post, and whiny to boot. Someone would just up and shoot the fool one day. He might even do that himself.

But until then, they had a job to do. Pa wanted horses or money, or both. And there would be no excuses. Cole had to bring what Pa wanted, or he couldn't go back. And he wanted to go back. That farm in Missouri wasn't much, but it would be his one day. Pa couldn't live forever.

"Why were you talking to that girl?" Darrell wiped his sleeve across his nose.

"Shut up, Darrell. It's none of your business."

Darrell grinned. "You sweet on her, Cole? Huh? You gonna kiss her?"

Cole mounted his horse, a fine bay gelding he had found on a farm in Virginia. The two others they had stolen that night had brought in some good money. He fingered the bag of coins inside his vest. Not enough though. He needed to get his hands on the horses the Amish had with them. Most of them were pure-blooded Conestoga, and the outfitters at the trailhead in Independence would pay top dollar for them.

Darrell and Hiram trailed behind him as he rode across the stream, and then back into the woods, following a deer trail he had found before it had gone clear dark.

Twenty-six horses would bring enough cash that there'd be no reason to take the money back to Pa. He might just get rid of Hiram and Darrell, too, and head out west on one of those trails. Oregon might be a good place for a smart operator like him. There was no telling what kind of deals he could wrangle.

But would even Oregon be far enough away from Pa once he discovered Cole's betrayal? He licked his dry lips. He'd have to think on it further.

When the deer trail reached the stream, Cole stopped and dismounted. The moon rode high in the sky, only a few days past the full. They'd wait until it drifted below the hills to the west before making their move. But once they got the horses moving, those Amish would never catch them.

"What are we doing, Cole?" Darrell's whine cut through the gurgle of the stream. "We gonna get a horse off of them Amish?"

"If you hadn't been so blamed quick to try to take one the last time, we'd have the whole string by now." Cole kicked at Darrell, who jumped sideways with his practiced step. "I told you to wait, but you had to try to sneak one out before the Amish fools were asleep." He snatched the front of Darrell's coat before the boy could react. "From now on, we do it my way. You hear?"

Darrell hung his head, avoiding Cole's stare.

"We'll do whatever you say, Cole." Hiram loomed at his elbow. "We know you want to make Pa proud."

Cole turned on him, shoving Darrell away. "He isn't your pa. How many times do I need to remind you? He's my pa. Not yours." He walked a couple steps away from both of them. "I can guess what kind of man your pa was."

"Don't start that again, Cole." Hiram's voice held a menace Cole hadn't heard before. "I know he's your pa, but he's all Darrell remembers. Let him share, like Ma said."

"Shut up, will you? Just shut up."

Cole aimed a wad of tobacco juice at their feet and moved toward the stream. He couldn't see the camp from here, but he could hear voices drift down the slope toward the bottom of the glade. He fished in his vest pocket for another chaw. The tobacco would help pass the time. Once the moon was gone and it was full dark, he'd make his move.

Jacob looked up at the moon, trying to guess the time. Not too long after midnight, if it was even that late. He still had a long night ahead of him.

He hadn't said anything after Andrew had told him about his feelings for Mattie and the conversation had drifted in another direction. For sure, she was the one he would choose to marry. The other two girls were fine enough, but Mattie . . . she had always been special. And Andrew would keep her laughing through their lives together. She might even be happy with him.

Jacob watched Andrew through the dying flames of the fire. The bed of coals gave off little light, but he could make out the other man's outline as he lay wrapped in his blanket. Jacob rubbed his fingers into his eyes, trying to soothe the sting from the wisps of smoke that blew his way.

That Andrew. He couldn't help it, the man was too likable to be mad at. The jokes he told as the fire burned low kept Jacob laughing until he had forgotten all about horse thieves and girls. He was becoming a good friend. Jacob laid another log on the fire, a dry, solid piece of oak that would burn slow. Just like the resentment that would build in his heart if he had to stand by and watch Andrew court and marry his Mattie.

His head dropped to his knees. His Mattie. For sure, she had been his, ever since he had first taught her to bait a fishing hook. She was his, and he wasn't about to lose her to Andrew. He let his eyes close, seeing Mattie's face in his mind. Strong, capable, good-natured. The little wren of a girl with brown hair caught up under her kapp. His mind drifted to a day on the banks of the Conestoga. Mattie's brothers teasing her, wanting her to bait her own fishing hook, and the grateful look she gave Jacob when he offered to do it for her . . .

A horse grunted and stamped its foot. Jacob woke up, lying on his blanket, curled up against the cold. The fire had gone out, and the moon . . . the moon had set behind the western mountains. The horse grunted again from the far side of the rope circle, and the horses nearer to Jacob shifted uneasily. Their pricked ears were silhouetted against the stars. Something had gotten their attention.

He crawled around the fire to where Andrew lay in his blankets, snoring lightly. Jacob jiggled his shoulder.

"Andrew."

"What—"

"Shh. Something is spooking the horses."

Andrew sat up and looked toward the corral. Every horse around the circle was alert, looking toward the opposite side.

"A wolf?" He scratched his head, then pulled on his hat. "Or a puma?"

"Or a horse thief." Jacob's jaw clenched. The Bates brothers? He had to find out. "I'm going to circle around the left, you go to the right. We have to protect the horses."

Andrew stood, pulling Jacob up with him. "We should stick together. Whatever it is, it might be dangerous for one of us to face it alone."

"All right, let's go."

Jacob led the way around the circle, careful to move quietly, but neither he nor Andrew were accustomed to sneaking through the woods. Last year's leaves rustled, and every few steps a stick cracked under a boot. When they reached the far side of the circle, the horses there were on the alert, looking into the forest, but they weren't panicked. Jacob's skin prickled. He could see nothing in the dark underbrush, but he trusted the horses' senses.

Andrew caught up to him, breathing heavily. He bent over, his hands on his knees. "You didn't have to run so fast."

"Shh. There's something out there."

A faint rustling from bushes twenty feet away sent Jacob's heart pounding. The rustling turned to shaking. A whiny voice swore, followed by a deeper, "Shut up." The noise retreated. After a few minutes, one of the horses nudged Jacob from behind. All was quiet and the horses were relaxed. The stars through the treetops above them were growing faint in the waning night.

"They're gone."

He could see Andrew's profile in the dusk.

"It was Cole Bates, wasn't it?"

"And at least one of his brothers."

"What can we do? Watch the horses every night?"

Jacob rubbed at the back of his neck. He was stiff from his night in the damp chill, and today they would reach the crest of the mountains. They all had a long trip in front of them, and worrying about Cole Bates wasn't going to make things easier. "We'll have to, I guess."

"Maybe we should just give one to him. Then he'd leave us alone."

Jacob couldn't tell if Andrew's suggestion was a serious one. His face was still hidden in the darkness. "There are the girls too. And our supplies. If we let him take part of what we have, do you think he'd stop there?"

"The world is very evil"—Andrew started walking back to their campsite—"but we have been taught not to resist evil. So, ja. Let him take what he feels he needs. Perhaps our kindness will change his ways."

Jacob pulled at Andrew's arm, forcing him to stop and face him. "Even if he tries to entice one of the girls away?"

Andrew stood for a moment with his head bowed. "Not if he tries that." He looked at Jacob. "We have to protect them."

"All right. If the Bates brothers continue to bother us, and I think they will, one or both of us will stay with the girls whenever they're near."

Andrew continued on to the edge of the clearing where they had left their blankets, Jacob following. A layer of mist floated above the ground between them and the wagons, and the sky was freshening to blue above them. Only one star still shone in the west, hanging at the crest of the mountains.

Jacob stirred the cold fire with a stick while Andrew stooped for his blanket, rolling it in his arms as he straightened. He stretched, then watched as Jacob kicked dirt over the few embers that still glowed.

"We've set ourselves a pleasant task, haven't we?"

Jacob looked at him, the dawn pink and orange behind Andrew's head. "What task?"

"Keeping company with the girls, of course." Andrew grinned. "I can't think of a chore I will enjoy more."

Jacob scooped his blanket off the ground and folded it as Andrew headed through the mist to the wagons. A pleasant task? For sure, it would be pleasant to have an excuse to be with Mattie and the others for the rest of the trip. But if they failed, he would regret it for the rest of his life.

9

Mattie wiggled her toes in the dust next to the line of wagons pulled off to the side of the road. Sunlight dappled through the spring-green leaves above to play on the surface of the pike, calling her to follow the rippling beams to the crest of the hill ahead. Daed had said to wait until they knew how long they were going to rest the horses after this morning's climb, but they were so near to the top of the mountain pass. They had to be. This was a wild area with no farms about, but that was no reason to fear for her safety. She wouldn't be more than a few hundred yards ahead of the group, but Daed still didn't want her to go.

The rest of the families strung out along the trail behind Daed's wagon, the children peering from the canvas covers and leaning over the sides of the spring wagons. The men met to discuss their next move, standing in a circle next to the Yoders' wagon, their hands clasped behind their backs while black hats tilted and bobbed like a flock of birds drinking from a puddle. In a few moments they broke up, and Christian Yoder announced, "We'll have our noon meal here to give the horses a chance to rest. Cold lunch for everyone."

With the announcement, the camp erupted into activity. Children poured out of the wagons, anxious to run while they could. The women met in the center of the line, no doubt discussing what to fix for a cold lunch. Mattie glanced up the road again. Reaching the top would have to wait. She trudged back to Mamm and the others. They would need her help.

"There you are, Mattie," Mamm said. "There is a wheel of cheese in the barrel in the back corner of our wagon. Go and fetch it, please. And also the loaf of bread."

Mattie climbed up the spokes of the front wagon wheel and climbed over the high board end and into the shadowy interior. She made her way to the back corner, balancing on the boxes and barrels that lined the floor like cargo in the hold of a sailing ship.

Naomi followed her in. "Mamm said to get some of the dried apples too. Everyone is hungry after the ascent we made this morning." She filled her apron with the dried apples and held the corners in one hand to form a bag. "Can you get the bread and cheese by yourself, or should I come back to help?"

"If you can take the bread, I'll bring the cheese." Mattie lifted the top of the barrel. A round loaf of dark rye bread rested on top, the last of the loaves Mamm baked before they left home. Underneath were several wheels of cheese, as wide across as she was, wrapped in linen and wax. She handed the bread to Naomi and reached for the cheese. She strained to lift it out of the barrel. She had forgotten how heavy it was.

"Naomi, can you give me a hand?" She turned around, but instead of Naomi, Jacob had just climbed into the wagon.

"I can help you. What do you need?"

"This cheese is pretty heavy, but I can get it. I thought Naomi was still here."

Jacob reached past her and lifted the cheese out of the barrel. "And I'm here now."

Mattie couldn't breathe in the confines of the wagon. Leaf shadows danced on the canvas cover, the flickering light pressing in on her as Jacob straightened, the cheese secure in one hand.

"Just one of them? I can take two if you think we'll need them."

She shook her head. "Mamm said one."

Jacob didn't move, but a slow smile spread over his face as he stood just inches away. "The folks might be pretty hungry after this morning's climb."

"We . . ." Her voice faltered as she looked into his eyes. Brown, warm, and inviting. This was the Jacob she had known when she was a little girl. "We have bread and apple schnitz too."

"Then we'll have enough to eat."

He turned away from her then, and took the cheese to the front of the wagon. As he climbed out, Mattie replaced the barrel lid and followed him.

Something had changed. Something that made her heart still pound when she thought of how close he had been as he took the cheese from the barrel. Before leaving the wagon, she took a deep breath. That hadn't been the first time she had been that close to a man. Andrew always sat close to her when he could, making sure their arms touched or their knees bumped against each other as they rode together.

And how many times had she and Jacob sat side by side along a creek bank when they were younger? How many times had he steadied her with his hand, or pulled her close to him when she tripped over a branch? Mattie drew another deep breath. They had been children then. His touch no different than if it had been from one of her older brothers. But the feeling that had made her heart pound when he stepped near today was nothing like the safe, protected feeling he had given her when they were children.

She stepped out from the wagon and joined the group gathered around a table made from sawhorses and planks from the Yoders' wagon, ready to eat. Mattie slipped into the circle beside Naomi just as Daed bowed his head. She wrestled her thoughts into a prayer of thanksgiving for the meal, and then the prayer time was ended.

As the ring of people rippled to form a line at the table, she raised her head and met Jacob's eyes from across the way, standing next to Josef. His mouth turned up into the same smile he had given her while they were in the wagon. That smile said he knew something she didn't, and he was pleased with it.

A hand grasped her elbow. "Would you like to sit with me while we eat?" Andrew's voice tickled her ear, soft and low.

Before she could answer, Jacob's smile had disappeared, his face growing red under the wide brim of his hat. He pushed his way to the other side of the group and disappeared. She turned to Andrew, catching Naomi's eyes on her.

"I'm glad you asked," she said, taking Naomi's hand. "Naomi and I would love to join you."

Naomi tried to pull her hand away, but Mattie grasped it more firmly.

Andrew looked from Mattie to Naomi, and back again. "There's a log across the road there in the shade. Meet me there after you fill your plates."

He backed away and Naomi pulled Mattie back toward

their wagon. "He wasn't asking me to eat with him. He was asking you."

Mattie looked at her sister's face, mottled pink and white. "I don't want to embarrass you, but I don't want to be alone with Andrew, either. Come and join us, and perhaps some of the others will too."

Naomi looked at her feet. "I can't."

Mattie circled Naomi's slim waist with one arm. "I know how you feel about him." Naomi's face turned a darker shade. "But he won't see what a wonderful girl you are if he doesn't spend any time with you."

"It's so easy for you, but you have no inkling of what it's like for me." Naomi took a deep breath. "All the boys like you, Mattie. You're sweet and pretty, and you can sew and cook."

"You can do all those things."

"But I'm not pretty like you are. Men like Andrew don't even look at me."

Mattie opened her mouth to protest, but Naomi went on.

"You go eat with Andrew and the others. Get Johanna to join you. I'd rather eat with Mamm and the other women than sit next to Andrew while he ignores me."

Naomi pulled away and went to the table to help one of the little Hertzler boys fill his plate.

Mattie glanced over the crowd. Andrew had gotten his lunch and had already found Johanna. The two of them were making themselves comfortable on the log.

On a grassy spot next to their wagon, Mamm sat on a blanket, holding Noah and Miriam's baby, Katrina, while Miriam took care of their three-year-old, Mary. Everywhere she looked, families were busy getting their lunches and finding a comfortable place to rest and eat.

Except one.

Behind the last wagon, Jacob stood with his staff in his hand, the flock of sheep grazing in the lush grass at the side of the road. At first she thought he was watching the group, but then realized his gaze was on her, as if no one else existed.

Mattie got into line behind Isaac's Emma. Her sister-in-law held baby Rebecca in one arm, a plate in her other hand, and was trying to direct three-year-old Leah to take items from the table to put on the plate.

"Let me help you," Mattie said.

"For sure, I need six hands today." Emma let Mattie take Rebecca from her. With one hand free, she could help Leah put pieces of cheese and bread on their plate. "I don't know where the boys have gone, but I hope they're with Isaac."

"They are. I saw Mose and Menno follow Isaac to the benches the men set up."

Once Emma had filled her plate, she looked for a place to eat.

"Mamm laid a quilt on the grass on the other side of the wagon. She's there with Miriam and her girls."

"We'll join them, then." Emma looked over her shoulder at Mattie's empty hands. "You didn't get your lunch."

"I'll go back after you're settled."

Emma stopped, facing Mattie. "I saw Andrew with the Hertzler girl. Johanna, isn't it?" At Mattie's nod, she went on. "I thought he was sweet on you."

Mattie smiled, thinking of Naomi. "Andrew is sweet on almost every girl. Someday he'll choose one, but I don't think it will be me."

Her sister-in-law went on, threading her way between the wagons. "Why not? It's time he settled down."

"We're friends, that's all. We've spent enough time together to know that nothing more will come from it."

Mattie held her squirming niece until Emma had settled Leah on the blanket next to Mary. Mamm's face was more content than Mattie had seen since leaving Brothers Valley. Saying goodbye to Annie had been hard, but Mamm had the rest of her children and her grandchildren to ease the pain of the separation.

Mattie headed back to the table. Everyone else had gotten their food and was scattered here and there in groups along the road. Andrew and Johanna sat close together on their log, laughing as they ate. She didn't want to join them and break up their fun. Naomi had found a place next to Hannah on a bench and was deep in conversation. Finally, Mattie dared to look down the road to where she had last seen Jacob.

He was still there with the sheep. As if she had called to him, he looked her way again. For sure, he would miss his lunch for those sheep, and to make sure Margli and Peter had their meal. Mattie took the last remaining plate from the table and filled it with slices of Mamm's rye bread, cheese, and dried apples in double portions, and took it to Jacob.

"What's this, then?" His eyebrows lifted as she approached.

"It's your lunch, and mine too, if you'll share with me."

"Andrew asked for your company, didn't he?"

"He's happy with Johanna, and I knew you hadn't gotten any food."

He grinned and motioned her toward two rocks alongside the road. Mattie sat on the largest boulder and he sat below her on the other. He took two slices of bread from the plate and laid a thick piece of cheese between them.

Mattie broke a corner off another piece of bread as he

took a big bite. "I've been looking forward to crossing these mountains for so long, it's hard to believe we'll be on the other side this afternoon."

Jacob looked up the road to where it curved and disappeared. "It's been slow traveling this morning, for sure. The horses have had to work hard to get up this far."

"Will it be easier for them on the other side?"

"It depends on how steep the grade is. They'll have the weight of the wagons pushing at them, and even with all of us helping to slow down the load, the horses will have to work hard to keep their pace steady."

Mattie contemplated the Conestoga wagons, lined up along the road. They not only looked like the sailing ships that had brought her grandparents to the New World a hundred years ago, but they seemed to be nearly as big as the vessels she had only seen pictures of. "It sounds dangerous."

"It is." Jacob took another bite of his bread and cheese. "But my daed and yours know what they're doing. Our families both came through the mountains east of Brothers Valley, and they are taller and steeper than these. You don't need to worry."

"You will help the other men with the wagons?"

"All afternoon."

"What about the sheep?"

Jacob made himself another sandwich with the last of the bread and cheese. "They'll graze here until all the wagons are down. Margli and Peter will watch them."

As Jacob ate, Mattie finished her own cheese. The families that were scattered around the wagons concluded their lunches, and the men started packing the benches and blankets back into the wagons. The crest of the hill called to her. They were so close . . . if she could only run ahead . . .

"It looks like we're getting ready to go." Jacob handed the plate back to her. "I know you want to see the other side. Why don't you go ahead?"

His words made her feet twitch. "I have to wait until the wagons have gone down."

"You could stop at the crest, just to have a look, and then come back."

Jacob's smile was infectious and she grinned back. "You're tempting me."

"Go ahead, before it's too late. It won't take long, and then you can come back to the wagons and help."

She stood up, then hesitated. Jacob stood behind her and pushed at her shoulders. "Go," he said. "You'll always regret it if you don't."

Mattie took a step, then three. She looked back at Jacob, and he shooed her on with his hands.

As she walked past the wagons, Naomi saw her. "Mattie, where are you going?"

"I'll be back," she said, not looking at her sister. "I won't be long."

Her pace quickened as she passed their wagon at the front of the line. Daed watched her pass as he hitched his wheel horses to the big wagon and smiled as he saw her intention.

"No farther than the top, Mattie."

His permission started her feet running up the road. Ahead was the crest of the mountain. The road went through a shallow cut, with laurel-covered mountain slopes rising on both sides. She ran through the cut and stopped on the other side. The road sloped down beneath her feet, winding to the left as it followed the side of the mountain. Farther down she could see where it turned to the right again, switching back to make the descent easy for the wagons. But straight ahead she could see only trees and more trees.

She climbed the slope on the left side of the road, pulling herself up by gripping first one shrub, then another. Every few steps she looked over her shoulder, but she could see only trees. Finally she reached an outcropping of rocks at the top and climbed onto them. She stretched as tall as she could, looking to the west.

There! There was the clear view she had been searching for. She moved to her right, and the trees opened even further. Between them, she could see to the other side of the mountains. Gazing at the rolling hills before her, she leaned farther to the right to get a better view. As far as she could see, tree-covered mounds fell away in a gentle lowering to the distant horizon.

That was the West? The land she had dreamed of seeing for so long? It didn't look any different than Brothers Valley. She stood on the rock, her arms crossed as she hugged her elbows. She had expected it to be exciting and new. Her chest ached with the familiar emptiness. How many years had she fed that empty place with the expectation of the new land she would see when she finally gazed over the crest of these mountains? There had to be something more than the same trees, the same road, the same chores, day after day. The hope she had held close for so long faltered like a guttered candle flame.

A sudden breeze from the west rushed up the mountain, stirring the leaves of the trees around her, but Mattie turned her back to its call. Below, her family and the others were hitching horses, gathering children, and doing all the other little chores that needed to be tended to before they set out again. She slid off the edge of the rock and started straight down the side of the mountain toward them. She didn't need to go back to the road, and she didn't need to look west again. There was no reason to.

∞

Jacob knelt to look Peter and Margli in their faces. Margli stifled a yawn.

"I'm counting on both of you to keep the sheep right here until we get the wagons down the steepest part of the slope. When they're done grazing, let them rest here. But don't move them until I come back. All right?"

Margli nodded, but Peter's attention was on a flock of crows calling from high up in the branches of an oak tree. Jacob sighed. He had argued with Daed about the wisdom of giving Peter and Margli this responsibility, but Daed said they were old enough. He had even reminded Jacob how he had been given even more responsibility at their age. Jacob surveyed the grazing sheep one last time, then handed Peter his crook.

"You're in charge, Peter. As long as the sheep stay here, you don't have to do anything. But don't go following after some deer trail or go off to hunt for birds' nests. You need to watch the sheep and keep them safe."

"Ja, for sure, Jacob. We'll take good care of them."

Jacob gave another sigh. He had to trust Peter and Margli, as young as they were. As he turned to catch up to the line of wagons, where Daed waited with the team, a movement in the trees up the mountain on his left caught his eye. Mattie was making her way down the slope, half sliding, half walking. He met her as she reached the road.

"Did you see what you wanted to see?"

She avoided his eyes, but her face was mottled with pink splotches. She had been crying. "It wasn't anything like I had imagined. There's nothing different on the other side. Only more hills and more trees."

Jacob worked to keep from laughing at her. She seemed as young as Margli, standing sideways to him and pulling at the leaves of a bush next to the road. "What did you expect? It's been the same all the way from the Conestoga. Some hills are higher than others, but it's all the same trees and mountains."

"But I thought it would be different. They say this is the last mountain range until the Ohio River, but you wouldn't know it." She snapped a branch off the bush. "I wanted to see . . . oh, I don't know. I imagined it would be a wide valley stretching away to the distance where the river would be a ribbon of shining light on the horizon." She turned to him. "I don't think I can stand another day of walking through this forest, uphill and down, only to make camp in another clearing next to another stream and cook another supper over another fire."

"There's nothing wrong with that, Mattie. This is a good life on our way to our new home in Indiana."

She snapped the twig in two and threw the pieces away. "But is that enough? Don't you yearn for something more?" Her arm swept toward the west, taking in the mountain, the sky, and everything beyond it. "There's a huge world out there, and I want to see it."

Jacob tried to see what she saw in that sweep of her arm,

but it held no lure for him. Everything he wanted was laid out in front of him, and the only thing he needed to do to find it was to keep his feet on the path. Everything except Mattie. If her heart was pulled toward some unknown place, would she ever be happy with him?

He glanced toward Daed. The horses stood in place waiting for the harness, but he wasn't there to put it on them.

"Mattie, if you keep thinking this way, you'll never learn to be content."

Pink blotches rose on her face again. She twisted the front of her apron in one hand. "How can I be content when I feel so empty?" Her eyes were dark and it seemed they opened into a swirling blackness. "I thought you would understand, Jacob. Tell me you do. Tell me you feel that same longing within you."

Something churned within him, but he shut it away. He stepped closer. "What are you looking for out there, Mattie? What do you want?"

Her shoulders slumped as she looked down at the ground between them. The distance was so small, if he moved his foot a few inches, the toes of their shoes would touch. But the expanse between their souls was immense.

"I don't know." Her voice was quiet, as if she was speaking from far away. Then her shoulders lifted and she looked up at him, her eyes bright and resolute again. "But I'll know it when I find it."

Jacob reached for her and took her elbow in his hand. "What if what you're looking for isn't out there? What if it's right here with your family and your friends?"

She shook her head. "If that was so, I wouldn't still feel this ache, would I?"

Her eyes pleaded, but he didn't have an answer. He resisted the urge to pull her close, to hold her until she rested in his arms.

"I hope you find what you're looking for, Mattie."

She wiped a stray tear from her cheek. "You must think I'm silly, talking this way."

Jacob released her elbow, pushing down that churning fear again. She was just a girl. A friend. Why did she make him want to sacrifice everything to help her? But he had to stay on his own path, whether Mattie was with him or not. He couldn't lose his focus in those bright brown eyes.

A shout from the line of wagons startled him back to the task at hand. "I must help Daed. He's waiting for me."

"Mamm needs my help too." She smiled and gave his hand a slight squeeze. "Denki, Jacob. You were very patient to listen to me. I'll be all right."

Mattie left him and made her way toward her family's wagon while Jacob pointed his feet toward his daed and the team that waited for him. A couple of days ago, he had been so sure that Mattie was the girl for him, but he never thought her dreams would be more important to her than a future with him.

10

Two days after descending the mountains, Jacob held the reins of Josef's team as the wagons waited for their turn to cross the Allegheny River near the town of Pittsburgh, the biggest river crossing on their route. The ferryman had limited them to one wagon and team at a time, and Daed's was the first to go. Josef had gone along on the ferry to help with the horses, and Jacob had volunteered to stay with his team to calm them. They were already nervous at the proximity of the rushing water and crowds of strangers on the road. He had left Margli and Peter to watch the sheep as they grazed in a grassy spot well away from the river, and his attention flitted from the horses to the sheep.

He rubbed the long brown nose nudging him. "You want more oats, do you? You've had enough for now, but you'll get more this evening."

The other travelers on the road, like the group of Amish, had been routed to this ferry by the men at the bridge toll gates in the city. The bridges, though they would be convenient, were built for city traffic like light carriages and pedestrians. This ferry, a few miles upstream from the center of Pittsburgh, accommodated the heavier traffic. Daed and the others had been glad to detour to the ferry after seeing the prices they would have been charged to use the bridge, even if they had been allowed to. The ferry was much more reasonable.

The other travelers on the road grouped behind the line of wagons. Freighters, mostly, but a few emigrants like their group. Two roads had come together several miles before this point: the one their group followed from central Pennsylvania and then up the east bank of the Monongahela River, and another main road leading from Maryland into Pittsburgh. The closer they had come to the city where the rivers joined to form the Ohio, the more travelers they met on the road.

Andrew left his wagon and joined Jacob. "Can you see how they're crossing from here? The river isn't too rough, is it?"

"I heard the ferryman say the river is high because of spring rains, but he wasn't worried. We'll have to trust his judgment."

Andrew stayed by his side as they watched the ferry crawl across the river. A tow rope was fastened to both riverbanks, threading through the ferry gear. A team of mules on the other side kept the ferry moving through the swell of brown water, even though the current pushed and pulled at the flat-bottomed raft, straining the tether rope. Daed's big Conestoga wagon bucked with the straining ferry, but the horses stood still with a man at each of their heads. Jacob whooshed out a breath he hadn't realized he was holding when the ferry reached the other side safely.

Andrew rubbed his hands on his trousers. "I'll be glad when we're all across and on the other side."

"For sure. We'll have to tether the sheep together to keep them from panicking." Jacob glanced behind the line of passengers waiting to cross to where Peter stood near the road, using his goad to keep the sheep in the grass. Coming along the road behind him were three familiar men on horseback.

"The Bates brothers, again. They could have taken the bridge across, yet here they are. If I didn't know better, I'd think they were following us."

Andrew glanced back at the familiar figures. "Almost every traveler heading to Pittsburgh and beyond has to take this ferry across, unless they're going into the city itself. It might be only that they wanted to avoid the congestion."

"Maybe, but they're the only ones in this line who are traveling on horseback."

Jacob kept watching as the three men rode past the line of people waiting, past the Schrocks' wagon, then the Bontragers'. Cole didn't look at Andrew and Jacob as they rode by, but Darrell grinned at them as he followed his brothers. They arrived at the ferry landing just as it returned full of travelers heading east. Cole approached the ferryman, and from his gestures, it appeared he wanted to go across before the rest of the people waiting for their turn. Their words didn't travel beyond the noise of the river, but the ferryman was gesturing toward the road full of travelers. Cole reached into his pocket, pulling out a small leather sack.

Andrew rose to his toes for a better look.

Jacob wished he was as tall as his friend. "What is he doing?"

"It looks like he's trying to give him money. He is trying to bribe his way to the front of the line."

The bribe must have been refused, because the Bates brothers stepped back as the ferryman signaled for Eli Schrock to drive his wagon onto the ferry. Josef and Mattie's brothers had ridden the ferry back across to help with the Schrocks' horses. Each stood at the nose of one of the huge animals. As Jacob led Josef's team to the front of the line, he could see the horses eyeing the rushing water under their feet, but with men's calm words and soothing pats, they stood quietly.

Cole Bates stepped forward again. "Let us ride with the wagon. Three more won't make that much difference."

The ferryman, red-faced and frowning, turned to him. "I said no and I meant it. The water is too high to risk overloading the ferry. If you don't like it, you can swim across, or go down to one of the bridges. Now get back in line and wait."

As the ferry pushed off, Mattie's face appeared at an opening in the back cover of the wagon and Jacob's mouth went dry. But his concern changed directions when he saw Cole watching her. The outsider's face slid into a grin, then he pushed his brothers toward the tavern at the side of the road.

"Take the horses over to the watering trough, Darrell. I'll order us some ale while we're waiting."

The three disappeared behind the tavern as Andrew turned to Jacob.

"What do you think of that? They gave up pretty quickly, didn't they?"

Jacob shifted his shoulders, releasing the tension that had built during the loading of the Schrocks' wagon. "I don't think it was a coincidence that Cole gave up trying to get across the river ahead of us when he saw Mattie in the wagon."

Jacob focused his attention back on the ferry, but his thoughts stayed on the trio waiting at the tavern. He remembered the cat that lived in their barn back along the

Conestoga Creek. For weeks, the cat had stalked a rat that had made its home under the horses' feed trough. No matter what time of day, or what the activity was in the barn that winter, the cat had never stopped watching for that rat. She would shift positions, from the barn loft, to the door, to under the wagon, to the grain bin, always moving a bit closer to the rat's hole. The funny thing was that the rat, cautious at first, got used to the cat's presence and grew more careless in his forays out for food—until the day the cat pounced.

As the ferry approached the opposite landing safely, Jacob glanced at the tavern. Cole Bates leaned against the hitching post by the front door, a mug in his hand, and his eyes on the wagon that was disembarking from the ferry.

Mattie peered out of the back of the wagon as she felt the ferry leave the landing. Her stomach turned as the wagon tilted, then righted again as the barge made its way across the river. Somewhere on the landing, Jacob was waiting his turn to cross. She scanned the faces of the strangers, and then a familiar grin caught her attention. Cole Bates stood at the river's edge, watching the ferry crossing. Not the ferry—her. When her eyes met his, he gave her a slow wink.

She dropped down to sit on the crate, her face heating at his boldness. It was a good thing the interior of the wagon was dim or else Naomi would be sure to ask why she was blushing. But instead, Emma passed a sleeping baby Rebecca to her.

"Mose and Menno won't sit still. Could you please hold the baby for me?"

Mattie took Rebecca in her arms as Emma grasped her sons by their hands and pulled them down to sit next to her.

Mamm reached over to tap each boy once on his head. "The ferry crossing is dangerous enough without you boys running from one end of the wagon to the other."

"But we're on a boat," Mose said.

"On a boat," Menno repeated. "Across the ocean."

"You can pretend all you like," Emma said, "but only if you sit quietly while you do it."

From her seat on the other side of Mamm, Miriam laughed. "I don't know how you keep up with those boys, Emma."

"Isaac helps, that's for sure. He keeps them busy with chores."

All conversation stopped as the wagon spun to the right. Mattie nearly screamed when Naomi grabbed her arm. After a long minute, the wagon righted itself again.

"We must have come to the stronger current in the middle of the river." Mamm's voice quavered a little but sounded calm. She squeezed Leah and Mary close to her. The three-year-old cousins smiled, safe in their *grossmutti*'s arms.

Even Mose and Menno were quiet for the rest of the crossing. Mattie watched baby Rebecca's sleeping face, but her mind was on the scene on the landing they had just left. Cole's appearance had been unexpected, but he hadn't looked surprised. He had been pleased to see her, as if he had been searching for her.

As she felt her face heating again, Mattie tried to turn her thoughts in a different direction. Jacob would be crossing last with the sheep, and all the men would help. He would have to do something to keep the ewes from going into a panic at the sight of the rushing water, but Jacob could do it.

When would Cole and his brothers cross? They were on horseback and could cross at the same time as Jacob.

Mattie forced her thoughts away from Cole Bates again, just as the wagon rocked, signaling their arrival on the far side of the river.

Emma kept her boys from jumping up to look out the end of the wagon as the noises outside told them that Daed was leading the horses off the ferry onto dry ground again, and it was all Mattie could do to keep herself seated. They were missing the most interesting sights, but she would be obedient and stay in the wagon.

"We want to watch the others cross," Mose said. He kept his eyes on Emma's face as his brother echoed his request.

Mattie passed Rebecca to Naomi. "We could lift the edge of the canvas and watch." Mamm nodded her approval, so Mattie continued. "The boys can watch with me, as long as we all stay in the wagon."

Mose and Menno grinned as they tumbled over the crates to join Mattie at the end of the wagon.

"Remember, we stay in the wagon." Mattie loosened the canvas cover and lifted the edge, tying it on either side of their heads. The boys knelt on a crate and leaned over the tailgate while Mattie sat next to them, leaning her arm on the edge of the wooden plank to watch the ferry cross back to the other side of the river.

The remaining wagons made the crossing without any difficulty, and then it was time to bring the sheep across. From this distance, Mattie could only see that Jacob was keeping the flock bunched together, but she couldn't see how. Sheep didn't like moving water, and if one of them became frightened, the whole flock could go off the edge of the ferry and drown. Only a skilled shepherd would be able to get them across safely.

Andrew and some of the other men assisted, surrounding the sheep and keeping them bunched as Jacob led them onto the ferry. Once they were settled near the front, the operator let a spring wagon join them for the crossing, then cast off.

Watching the ferry from the safety of the riverbank, Mattie remembered each bump and swing of the barge from her own crossing. When the ferry reached the stronger current, it swung on the tether rope, but the pulley system linking the barge to both shores held firm, and it continued on its way. As it came closer, the baaing of the sheep carried across the water.

"Why are the sheep bleating so?" Mose asked.

Menno echoed his brother. "Bleating so?"

Mattie shifted so that she was kneeling between her nephews and put an arm around each one. "The poor sheep don't like the water and they're frightened. But Jacob and the others will take care of them."

Mose pointed. "That one jumped off!"

Before Mattie could realize what was happening, Bam, the young ram, had slipped from Jacob's grasp and run off the side of the ferry. Jacob threw off his hat and coat and jumped into the water after the sheep. Mamm and the others crowded behind Mattie and the boys, watching.

"That sheep is going to drown and take Jacob right along with him," Miriam said.

Emma hushed her. "Let's see what happens."

"And pray," Mamm said. "And pray."

Mattie couldn't move or think. Jacob's head was a sleek, dark ball on the surface of the water, just a few yards from the riverbank, but the sheep was nowhere to be seen. He dove beneath the brown water, while Mattie held her breath, waiting for him to surface again. After long seconds, his head appeared again, but many yards downstream, nearly even with their wagon. This time he was near enough the shore to stand, clutching the young ram even as the current tried to pull it from his hands.

"I have to help him." Mattie climbed out of the wagon, slipping from Naomi's grasp.

As she ran toward the riverbank, she could hear Mamm's faint voice telling her to stay out of the water, but it wasn't necessary. Jacob reached the reeds at the river's edge the same time she did, and she grabbed a handful of soaking wet wool and helped him heave the sheep out of the river and onto the bank, water dripping out of the ram's thick wool coat. Jacob laid the animal on its side, and pressed its ribs, over again, and then again, until water poured out of Bam's mouth and he tried to struggle to his feet.

Mattie grabbed the ram before he could run away, while Jacob sat back on his heels, coughing.

"Are you all right?"

Jacob nodded. He coughed once more, then tried to catch his breath. "I thought we had lost him."

Mattie's hands were shaking. "I thought we had lost you! What did you think you were doing, jumping into the river like that?"

Jacob looked at her then, his hair plastered on his forehead and in front of his eyes. He wiped it away. "I had to save Bam. He's the only ram we have, and without him we don't have a flock."

"You could have drowned." Her voice was shaking too.

He grinned at her. "Would you miss me if I had?"

"This is nothing to make jokes about."

Jacob started to reach for her, then stopped, water dripping from his arms. "I can joke about it because everything is fine."

Mattie bit her lip. Her fingers were still entwined in Bam's wool, and the smell of wet sheep was overpowering.

"Mattie, look at me."

She met his eyes as he touched the end of her nose with one finger. "I'm fine. There's nothing to be upset about."

The ferry had reached the shore and the rest of their group was running toward them over the stony road. With the sound of their feet, Mattie's fear suddenly turned to a churning anger. "I'm not upset." She stood, pushing Bam toward his shepherd. "If you want to care more about a stupid sheep than . . . than any of us, then so be it." She started back toward the wagon.

"I know upset when I see it, Mattie." His words carried after her. "You were worried. I know you were."

Mattie grasped the high wagon wheel, ignoring her nephews' questions and Mamm's concern. Of course she had been worried. The churning anger had passed as quickly as it had come, and in its place was a relief that made her knees go weak.

She looked back at the crowd gathered around Jacob. His mamm had brought a blanket for him, and Andrew walked beside him toward the Yoder wagon. As they passed her, Jacob reached up and ran his fingers through his hair, shaking off the drops of water. His eyes met hers, but instead of the mocking laughter she expected to see, the look he gave her held concern. She smiled, he returned it, and that quickly they were friends again.

11

They stopped for a late lunch after the river crossing. They had pushed on along the northern bank of the Ohio until they were well beyond the edge of Pittsburgh and finally halted where they found a sloped meadow leading up from the river. After receiving permission from the farm's owner, the group set up a quick noon camp in the early afternoon sunlight.

Jacob and Andrew helped picket the horses between the wagons and the tree-covered bluffs, well away from the road and near a bubbling creek that rushed down the slope toward the river. Mattie and Johanna walked past them, carrying pails and giggling as they hurried on their errand. Jacob turned back to Andrew. His friend had a smile on his face as he watched them dip the pails into the water.

"I think dinner is ready." Jacob turned toward the camp. He hoped Andrew would follow him, but the other man went toward the girls instead, reaching to take their full water pails from them. Jacob kept walking, Mattie's laughter ringing in his ears.

Mamm and the other women had made a stew out of some crayfish Peter and the other boys had caught in an eddy where the creek nosed its way into the Ohio, along with some dried onions and string beans. Cornbread left over from the night before rounded out the meal. The whole camp served themselves from the common pot after the prayer.

Jacob took his bowl and spoon to the edge of the meadow where the sheep had settled themselves, resting in the grass. He found a rock to sit on and started his meal. As he ate, he gazed around the camp. Andrew was sitting between Mattie and Johanna on one of the benches. Naomi and Hannah sat on a quilt spread on the grass with their mothers, Mamm looking hot and uncomfortable. The rest of the families were scattered in a loose circle around the fire. The children had eaten quickly once they were served and had started a game of tag on the other side of the wagons. Younger children sat in their mothers' laps, already nodding off. Even William had forgone the games and lay on the grass with his head in Mamm's lap. The group would rest here for an hour or so before pushing on.

He couldn't keep from watching Andrew. Whatever he was saying, he kept the girls laughing. Finally they went to help wash the dishes and left him sitting alone. Jacob finished his soup and took his bowl to the dishpan, but none of the girls seemed to notice him as he helped himself to one of the remaining pieces of cornbread and joined the circle of men resting in the shade of the wagons. Daed and a couple others were lying in the grass with their hats over their faces, but Jacob sat next to Josef as he talked with Mattie's brothers, Isaac and Noah.

The conversation moved from planting methods to raising

children, and Jacob's mind drifted as Isaac and Noah debated the best age to start having their sons join them with the daily chores. His mind wandered when Isaac pointed out that Noah had only two daughters so far, so he should pay attention to his older brother's experience. Jacob leaned back on his elbows and let his gaze move from group to group around the camp. The girls had finished washing the dishes and went toward the woods at the foot of the bluff, carrying pails. Hannah didn't go with them but sat near Mamm and William. He leaned back into the long grass, relaxing into the soft bed. Josef brought up the question of whether oxen or horses were best for plowing, but Jacob let his eyes close and lost the train of the conversation.

He woke when Josef patted his knee.

"Time to get going. The noon hour is long past and we need more miles before we stop for the night."

Jacob stretched and rose to his feet. The camp was bustling again, and voices rose in the warm light of early afternoon.

Daed walked past him on his way to their wagon. "Bring the horses up from their pickets, Jacob. Time to get going."

"Ja, for sure."

When he had gathered the horses and started back toward the wagon, Magdalena Hertzler stopped him. "Have you seen Johanna? She went to pick dandelion greens with the other girls after dinner, but they haven't come back."

"They probably lost track of time. I'll go look for them while Daed hitches up the team."

Telling Daed where he was going, he tried to keep from worrying. They couldn't have gone far and nothing could happen to them in this settled part of the country. He hoped they had only gotten turned around in the woods. The look on Cole's face as he had watched the Schrocks' wagon cross the river came back to him, but the Bates brothers had lingered in the tavern until the Amish group had all crossed and gone on their way. They were probably still lounging there, waiting for their turn at the ferry.

Jacob started toward the spot where he had seen the girls go into the trees, and Andrew jogged after him.

"I heard that Mattie and the others haven't come back yet. Do you want some help looking for them?"

He didn't want Andrew coming with him to fetch Mattie, but he pushed down the bitterness that rose with the thought. Andrew had as much reason as he did to be concerned about them. "For sure. Two will be better than one."

When they climbed past the thickets at the edge of the trees, the interior of the woods was shaded and cool. The trees were thick enough to keep the undergrowth from hindering their passage.

Andrew stopped to survey the quiet grove. "They wouldn't find any greens here."

"There's a sunny patch up ahead. Let's check there."

As they drew closer, Jacob saw that the sunny patch was at the edge of a large meadow at the top of the bluff. On the far side the girls were gathered together talking with some men.

Jacob stopped Andrew. "Who are they talking with? No one from our group."

"It's the Bates brothers." He walked faster and Jacob trotted after him. "I knew we needed to worry about them."

By the time they finally found the meadow on top of the bluff that was dotted yellow with spring dandelions, Mattie was hot and thirsty. Johanna and Naomi didn't seem to notice but sat in the grass and fell to picking as many of the soft greens as they could reach. This hadn't turned out to be the adventure Mattie had hoped for when Johanna suggested it while they were washing dishes. She thought it would be a chance to see something new, but the trees were too thick to see beyond the meadow. Then she turned toward the river and was rewarded with the view she had been looking for. The water, brown with spring silt, flowed with a power that showed itself here and there where the silky surface was split by a rock or log snag. Beyond the river, farmlands interspersed with wood lots stretched into the distance.

Mattie stooped to pick the delicate leaves, searching among the long grass for the tenderest shoots. She pushed a strand of loose hair behind her ear and straightened her back. Her pail was half full. Johanna and Naomi chattered together as they filled their buckets, moving away from Mattie as they worked. Mattie went the other direction, to a part of the meadow they hadn't reached yet, a shallow dish of green near the edge of the forest, full of dandelions. She bent to pick a handful, then took another step to grab some more of the choice leaves.

"Those will make a mighty fine mess of greens for your man." The words were English, the voice warm and friendly.

Mattie hesitated, and then looked up. Cole Bates strolled toward her from a road that ran along the crest of the bluff. His brothers sat on their horses behind him, holding Cole's bay gelding by the reins.

"Yes, they're fine greens." A thrill ran through her. Cole seemed handsome and friendly in the afternoon sunshine, and she felt nothing of the fright he had given her that night on the other side of the mountains. She glanced toward Naomi and Johanna, but they were around the bulge of some brambles, out of sight.

"Will you fix them with ham hocks?" Cole had reached her side. He bent down to pick a few of the leaves and dropped them into her pail, leaning close to her. His nearness, combined with the odor of stale beer and horse sweat, made her take a step back.

"Perhaps."

He grinned at her. "And your man?"

She felt her face turn red-hot. He must have meant to ask if she had a husband. "I don't have a . . . a man."

He grinned again and moved to her other side, placing himself between her and the other girls. He picked another handful of greens and threw them into her pail. "Then maybe you could make that mess of greens for me."

He winked and she turned her head away. She had been staring at him. He wore his hat at an angle that gave him a daring look, and his black hair, black mustache, and black eyes, with a neckerchief tied around his throat, completed the picture. His shirt collar was open, and he wore a patterned vest. Even his boots had fancy silver trim on the sides. Just like the other times she had seen him, she couldn't tear her eyes away.

"What do you say?"

His grin was like a child's, open and carefree. She couldn't help it. She smiled back. "My daed wouldn't like it."

He leaned close to her with another wink. "Your dad needn't know."

"Mattie?" Naomi called to her. "Where are you?"

Cole put his finger to his lips, but Mattie shook her head. "I'm over here," she answered in Deitsch.

"We need to start back to the camp. Johanna and I filled our—" Naomi stopped abruptly as she rounded the curve of a patch of berry brambles and saw her with Cole.

Cole never turned to look toward Naomi. Instead, something beyond Mattie's shoulder had caught his attention. Mattie glanced back and saw his brothers coming up behind her. Turning back to Naomi, she saw Johanna step up next to her. Both of their faces were shocked and wary.

"Ja, Naomi, you're right. We need to get back."

She moved to step around Cole, but he grasped her arm. "You girls don't need to talk that Dutch stuff. We're just getting acquainted. There are three of us and three of you." He pulled Mattie closer and leaned toward her ear. "And that seems just about right, doesn't it?"

Mattie looked into his eyes. Sharp and black like obsidian, a person could lose herself in them. He smiled then, as if he was confident she would agree with him.

A shout from across the meadow drew their attention.

"Mattie, it's time to go." It was Andrew, and right behind him was Jacob.

What was she doing? She should never talk to an outsider like this. She pulled her arm from Cole's grasp. "I need to go."

His handsome face twisted for a second, then he smiled at her again. "Until another time, then."

Cole joined his brothers as they made their way back to their horses. Mattie watched them until they mounted and rode off. Her insides quaked as she turned to her friends.

Andrew and Jacob had caught up with them. Andrew reached out one hand. "Come, Mattie. The noon stop is over and the wagons have started moving again. We need to catch up with them."

"Ja, for sure." Mattie smiled, keeping her voice bright. If it quavered a bit at the end of her words, no one seemed to notice.

Andrew took the lead, heading back toward the river and the camp between the river and the bluff. Johanna followed him, with Naomi right behind her. But Jacob stepped in front of Mattie.

"What did he want from you? That Bates fellow?"

Mattie looked at Jacob's boots, grass stained from his walk through the meadow. Cole hadn't said anything wrong, but the way he turned his words made his meaning mysterious.

She laughed as she met Jacob's gaze. "He wanted me to make a dish for him from the greens."

He held her gaze as he stepped aside to let her follow the others. "Some greens? That's all?"

"That's all."

"He's a dangerous one, Mattie. He looks fair, but feels foul, if you know what I mean."

Mattie looked into his eyes, comparing them to Cole's. Brown, warm, and inviting. Hiding nothing. She passed him and ran to catch up with Naomi and Johanna. Jacob's eyes held a promise of comfort and stability. But Cole? His eyes held adventure.

12

Jacob watched Mattie catch up to the other girls. Whatever she said, Cole's interest in her couldn't be as simple as asking her to cook him some food.

He let the others go on as he doubled back, following the Bateses' trail through the long grass on the top of the bluff to the road they had come from. The narrow track clung to the edge of the ridge, offering an unobstructed view of the rolling farmland across the way, the river with its flatboats poling through the swift current, and the larger river road below. From this vantage point he could see Eli Schrock's wagon leading their group, with the Yoders' wagon close behind. The other wagons followed, then he saw Andrew and the girls come out from the trees below him and run to catch up with the group. Last of all came the little flock of sheep, with Peter walking in the lead with Bam. The ram, still damp from his adventure in the river, pranced and bucked next to Peter before snatching a bite from the grass along the road.

As quickly as the Bates brothers could travel on their

horses, Cole Bates could have been watching them all the way from Pittsburgh and waited until he knew he could talk to the girls alone. Jacob cast a glance along the bluff top. Somewhere ahead of him on this trail, the Bates brothers could be watching Mattie even now.

Jacob forced his tight fists to relax. Even if he wanted to fight Cole, he would never come out of such an encounter as the winner. Cole was wise in the ways of the world and had surely been in his share of fights. Fighting wasn't the way to prevent the Englisher from taking what he wanted.

He and Andrew, and the other men, too, could keep watch over the girls. But even that wouldn't be enough against a determined foe. Cole would only wait until their guard was down. Was Mattie to be a prisoner forever, just because some Englisher had taken a fancy to her?

As Mattie and Naomi caught up to their family's wagon, they hopped onto the lazy board, the seat running along the far side of the wagon, and disappeared from his view. He took one more look along the top of the bluff, but saw no one, then started down the steep hill toward the river. He hadn't missed the interest showing in Mattie's eyes when she was talking to Cole. He would never understand a girl's mind. Never. There was nothing about that man to draw her, and yet she had spoken to him. Had let him take her arm. She couldn't be interested in him. Not Mattie.

When he passed the place where he and Andrew had found the girls, Jacob stopped to get his breathing and his feelings under control. Not only would the sheep notice his agitation, but Peter and Margli would too. It wouldn't do any good to worry them. He leaned over, resting his hands on his knees, taking a deep breath. He whooshed it out, then took another one. His eyes focused on the bent grass blades below his feet, and one stray dandelion leaf, already wilting. Mattie must have dropped it, possibly when Cole grasped her arm.

The memory made him straighten with a groan. If Mattie wanted to go with that man, to leave her family, there was nothing to hold her back. She hadn't taken her baptism vows yet, so there was nothing to hold her to the church. Love of family and home hadn't been enough to keep Liesbet from straying, and he couldn't count on it being enough for Mattie, either.

And her longing to see beyond the land in front of her feet haunted him. He groaned again, pushing the heels of his hands into his eyes. If only he could rid himself of the memory of the look in her eyes when she spoke of seeing new lands. There was nothing he could do to keep her at home, not if she wanted the adventures Cole could promise her.

Adventures leading to her destruction.

As little as Jacob had seen of the world, he had recognized the look in Cole's eyes when he held Mattie close to him. Mattie deserved a man who would love her and care for her. A man who would protect her. Cole had no thought beyond how he could use her. There had been no love in his expression.

An idea flitted through Jacob's mind, leaving him cold. The one way he could ensure that Mattie wouldn't willingly follow Cole Bates. He snatched off his hat and ran his fingers through his hair. An idea so preposterous . . . but it might work. Mattie hadn't yet taken her vows to God, to become a member of the church, but what if she gave her vow to him? If he could persuade Mattie to pledge her life to him, a promise of marriage, perhaps that would be strong enough

to keep her from leaving her family—and him—and keep
her from following Cole to disaster.

By the time the group stopped to make camp, they had
gone fifteen miles from the ferry crossing of the Allegheny
River, had forded countless streams flowing into the Ohio
River, and passed through half a dozen small towns along the
riverbank. Tomorrow, Yost Bontrager had said, they would
reach the Indian trail that would take them west, away from
the river and deep into Ohio, to the Amish settlement there.

Jacob could only feel relief at the thought of leaving the
river behind. All afternoon he had kept scanning the bluffs
above the river, watching for any sign of the Bates brothers.
Not seeing them didn't settle his mind at all. He'd rather
know where they were lurking.

The night's camping spot was a wide meadow filled with
coarse swamp grasses. Earlier in the spring this would have
been a swirling eddy in the flooded river, but as summer approached, the marshy ground was nearly dry. They halted
the wagons back from the river, under the brow of the ever-
present bluffs where the ground was higher, and picketed
the horses in the lower meadow, where the coarse grass grew
thick. Jacob settled the sheep near the wagons where they
could browse on the brush growing on the side of the steep
slope rising above them.

After the meal, when evening prayers had been said and the
campsite cleaned up for the night, most of the travelers went
to bed. Jacob joined Henry, Andrew, and the girls around
the fire. This gathering time, while the parents settled their
young children for the night and the older members of the

group sought rest and quiet, had become a pleasant habit for the young people. Sometimes they sang together, soft hymns that lulled them all to a quiet night's rest. Rarely, one of their fathers had to reprimand them for laughing too loudly at Andrew's jokes.

Tonight Jacob took the spot on a log next to Mattie. Naomi and Henry sat on her other side, with Andrew and Johanna on their own log across the fire. Jacob rubbed his hands together to warm them against the chill air along the river. He wanted to spend time alone with Mattie, but how could he get the others to leave them alone by the fire?

His question was answered when Andrew gave a big yawn. He scooted closer to Johanna, and then leaned forward to stir the coals. "It's been a long day. How about just one song, and then we call it a night."

Naomi wrapped her shawl more tightly around her shoulders and leaned toward the dying fire. "That sounds good to me. I can hardly keep my eyes open."

Andrew started singing a hymn, one of Jacob's favorites. Their voices blended under the starry sky as Andrew led them through the verses.

When the song ended, he stood. "I'd volunteer for the first watch tonight, Jacob, but I'm afraid I'd fall asleep. Do you mind?"

"Not at all. I'll wake you when it's your turn."

When Naomi started toward the wagon with Henry, she hesitated, looking at Mattie. When Jacob took Mattie's hand in his, she said, "You go ahead, Naomi. I'll be along soon."

Johanna took Naomi's arm and they giggled together before saying good night and separating to their own wagons.

Jacob didn't release Mattie's hand, even when they were

alone, and she didn't pull it away. He pushed all thoughts of Cole Bates out of his mind as he ran his thumb along her slender fingers. His Mattie.

"What did you want to talk about?" She didn't look toward him as she spoke, but stared into the pulsing red coals.

His mouth went dry. All afternoon he had been rehearsing what he would say, the reasons he would give her, telling himself that securing her pledge was right and good. It was to keep her safe. But now that the time had come, the words stuck in his throat.

Mattie took a stick and poked at the dying fire. "Are you going to keep the fire going all night?"

He pushed off the log, releasing her hand. "Ja, ja, ja." He put three small logs on the coals and dropped some kindling between them. He blew gently until the kindling caught, then fed the small fire with Mattie's stick.

She leaned back with her fingers laced around one knee. "Do you remember the night before my family left the Conestoga? It was a night like this one."

Jacob gazed at Mattie's face in the firelight. "You were crying, and came to see me."

"I didn't want to leave you behind. I wanted to go west, but I wanted you to go with us."

"That was a long time ago. You were just a little girl."

She turned to him then, and he sat beside her on the log again. "I might have been a little girl, but I knew what I wanted."

Jacob swallowed, his mouth full of cotton. "Do you know what you want now, Mattie?"

She looked into the fire again. "I think I do, then something happens, and I don't know what to think."

"You mean Cole Bates."

Mattie nodded, and Jacob held back the words he wanted to say. Words that would tell her what a fool she was for even considering that man worth a moment of her time. Words that would berate her and condemn the man who held her thoughts.

He took her hand again and held it until she met his eyes. "Think back to when we were children. What did you want then?"

She laughed, hiding her mouth behind her hand. "I wanted you to be my brother, so we could live together forever. Isn't that silly?"

Jacob's breath caught at the simple beauty of her expression. His Mattie, pure and innocent. His breast burned with the need to protect her. "I don't think it's silly. I knew even then that we were meant to be together."

"But no matter how hard I prayed, you never became my brother, and we moved away. I thought I'd never see you again."

"Your prayers were answered."

She laughed, keeping her voice quiet. "You aren't my brother, Jacob."

"I can be closer than a brother." He reached toward her and dared to stroke her cheek as he tucked a stray bit of hair behind her ear. "You've always been part of my heart. Ever since you were a little girl."

He felt her hand tighten on his. When she spoke, it was a whisper so soft, he had to lean close to hear it. "And you've always been part of mine."

"I give you my pledge that I will always care for you. I'll protect you from all harm, and provide for you and our family."

Her eyes grew large as he spoke, her expression solemn. "What are you saying, Jacob?"

"I want you to pledge yourself to me. Promise that you'll stay with me. That you won't let anyone or anything come between us."

Mattie's fingers twined with his, and she covered their joined hands with her free one. She didn't answer for several minutes while Jacob's heart pounded.

"I don't mean to say that I would ever let someone like Cole Bates come between us"—Mattie pulled her hands away and turned toward the fire again, hugging her knees—"but I want more than this ordinary life. All I've known is doing the same thing over and over again, living a plain, simple Amish life. But there has to be more, doesn't there?"

Jacob picked up a stick and stirred the fire. "There might be something different out there, but I don't think you'll ever find more than what we have right here. Don't we have enough? We have all the food we need and work to do. Family, friends, a future. It's a life of living the way God has ordained. How could you want anything else?"

"It may be the way God has ordained for you, but what if he has something different for me?"

Mattie had drawn her knees up and rested her chin on them, her hands clasped. Huddled into herself like that, she had shut him away from her as firmly as if she had refused his request.

She reminded him of a ewe lamb they had once who wouldn't stay with the flock. It had jumped every fence they put it behind and sought its own pasture, away from the others. Daed had finally said to leave it be until it got lonely, and then it would come back. He had been right. The ewe lamb spent a night outside the fold, but then was bleating at the gate the next morning. It never tried to leave the flock again.

He wanted to pressure Mattie to give him her pledge, but what kind of promise would that be? She would never keep it, and before he knew it, she would jump the fence and be off again.

The fire shifted and he pushed the half-burned logs back together again. He would have to let her go. Let her find her own way. He could still try to protect her, but he couldn't force her to love him. He would have to leave that part up to God.

That evening Cole Bates hefted the sack of gold pieces in his hand. The detour to the towns along the southern bank of the Ohio River last week had been lucrative. These movers heading west were too trusting for their own good. Stolen horses brought a good profit, if a man knew where to sell them, and Cole knew. But like Pa always said, once you made some headway, it was time to lay low for a while. They didn't need to go pressing their luck.

"Why don't we spend some of that money on food?" Darrell lifted his stick out of the fire. The rat he had skewered dripped fat onto the coals, releasing an appetizing sizzle.

"There's nothing wrong with rat." Hiram bit off a chunk of his own and Cole shuddered. Hiram was never patient enough to cook his meat all the way through.

Cole dug the last hoecake out of his sack. The cakes had been fresh when Hiram had snatched them out of a settler's kitchen two days ago, but now the cornmeal crumbled in his mouth.

"Cole? We got to buy some food." Darrell's whine worried Cole's ears like a mosquito. "Pa won't miss a dollar or two of the money."

"Do you want to be the one to tell him we spent the money on food when he taught all three of us how to live off the land?"

That shut Darrell up. He knew as well as Cole that Pa would get one of them to tell, and then they'd all get a beating.

"Tomorrow you two can do some hunting. Maybe you'll find a rabbit or groundhog and Hiram can make some stew."

Hiram's grunt was his agreement. Darrell hunched his shoulders and stuck his rat back over the flames.

"And no stealing. We'll stay here a day or so, then move on into Ohio."

"You still looking to get them horses off the Amish?"

Cole glanced at Hiram as his brother sucked the meat off a tiny bone. "Those horses are the best we've seen. Matched teams like that will bring a good price."

"They won't be easy to get." Hiram threw the remains of his supper into the bushes behind him and wiped his fingers on his trousers. "You were wrong about those Amish. You said they'd be easy pickings."

"I misjudged them." Cole shrugged. "But we'll get the horses."

A guffaw sounded from Darrell's side of the fire. "You going to get that girl too? She's a pretty one." Darrell took a bite from his rat. "She'd be nice to cozy up to on a cold night." He laughed again, ignoring the juices dripping down his chin.

Cole turned away from both of them. "I'm going to scout the trail up ahead before it gets dark. You two stay here."

"If you bring that girl back, make sure you bring her friends too!" Darrell collapsed on the ground, laughing at his own words.

Ignoring them, Cole made his way to the trail along the top of the bluff and walked for a little less than a mile, until he could see the Amish camp. They had picketed the horses too near the wagons for his liking and probably were setting a watch. Those Amish weren't fools.

He settled along the trail, lowering himself so he could peer through the long grass at the edge of the bluff without being seen. The camp below was quieting down in the evening dusk. He watched one young woman coaxing a small boy to leave the flock of sheep. The boy came to her and she lifted him in her arms, hugging him as she did. Cole swallowed a lump down in his throat. He barely remembered his mother, but he knew she had never hugged him like that. Pa would never have allowed it.

Catching sight of the girl, Mattie, he risked raising his head over the top of the grass. She carried a dishpan to the edge of the camp, and the water flew in an arc onto the patchy swamp grass. She was a pretty thing and not afraid of hard work from the looks of it. His hand clenched, remembering the feel of her soft arm in his hand. The flowery smell of her seemed to waft its way toward him on the evening breeze.

As the other members of their group made their way to their tents and wagons, Mattie and the other young people gathered at the fire. One man, the one called Jacob, sat a little too close to her, but no matter. She told him she had no man, and even if she did, Cole knew how to take care of a rival. He waited until darkness fell and the fire died. Once he could no longer see her, he moved back away from the edge of the bluff and started down the trail back to camp.

The idea of going west had grown on him during the past week. Those Conestoga horses would bring top dollar in

Independence. The only problem was what to do with Hiram and Darrell. Darrell couldn't keep a secret to save his life, and if Pa asked the weasel-faced kid why Cole hadn't come home, Darrell would blurt out the whole story. After that there would be no rest. No starting over. He'd never be able to get away and live on his own. Pa would follow him to the ends of the earth to take revenge for his betrayal.

No, if he was ever going to get away from Pa, he'd have to do it in secret. That wouldn't be too hard. He'd change his name, head west with that Mattie girl and a good team of those Conestogas, and he'd never have to worry about Pa again.

But Darrell and Hiram were a problem. They'd have to up and disappear. They couldn't go home to that hardscrabble farm of Pa's in Missouri, and they sure weren't going to tag along with him. Darrell was a real liability with his stupid, thick head and constant whine. And he could never keep a leash on his tongue. More than once on this trip he had spoiled their chances to grab a horse or two because his whining had alerted the owners.

Then there was Hiram. There was something wrong with that boy. No, not a boy anymore. Hiram had gotten his full height a couple of years ago, towering over Cole's near six feet, but on this trip he had filled out with pure muscle. He didn't talk much, but he wasn't dumb like Darrell. He was sly, and a cruel streak ran through him a mile wide and two deep. It was only a matter of time before he decided he should be the leader of the group, and Cole didn't want to be around when he did. He grew cold just thinking about it.

If he was ever going to be free of Pa, he'd have to act soon. The rumors he had heard of that place called Oregon made it sound perfect for a man like him. A place to start over, to make his way without Pa looking over his shoulder. With a girl like Mattie, he could raise a passel of sons to be just like him—tough and able, willing to take whatever that new land had to offer.

He'd need to get those horses and the girl, and get to Independence by the end of May if he was going to join up with a wagon train this spring. If he didn't get there in time, he'd have to wait until next year. And he wasn't a man to wait when he knew what he wanted.

13

Mattie slipped around to the far side of the wagon from where Jacob watched her from his spot by the fire. She should climb into the wagon, take her place on the pallet next to Naomi, and go to sleep. But she couldn't. As hard as her heart was beating, she would wake Naomi and the rest of the family for sure.

Jacob's promise to protect her, to take care of her, was what she had dreamed of before Daed had gone west last year and come home with stories of the land he had seen in Iowa. But even with her longing to see those western prairies, knowing that Jacob felt something for her pulled at her heart. How could she refuse him?

She held trembling fingers to her lips, took a deep breath, then another. Slowly her heart quieted until she could once again hear the croaking of the frogs along the river.

The sheep had settled in groups of two or three on the grass, patches of white in the darkness. Jacob had staked a rope around them as he often did at night, just enough to remind them not to wander away, he had said. If they did wander, he, Andrew, Josef, or one of the other men keeping watch would see them before they got too far away. Mattie walked toward the nearest white shape, and the sheep lifted her nose in greeting. It was Bitte, the lead ewe. Mattie patted her head, then looked up through the branches at the edge of the woods to the canopy of stars. The northern sky was blotted out by the trees and the bluff rising steeply, but overhead the night sky shone silvery white. There was no light except the stars and a faint blue in the west left from the evening sunset.

Mattie hugged herself, rising up on her toes. Then she flung her arms out. Nothing could keep her from flying up to those stars tonight. Jacob Yoder said he cared for her. She twirled around twice, three times, then hugged herself again. Closing her eyes, Mattie let her mind go back to the first time she had realized how much he meant to her. It was just before her family had left the Conestoga to move to Brothers Valley. Jacob had changed that summer, like many boys did when they turned fourteen. But even with all the grown-up mannerisms and obvious disdain for the younger children in their church, he had never changed how he acted toward her.

One Sunday afternoon, he and the other older boys had found her sitting high in her favorite tree. She had often gone there the last few months before they moved, letting the wind sway her while she thought about her dream—the dream she had several times that spring. The dream she had again just before they left Brothers Valley.

When they had spied her in the tree, the other boys teased her, calling her a tomboy and other nasty names, but Jacob had intervened. He stood up for her against them, and after they went on to some other pursuit, he climbed into the tree with her.

"What are you doing up here?" he asked.

Mattie looked at him then. At the whiskers he had missed in his early attempts at shaving. At his long legs and arms that had made his climb awkward. And at his eyes. Jacob's serious, gentle eyes. "Do you have dreams, Jacob?"

"You mean at night, while I'm asleep?"

She nodded.

"Sometimes. But mostly they disappear when I wake up."

"Do they ever come back? Do you dream the same thing more than once?"

"Maybe. I don't remember. Why?"

Mattie shrugged. "I keep having this dream that I'm trying to get somewhere, but I can't get through the wall. It's a high wall, like the picture of the mountain cliff in my schoolbook. And in my dream, I'm looking for a secret passage."

She waited for Jacob to laugh, but he didn't. He only broke a twig off the tree branch and rubbed it between his fingers. "What is behind the wall?"

"I don't know. But it must be something wonderful. I feel like it's calling to me, inviting me to come in, but I can never find the way."

"Are you alone in the dream?"

"There are a lot of other people outside the wall with me, but they aren't trying to get in. Only me."

Jacob waited then, twirling the twig until the bark wore off. After peeling the twig all the way around, he tossed it to the ground. "I had a dream once where I was looking for something." He broke another twig off the branch.

"Did you ever find it?"

He shrugged. "I don't know. But I never had the dream again. Maybe when you find what you're looking for, you'll stop having your dream."

"You don't think it's silly? Having dreams like that?"

He smiled at her, then climbed down the tree. "Mattie," he said, reaching up and tugging gently at her dangling foot, "I don't think anything you do is silly."

Jacob walked away then, but he had stolen her heart. From then on, she compared every boy she met to Jacob, and none of them had come close.

Mattie reached down to pet Bitte again, scrunching her fingers into the sheep's woolly head to scratch the soft skin behind her ears. And now Jacob had asked her to give him her pledge. He wanted her to be part of his future . . . her fingers slowed. He wanted her to live forever with him on his farm in Indiana.

She looked toward the west, where the faint blue had darkened into the black night sky. Stars shone in a white carpet overhead, with a few wispy gray clouds hanging in the air between the night and her outstretched fingers. Her hand dropped to her side. If she pledged herself to Jacob, she would never go west again. Never see the western mountains, or the ocean. She would never know if Oregon was as wonderful as the travelers going by their Brothers Valley farm had claimed.

Her dream came back to her. The high, gray cliff looming above her, and the certainty that there was a way through. But what was behind the wall? Was it Oregon? Is that what the dream was telling her, that she was meant to go farther west?

If she did what Jacob had asked, she would never know. She sighed and gave Bitte a final pat before turning back toward the wagon. She couldn't live not knowing what the west was like. Even now her heart was about to burst with longing, but for what? For Jacob, or for adventure?

The second day after the group had left the river, Annalise grabbed the edge of her bench seat as the wagon lurched, stifling a groan. Ever since they had headed west, the rain had been relentless. Now the track they were following had turned to a sticky mire. Every few miles the men had to halt the teams to knock the clumps of mud out of the big spoked wagon wheels, but the mothers with small children were forced by the weather to stay inside the crowded wagons. The young people—Hannah, Mattie, and the rest—chose to ride in the open spring wagons, but Annalise wouldn't risk the little children's health.

Margli and Peter sat across the wagon from her, playing cat's cradle with a bit of yarn, but little William was at loose ends. His wooden cows and horses lay scattered on the bench where he had left them.

"Memmi, tell me a story." William, three years old and used to being active all day, climbed onto the bench beside her. His voice was almost a whine, but she couldn't reprimand him. Not today.

Gathering him close, Annalise rubbed her belly to ease the pressure of the babe's protesting push. "What story would you like?"

"*Grossdawdi* Isaac and the ship." William squirmed around until he was seated on his bottom. "Tell me about the rats."

"Haven't you heard that story enough?"

William shook his head and leaned against her.

"Many years ago, Grossdawdi Isaac had to leave Europe with his wife and three children."

"Nancy."

"Ja, his wife's name was Nancy. Do you remember the names of the children?"

"William, like me, and Suzanne and Mary. She was the baby."

"That's right. They traveled by ship on a long voyage across the ocean."

"Storms." William spoke around the thumb he had stuck in his mouth. His head slipped down to her knee and he laid down on the bench.

"There were many storms that tossed their little sail ship to and fro. There wasn't enough food to eat, and they had to fight the rats to keep them from eating the supplies. Many people got sick."

William's blue eyes stared up at her. He popped his thumb out of his mouth. "Mary died."

"Ja, Mary died." Tears filled her eyes, as they always did at this part of the story. "And their memmi, Nancy, died too."

"Not William and Suzanne."

"The other children survived, and so did Grossdawdi Isaac. When they arrived in Philadelphia, an Amish family was waiting for them. Grossdawdi's cousin, Christian. They walked from Philadelphia to Berks County. To the Northkill Settlement."

"That's where they were attacked by the Indians," Peter broke in.

"But first something else happened."

Margli didn't look up from the complex design she was

attempting with the yarn. "Grossdawdi Isaac got married again. He met Grossmutti Fanny, and she was William and Suzanne's new memmi."

Annalise felt faint as the wagon lurched again. Was she going to be sick? She rubbed at her belly, waiting for the dizzy spell to pass. These spells were coming often, almost every day. She should speak to Mary Nafsinger about them.

William wiggled. "The Indians, Memmi."

"Ja, the Indians." She rubbed at the small of her back. "The Indians were friends with the Amish settlers at Northkill. The settlers shared their food with them and never threatened them with a gun. They lived in peace for many years."

"But then war came." Peter continued the story.

"Ja, war came. Some Indians fought for the French and tried to drive all the settlers off of their land. One night, a group of Indian soldiers attacked the Hochstetler family. After that, Grossdawdi Isaac moved to the Conestoga with his family."

"He built the log cabin."

"Ja. And the smokehouse and the barn. But William, his son, built the house." The lovely house on the Conestoga. Annalise sighed and pushed her fist into her back, right above her hip bone, where the twinges of pain always started and radiated down her leg.

"And William was Jacob's father, and then Grossdawdi Jacob was Daed's father," Peter said.

"Ja, that's right." Annalise heard her own voice as though through layers of wool batting. A gray haze covered her vision, and then all went black.

Annalise opened her eyes to see Christian leaning over her.

"Annalise, are you all right?"

"Did I fall asleep?" She was lying on the floor of the wagon, looking up at her family. Margli's face was white.

"You fainted. When you fell off the bench, the children called me."

Annalise tried to sit up, but Christian held his hand on her shoulder.

"How long have I been lying here?"

"Not long. I sent Peter to get Mary Nafsinger."

Annalise relaxed. Mary's midwife skills would help her know what was wrong with her. She rubbed her stomach as the baby kicked. At least she knew it was safe and well.

Christian sent the children outside when Mary came. The rain had settled into a light drizzle, so they would get wet, but not soaked through. Hannah would take care of them.

"Peter said you took a tumble right onto the floor," Mary said.

She motioned for Christian to help her and they brought Annalise to a sitting position.

Annalise tried to smile at Mary, but her mouth trembled. "I think I fainted."

"How do you feel now?"

"Better." Tears filled Annalise's eyes. "I don't know why, but I feel very weak."

At a look from Mary, Christian left the wagon, leaving Annalise alone with the midwife.

"Do you feel like you can sit on the bench?"

Annalise looked at the board she had fallen from. It seemed as high as a mountain peak. "Maybe. If you'll help me."

Mary supported Annalise's arm as she slowly got to her feet. But instead of sitting on the bench, Annalise lay down on her pallet on top of some boxes. She nearly started crying again when she saw the concerned look on Mary's face.

"You told me you don't expect the baby until summer, ja?"

"Not until July, I thought. But then you thought it could come as early as May."

"The babe is quite large. Do you feel any of the birthing pangs? Even small ones?"

"Small ones, but nothing strong enough to make me think my time has come."

Mary peered at her face, feeling her cheek with the back of her hand. "Your color is coming back, so that is good. Lying down seems to be helping." She leaned back and looked at Annalise's stomach. "I need to feel the babe, to make sure all is well. Please turn onto your back."

Annalise tried to remain still as Mary gently felt the tight round ball of her belly.

"Do you feel the babe kick much?"

"All the time. I don't think this one ever sleeps."

"Um-hmm. Ja, for sure." The older woman straightened up. "Have you considered that there might be more than one babe?"

"More than one?" Annalise pushed herself to a sitting position. "Do you mean twins?"

Mary smiled. "Could be. All the signs point that way."

"Is that why I fainted?"

Mary's smile faded. "The strain of two babies is hard on your body. You need to rest more, eat better, and stop riding in this bumpy wagon. It could bring on an early birth."

Annalise pressed a hand against her stomach. "Are they in danger? Could we . . . could we lose them, even before they're born?"

The midwife sat next to her on the pallet and placed her own hand on the babies. "Yes, there is a danger, a danger to all three of you. We are close to my son's farm. Daniel said we should reach it by tomorrow. I think if you make it that far, then you should stay there until your time comes."

Annalise bowed her head, rubbing her swollen belly. God couldn't take these babies too. He couldn't.

Even though it was only midafternoon, Peter came running down the road to Jacob and the sheep with the news.

"We're camping just up ahead for the night."

"Why? We could go another few miles today, even with the rain."

"Mamm took ill. She fell on the floor, and Daed said we're not going any farther today."

Mamm. Jacob shoved his crook at Peter. "Look after the sheep, and bring them up to the wagons. I'm going to see what's happening."

Jacob sprinted toward the wagons, running through the wet grass alongside the muddy, rutted road. When he reached the Bontragers' wagon, he slowed. How ill was Mamm? He changed course and stopped at the small green wagon. Hannah would know.

He scratched at the canvas wagon cover. "Hannah?"

"Just a minute." Her voice was nearly a whisper, it was so soft. She climbed out of the wagon, closing a flap of canvas over the front opening. "I just got William to take a nap. Peter told you about Mamm?"

"All he said was that she took ill. Is she all right?"

Hannah laid a hand on his arm. "She's all right, and the babies are too."

"Babies?"

"Mary says there are twins, and that's why she's been having a hard time. But she's all right now, and resting."

"But Peter said we were camping here tonight. Why can't we continue on if Mamm's all right?"

Hannah's eyes looked tired and worried.

"Is there more you aren't telling me?"

"Ne, nothing more. But Mary said Mamm shouldn't travel any farther until the babies are born."

Stay in Ohio? Jacob shook his head, trying to clear it. "I need to talk to Daed."

"The men are gathered up by the Schrocks' wagon. They're talking about it now."

Jacob found the group of men discussing the issue, just as Hannah said. The circle parted to allow him to join, and as he looked from face to face, his panic subsided. They were part of a community. These families would face this complication with them, giving help and advice, and supporting Daed's decision, whatever it was.

"Jacob," Daed said. He stood on the opposite side of the circle, flanked by Josef and Elias Hertzler. "You've heard the news?"

"Hannah told me."

"I was just telling everyone else that I will stay in Ohio until the end of the summer. We will stay with the settlers there, and join the rest of our group in Indiana by September."

September? They would be in no position to survive the winter in a fledgling settlement if they arrived that late in the season. Jacob glanced around the circle. Every man was looking at him.

"I can't risk the journey, Son. Not with your mamm in such a condition."

Daniel Nafsinger ended the impromptu meeting with a prayer, and then the men separated to take care of the business of setting up the camp. Andrew made his way across the disintegrating circle to him.

"I'm sorry about your mamm, and that your family is having such trouble."

Jacob looked into Andrew's eyes, but the usual mocking glint was gone. "How long will you stay in Ohio before heading on to Indiana?"

"I heard Eli Schrock say that they plan to rest for a week. The women want to do laundry, once this rainy weather clears. And we all need to rest and have some real food to eat."

Jacob scanned the groups of people working to set up the camp, but Mattie wasn't in sight.

"Don't worry about Mattie, Jacob. I'll take care of her for you."

This time the glint was there. He couldn't leave Mattie in Andrew's care. She could be married to the man by the time Jacob made it to Indiana.

14

The rain ended overnight, and a radiant dawn lifted everyone's spirits. Mattie had chosen to ride in the spring wagon with her sisters-in-law, Miriam and Emma, and their little girls since the trail was still muddy in the ruts.

Glancing behind her at Jacob urging the muddy sheep along the trail behind the wagons, she shifted in her seat. Avoiding the mud was only part of the reason for her decision to ride in the spring wagon. Avoiding Jacob was the biggest part. Since the evening he had asked for her pledge, the weather had been rainy. No one lingered over their cold meals and there was no campfire for the young people to gather around at night. The more time passed, the more reluctant she was to give Jacob an answer. Whatever she decided, she would have to live with it for the rest of her life. She bounced three-year-old Leah on her knee. It might as well be forever.

The sun was only halfway until noon when they came to the first Amish farm along the road.

Daed, in the lead wagon, halted the caravan and shouted a greeting. "Hallo."

An Amish man flanked by two young boys appeared in the barn door. He waved his answer, then came to the side of the road to speak with Daed. Mattie took in the comfortable-looking frame house, with outbuildings scattered in the open area around a stone, two-story barn. If all the farms were as prosperous as this one, then Ohio must be a good place to live.

The man gestured down the road, the way they were traveling, then indicated a turn to the right. With a final wave, Daed started his team again, and they were on their way. As Emma drove the spring wagon past the farm, Mattie waved to the man's wife, who had come to the door of the house. The woman leaned over the Dutch door, waving in reply. She had set a little boy on the bottom half of the door, but he wasn't watching the wagons. He pointed toward a girl about Leah's and Mary's age who was throwing grain to the chickens pecking in the gravel path that led from the door to the barn. It all looked so clean and picturesque, and the hominess of it all made Mattie turn in her seat to keep the little farm in view after they drove by.

As she turned to face the front again, she swallowed a lump in her throat. Would a home like that ever be in her future? The desire to go west made her heart race, but a home . . . Jacob had said he wanted a home that he would never have to leave. A home for his children and grandchildren through the generations to come. At times like this, she could understand his dream, and the longing to join him was so great it made her bones ache.

She rubbed at her elbows, and then helped three-year-old

Mary climb onto her other knee. Hugging both little girls close, she smiled, banishing her mood.

"We'll be there soon, I think." Miriam leaned to the right, trying to see beyond Daed's wagon ahead.

"The Nafsingers' son lives near Walnut Creek, doesn't he?" Mattie asked, trying to remember the details of the adults' conversations over the past couple of weeks.

"Just a little north, Daniel said." Emma pointed ahead, where Daed was turning onto another road heading to the right. "Here's our turn."

The road leading to the north was narrower than the one they left, and led up a hill, then down into a long valley on the other side. At the bottom of the valley was a creek, swollen and brown from the recent rains. Farms spread out on both sides of the road with freshly plowed fields and open meadows separated by wood lots. Here and there along the valley were more of the white frame houses like the one they had just passed. Mattie counted four farms in this valley alone. The Ohio settlement seemed to be as large as the one in Somerset County.

Daed turned into the lane leading to the second farm on the left. The lane forded the creek at a shallow spot where gravel had been laid to make the way smooth, and then wound up a slope to the buildings. Hills rose above the house and barn, and cows dotted the meadow beyond the barn. Before they stopped the wagons, the family came out of the house. Mattie glanced behind her to the small green wagon, where the Nafsingers were riding. Mary stood at the front opening of the wagon, waving. Josef halted the team, and the old couple were in the arms of their son and daughter-in-law.

Mattie swallowed back tears at the sight of Mary's face,

until she saw the three grandchildren hiding behind their mother's skirts. Then as Mary's face crumpled into tears, Mattie let hers flow too. Mary's tears of joy were contagious as she met her grandchildren for the first time.

Daniel's son left the reunion long enough to point out their camping spot, a clear area just north of the barn, and then rejoined his family as the wagons drove on.

"What a happy sight!" Miriam sighed. "The Nafsingers have never met their grandchildren, have they?"

Mattie shook her head. "And there are two other families for them to meet. I think Mary said their other son and their daughter each have five children."

"They all live close by?"

"I don't know, but I hope so."

Making camp was leisurely that afternoon since they had arrived at their destination so early. Mattie looked for Jacob, but he was busy settling the sheep in the upper pasture. After that, she saw him in the barnyard with the other young men, setting up tables and benches in a level spot.

After getting their wagon set up and everything comfortable for their stay, Mattie looked out over the valley from their camping spot halfway up the hill. Walnut Creek had been settled almost thirty-five years ago, and much of the thick forest had been cleared. She could see the road they had traveled on winding away back to the south and then east. It showed again on the crest of a hill in the distance but disappeared as it tumbled down the other side. Everything looked settled and peaceful, like the vision Jacob had for his home in Indiana.

A twisting, uncomfortable thought made her move her gaze away from the road. Somewhere back there to the east was Cole Bates. Turning the thought over in her head, as she had many times in the days since she last saw him, gave the same awful pleasure as scratching a mosquito bite. He was forbidden, worldly, and not someone she should hold in her thoughts. But the very danger she should flee from called to her. A man like Cole Bates would never settle for a neat, white frame house on a little farm.

Jacob followed Ulrich Nafsinger up the slope behind the barn.

"Your sheep will do well in the upper pasture, I think."

Jacob lengthened his strides to keep up with the youngest of Daniel and Mary's sons. "You've heard that our family will need to stay on until autumn, haven't you? Will that be a problem?"

"Not at all." Ulrich bent and swung between the fence rails. "We'll enjoy the company. Your daed said you'll need a lambing pen." He gestured toward the southeast corner of the meadow where the fence ran under the shelter of some overhanging trees. "That spot will be protected, and since it slopes toward the southeast, your sheep will have the advantage of the sunlight. The rest of the meadow is well-fenced, with plenty of grass for both the sheep and my cows."

"Denki. We'll bring the flock up right away and get them settled."

Ulrich led the way back down the slope. "You'll be staying here with your folks, then?"

"Daed hasn't said any different. They'll need me to help when lambing time comes, for sure."

"I thought you'd be anxious to get on to Indiana."

Jacob pushed his smoldering resentment into the background. Daed needed him here. Building his new life in Indiana would have to wait. "I admit I'm disappointed that I'm not going with the others—" he paused as he caught sight of Mattie near the wagons, playing with her young nieces—"but it can't be helped."

Meanwhile, Mattie would go on to Indiana without him. He hadn't talked with her since he asked for her pledge along the Ohio River, and he had no idea what she might be thinking. It would be so simple for her to agree, and they could make their plans. She could stay here in Ohio until autumn, so they could court properly.

If only she would give him her pledge, and he could trust her to keep it. He blew out a whooshing breath. He had thought of confiding in Daed several times in the last few days, but he already knew the advice he'd get: Wait for God, be content with what he has given so far, and pray.

Waiting had never been so hard.

Supper was ready by the time Jacob, Peter, and Margli, along with Henry's and Andrew's help, had gotten the sheep into Ulrich's pasture. Jacob waited until the sheep were grazing and Bam had explored the entire meadow. When the ram settled in to grazing also, Jacob joined the other men at the tables.

Moses Stutzman, Daniel's son-in-law, leaned his elbows on the table and took a forkful of schnitz pie. "How are things going in Pennsylvania?"

Eli Schrock glanced at Moses as he cut the point off his own piece of pie. "What do you mean?"

"I mean since the conference in your district there in Somerset County, the Glades, six years ago. The ministers put down some harsh rulings, didn't they?"

Daed leaned forward, his forearms bracketing his plate and his fork grasped in one hand. "It depends on what you mean by harsh, Brother Moses."

Moses shrugged. "I think it's a hard thing when we shun our own members who choose to join one of our sister churches, the Mennonites or the Dunkards. It isn't as if they've joined a church that teaches infant baptism rather than believer's baptism."

Eli raised his eyebrows. "So, that's still a topic of discussion here in Ohio?"

"Ja, for sure." Moses balanced another bite of the pie on his fork. "Some say the whole controversy was settled back in 1837 with the Glades Conference, but others say it is still undecided."

Jacob Nafsinger, Ulrich's older brother, laid his fork on his empty plate. "Only you folks up in Oak Grove still bring that up, Moses." His voice was mild. "The rest of us have no question about it. If a member leaves the Amish church to join with another, it is as much as if he has forsaken his marriage vows. He is to be shunned and put under the *bann*."

Yost Bontrager cleared his throat, stretching his long legs out under the table until Andrew and Jacob, across from him, had to shift aside. "In the Glades, including Brothers Valley, we hold to the directives of the 1837 meeting. There are other districts in Pennsylvania who have trouble remembering what the directives say, though."

"It would be difficult to remember all the rulings," Moses said. "The ministers at the conference came up with quite a few of them."

"Ja, well, the directive against bundling is quite often

ignored"—Yost stroked his beard—"much to the shame of our young people."

Andrew shifted in his seat and Jacob looked over to see his face reddening. Had he ever indulged in the practice?

"It is the parents' job to keep their young people in line," Jacob Nafsinger said.

Moses pushed his empty plate away. "Sometimes the parents encourage the behavior in order to get their young people to marry early, instead of waiting until they're in their twenties." He looked pointedly at Andrew when he said this.

Eli Schrock bowed his head. When he spoke, his voice was sorrowful. "It is a sad day when the ways of the world rear their heads among the faithful in the church."

Jacob found his head was nodding in agreement with Eli, along with several others.

"It isn't only the ways of the world, brother," Daed said. "The influence of other churches can be deadly."

Andrew rose from the table then and Jacob followed him. "Andrew, wait."

Jacob caught up with him and they walked together toward the upper pasture.

"The talk back there made you uncomfortable."

Andrew leaned on the top rail of the fence, watching the sheep. "It came a little too close to home for me."

Jacob shifted, but he had to ask. "Did you . . . have you done that?"

"Bundling?" Andrew looked sideways at Jacob. "What you want to ask is if Mattie and I have ever spent the night like that."

Jacob nodded, his face burning.

"Never Mattie, and her father wouldn't allow it." Andrew

kicked at the grass along the fence. "But there were always girls who wanted to, and even a couple fathers who proposed it, like Moses said." He leaned on the fence again. "I have to admit, I was tempted. I thought it might be fun." His fingers picked at a loose splinter on the top fence rail. "I'm glad I didn't, though."

"Why?"

"One of the girls in our church ended up expecting a child. She and Abe Glick got married before they had intended to. They were only seventeen." He tore the splinter off the fence rail with a jerk.

"I've never heard of the Amish in the Conestoga district acting like that. It seems like the wrong way to court a girl."

Andrew leveled his gaze at Jacob, his brows lowered. "I wish the folks in Somerset County didn't either." He stared at the fence rail where a golden wound gleamed in the weathered wood. "All I can think is how hard it must be for Abe and Bethann, starting out their marriage that way."

"Why did they do it in the first place, when it's against the Ordnung?"

Andrew smiled, but his face held no humor. "Sometimes I think you're awfully young, Jacob. Some fellows think the church and the ministers don't know everything, and they can choose how they're going to live their lives."

"But if they've been baptized—" Jacob cut off his words, remembering that Andrew hadn't yet been baptized.

"Why do you think so many of them go over to other churches? Or never join any church? The Amish aren't the only ones who know the right way to live."

"Would you do that? Join another church?"

Andrew shrugged again. "I don't have any reason to, and

I don't want to be separated from my family. As long as I haven't taken my baptismal vows, I don't have to worry about it."

He headed back down the hill in the dusk, leaving Jacob with the sheep. Andrew's casual attitude hid a troubled man. Jacob scratched the day's growth of whiskers on his chin. He was thankful for the directives and the Ordnung. Living in obedience to Christ was hard enough, and the Ordnung gave guidelines to make it easier. It looked like Andrew had learned that lesson the hard way.

Even though the rain had ended hours ago, gray clouds still hung in the air. Finally, sunset broke through the scattered clouds to the west. Cole Bates tossed the dregs of his coffee onto the feeble fire Hiram had coaxed from a pile of wet sticks and threw his cup into his possibles bag.

He had lost the Amish movers and their horses. Or rather, Darrell had lost them. Cole had trailed the Amish group along the Ohio River, staying far back so he wouldn't raise anyone's suspicion. Eventually the group would leave the river and head into the interior. All the movers did, whether they stuck to the road or took flatboats. But now they were almost to Wheeling and they hadn't seen a trace of the Amish for days. Darrell was supposed to be the tracker, but he had missed their western trail. That's all there was to it.

"What happened to the fire?" Darrell dropped an armload of wet sticks on the ground. He looked at Cole, his left eye swollen nearly closed.

Cole turned away from him. He should have given him two black eyes. "It was going out. I doused it."

"I brought more wood." Darrell's whine pushed Cole's nerves dangerously close to the breaking point. "I haven't cooked the rabbit yet."

Cole glanced at the wet, skinny carcass Hiram had brought to the camp. The thing was full of crawling fleas and bloated ticks. "We don't want to eat that. It'll make us sick. Hiram should have let it die where he found it."

"But I'm hungry."

"Shut up, Darrell. Make the fire again if you want to."

He left Darrell at the fire, poking at the wet coals and blowing on them, trying to find a spark. Cole made his way toward the river, keeping an eye out for Hiram. He had disappeared after delivering the rabbit to the camp. Probably found a tavern somewhere. Just like him to keep the news to himself.

A camp of movers had set up for the night below the bluff. Cole squatted at the edge next to a clump of bushes and watched them in the fading light. Five wagons with a single team for each. A few women and children. From the looks of their outfit, they were going a ways. They could even be heading to Oregon. But from what he had heard of that trail, a single team of horses would be dead by the time they got halfway across the Great Plains.

Cole watched as the men picketed the horses and fed them each a couple handfuls of grain. The women started cooking fires, each setting up a tripod and stew pot. They were green, that was certain. The kids played wildly, kicking dirt into the food until the women yelled at them to go somewhere else. They ate their meal, and then as it grew dark, they all scattered into their wagons, leaving the fires to go out on their own.

A grin made its way across Cole's face. No dogs, no guard watching. He was probably saving those folks from a slow death on the trail by stealing their horses. They should thank him.

He backed away from his hiding place before rising to his feet. If Hiram was back at the camp, the three of them could go to the movers' camp for the horses and light out for the buyer in Pittsburgh before dawn. Or if Hiram wasn't at the camp yet, he and Darrell could do the job, sell the horses, and leave their brother out of it.

A sudden thought of what Hiram would do if he thought he had been double-crossed made a cold sweat break out. Cole slowed his pace. Pa had given him the job of keeping his brothers in line, but Hiram had outgrown any power Cole had over him. He couldn't risk double-crossing the man. Pa and some others Cole knew were mean, ornery cusses, but the side he had seen of Hiram in the last week or so showed an evil that Cole hadn't come across before. He shuddered as he remembered the look on the man's face when Hiram had twisted the rabbit's neck. So far, he was on Hiram's good side, but how long would that last?

He might as well be living with a mad dog.

Walking into the cold camp, he found Darrell still poking at the wet coals.

"You seen Hiram?"

Darrell yawned. "Yeah. He came back a while ago. Rolled up in his bedroll with a bottle that he won't share."

The last three words were thrown in the general direction of Hiram's bedroll, but the only response was a grunt. Cole tried to shake off the cold feeling that had been creeping up on him since Hiram had disappeared that afternoon. If he

Jan Drexler

was already drunk, he'd be more of a liability than a help on this job. He walked over to the tree where Hiram leaned against the trunk, wrapped in his bedroll and with a bottle in his hand. There was some liquor left in the bottle, so maybe he wasn't too far gone yet.

"I found us a bunch of horses."

The only answer he got out of Hiram was a grunt, but Darrell got to his feet. "You found them Amish?"

"No. It's a bunch of movers. Ten horses picketed with no guard."

Darrell snuffled. "Dogs?"

"Nope."

Darrell laughed. "Hey, now that's what I call easy pickin's. We gonna go get them, Cole?"

Cole nudged the end of Hiram's bedroll with his foot. "You up for it?"

"No." Hiram struggled to his feet, throwing off the dirty blanket. An empty bottle rolled with it. Cole backed away. "I'm done with you, Cole. I'm done with you deciding what horses we steal and when." He rose against the backdrop of the surrounding trees, staggering a bit. A darker shadow against the dark woods. "Give me my share of the money. I'm heading out."

Cole's wet palms itched, but he wasn't going to let Hiram see he was nervous. Darrell stared at Hiram as the big man rolled his blanket into a ball and took another swig from his bottle.

"What are you doing, Hiram?" Darrell's voice faltered as he looked from his brother to Cole. "Cole's the oldest. He's always been in charge. Let's just go get the horses like he said."

181

Hiram ignored Darrell and shuffled toward Cole, the smell of the cheap whiskey and vomit pushing ahead of him. Cole took another step back.

"Come on, Hiram. You know Pa wants us to stick together. Once we get the money Pa sent us for, we'll head home, and then you can go wherever you want."

Hiram stopped, swaying on his feet. "I owe your pa nothing. Give me the money, or I'll kill you for it."

Cole swallowed, his clammy hands clutching at the purse inside his vest. Hiram's voice was cold and deadly. Cole had no doubt he would carry out his threat. He pulled out the purse and emptied the coins into his hand. Squatting on the ground by the fire, he cleared a spot in the dirt and divided the coins into three piles. He flinched when Hiram stooped, but the other man only gathered one of the piles in his big hand and thrust the coins into his pocket.

Hiram picked up his saddle and threw it on his horse's back.

"Hiram?" Darrell peeped like a lost chick. "You aren't going without me, are you?"

"Why would I want you along?" Hiram pulled the saddle girth tight and turned toward his brother. "Stick with Cole. He'll feed you, at least."

Hiram mounted his horse and disappeared into the darkness.

Darrell turned his gaping face to Cole. "What are we going to do without Hiram?"

Cole put the remaining coins back in his purse and straightened. A great weight had lifted now that Hiram was gone. "We're going to get those horses down by the river."

He saddled his horse and checked his rifle and pistol. Primed and ready to go. He mounted and started toward the trail down the slope of the bluff, leaving Darrell to catch up.

When they reached the camp, all was quiet. Just as it had been a couple of hours earlier. Normally, Darrell would stay with their horses a distance from their target, holding them so they wouldn't run off. But without Hiram, Cole needed Darrell's help. Looking at the kid, Cole couldn't help but feel sorry for him. Stupid as a rabbit without enough brains to outrun the fox, but at least he could pull picket pins and lead horses without messing up. He tied both horses to a driftwood log at the side of the river and they started toward the movers' camp.

Cole signaled Darrell to head to the left of the picketed horses, while he approached them from the right. He took a handful of cattail roots out of his pocket and held one out to the nearest horse. Its neighbor gave a nervous nicker, but quieted when he got his own root. Cole pulled their picket pins, then went to the next team. He saw Darrell on the other side of the group, making his way through the horses. Cole hurried to the next picket.

All was going well when suddenly the air exploded with a horse's neigh. One of Cole's horses had lashed out at one Darrell was leading, and the rest of the horses balked and pulled at their ropes. Cole grabbed at one, but the line slipped away and the horse ran off downriver.

"What's going on out there?"

The shouting voice was answered by a shot from Darrell's direction. The stupid kid had started a fight. He knew if they ran into trouble, the plan was to leave as quickly and quietly as they could. But there he was, firing a second shot from his pistol.

"Horse thieves!" That shout was from another wagon, and suddenly the air was filled with gunshots.

"Stop shooting!" yelled a third man. "You'll hit the horses."

Cole dropped the ropes he held and pulled out his pistol. Where did Darrell go? He fired a couple shots in the direction of the wagons and ran toward the spot where he had last seen the kid. He bumped into a horse that was pulling back, straining at his picket line. Grasping the rope, Cole followed it down to the picket pin. But it wasn't fastened to a picket pin. It was held tightly in Darrell's fist. Bullets whizzed all around, and he heard a scream as one of the horses was hit.

"Stop shooting!" the third voice yelled again. "You fools, stop shooting!"

Cole shook Darrell's arm. "Come on, kid. We've got to get out of here."

Darrell didn't respond and Cole bent closer to the dark form. Starlight glinted from staring eyes.

Cole cursed, then bending low and keeping the few horses left between him and the wagons, he started toward the river and his gelding.

Shots rang out from the wagons and Cole froze. Any noise or motion could betray his position. He thanked his lucky stars the moon was dark and clouds were moving in, hiding the stars. The dark night was his only cover.

Seconds turned into minutes. The horses calmed down. The chorus of frogs started again. He heard movement from the direction of the wagons. The men were venturing out to see what they could find. He had to make it back to his horse before the men discovered it.

He crawled sideways on his hands and feet, crab-stepping to the riverbank. He slid into the cold water, holding back a gasp as it soaked through his clothes. He let the current take him downriver from the movers' camp as he watched the men's shadows drift among the few horses still fastened to their pickets. One raised a shout when he discovered Darrell's body.

Cursing under his breath, Cole waited until he was far downstream before swimming to shore. He made his way to the spot where he and Darrell had left the horses. His horse still stood, but Darrell's was long gone. Silently thanking the horse's former owner for training the gelding so well, Cole mounted and started south. Once he was sure he was out of earshot, he pushed the horse as hard as he could before the movers made their way that far down the riverbank in search of their own horses. It was too late for Darrell. He had already found his own way out of this mess.

After heading downriver for several miles, he turned the horse up a road leading west, away from Wheeling and away from the river road. He needed to be far away before dawn.

15

On Monday, their third night in Walnut Creek, Johanna found a seat next to Mattie on the log the boys had placed next to the communal campfire.

"It feels so good to stay in one place for a while, doesn't it?" Johanna scooted closer to Mattie as Hannah joined them.

"Somehow chores seem easier when you aren't expecting to leave again first thing in the morning." Hannah tucked her skirt around her legs. "And the children are enjoying the time to play. Did you see them this afternoon?"

Mattie laughed. "The boys sure got wet and muddy building the dam across the creek, didn't they?"

Johanna looked up at the stars that appeared in the deep blue sky as dusk turned to night. This was her favorite time of the day on this trip. The children were all asleep with their parents, and she and her friends had the campfire to themselves. Every evening as she watched Andrew tell his jokes and lead the singing, she let herself be caught up in his laughter. From the cleft in his chin to his blond hair with the little flip over his left ear, she couldn't stop looking at him. And when he looked across the fire and captured her gaze with his own—

"Should we build the fire up?" Jacob had joined the girls, and behind him were Andrew and Henry.

"For sure." Andrew answered for them all. "We want to chase the evening chill away for a while, don't we?"

Jacob placed a couple more pieces of split oak on the fire, then took a seat on the second of the three logs around the fire and motioned for Henry to sit beside him.

Naomi was the last to join the group, and she hesitated just outside the ring.

"What are you doing, standing out there?" Andrew grabbed her hand and pulled her toward the third log. "You can sit here by me."

Naomi didn't answer but took her seat. Her face was pink in the firelight and her eyes glowed as she smiled at Andrew. He grinned back at her and looped his arm around her shoulder.

Josef joined them then, sitting next to Jacob. "It's been a long day, ja?"

"How are the horses holding up?" Jacob asked. Johanna had seen Josef inspecting each of the horses' hooves, filing them and fixing loose nails.

"These horses are so strong they could pull the wagons all the way to Iowa," Josef said.

He grinned around the circle, his glance pausing as he looked at Hannah. Johanna felt that twinge again, watching them. She wasn't jealous, not really. But watching Hannah and Josef exchange glances and smiles when they thought no one else noticed reminded her of her own longing for someone special. Someone who could make her blush with his smile. Someone who had the right to kiss her whenever he liked.

Andrew moved his arm from around Naomi's shoulders, then leaned close to her, whispering something in her ear that made her laugh. As she enjoyed Andrew's attention, Naomi looked happier than she had since they left Brothers Valley. Then Andrew looked across the fire and winked at Johanna, and a hot bubble simmered in her breast. He wasn't serious about Naomi, or Mattie. Was he even serious about her? All the things they had talked about as they ate their noon meals together, or when he met her behind her wagon after all the others had gone to bed . . . had those moments meant anything to him?

Her face grew hot as she tried to concentrate on the conversation between Jacob and Josef, but their words slid past her. She watched Andrew catch Naomi's eyes with his own, holding her captive. Naomi's smile was radiant as she watched Andrew's expressive face. He shared another joke with her and she laughed a little too loudly.

The simmering bubble rose in her throat. Andrew could flirt with any girl he pleased, but Naomi thought he was serious. She loved the attention from him, but she was in for a big fall when he turned his attention elsewhere. Johanna bit her lip, remembering when she thought Jacob was paying attention to her in the same way, and the hollow hurt when she realized he was only being nice to her for Hannah's sake. Naomi was too sweet to go through that kind of disappointment, but Andrew kept leading her right along.

"What are we going to sing tonight, Andrew?" Jacob said as he stirred the dying fire.

Andrew didn't answer, but started "das Loblied" in his

188

deep voice. Johanna joined in the singing with the others, their voices softly chanting the old tune. The words of the familiar hymn washed over her, praises to God above taking her mind away from Andrew and everything else. The music pulsed in the same slow rhythm as the glowing coals.

When they had sung all the verses they knew, Josef stood and stretched.

"Ach, it's to bed we should be going. Morning very early comes."

Henry rose from the log where he had been nodding off and held his hand out to Mattie, who took it, and they went toward the Schrock wagon together. Jacob followed them, while Hannah and Josef went toward their tent.

Andrew stood and stirred the fire, spreading the coals.

"Good night, Naomi," Andrew said as she moved to join him by the dying fire.

Naomi stopped. It was too dark to see her face, but Johanna saw the tilt of her head against the stars as she looked toward the log where Johanna sat.

"Good night." Naomi pulled her skirts in as she walked past Johanna. Once outside the ring of logs, she ran toward her family's wagon.

Andrew leaned the stick against the log he had been sitting on and lowered himself down next to Johanna.

"I guess it's just you and me now, right, Jo?"

She knew he was grinning at her, but she only scooted a few inches away from him and leaned toward the fire. The coals were cooling, changing from orange to black, but still pulsing with heat.

Andrew caressed her elbow, then pulled her back toward him. "What's wrong?"

The expression on Naomi's face in the firelight earlier gave her the strength to say what she needed to say. "How could you treat Naomi like that?"

"What?" He sounded surprised.

"You don't have any intention of pursuing marriage or anything with her, but you lead her on until she thinks there's a possibility." The words rushed out, and when they were done, Johanna bit her lip. He would never speak to her again after this.

"I was just being friendly." Andrew shrugged, his palms up in supplication. "All the girls like a little attention, don't they? Naomi isn't any different."

Johanna turned toward him, even though she couldn't see his face in the dark. "That's the problem. Naomi is different. She thinks she's in love with you." She was glad the darkness hid the tears in her eyes. "You don't know what it's like to have a broken heart, do you, Andrew Bontrager? You think it's fun to laugh and joke with a girl, and even kiss her, but then just when she thinks you actually have feelings for her, you turn around and do the same thing with the next girl."

"We're just having fun."

"It isn't fun for Naomi. You treat her like some fish you have on a line, giving her hope that she has a future with you, but then you laugh and let her go again. It's cruel."

Andrew leaned with his elbows on his knees, quiet for once. Johanna let the silence between them grow while the simmering bubble inside her cooled after her outburst. When he took off his hat and ran his hand through his hair, she stifled a sob. She was as bad as Naomi, loving the wrong man for all the right reasons. But she wouldn't let him make a fool of her. He wasn't going to break her heart. Tears trickled down her cheeks.

She stood and he grabbed for her hand. "Don't go."

Shaking her head, she pulled away. "I can't stay. I'll see you in the morning." She turned her back on him and stumbled across the rough meadow grass to her family's wagon, letting the ebbing anger carry her forward until she reached the wagon tongue in the shadows far from the fire. She sank onto the sturdy wood, her face in her hands, and let the hot tears flow.

Andrew took a couple of steps to follow Johanna, but stopped. She didn't want him near her. That much was clear.

He turned to the fire, kicking up dirt from the edges of the circle to cover the dark red coals. The fire would go out without the smothering, but kicking at the black soil felt good. When he reached the log he had sat on with Naomi, he kicked it too. It felt even better and he kicked it again.

Fool, fool, fool. He had done it again. Gone too far. Stuck his stupid foot in his stupid mouth.

He slumped down on the log. He wasn't interested in Naomi, so why did he flirt with her tonight?

Because he loved seeing that look in her eyes. Any girl's eyes. She adored him, and he liked girls who looked at him that way.

The way that led to such trouble back home. Jo was wrong. He knew what it felt like to have his heart broken. He had been on the receiving end of that game when Bethann had married Abe Glick.

He snatched off his hat and then shoved it down on his head again.

Jo knew he was only playing with Naomi. She saw right through him.

Ja, and Mattie knew too. But Mattie didn't bother him.

But Jo . . . had he lost her tonight?

He was just being himself, wasn't he? Everyone liked him. Everyone laughed at his jokes. The jokes he told to keep the memories at bay. The games he played to keep himself from getting serious about another girl.

But Jo . . .

His eyes itched and he swiped at them with one hand, feeling the hot wetness. If Jo saw through him, what did the others think?

Jo had seen the real Andrew tonight and she had walked away. If Naomi or even Mattie had done that, he would have shrugged and laughed it off.

He would have forgotten it and gone on to the next girl. Anything to show he wasn't hurt.

A sob rose in his throat, and he swallowed it down. There wasn't anyone else like Jo. When he kissed her, it was real. With other girls, it was part of the game, but with her, it was like she opened a place in his soul and joined herself to him.

He lifted his head and stared in the direction of the Hertzlers' wagon, even though he could only see black shapes in the darkness. Had she gone inside the tent she shared with her sisters, or was she waiting for him?

Andrew bent his head. He didn't deserve a girl like Jo. But without her . . . He swallowed another sob, forcing it down. Without her, life would be nothing. He would be nothing. If he let her get away . . .

He jumped to his feet and lurched toward the Hertzler wagon. As he got closer, his steps slowed, and he walked with caution, feeling his way past the big wheels toward the front of the wagon. Even in the shadows, he could see her hunched on the wagon tongue.

He stepped up behind her, laying a hand on her back. She turned toward him and he pulled her into his arms. "We have to talk."

She nodded and sniffed. "Not here. We'll wake someone up."

He took her hand, warm and soft, and led her to the pasture where Jacob had put the sheep, up the hill from their camp. The starlight was bright out here in the open, and when Andrew stopped and Jo lifted her face toward him, he could see tears shining on her eyelashes. His gut wrenched. Those tears caused by his stupidity.

"Never again," he vowed, whispering. "Never again."

"Never what?"

"I'll never do anything to make you cry like this, Jo. Never."

She sniffed again and lifted the hem of her apron to wipe her face. "How can I believe you? You're never serious about anything. You play with people's lives like everyone is a character in a story, and you don't care about anyone but yourself."

Andrew took a step back. "You're right." He dropped to his knees in the thick grass, sitting back on his heels. "I've been a stupid fool and you've known it all the time. How could you stand to be around me?"

Jo knelt next to him and took his hands in hers. "You're not just a stupid fool."

He groaned. "What else? How bad am I?"

She tugged at his hands. "That's not what I mean. You are smart, and you have a gift for bringing people together." He looked at her and caught the beginning of a smile. "Sometimes you do some pretty foolish things."

"Like flirting with Naomi tonight."

"That may have been the most foolish of all. You need to apologize to her."

Andrew pulled at the grass in front of his knees.

Jo went on. "And no more games."

Andrew's eyes stung. So this was what it felt like when God taught you humility. This little slip of a girl telling him how he needed to act. The stiff rod in his back melted. This little slip of a girl who cared enough about him to give him the hiding he deserved.

"I need to apologize to you too." His words came in a rush, before he could have second thoughts about them.

When she didn't say anything, but only gripped his hand tighter, an unfamiliar feeling spread through his chest. So he was doing the right thing for once. It felt better than blindly forcing his way along, casting people's feelings aside as he went.

"I'm sorry, Jo. I didn't mean—I mean, I didn't think. I promise, I'll never do anything like this to you again."

"Why? Because it makes you feel bad?"

Andrew let the question sift through his head, pushing away his usual casual remarks. He needed to learn a new way to talk to girls . . . to her.

"Not because it makes me feel bad, but because it hurts you." He took her face in his hands and rose up on his knees, tilting her face toward him and the starlight above them. "I love you, Jo. You make me complete. You make me a better man."

She stroked his cheek with her hand and circled his neck, pulling him to her. "I love you too." Their lips met, and Andrew felt Jo tuck herself into his heart.

Christian Yoder looked toward the blue Conestoga wagon nestled under the branches of the maple tree again, the hammer forgotten in his hand. Every thought the last few days was of Annalise. Was she well? Was she comfortable? Would everything be all right?

Elias, nailing his own end of the board to the upright of the table they were building, finished his work with a final hard blow that made Christian jump.

"You need to quit standing here and go talk to her." Elias talked around the nails in his mouth as he held the next one ready for his hammer blows.

"I don't want to disturb her."

Elias drove the nail home with three blows. "If our sawing and hammering hasn't disturbed her, I don't know what will." He gestured with his hammer. "Go on. I can finish this."

Christian put his hammer in the toolbox and started toward the wagon. He shouldn't be nervous when it came to talking to his own wife. Climbing up the spokes of the wagon wheel, he peered into the dim interior. Her form was a dark mound on the pallet bed.

"Annalise." He kept his voice quiet, hoping she was asleep.

But her reply was immediate. "Christian?"

She struggled into a sitting position, and he climbed into the wagon box to kneel at her side.

"Don't try to get up. I just came to see how you are feeling."

As his eyes adjusted to the shadowed light, he could see the soft love in her eyes as she smiled at him. "I'm feeling fine, but more than a little bit at loose ends."

"Where are the children?"

"Hannah took them out to play so I could rest."

He pulled a keg closer to Annalise's pallet and sat near her. He took one hand in his and kissed it. "And yet here you are, wide awake."

She smiled, intertwining her fingers with his. "I've rested so much that I'm tired of resting. There is so much to do, and yet I lie here doing nothing."

"You are doing something very important. You are keeping yourself and the baby healthy. That's the most important job you can do right now."

Annalise sighed. "You remember that Mary said there are two babies. Twins, Christian." She stroked her swollen belly and smiled at him. "Two wee babes waiting to come into the world. We are truly blessed."

"I know Mary claims there are twins in there, but she isn't the Lord. Remember, he's the one who told Rebecca in the Good Book that she carried twins, not the midwife. I'll wait until your time comes before I believe it for sure."

A shadow passed over her face then, and she stared toward the front opening of the wagon.

"What is wrong? Something worries you."

She glanced at him and squeezed his fingers. "You know me so well." She smiled as he chuckled. "I think often of Liesbet these days. How she should have lived to give birth to our grandchild."

"Are you afraid of your own confinement?"

Annalise nodded. "Every time a woman gives birth, there is danger of something going wrong. I try not to be afraid, but I don't want to lose these babies."

"And I don't want to lose you. We need to trust that the Lord will do what is best."

She looked down at her swollen stomach, her bottom lip between her teeth. Christian lifted her chin.

"Something else bothers you. What is it?"

"I also worry about our other children. If I don't survive, you must marry again. Don't let the little ones grow up without a mother."

"But—"

"Promise me."

"You won't—"

She struggled to stand up. "Promise me."

Christian pushed her gently back down onto the pallet and lifted her feet up onto the bed.

"All right. I won't let the little ones grow up without a mother." He sat next to her, cradling her in a hug. "But I refuse to believe that you will die giving birth to this baby," he whispered in her ear.

"Ach, Christian, just like you refuse to believe there are two babies."

She laughed as she said it and he laughed with her, leaning his forehead on hers.

He held her like that for several minutes, neither of them speaking. His Annalise. How would he ever live without her?

"I love you." He sat back to look at her face, swollen with the pregnancy, but beautiful. "You are the light of my life."

"And you are mine."

"Do you need anything?"

"A drink of water, and my knitting."

He fetched a dipper full of water from the bucket at the side of the wagon, and then got her knitting basket from its hook on one of the wagon bows.

"Anything else?"

She shook her head. "You need to get back to work."

"Not yet. Since we aren't going on to Indiana with the others, my work isn't pressing."

"I worry that we won't be able to buy our farm in time to grow any food for the winter. Should we stay here until spring?"

Christian shook his head. "Don't worry about that. There will be a solution. Perhaps the other families will be able to plant our seeds for us."

"What about a house to live in? And a well? A barn for the animals? There is so much work to be done."

He pushed the rising doubts away. She was right, but she shouldn't be worrying about it.

"All of the work will get done in its own time. We have neighbors. Our friends. We will not starve."

"We can't expect our neighbors to do all of our work for us. They have their own farms to buy and build."

"Maybe I should go on to Indiana and come back for you and the children in the autumn."

Annalise was silent at this suggestion, but her hands twisted the handle of her knitting basket. He laid his hand on hers, stilling her fidgeting fingers.

"We don't need to make any decisions right now. I will consider what needs to be done and talk it over with the others. There will be a solution."

She nodded. "That is a good plan." She yawned. "Perhaps I'll try to sleep now."

Christian hung the knitting basket from a hook that was closer to Annalise so she could reach it when she wanted it, then kissed her forehead.

"Sleep well."

She nodded, her eyes already closing, and Christian left the wagon as quietly as he could.

Elias had finished the table, a rough one made for using outdoors, and placed it between the wagon and the community campfire. When the rest of the group left for Indiana, this would be their home until after the baby was born.

Christian ran his fingers through his beard. If Mary was right, and there were two babies, what would they do? The danger was greater when a woman gave birth to twins, but there were successful births also. Look at Rebecca and Isaac. They had twins and both of them lived to see their boys grow up, even though Rebecca's pregnancy had been difficult from the account in the Good Book. He had no reason to worry that it would be any different for Annalise. Since they had stopped traveling and she had been able to rest, she was feeling much better. And she had Mary Nafsinger to help her, a midwife experienced with this kind of pregnancy. They only needed to trust the Lord and wait.

16

After the noon meal on Thursday, Jacob took his tools to the corner of the pasture where he was building the lambing pen. He had plenty of time to finish it, since he didn't expect the first ewe to drop her lambs for another three or four weeks.

By then, Mattie would be in Indiana. Jacob missed the nail he was aiming at and hit his thumb instead. He stuck it in his mouth and sat on the nearby pile of lumber.

Normally, he would tackle a task like this and get it done. Get it over with and move on to the next thing. But this life wasn't normal. Sitting around here in Walnut Creek while the rest of their group prepared for the next stage of the trip made his feet itch and his head hurt.

At least Mamm was doing better. Mary Nafsinger had been right, that she needed to rest. But that didn't mean Jacob needed rest too. He had been anxious to get to Indiana for six months, and this delay ate at him.

And Mattie still hadn't given him an answer. He grabbed another nail and started in on the lambing pen again. In fact, it seemed she had been going out of her way to avoid talking to him. He concentrated on the nail, driving it into the wood with three sharp raps of the hammer, then went back to the nail he had missed and drove it home just as neatly.

At least he hadn't seen any sign of Cole Bates and his brothers since they left the river road.

"Jacob!"

Jacob shaded his eyes against the afternoon sun and looked across the pasture. Hannah stood at the far fence, waving to him. He waved to show he had heard her, then put his tools away, gathered a few stray nails, and walked down the slope toward her.

"Is it suppertime already?" he called as he came closer.

"Not yet, but Daed wants to talk to you. He and Josef are waiting."

Jacob climbed over the fence and fell into step beside her as they walked toward the group of wagons. "What does he want?"

Hannah's smile told him she knew. "I'll let Daed tell you. But I think you'll like his idea."

When they reached the wagon, Daed got right to the point. "Your mamm can't travel any farther until September. I won't risk her health, or the child's."

Jacob looked down at his feet to hide his amusement. Daed spoke of the coming babies as one, maintaining that Mary Nafsinger didn't have God's knowledge. But Jacob thought that perhaps he still hadn't accepted the idea of having two children added to the family at once.

"But we still need to buy our land and get our farms established before winter," he went on. "I'm going to send you ahead to Indiana with Hannah and Josef."

Jacob exchanged glances with his brother-in-law.

"You trust us to choose your land as well as our own?" Jacob's throat filled as he said the words. His own land. His future.

Daed stroked his beard. "I would rather do it myself, but I need to stay with Annalise. You know the kind of land we need. Pasture for the horses, cows, and sheep is most important, along with farmland. And before spring turns to summer, a garden needs to be planted." Daed sighed. "I feel like I'm giving you a great burden, Jacob, but I can't be both here and in Indiana."

Jacob leaned against the wagon wheel. "I'll do my best to find good land for both of us."

"Josef will be seeking a place too." Daed held Jacob's gaze. "I'd like all three farms to be close to each other."

Jacob nodded, and Daed went on. "But the most important thing is that we settle near the other Amish families who went to Indiana last year. We want to form a community, and we can't unless we live near each other."

"Aren't the Hertzlers, Schrocks, and Bontragers looking for the same?"

"Ja, ja, ja. I hope you will take their advice when searching for our land."

Jacob kicked at a tuft of grass. Looking for his own land was one thing. He knew what he wanted, what he had dreamed of. But being Daed's representative was different.

"You're sure I can do this?"

Daed grasped Jacob's shoulder. "I know you can, Son. And if something unforeseen happens, you can ask the other men for advice on how to proceed."

Jacob stood straight, adjusting his trousers. "Well then. I'll try to act as you would."

"You always do."

Daed squeezed his shoulder, and then climbed into the wagon. Josef beckoned for Jacob to follow him, and they walked toward Hannah and Josef's green wagon.

"Your daed has much confidence in you, ja? You will honor his wishes, I know."

"I'm glad you'll be there too, Josef. You can help me find the right land."

"I will be helping you. No job is too large when brothers work together."

"For sure." Jacob's gaze caught sight of Mattie as she walked toward the Hertzlers' wagon with a skein of yarn in her hand. "When do we leave? I haven't been paying attention to the plans."

"In four days. We want to worship with the congregation here on the Sabbath, then we will leave early Monday morning. The men are meeting tonight to discuss our route."

"I will be there."

Jacob took a step away, and Josef's eyebrows went up. "And now I'm thinking you want to tell someone the news, ja? A fraulein, perhaps?"

Josef gave him a friendly push in the direction of the wagons, but Jacob headed toward the campfire. If Mattie hadn't sought him out in the last week, then perhaps she didn't want to speak to him at all. Would the news that he was joining the group for the rest of the way to Indiana be welcome, or not?

Movement near the Hertzlers' wagon caught his eye. Johanna and Mattie examined the bundle of yarn and compared it to one Johanna held. He smiled at Mattie's expression as she talked with her friend, and tried not to watch as Mattie walked back to her family's wagon. But he couldn't help noticing her quick step and the pretty way she swished her skirt to the side when she climbed the wheel spokes into the wagon.

He had asked for her pledge so that he could protect her, but as time passed with no sign of the Bates brothers, that pressing need had eased some.

At the same time, it had been replaced with something else. For so many years he had thought of her as his Mattie. When he was a boy, his thoughts had never gone beyond the friendly companionship they had enjoyed, and even while she lived in Brothers Valley, he had always hoped they would pick up where they had left off someday. Lately though, his musings had taken a different direction. Instead of the shadow at his heels, Mattie had become the prize at the end of his quest. She was the reason to build his home in the wilderness of Indiana.

But without her pledge, her promise, he couldn't be sure that she would ever share his dream.

Mattie couldn't avoid Jacob forever, but she could put off the confrontation for a little while longer. She peered around the edge of the wagon cover. Jacob was still talking with Andrew near the campfire, so she climbed out on the opposite side and hurried to the grove of trees up the slope beside the cow pasture.

Part of her made her want to go right up to Jacob and say she would give him her promise. The thought of being with him all her life felt so right and good. As Jacob's wife, she would enter into that stream of history that started so long ago when both their ancestors made the decision to follow the Anabaptist teachings. Whenever Mattie heard the stories of the *Martyr's Mirror* read, a rod of iron seemed to give her strength to face whatever adversity might come. Those men and women were her forebears, and Jacob's too. Their children would be part of a great heritage and a great faith.

But—

Always, there was that hesitation. As if to walk down one path toward Jacob, she was turning her back on all other possibilities for her life.

Mattie sat on a stump in the midst of the grove. From here she couldn't be seen from the camp, but she could look beyond the trees to the rolling hills that undulated to the horizon in all directions. These hills in Ohio weren't as tall as the mountains surrounding Brothers Valley, but they were peaceful, with patches of meadows and farm fields making breaks in the trees. Could Indiana be as beautiful as this?

She was so lost in thought, she didn't hear anyone coming until Hannah parted the shrubs in front of her.

"Mattie? I didn't know anyone was here."

"That's why I like this spot. It's so secluded, no one can find me."

"That's why I like it too." Hannah turned to leave.

"Don't go." Mattie scooted to the edge of the big tree stump. "We can share. Sit here beside me."

Hannah smiled and joined her. "You must have been thinking of something important. Your face had a faraway look just now."

Mattie hugged herself, wondering how much she should tell Hannah. Of course, if she married Jacob, she and Hannah would be sisters. The thought made her smile. "I have a secret to share with you, and I could use your advice."

"It must be a good one to have you smiling like this. What is it?"

Mattie leaned her chin on her hand. "You know how Jacob and I were always close as children." She waited for Hannah's nod. "He told me a few nights ago that he wants my promise to marry him."

Hannah gasped and clapped a hand to her mouth. "When? How? I mean, you said yes, didn't you?"

"Shh! I didn't say anything, yet. This isn't a decision to make lightly."

"Of course not." Hannah turned toward Mattie and took her hand. "All the time we were growing up, he's never been interested in any of the girls around the Conestoga. I thought he would never get married, but he must have been hoping to see you again." She squeezed Mattie's hand. "I can hardly wait until we're sisters."

Mattie tightened her grip on Hannah's hand. "But Jacob will be buying a farm in Indiana. He says he'll never move again."

"That's right. He has his heart set on that."

"I've never lived anywhere for more than a few years at a time. Daed always wants to move on, to see what is farther west, and I've always been happy to go with him. I'm not sure I'd be content to stay in Indiana for the rest of my life."

Hannah leaned toward her. "You'll be surprised to find out what you'll do when you're in love."

Mattie chewed her bottom lip, thinking of Annie. Her sister had given up her family to be with her husband. Someday, Daed would want to leave Indiana—would Mattie be the one to stay behind with her husband then?

"You do love him, don't you?"

Mattie looked at Hannah, not knowing how to answer. Jacob had stolen her heart so many years ago, but did that mean she wanted to marry him? How could she make a decision that would change her life like this? "How did you know you were supposed to marry Josef?"

Hannah let go of Mattie's hand. "I didn't at first. Josef was sure we were to get married, but there was so much I had to sacrifice if I married him. It took months for me to decide."

"What made you say yes to him?"

Hannah didn't answer for so long that Mattie wasn't sure if she had heard the question. A breeze from the west brought the sounds of a neighboring farmer calling his cows in for milking.

"When Liesbet died, I realized I was trying to hold on to the past when God wanted me to look toward the future he had for me."

Leaving the past behind was not Mattie's problem. She could hardly wait for the future to arrive. "But how did you know that Josef was the right future? Don't you wonder what might have happened if you had chosen to do something else?" Mattie bit at her lower lip. "What if you had decided that you didn't want to sacrifice anything?"

"Every decision one makes means denying something else." She opened one hand. "When I decide to have mush for breakfast," she opened the other hand, "then I have decided not to have gravy and toast. When I decide to spend the morning sewing, then I've decided not to spend the morning knitting."

Mattie pushed some brown leaves aside with her foot, revealing a flower that had been nestled in their midst. She leaned close to touch the Dutchman's-breeches with a careful finger. She could choose to pick the flower, or she could leave it growing at the base of the tree stump. But whichever she chose, she couldn't go back in time to change the decision. She wouldn't be able to fasten the flower back on the plant once she had plucked it, and she couldn't come back to marry Jacob if someone like Cole Bates took her west to the far mountains.

Hannah went on. "Every decision you make is like walking through a door. When Josef wanted to marry me, I felt like I was in a room with many doors. I thought I had the power to decide to choose any of those doors, but the Good Lord knew exactly which door was best for me and helped me make that decision."

"But how do you know it was the right decision?"

"Because of the peace it gave me. Every other one of those choices didn't give me the peace that the thought of marrying Josef did." Hannah squeezed her hand one last time, and then stood to go. "I asked God to make me content with the choice I made, and he has. I can't imagine living any other life than the one I have now. Pray about your decision, Mattie. God will help you know the right thing to do."

Mattie watched Hannah slip through the underbrush in the small grove and back toward the wagons.

Contentment. She had never learned to be content with anything. As long as she could remember, she had been striving for something more—something different—than what she had. Would marrying Jacob make her content? She smoothed a fold in her apron. Perhaps there wasn't anything that would make her feel the contentment and happiness Hannah had described.

Her dream came back to her. The high cliff looming above

and knowing that there was an entrance into the elusive world on the other side. Somehow, if she could get through to that wonderful place, she would have her answer. Perhaps she would be content there.

Supper the next evening was a feast of fresh venison. Mattie celebrated along with everyone in the group when Andrew and Henry came back from a morning of hunting with two deer. Since then, the younger married girls had been baking bread and pies to go with the meal. The older women, except for Annalise and Mary, had gathered greens, and their Ohio hosts had added potatoes to the meal.

Mattie filled her plate after helping to serve the men and older women and took it to a quiet end of one of the tables to relax and eat. The men had said they expected to arrive in Indiana in less than two weeks by taking the new Stone Road north through the Great Black Swamp, and then west. Even though the tolls would use precious cash, going around the swamp would take weeks longer. Mattie suppressed a shiver at the thought of a swamp so vast and dark that a man could get lost forever in its depths, but it wasn't a shiver of fear. The descriptions she had heard from the Ohio settlers were unbelievable, and she was anxious to see the swamp for herself.

Johanna slid onto the bench beside her with her own plate. "Isn't it wonderful good to have fresh meat?"

"And potatoes."

"Mamm hopes we'll be able to plant our seed potatoes soon, and our vegetable seeds. But Daed says we have to wait and see what the farms are like. He's afraid the land we buy won't be cleared yet and we'll have to work so hard to make it produce that we won't be able to have a garden this year."

Mattie let Johanna talk on, only half listening. Across the way, at a table with Andrew and the other young men, Jacob sat facing her. If she looked in that direction, she would catch him looking away, as if he had been staring at her.

"What do you think, Mattie?" Johanna poked her shoulder. "Mattie, wake up."

"What?" She felt her face heat when she saw Johanna's knowing look.

"You and Jacob. You've both been moping around the whole time we've been in Ohio. Haven't you heard that he's coming to Indiana with us, even though the rest of his family is staying here until September?"

"I hadn't heard."

"Haven't you talked to him at all?"

Mattie shrugged. "I don't know what to say to him."

"I agree. He isn't easy to talk to, that one. He never answers more than a grunt, does he?" Then Johanna leaned close, her face blushing. "Can you keep a secret?"

"Ja, for sure."

"Naomi told me you were sweet on Andrew once. Do you mind if he pays attention to me?"

Mattie put her arm around Johanna's shoulders. "I don't mind. We were never serious about each other. But I haven't known Andrew to be sweet on any one girl. I'm not sure he's ever going to settle down."

"I think he might be changing. I'm in love with him, and he says he's in love with me."

Mattie's arm dropped. "What?"

"Shh!"

Johanna glanced around. Mattie followed her gaze and saw Naomi watching them, her face sad and withdrawn. When their eyes met, Naomi turned and ran from the gathering.

"I wanted to ask you, since you know him so well—" Johanna hesitated, her bottom lip caught between her teeth. "Can I trust him? I mean, does he have a habit of telling girls that he loves them?"

"All the time I've known him, he's never once used that word around me." Mattie gave Johanna a smile. "He's always been ready for a fun time and is quick to let a girl know when he likes her, but love? That doesn't sound like Andrew to me."

Johanna gazed across to the table of young men and sighed. Mattie looked over and caught the look on Andrew's face before he turned back to his friends. She had never seen him look so joyful. Every trace of his usual sarcasm was gone.

"I think you can trust him, Johanna. Andrew has changed since he met you. You've been good for him, and I'm glad you told me. Don't worry, I'll keep it a secret." She gave her friend a hug, then rose from the table. "I need to go find Naomi. I'll see you around the campfire tonight."

She followed Naomi's path between the wagons, then up the hill to the cow pasture where Jacob had penned the sheep. Ahead of her, Naomi strode up the hill toward the far fence and the woods beyond.

"Naomi!" Mattie gathered up her skirt and started running. "Naomi, wait!"

She finally caught up at the fence where Naomi had paused.

"Don't follow me, Mattie. Just let me be alone."

Mattie grabbed her sister by the arms and turned her around so she could see her face. "I knew you were crying. Why?"

"You wouldn't know, would you?"

"What do you mean?"

Naomi slumped against the fence post. "You've never had a boy ignore you."

Mattie backed away a step. "That isn't true, Naomi. But I do know how you've always wished that Andrew would notice you."

Tears dripped from Naomi's chin as she sniffed. "Andrew has never looked twice at me, except to tease me. But he took you out riding whenever he could, and you don't even like him." She hiccupped.

"Andrew has been a friend, but nothing more. Why are you so upset about this now?"

Naomi took the handkerchief Mattie handed her and wiped her nose. "I saw Johanna with him last night." She folded the damp handkerchief and sniffed again. "I wasn't spying on them, but if I moved, they'd know I was there and they'd laugh at me." A sob escaped. "I couldn't bear to have Andrew laugh at me." She wiped at her eyes.

"So you saw them together. You should be happy for them."

"But I love him. I've always loved him." Naomi hiccupped again. "I've never loved any boy except Andrew, but now he and Johanna—"

Mattie gave her sister a hug. "There will be a man for you, Naomi. Someone more wonderful than Andrew."

Naomi took a deep, shuddering breath and released it with a sigh. "I don't think so." She wiped her eyes again. "It would take someone pretty desperate to love me."

"That isn't true."

"Look at me." Naomi took both of Mattie's shoulders. "Do you remember what the Good Book says about Leah and Rachel? Rachel was beautiful, but Leah had weak eyes.

That's me, Mattie. I'm Leah. No man will ever think I'm beautiful."

"I never knew your cast eye bothered you. I've always thought you were beautiful, much prettier than I am with my dumpy figure. Besides, a man who would let something like your eyes blind him to your true qualities doesn't deserve you."

Naomi's lips curved in a half smile. "I guess I'll have to ask the Good Lord to bring him to me, like Daed said during our morning prayers."

"He said we could ask God for anything, but do you think he meant a husband?" Mattie wanted to laugh, it sounded so ridiculous.

"Even a husband." Naomi pushed away from the fence post. "Denki, Mattie. You're a good sister, and you've made me feel better. I'll get over Andrew eventually."

"Where are you going?"

"Back to the wagon. I think I'll go to bed after the dishes are done." She looked down the meadow toward the camp. "Meanwhile, you need to stay here. Jacob is coming."

Mattie turned. Naomi was right, Jacob was climbing the sloping hill straight toward them. "I'll go back with you."

Naomi pushed her back toward the fence. "You won't. You'll stay here and talk to Jacob. You've ignored him ever since we got to Ohio, and you need to tell him why. He deserves that much."

Mattie chewed her bottom lip as Naomi headed toward the camp, stopping to exchange a few words with Jacob as they passed. Her sister was right, and so was Johanna. She should talk to Jacob. But how could she talk to him when she didn't have an answer for him?

Jacob didn't greet her as he approached. He leaned against the board fence next to her and gazed up at the dusky evening sky. The sun had neared the western horizon, and the shadows had crept east, making pockets of darkness at the edges of the meadow, hard by the forest.

"Good evening, Mattie." He didn't look at her as he finally spoke. "The sunset is fiery red tonight. It will be a fine day tomorrow."

She hadn't noticed the clouds turning from pink to orange as the sun dipped lower. "Ja, a fine day."

"So you do hear my words? Do you see me too?"

"For sure I see you." She turned to see a teasing light in his eyes. "Why wouldn't I?"

He shrugged. "I thought perhaps I was invisible, since you haven't spoken to me for the last week."

Mattie moved a step away from him. She hadn't sought him out, but she hadn't thought he noticed she had avoided him on purpose. But what could she say to him when she didn't have an answer to his question?

"Maybe I spoke too soon," he went on. "I wanted you to know how I felt, and I've let you have time to think. Do you have an answer for me?"

Mattie ran her finger along the top rail of the fence. "It isn't an easy decision to make."

"I had hoped it would be, and that you felt the same way I do."

"I do, I think. But there's more to this than how I feel today. What if my feelings change tomorrow?" She bit her lip, stopping herself from saying what she really feared, that she would give him her promise and then regret it when a new opportunity arose.

"A decision like this isn't based on feelings." He turned to look at her. "That's why two people make a binding promise when they marry. Feelings can't be trusted."

Mattie looked down at her bare feet. On an impulse, she grasped some blades of grass with her toes and picked them. When she released her grip, the grass fluttered to the ground. Jacob was right, she couldn't trust her feelings. But she wasn't sure she could keep a promise, either. Left to herself, she would make some rash mistake and Jacob would end up regretting he had ever asked her to marry him.

She looked into his serious eyes, dark in the fading light. Loving him was easy. But making the pledge he had asked her for was something altogether different. "I can't make the promise you want, Jacob."

He grasped her arms and pulled her to him. "Why not, Mattie? What is holding you back?"

Mattie pulled back for an instant, and then relaxed in his grip. "I can trust you, Jacob. You're strong and faithful. You know what your future holds and you know how to achieve your dreams. But I don't trust myself. I don't know if I could keep any promise I make to you."

He pulled her closer. "But when you make a pledge, you can trust God to help you keep it. Rely on his strength."

Trust God to do what she couldn't? The idea made Mattie's stomach turn. She wouldn't take that risk.

She shook her head, and Jacob's face fell. He rubbed at the back of his neck as he stepped away. Looking back at her once, he started down the hill toward the camp, his feet shuffling in the long meadow grass.

Monday morning dawned clear and cool. Jacob scanned the northwestern sky as he jogged up to the meadow for one last check on the sheep before they left. Only a few wispy clouds caught the morning sun, but no sign of rain. A good day to travel.

Daed was leaning against the fence, waiting for him.

"I thought you would come up here this morning."

Jacob grinned at him. "I know I'm leaving the sheep in good hands, but I've grown attached to them over the past few weeks."

"And they to you." Daed nodded at the sheep. Bam trotted toward them with his nose in the air, looking for a treat, while the twelve ewes followed behind, bleating as they came. "You've done a good job with them, and they trust you."

Jacob leaned down to scratch the thick wool around Bam's short horns. "I never thought I'd come to like them as much as I have."

"You're a good shepherd, Son. You put the sheep ahead of your own comfort, and you risked your life to save the ram. Those qualities will make you a good farmer and a good husband."

"I'm not sure I'll be a husband anytime soon." Jacob fed Bam the stub of a carrot he had brought for him.

"I've watched you and Mattie Schrock together. It might be sooner than you think." Daed lifted one foot to the lower rail on the fence and looked at Jacob. "She's a fine girl."

Daed hadn't heard Mattie's answer, or he wouldn't think marriage to Mattie was going to happen at all. "I don't know if Mattie is the one. She doesn't want to make any promises."

"She's young yet. Younger than Hannah. Give her time."

Jacob gave Bam another carrot. He always had trouble

216

remembering that Mattie was the same age as Liesbet, but she would never be as foolish as his sister had been, running off to marry an outsider. "You think she might accept me eventually?"

"If you treat her as a man ought to, with patience, kindness, and gentleness. Trust God for the outcome, not your feelings, and encourage Mattie to do the same. He'll make the way clear to you."

Patience. It seemed he had already shown the patience of Job when it came to Mattie. "I'll come back in September to help you move on to Indiana. The lambs should be old enough to travel by then."

"Your mamm, also. The babe will be a few months old." Daed turned to him. "I know you worry about her."

Jacob swallowed the lump that was nearly choking him. "I'm afraid of what might happen while we're in Indiana."

Daed laid his hand on Jacob's shoulder. "Leave it in God's hands. Worry and fear will change nothing. This baby—" He held up a hand against Jacob's sound of protest. "Or babies, if Mary is right, will come in God's time and in his way. All we can do, and the best we can do, is to pray." He leaned on the fence again. "I'm counting on you, Josef, and Hannah to prepare the way for us in Indiana. Find a good piece of land, one your mamm will like."

"We'll do our best."

They started back down toward the road where the wagons were already lined up, ready to go. Peter and Margli were saying goodbye to their friends in their own ways. Peter and Mose Schrock were racing from one end of the line to the other, while Margli and Barbli Hertzler clung to each other.

As Jacob approached, Mamm released Hannah from a hug and turned to him.

"I hate to see you go." She drew his face down toward her and gave him a kiss on the cheek. "I'll miss you."

Jacob's eyes misted over. He pushed away the dark thought that this might be the last time he would see Mamm, but put his arms around her bulky form and held her tightly. "I'll miss you too. I love you."

She looked up at him, her own eyes brimming with tears. One caress with her hand on his cheek, and then Peter rushed up to them.

"You're really going, Jacob? I wish I could come too."

Jacob drew his brother aside and crouched down to look him in the face. The face that mirrored his own. "You're needed here, Peter. You're the oldest boy now, and Daed needs your help."

"I'm no help." Peter stared at the ground between them. "I'll never be able to help Daed like you do."

"Look at me." Jacob waited until Peter's eyes met his. "You know a lot already, and you're getting bigger and stronger every day. Daed is going to need you when the lambs start coming, and Mamm will need you to play with William and keep him out of trouble. I'm counting on you to stand in for me while I'm away."

Peter gave him a quick grin. "You really think I can be you?"

Jacob grabbed the boy close in a rough hug, then released him. "I know you're going to do your best."

Peter launched himself back into Jacob's arms and clung to him for a long minute. "You're going to be gone forever."

Jacob buried his hand in Peter's curly hair and pressed him close. "September will be here before you know it."

Eli Schrock's whistle announced that it was time to go. Jacob gave Mamm one last kiss, shook hands with Daed, and joined Josef and Hannah at the smaller wagon. As the group started out, Jacob took one last look. Mamm and Daed stood together at the side of the road, with Peter and Margli on each side of them. William ran down the road after the wagons until Daed called him back. Jacob waved, and then the wagons rounded a bend and they were out of sight.

Hannah took his arm as they walked behind the wagon. "I saw you saying goodbye to Peter. You really love him, don't you?"

Why did his eyes keep blurring? "You know, better than anyone, how hard it was to love the younger ones after . . . after losing Hansli and the girls." He felt Hannah squeeze his arm, and he continued. "But things change." He shrugged. "I don't know. Maybe I'm growing up."

She laughed. "I hope you're growing up, Brother Jacob. You're going to be a husband soon, and before we know it, a father."

"Who said I was getting married?"

"No one needs to say anything. I have eyes, you know. I see the way you and Mattie are when you're together."

Jacob let her comment settle in as they walked along the road, heading north. Both Hannah and Daed assumed he would marry Mattie, but they didn't know about Mattie's hesitation. Was Daed right, that he should trust God and leave the outcome to him? It didn't seem he had any other choice.

17

Cole cradled a dusty brown bottle between his hands. He had stolen it from a wayside tavern the night before and then rode ten more miles before he dared to stop and take a drink.

He cursed his shaking hands as the stopper slowly twisted off, then upended the bottle. He choked as the fiery whiskey hit his throat and coughed, spitting out most of what had gone into his mouth. Pressing the heel of one hand into his aching forehead, he tried another drink. This time the liquid floated down his gullet and burned deep in his empty belly.

The sky lightened in the east, but he barely noticed. He had barely noticed anything since that disastrous night along the Ohio. Darrell might not have been of much use, but he was an extra pair of hands when he needed them. Hiram—he wasn't sorry Hiram had gone off on his own. The thought that Hiram might come back to avenge Darrell's death made him take another swig of the whiskey. All he could hope was that Hiram had gone far enough that he'd never hear about what happened that night.

Pa, now, he wouldn't miss them either way. Pa didn't care what happened as long as he got his money and no one brought the law down on him. Cole felt the poke tucked in his vest. If it was up to him, this money would never make it back to the farm in Missouri. The law didn't bother him, but Pa did. Cole didn't know how long he had before the old man came looking for his money, but he wasn't going to stick around to find out.

He took another swallow from the bottle.

Even with all that had happened, he couldn't put that fine string of Conestoga horses out of his head. The Amish movers surely had made their way to the Amish settlement in Ohio by now, unless they were moving on west. He let his mind drift to Mattie. That girl just wouldn't leave him alone. At night, when he did sleep, he dreamed of her, of what he would do when he finally had her alone, without the constant interfering presence of her family.

With that thought he got up from the rotting log he had been sitting on and mounted his horse. If they were moving on west, they'd take the Stone Road. Every mover heading west took that new road through the Great Black Swamp. There might be an opportunity or two to steal a couple horses from the settlers in the Swamp even if he didn't find Mattie and her group.

Fastening the stopper on the bottle again, he stowed it in his saddlebag. He'd need a clear head to take him to the next step.

He reached Fremont, at the southern edge of the Swamp, just after noon the next day. The Stone Road began here and went straight northwest to the Maumee River on the northern side of the Swamp, cutting a straight line of stone atop a dike, providing a dry road through the vast wilderness of wetlands and standing water. He stopped at the inn near the tollbooth, and as he dismounted in front of the steps, a boy came to take his horse.

"Make sure you clean him up and give him a good feed." Cole flipped a coin at the boy. He may as well spend Pa's money on his own comfort.

When he walked into the inn, the woman behind the counter kept a sour face until he plunked down a five-dollar piece on the wooden surface. "I want a bath and a room for tonight. Supper, and whiskey if you've got it."

The woman nodded, her frown turning to a simpering smile at the sight of the money. "Yes, sir. You must be traveling." She turned a register toward him for his signature.

"I am. I need someone to clean my clothes too." He scrawled an X with his dirty finger on the line she indicated.

The innkeeper walked into the low-ceilinged hall then, brushing dirt off his hands before sticking one out in Cole's direction. "Mighty glad to have you stay with us, sir." He eyed the coin still lying on the counter. "Whatever you'll be needing, just let us know."

Cole looked the man up and down. "I'd like to know a bit about the road ahead. Maybe we could talk over supper."

"Yes, sir. There should be a few others in the tavern around that time, and they'll be glad to tell you what you need to know."

"That's fine." Cole picked up his saddlebag and turned to follow the woman up the stairs to his room. He stopped, not looking toward the man, and keeping his voice casual. "I don't suppose you've seen a group of movers go through here in the past week or so. Amish folk. Several families with Conestoga wagons."

"Yes, sir, we sure did. Don't see many of them around here, since their settlement is down south a bit. But two days ago, just like you said. Some of those Conestoga wagons. They went on up the Stone Road. Seemed anxious to get on and didn't stay to visit any."

Cole struggled to keep his expression bland. "They're some friends of mine. If they're only a couple days ahead, I'll be able to catch up with them." He paused, as if he had just thought of something. "I'll be leaving early in the morning, before dawn. Will I be able to get my horse, or do you keep your barn locked?"

"We never lock the barn. You can leave whenever you wish."

"You don't lock the barn?" Cole put a surprised look on his face. "You must not be bothered with horse thieves here then, the way the innkeepers are down south."

The innkeeper's face blanched. "Why no. We never have."

Cole smiled, as if he was relieved. "I'm sure you won't be a victim of those rascals. But you never know where they might strike next."

By the time he had taken a bath in the room off the kitchen and dressed in clean clothes straight from the clothesline, it was suppertime. He shaved carefully, scraping off a two-weeks' growth of beard, and trimmed his mustache. Darrell and Hiram might not have cared where or how they camped, but Cole hated the creeping dirt that never came off in a quick dip in a stream. Only a hot bath and lye soap would get him clean enough. He grinned at his reflection in the flecked mirror over the chifforobe. With any luck, he'd catch up with the Amish movers by tomorrow night. Somehow he'd get those horses. He smoothed his mustache. That Mattie girl too, if he had read the expression in her eyes right.

He let himself sleep less than two hours, after spending a long evening in the tavern talking with a couple salesmen from Toledo. He dressed quietly and crept down the stairs, avoiding the two steps that had squeaked beneath his tread the night before. He let himself out the kitchen door and walked toward the barn, estimating the time by the stars. Only a few hours until dawn.

The barn door opened with a quiet groan and he stopped, waiting to hear if he had roused the stable boy. When no one stirred, he left the door open to the moonlight and went to his horse. He saddled him quickly and tied him to a post.

"Now you wait here," he said, calming the bay gelding. "We'll see if we can get any friends to take with us."

The salesmen had driven a carriage pulled by a pair of sleek blacks with matching white stockings. Cole brought them out of their stalls and strung their halters together with a lead. They came willingly enough when he gave them each a handful of grain out of the bin. He closed the barn door behind them and mounted, leading the blacks.

The tollbooth was closed, just as the innkeeper had told him it would be this early. The gatekeeper expected night travelers to leave their toll in a box, but he walked the horses past the gatehouse and around the single pole barrier. He continued walking them on the grass trail next to the stone and tar surface of the road. Once out of earshot of the town, he pushed the horses into a trot, their hooves muffled by the grassy verge.

Cole looked back at the sleek blacks. Not a bad night's work. He grinned and settled into the mile-eating pace that would catch him up to his prey.

∞

224

Even on the second day of travel on the Stone Road, a week after they had left Walnut Creek, Mattie couldn't get enough of the mysterious swamp around her as she walked on the grass trail beside the wagon. The road, straight as an arrow and covered with a macadam surface made of tar mixed with stone, marked the miles-long gash in the canopy that rose on either side. Below the raised road, water stood in pools on either side. Trees rose long-legged from the bright green duckweed, reaching to vast heights where their narrow crowns searched for the sunlight. On the grass-covered slopes of the dike, Mattie saw signs of animals. The splash of an otter disappearing under the water as they passed or the white flag of a deer's tail were common enough. But as she peered farther into the murky depths on either side, the only signs of life were the drumming of unseen woodpeckers or the flash of a blue warbler flitting through the high branches.

The night before, as they camped on a raised island, the mosquitoes had pestered them endlessly. The men had made a smudge of the cooking fire, hoping it would keep most of the insects away, but the pests found bare skin even through the thick smoke. Naomi had hunted out some jewelweed, and they had picked handfuls of it, applying its sap to the bites on the children's arms, legs, and faces. Morning had brought a cool north breeze blowing through the tunnel of a road, bringing some relief, but Mattie knew mosquitoes. They would be back as soon as the breeze died down in the evening.

They stopped at noon, gathering together on the grass alongside the road. Jacob kept to his wagon, not looking at Mattie at all. Mattie continued to ignore him as well. Never mind the nagging desire to watch him work with the horses or to go with him along the drier ridges leading into the Swamp on a search for firewood. She also ignored the sick feeling in her stomach. It must have been something she ate that made her uncomfortable. It couldn't have anything to do with Jacob.

Mattie tried to amuse three-year-old Leah by making a handkerchief baby while the child's mother, Emma, dealt with a fussy Rebecca.

"This poor baby has so many mosquito bites, it doesn't surprise me that she can't sleep." Emma patted at Rebecca's face with a wet cloth while the baby twisted her face away.

"The last mile marker I saw was thirty-two, so we only have eight more miles to go." Mattie took the tired handkerchief from Leah's hands and re-formed it into a doll one more time. "We should be out of the Swamp by tonight, and then we'll be able to camp on higher ground."

Emma stood and rocked back and forth, trying to comfort her daughter. "We can't be away from this evil place quickly enough for me."

Mattie gave Leah a cluster of yellow dandelions, laughing as the little girl giggled and picked it apart, scattering the flowers. "I don't think the Swamp is evil. It's beautiful and mysterious."

"It's dangerous, if you ask me. I know I heard a bobcat prowling around our camp last night. And we've met so many men on this road. How do we know one of them isn't a thief?"

"Most are just travelers, like us. Like those salesmen from Toledo we saw yesterday. They were nice enough."

"Fancy men. Outsiders." Emma slowed her rocking as Rebecca's cries softened. "We can't trust outsiders." She nodded her head down the road behind them. "Like that one. Why does he have three horses? And why is he hanging back, almost out of sight?"

Mattie stood to see who Emma was talking about. For sure there was a man back there. Far enough away to be nearly indistinguishable in the distance. A sudden memory of Cole Bates sprang into her mind. This man reminded her of him, with his black hat and bay horse. But no one had seen him or his brothers since they left the Ohio River.

Isaac came up to them and lifted Leah from her seat on the ground. "We're starting out again. It will put a strain on the horses, but we want to get to the end of this swamp before we camp tonight."

While Emma followed him to the wagon with the sleeping baby, Mattie waited, looking for the man behind them. But while she had been distracted by Isaac, the traveler had disappeared from view. She took a few steps down the grassy trail. There was no sign of him.

"Mattie," Daed called to her. "Keep up with us."

"I'm coming." She took one last look down the road. Had she seen movement in the green undergrowth?

Once the horses were hitched to the wagons, the men kept them going at a fast pace. Mattie followed behind. Daed's wagon was last in the group today, following the Bontragers and Hertzlers. Josef Bender's wagon led the way, with Jacob driving from his seat on the wheel horse. She could see him far ahead. As far away as he had ever been since their talk back in Holmes County. She was glad to follow behind the last wagon this afternoon, alone for once. Perhaps she would be able to make some sense of her jumbled thoughts.

Mattie kept up with the wagons as they passed the next mile marker, but then she saw a flash of red flying through the trees. She stopped to find the bird, searching the dark canopy. The bright red feathers belonged to a large woodpecker. But as soon as she spied it, it hopped around to the other side of the tree trunk it clung to. She walked farther along the path. There, it came back into view. She watched the black-and-white bird, as large as a hen, hammer its red head into the wood. The drumming sound echoed in the trees, then it flew off into the woods.

Looking around, Mattie saw that the wagons were far ahead of her on the road. She had stopped to watch the woodpecker for longer than she thought. She slapped at a mosquito and climbed back up the dike to the sunny surface. She had also wandered much closer to the Swamp's black waters than she had thought. She shook her head. It wouldn't do to let herself be distracted like that. Woodpeckers or not, she would have to hurry to catch up with the others.

As she started down the road, the sound of hoofbeats drifted toward her from the road behind. She turned to see the man with three horses coming up on her. She looked toward the wagons again. They were too far away to call to, and too far for her to catch up before the stranger would be upon her. A creeping tingle went down her back and she flexed her hands, suddenly cold. She started walking as quickly as she could. Maybe he would pass by without a word.

The hoofbeats grew closer, then stopped just behind her.

"Mattie-girl. I was afraid I wouldn't see you again."

Cole Bates flashed his handsome smile at her when she looked toward him, but she turned her back and kept walking. The horses followed her.

"You've let yourself get left behind by your folks." He caught up to her, walking his horse beside her. "I have to wonder if you did that on purpose, knowing I was following behind."

She refused to answer, but he kept on.

"I also have to wonder why such a pretty girl keeps on with these plain folk. You don't look like one of them, you know."

In spite of her resolve not to, Mattie glanced at him. Lies and trouble. He was a thief and a liar, just like the evil one. She walked faster, ignoring the stitch coming in her side. The wagons continued on, just out of calling distance.

Cole turned his horse in front of her, standing between her and the rest of the group, the horse hiding them from her sight. "I have an idea, Mattie-girl."

"Don't call me that." She tried to walk around the horse, but the other two, following Cole on a lead, surrounded her.

He smiled at her. "You're a pretty one. And I have a feeling you'd like a more adventurous life than you'll ever have with those Amish."

The way he dismissed her family made her shudder. As if they were the outsiders, and she belonged in Cole's world.

The horse moved restlessly as he kept it reined in, trapping her. "I'm heading to Oregon."

She was compelled to meet his eyes.

"Aye, you've heard of it, haven't you? I think we'd do well together on the trail, you and me." He leaned down from his saddle, his face close to hers. "I'll take you to see things you've never even imagined, Mattie-girl."

In spite of herself, Mattie couldn't look away from him. "Have you seen the mountains?"

Cole dismounted and stepped close to her. She backed against the crowding horses circling the two of them. "I never have, but I'm going to." He reached out and touched her cheek with the back of his hand, a single caress. "You have a mind to see them, Mattie-girl? Just say the word, and I'll take you there."

His hand slipped down to her shoulder, then to her waist. He drew her closer until she smelled the alcohol on his breath. His black eyes held hers.

"No." Mattie shook her head and pressed back against the horse. Her heart pounded and she shivered with a sudden chill of cold sweat. "No, I can't go with you."

Cole smiled. "Oh, Mattie-girl, I think you will. But not now. I need the horses too, you know." He shifted his hand from her waist to the back of her head and bent to capture her mouth with his. The kiss was hard and forceful, and she struggled against him until he moved his lips to her ear. "Watch for me. I'll come get you one night."

And suddenly she was free. She took one look at his face, cocksure and laughing, then turned and stumbled, catching her balance as she fought her way between the surrounding horses. She ran along the trail, dreading the sound she knew would come—the sound of the bay gelding's hoofbeats overtaking her.

But the only thing she heard was Cole's laughter. "You'll come with me, Mattie-girl. I know you will."

18

By the time Jacob drove past mile marker thirty-eight, signs that they were approaching the town of Perrysburg were abundant. He could see higher ground on the other side of the river, where the town was located, and the occasional isolated cabin turned into farms with a few acres of meadowland even here, where the ground on either side of the raised road was still mostly marshes and reeds. He glanced behind often, watching for Mattie. He had lost sight of her soon after they had started out following the noon stop. Her habit of stopping to gaze into the depths of the Swamp worried him, but so far she had always managed to keep up with the wagons. Even so, anything could happen when she was out of his sight.

When she finally caught up with them again, he sighed with relief. The two days of travel through the Swamp had been monotonous, but not without worrisome reminders of the life that many worldly people led. More than once they had driven past cabins in the Swamp that were little more than shacks built of logs. The men who stood before them, silently watching their progress, reminded him of George McIvey, the English outsider Liesbet had married. One man in particular, unshaven and belligerent, had kept his family behind him—three or four grimy children, and a woman in the shadows of the doorway, with staring eyes and expressionless faces. The scene had haunted him ever since, seeing what Liesbet's future with McIvey could have been if she had lived.

What Mattie's future without belonging to the church could be. Her face the last time they had talked reminded him of Liesbet's, just before she ran off with McIvey. He felt the familiar wave of helplessness wash over him. There was nothing he could do except watch, wait, and pray.

Jacob straightened his back. Mattie hadn't given him her pledge, but at least she was still with her family, and he hadn't seen anything of Cole Bates and his brothers. He could hope Bates had lost their trail when they stopped in Holmes County, but a twisting in his gut told him that he couldn't assume they were rid of him.

It was suppertime when they reached mile marker forty and crossed the Maumee River at the edge of the Swamp, but Jacob kept the group's pace as fast as ever. Last night's camp had been a misery, and all the men agreed they were willing to push harder today in order to spend the night in a camp on higher ground. They still had an hour of daylight left before they had to stop for the night, and the higher into the uplands beyond the Swamp they were able to go, the better.

When he reached a likely looking spot two miles beyond the town, he pulled up.

"What do you think, Josef?"

Josef jumped off the lazy board along the side of the wagon

and trotted up to meet Jacob as he dismounted from the wheel horse. "I like this spot." He turned to wave Yost Bontrager and Elias Hertzler to come forward.

While the older men went to the nearby house to ask for permission to camp on the land, Jacob walked back to tell the others what they were doing. Mattie came to meet him as he reached the final wagon.

"It's a good spot to rest." Her face was pale in the lowering light, but he shoved aside a flash of concern for her. They were all tired after the two-day push through the Swamp.

"I'm certain there will still be mosquitoes."

Jacob tried to control his breathing. So she had spoken to him, but it didn't mean they had returned to the closeness they had enjoyed before he had asked her for her pledge. "But they won't be as bad as in the middle of the Swamp."

Mattie hugged her elbows and shuddered a little, stepping closer to him.

"You liked the Swamp, didn't you?" Jacob risked looking at her eyes, but she wouldn't meet his. "I often saw you looking into it, as if you wanted to explore it."

She bit her lip. "I did at first. It's a wild place, isn't it? I can't imagine it will ever let itself be tamed, even though people built such a fine road through it, and some even live there."

"At first? You mean you grew tired of it?"

She glanced behind her, back down the way they had come, but the road was empty. "I'm glad to be out of it and onto dry land." She still didn't meet his eyes.

"Elias and Yost are returning. It's time to make camp." Jacob started toward the front of the wagons, but stopped when Mattie plucked at his sleeve.

"You'll make sure the horses are secure?"

"Why are you concerned about the horses?"

Mattie looked at her feet, then at him. "We're among strangers here, so we should be wary."

"For sure."

She gave him a half smile, then turned to climb into one of the spring wagons with her mother and the other women and children. Jacob jogged up the road to his wagon, shaking his head. Something was bothering Mattie, something about the Swamp, but she might never tell him what it was.

The families made camp in the meadow. A nearby stream flowed clean and fast over a bed of rocks, and they filled their water barrels. Andrew started the campfire, but no one cooked food for the late supper. Dried apples and bread that had been baked before they left Holmes County were enough after a tiring day. The meal was quiet, and most families looked for their beds before it was fully dark. Andrew slapped Jacob's shoulder as he walked by with Johanna.

"Do you think we need to keep watch tonight? The horses seem safe enough here, don't they?"

Jacob shook his head, as uneasy as Mattie. "I'll sleep near them, at least. We haven't seen the Bates brothers, but that doesn't mean other troublemakers aren't around. You go ahead and find your bed."

Andrew almost laughed, but his grin turned to a wry smile when he saw Jacob was serious. "Whatever you want. Wake me up if anything goes amiss."

He went on with Johanna toward the Hertzler wagon while Jacob put another small log on the fire. The look in Mattie's eyes when she asked about the horses still worried him. What had she seen on the trail through the Swamp?

Mattie had gone toward the Schrock wagon with one of

her nieces, but now made her way back to him. The first stars were showing in the darkening sky behind her, but he could see her silhouette against the faint light. It was only when she came close to the fire that he saw the worried look on her face.

"Shouldn't you be with the horses?" She took a seat on the bench near him.

He would put the boards away out of the damp before he found his bedroll, but for now the makeshift seating was scattered around the fire. "They're safe enough on their pickets. I'll move them closer before I turn in for the night."

She glanced toward the edge of the meadow where the horses were scattered over the dark grass, grazing.

"What is it, Mattie? You haven't been worried about the horses before. Did you see something that makes you think they're in danger?"

She didn't answer, so he moved to the bench next to her and took her hands in his. They were cold in the night air.

"What's wrong?"

She squeezed his hands. "I saw Cole Bates."

His stomach churned. "You saw the Bates brothers?"

She shook her head. "Only Cole. He . . . he was following us along the swamp road."

"Did he say something to frighten you?"

"He . . ." She stopped. Her voice dropped to a whisper so quiet he had to lean close to hear. "Did you mean it when you asked me to give you my pledge, Jacob? To give you my promise?"

His breath caught. "For sure, I meant every word. But can you keep your promise?"

She didn't look at him, but drew her hands back and gazed into the fire. "I think I can."

It was Jacob's turn to look into the fire, as if a solution was in the shifting flames. He needed to know. He needed to be sure. His arms ached with the desire to hold her close to him, but he didn't move. If she was going to give him her pledge, it had to depend on more than her thinking she could keep it. He glanced at her profile outlined against the firelight.

"I hoped that promising to marry me would keep you safe, but if you aren't sure that is what you want, then your word won't keep you from following whatever whim comes into your head."

"You make me sound like a flighty little girl." Her voice rose in protest. "I know exactly what I want."

"And what is that?"

Mattie didn't answer, but looked down at her hands lying in her lap. She opened one, and then the other. When she looked at him, a frown darkened her face.

"Maybe I don't know yet."

Jacob's gut wrenched.

"Did you only ask me to make that promise because you wanted to keep me safe?"

It was Jacob's turn to look into the fire. He would never give his heart to any other girl, but could he tell her that he loved her? Loving someone held risks. He had loved his brother, Hansli. And Liesbet. But his love hadn't been enough to protect them.

"I want you to be my wife. I want you to help me build our farm, our family. To build our lives together."

Mattie reached for a stick and stirred the glowing coals of the fire. "What if I don't want to live on a farm? What if I want to . . . to see the mountains and the ocean? Would you take me to see them?"

Jacob watched Mattie as she pulled the stick out of the coals. The end had caught fire, flames circling the tip like a crown of liquid light.

"Is that really what you want? To travel on to the west, never having a home?"

"I want a home someday." Mattie blew out the tiny flame. "I could go west to Iowa, or to . . . to Oregon." She pushed the end of the stick into the coals again. "And then I could come back and be your wife."

"Ne, Mattie. If you went west, you would never come back. You'd be lost from us forever." He gazed at her profile against the firelight. Her delicate features were overshadowed by the shape of her kapp and the Plain clothes she wore. "And besides, how would a girl like you go west?"

"I could find someone to take me."

"No Amish man would do that." He pushed against the fear rising. Would she go anyway? Or would someone else take her away? Someone like Cole Bates?

She dropped the stick and rose to her feet. "It's only a dream, Jacob. A thought." She started toward the wagons. "I'll probably never see those western mountains."

She left him sitting by the fire with his gut churning. Jacob reached down to pick up the stick again, and blew out the tiny flames that were trying to claim it.

Mattie gave up trying to sleep. Every time she closed her eyes, she saw Cole's mocking smile, his outstretched hand as he invited her to come away with him. To go to Oregon with him. She turned her mind away from the memory of his kiss. It had been rough and frightening. Andrew's kisses had never felt like that. It was like Cole wanted to control her, to possess her.

She slipped from her pallet to the seat Daed had built on the front of the wagon. She hadn't ridden there, but Naomi and Mamm had when they hadn't ridden in the spring wagon. They talked as they rode, knitting to pass the time.

Pulling her blanket around her, Mattie made herself comfortable on the plank seat high off the ground. All was quiet in the camp. Jacob had shortened the horses' picket lines and brought them closer to the fire. She could see the mound of his body lying by the glowing coals, as close to the horses as he could get. But if Jacob was sleeping, Cole could still sneak in and make off with some of the horses. The hair on the back of her neck prickled at the thought. Cole could be here now, watching the camp.

Watching her.

She pulled the blanket tighter, glad that the soft gray wool covered her white muslin sleeping gown. Now that she wasn't alone on the road in the Swamp and she wasn't hemmed in by Cole's horses, she could let her mind play over the memory of his invitation with only a shudder of excitement rather than the panic of fear she had felt then. His words circled in and out of her mind. He was going to Oregon. He said he wanted to take her with him.

She would never go with him. She could never do that.

But the thought of it . . . What would it be like to go with a man like Cole Bates? She had told Jacob that she could travel west and then come back to him, but he was right. That would never happen. If she was ever brave enough to take a step like that . . .

Or foolish enough.

It would be foolish. The Good Book was full of warnings about fools and what their end would be.

If she did something like going west with Cole, it wouldn't be only Jacob that she would be putting behind her. It would be Daed and Mamm, Naomi, Isaac, and Noah. But Henry would follow. At fourteen, nearly fifteen years old, he wouldn't worry about any risk. He would try to find her. She was as sure of that as she was sure that the sun would rise in the morning.

Mattie slapped at a mosquito whining its way around her head and pulled the blanket up around her ears.

So, she had made her decision. She wouldn't follow Cole Bates anywhere, not even to Oregon. She'd do it for Henry's sake, and for Mamm's. Someday she would go, though. Perhaps when Henry was older, they could go together.

She brushed at the prick of a mosquito biting her forehead.

If she married Jacob, though, she would never see any place beyond Indiana. No good Amish man would want to leave his farm and church behind just to let his wife see what was beyond the horizon. And no good Amish woman would want to go, either. Hannah was right. She needed to learn to be content with what God had provided for her.

Mattie squirmed on the hard plank. She was old enough to be baptized, but she hadn't joined the baptism class the last time the ministers held it. There was too much to do and see before she tied herself down. But if she wanted to marry Jacob, she would need to be baptized first. She sighed, leaning her chin on one hand. If she chose to join church and marry Jacob, the door to the west and Oregon would be tightly shut. She wouldn't go back on her vows, and she would never leave Indiana.

She glanced over at the fire again, at the soft mound that was Jacob. Could she be content with him, building their life together on an Indiana farm? A farm like the one she had seen when they first arrived in Ohio, with a white frame house, a Dutch door, and children feeding the chickens on a gravel path?

One of the horses lifted its head, ears pricked, and Jacob sat up. Mattie tried to see into the darkness on the other side of the fire, but there was no movement and no sound. The horse resumed its grazing, but Jacob stayed sitting up. Mattie counted to ten, slowly, but nothing happened. Jacob didn't move. He must have heard something.

Climbing slowly down the spokes of the wagon wheel, Mattie paused when she reached the ground. It was silly for her to go to the fire, to see what Jacob had seen or heard, but she gave in to her curiosity. When she reached the fire, Jacob jumped.

"What are you doing here?" He whispered so quietly that she had to lean close to him to hear.

"I couldn't sleep, and then I thought one of the horses heard something in the woods."

He pulled her down to sit on the ground next to him. "There's something or someone out there. You should have stayed in the wagon."

"I saw that you were awake, and I had to see what was going on."

"Stay here now, and be quiet. Watch and listen."

The fire had died down to a few glowing coals that gave no light. The moon was a thin sliver near the horizon, and starlight filled the sky, but the horses were only black shadows on the dark field. Nothing moved except when one of them took a step to reach another bite of grass.

Mattie leaned close to Jacob's ear, feeling safe near him. "How can you tell something is there?"

His lips brushed her cheek as he turned to whisper in her ear. "The frogs."

He didn't move away from her but held her close. She felt his soft breath on her cheek as she waited, listening. Then she understood what he meant. The frogs along the meadow opposite them were silent. Behind the wagons they continued, but beyond the horses all was silent, as if the frogs were waiting for something to happen.

"I'm going to go over there. You stay here."

Jacob didn't wait for her to answer before he was gone, threading his way between the horses. She could hear his progress as the horses stepped away from him or shook their heads in the dark. Everything else was silent, until a hand from behind covered her mouth.

A scream caught in her throat as she tried to wrest out of the tight grip that held her.

"Shh, Mattie-girl. You'll wake the whole camp."

She froze, bile rising in her throat.

"And you don't want your sweetheart hearing you and coming back here to get a knife in his gut, do you?"

The hand covering her mouth and nose restricted her breathing. She clutched at Cole's hand, trying to get some air in her lungs.

He turned her face toward his and leaned over her. "I'll let you breathe if you promise to be quiet. If you make the least noise, someone is going to get hurt."

She nodded and he released his hand. She gasped for breath, nearly coughing at the rank odor of stale tobacco smoke and whiskey that accompanied him.

He stroked her cheek with one hand, while the other one circled her waist, more closely than any man had held her before. "Oh, you're a sweet morsel, you are."

She turned her face away, but he grasped her chin and turned her toward him again.

"Here's what you're going to do." He leaned over her. "You're going to call your sweetheart to come back to the fire. Tell him you're scared or something. And then you do your best to keep his mind off the horses." His finger traveled from her chin to her neck. "I'm sure you'll think of something to keep him from noticing what I'm doing."

"What . . . what will you be doing?"

Cole chuckled and bent to kiss her cheek. "You don't worry about me. Just keep that fellow busy." He stood. "Count to ten, then call him. Do you understand? If I find him out there, I'm going to have to hurt him. So if you want him safe, make him come to you."

He disappeared into the darkness. Mattie's teeth chattered, but she counted to ten.

"Jacob." She called his name softly, not wanting to wake up anyone in the camp. She didn't doubt that Cole would keep his promise to hurt Jacob, or anyone else who got in his way.

She clutched the blanket around her and stepped around the fire, toward the horses in the direction Jacob had disappeared.

"Jacob," she called again.

He appeared out of the darkness. "What is it? Did you see something?"

Her knees shook. "I'm . . . I'm scared. I want you to stay here with me."

Jacob grasped her hand. "I'll take you back to your wagon. I need to watch the horses."

"Ne, I can't." Her voice rose in her panic. If she didn't keep him here by the fire, Cole would hurt him, possibly kill him.

"Mattie, I need to take care of the horses. You must do as I say."

"You can't go back out there." She thought of flinging herself into his arms, to force him to stay with her. Cole had said she would think of something. "I . . . I need you."

"What is wrong? Did you see something?"

Mattie clenched her teeth to keep them from chattering. If she told him about Cole, he would go off into the darkness to find him. But if she remained silent, Cole would take their horses and they would be stranded along the road. A sob broke through.

"Cole is here." She clung to Jacob's sleeves as he tried to pull away. "If you try to stop him, he'll kill you." Jacob wrenched one arm out of her grasp. "Jacob, don't go out there."

"I'm going to get Andrew and Josef. We can't let him take the horses." Jacob pulled her toward the wagon. "You get in your wagon. Tell everyone to stay inside."

As Jacob roused the other men, the camp exploded into light and sound. The men lit torches from the dying coals and encircled the horses. Mattie watched their progress from inside the wagon, peering out through the front opening in the canvas. Finally, the torches made their way back to the camp. The men gathered the horses closer to the wagons, tying them to wagon wheels rather than leaving them on their pickets in the meadow.

Daed stopped at their wagon when he saw Mattie watching.

"We saw nothing out there. If there was someone, we must have frightened them off."

Jacob and Andrew stood behind Daed, and Mattie saw them exchange glances. Again, Jacob was asking the others to trust his word with no evidence, but Mattie knew. And for sure Cole Bates would try again.

19

The next morning was hot and humid as soon as the sun peeped over the tops of the trees on the eastern horizon. The women brought out a cold breakfast of dried apples and cheese, and Johanna took her serving to the bench near her family's wagon where she and Andrew had eaten supper together the night before. She sat fingering her dried apples as she waited for him to finish helping the other men put the horses back on their picket lines in the grassy meadow. Had Cole Bates really tried to steal the horses last night, like Jacob and Mattie said? Jacob wouldn't lie, but surely he had been mistaken. No one could be so mean as to steal horses, not in modern times like these.

Andrew finally came walking toward her, rubbing his arm.

"Did you get hurt?" Johanna moved to give him room on the bench.

"I don't know." Andrew sat next to her with a thud, making the bench shake. "Maybe I slept on it wrong. Or I slept on everything wrong." He stretched, rolling his shoulders. "I ache all over."

"Here." Johanna offered him her plate. "You take my breakfast and I'll go get more."

He shook his head. "I'm not hungry." He leaned his elbows on his knees, rubbing his face. "It's cold this morning." He glanced at her. "Aren't you chilly?"

"Are you becoming ill? If you're achy and chilled, it sounds like you need to go back to bed."

"Only babies go to bed in the daytime."

Johanna stood, leaving her plate on the bench and taking his arm. "Come with me. We're going to find your mamm."

As she pulled a reluctant Andrew toward the Bontragers' wagon, Johanna waved Nancy, Andrew's mother, over to help her. Andrew seemed to be falling asleep on his feet and leaned against her so heavily that she was afraid he would fall to the ground.

"What is wrong?" Nancy took Andrew's other arm as she joined them.

"I'm all right." Andrew tried to shake off their help, but Johanna kept her hold on him easily. Too easily.

"I think he is sick."

Nancy looked at Andrew's face and the eyes that seemed ready to close. "You're right. It's to bed with you, young man."

She called her husband, Yost, and son-in-law, Thomas, to help lift Andrew into the wagon, and Johanna helped her lay Andrew on a mattress.

Nancy felt his forehead. "He is burning up with fever."

"He complained of being cold."

Andrew turned to the side with restless movements, his teeth chattering as if he was chilled to the bone.

Nancy frowned as she covered Andrew with a blanket. "Chills and fever. I've seen it before. We need to keep him warm, and watch for the fever to break." She looked at Johanna as if to judge her abilities. "Will you help me? We'll need to watch him day and night for the next couple days."

"For sure, I'll help. Is it catching? Should we warn the others?"

"I've never heard of anyone catching it from another, but I wouldn't be surprised if more of us come down with it. People contract it along river bottoms and swamps."

"Just where we've been during the last week." Johanna laid the back of her hand on Andrew's cheek. Nancy was right, he was burning with fever.

"If you can stay with him, I'll get some water and cloths so we can try to cool him off."

As Nancy left, Andrew turned his head to the side and gave her a crooked grin. "Ma says I'm sick." His words were slurred. "I'm glad . . . you're . . . here . . ." Andrew's voice faded as he fell asleep.

Tuesday night's events stayed with Jacob through the next day and into Thursday. There had been no more sign of Cole Bates, but Mattie stayed close to her family's wagon, even riding with her mother and Naomi rather than walking nearby.

Jacob was glad to see it, although he would have enjoyed her companionship as he walked along next to the smaller wagon he shared with Josef. He swished the willow pole he carried through a tall stand of grass next to the road. He missed the hours they spent together herding the sheep before they had reached Ohio.

That led his thoughts back to his family. Anything could happen to them before he and Josef were able to return to

Ohio. He sighed. Daed had said they needed to leave the outcome of the situation in God's hands, but sitting back, yielding to God's will, didn't seem like it was enough. There must be something he could do to help Mamm, but every time he thought about sending Josef on to Indiana without him and retracing his steps back to his family, he knew it would be useless. Even Daed, there with Mamm, was help-less. They could only wait.

Thursday night they camped in the driest spot they could find, strung out along the roadside. Marshy spots had been abundant along their route, sometimes opening into lakes, and sometimes narrowing to a small stream that meandered to the next marshy spot. The mosquitoes were still ferocious. Jacob gathered swathes of green grass to smudge the fire as the sun moved toward the western horizon. Mattie's brother, Noah, had fallen ill with the fever 'n' ague the afternoon after Andrew had taken to his bed.

They had passed some farms along the way, and the families had warned them against milk fever. It was prevalent in this area, they had said. So after milking the three cows they were taking to Indiana, Henry poured the milk out onto the ground.

"Better to have the little ones go hungry rather than die of the milk fever," Isaac told Jacob, his face grim.

All of the men's faces were grim, his included. Jacob rubbed at his forehead, trying to ease the tension that had settled there. He watched Isaac walk back to his family. The man's shoulders were slumped as if he carried a heavy weight. Worry about his four children, his wife, and the unknown waiting for them in Indiana were all plain to see with each step he took.

Only Eli Schrock and Yost Bontrager remained cheerful.

"We'll soon be away from the swamplands," Eli said as

Jacob joined the group of men gathered around the smoky fire. "The land Yost and I saw last year is dry ground, with running streams here and there. Once we get to Indiana, the travel will be much easier."

"If we don't all fall ill of the fever 'n' ague first," said Elias Hertzler. "I'm beginning to wish we had stayed in Pennsylvania."

"Don't lose sight of our goal, Elias." Eli Schrock clapped a hand on the other man's shoulder. "We can't let a few hardships discourage us."

"What about that horse thief Jacob saw the other night?" Elias crossed his arms and scowled. "If the boy is right, and I'm not saying he isn't"—he nodded in Jacob's direction—"then we know this fellow won't give up easily. He knows his horses, and he wants ours. What if he is successful? How many horses does he need to steal before we take action?"

"What kind of action are you thinking of?" Isaac's quiet voice cut through the men's murmuring responses to Elias's statement. "Do we resist the man who would steal from us?"

Jacob rubbed the sweat off his face with his shirtsleeve. "There's nothing that says we can't act to prevent the thief from being successful. We can keep watch on the horses, tie them close to the wagons at night."

"And if we catch the thief in the act, what then?" Elias peered around the circle of faces through the smoke.

Eli Schrock stroked his beard. "The Confession teaches us that Jesus Christ has forbidden revenge and resistance. We are to bless those who persecute us."

The men around the circle nodded in unison.

"Ja," Yost said, "we will bless the one who wishes us harm. We will pray for him and turn our cheek if necessary."

"I will give of my horses," said Eli, "since it seems that is what he desires." He looked from face to face. "If any of us catches this man in the act of trying to steal a horse from us, then offer him my team, and bless him as he goes on his way."

"Denki, Brother Eli." Yost nodded toward his friend. "We will all support you in this gesture and assist you in your work until you are able to replace your team. Meanwhile, I propose that we start our journey earlier than normal in the morning. It appears that we have unsettled weather ahead, and we may not be able to travel in the later afternoon if there are storms." He looked toward Jacob. "Will you watch the horses tonight?"

Jacob nodded in assent. "I will watch the entire night and then sleep in the wagon while we travel tomorrow."

The men separated to their own wagons, drifting off in twos and threes. Eli Schrock stepped close to Jacob. "Remember what I said about my team. We must not disobey the teachings of Christ."

After Eli left him, Jacob sat on a stone in the thickest part of the smoke, holding his sleeve over his nose, his eyes watering as he sought a brief respite from the insects. He was glad the men were finally taking the threat of the horse thief seriously, but he couldn't shake the feeling that Cole's interest in Mattie was a more serious threat. He rubbed at the back of his neck, chasing off a mosquito.

With the illness of two of their members, the entire community seemed to be waiting for the next blow to fall. Jacob was on edge as much as the others. But without knowing when or what the disaster might be, there was no way to guard against it, or to protect themselves.

Daed would say to trust God. He would tell him that worry

and fear would only eat at him and make him miserable. Jacob scattered more green grass on the fire. Daed was right. He was miserable, for sure, and the more the worry took hold, the closer that lapping sea of darkness came to the edge of his consciousness.

Worry added to worry. Would it ever end?

He rubbed at the back of his neck again. It prickled as if tiny mosquito feet were crawling along his skin, seeking a vulnerable spot to attack.

Trust God. There was nothing else he could do.

As voices quieted in the wagons, he walked up the line, checking each horse's tether. When he reached the far end, he stretched and slapped at a mosquito. It promised to be a long night.

Toward midnight the wind freshened, bringing a breath of cool air from the northwest. Jacob walked up the line of horses again, more to stay awake than from any worry that the quiet would be disturbed. But as he reached the end of the half-circle of wagons, he heard a voice and ducked behind the corner of the Schrocks' wagon.

"Whoa, there, beauty."

The voice was low, the words English. Jacob left his cover and crept along the line of horses until he reached the third horse in the line. Beneath its neck he could see the intruder. Even in the dark he recognized the man's build and the shape of his hat. Cole Bates.

Jacob ducked under the horse's neck. "Hello, Bates." He kept his voice low also. He didn't want to wake the Schrock families sleeping on the other side of the canvas wagon cover.

The man jumped, startling the horse he held by the halter.

Before Jacob could say anything more, he saw the flash of a knife blade in Cole's free hand.

"Stay back. Let me take the horses and no one will get hurt."

"You're right. No one will get hurt."

Cole untied the horse's tether. It was one of Eli Schrock's team. Jacob clenched his fist at the thought of what he had to do. It didn't seem right to let a thief take the horses, but that was man's thinking, not God's. No matter how he felt, he needed to obey the men's decision.

He reached to untie the rope of the second horse in line, the teammate of the first. "Take this one too. Take the team, and go with our blessing."

Bates froze. "What's this?"

"Take these two horses, then be on your way."

Starlight flashed on Cole's teeth as he gave a short laugh. "You're trying to pull one over on me, right? As soon as I leave, you'll come after me and try to catch me as a horse thief. Nothing doing. It's all of the horses or none."

Jacob shrugged. "We won't fight you or come after you. It isn't our way." As he spoke, he realized that Cole was alone. "Where are your brothers?" He half turned, expecting to see the rest of the horses being led off by the other thieves.

"I'm working alone now, and no deal. I take all the horses or none of them."

"No. Only these two. But take the horses as a gift. We won't force you to steal them."

Cole dropped the rope and backed away. "What are you getting at?" He moved the knife back and forth. "Where are the rest of them? Why are you out here alone?"

"It isn't a trick. You don't have to be a thief." He took a step closer and held the second horse's lead rope out to the other man. "Take these horses as our gift. Go somewhere and start over. We won't try to stop you."

Cole looked one way, then the other. "That Mattie-girl, did she put you up to this?"

"Mattie has nothing to do with this."

"She's a sweet one, she is. This sounds like something she'd think of." The man's teeth gleamed in the starlight.

Cole's intimate tone slid into Jacob's consciousness, setting his teeth on edge. How well did Cole know Mattie?

"Take the horses and leave." Jacob's voice came out harsher than he had ever heard before. Another minute and any thought of peaceful nonresistance was going to run right out of his head.

Bates chuckled and slid his knife into his belt. He picked up the two lead ropes and looped them over the wagon wheel. "Forget it, farmer. I'll wait until I can get the whole package. All the horses, and the Mattie-girl too. Did she tell you she's going to Oregon with me?"

He backed away into the darkness, and then was gone without another sound. Jacob took a deep breath and retied the two horses' lead ropes to the wagon wheel.

A soft noise from the wagon drew his attention. Mattie had pulled back the wagon cover enough to peek through at him.

He held her gaze. "You heard what he said?"

"I did."

"Is it true? Are you going to Oregon with him?" She didn't answer right away, and he stepped closer to her. "Mattie? You wouldn't go with him, would you?"

"Of course not. He's a thief and a liar and a dangerous man."

"What would make him say that? How does he know you? Have you been talking with him?"

"Not really. I mean, he has talked to me."

Jacob pushed his ire down. Anger that had risen so quickly it took him off guard. "Go back to sleep, Mattie. We'll discuss this in the morning."

Then he saw Naomi behind Mattie, her eyes wide as she listened to their conversation. For sure, the whole Schrock family would have been awake ever since he confronted Cole.

"Good night, Jacob." Mattie let the cover down again. He could hear her moving inside the wagon, then all was quiet.

He started back down the line to the Bontrager wagon, checking the knot on each horse's lead rope. He didn't doubt that Bates would try to steal all of the horses, but he would certainly resist any attempt of Cole's to take Mattie away, whether she wanted to go with him or not.

Jacob reached the last horse in line and slumped down, his hands on his knees and his head hanging between his shoulders. Ja, whether she wanted to go west with the thief or not.

For two days Andrew had alternated between shaking with the cold chills and burning with fever. Johanna had been at his side each afternoon when the fever broke, his clothes and bedding soaked with sweat. But then he would grow hot again, his skin parched and dry, and soon he would be shaking from the chills. The group continued traveling, and the occasional jolts of the wagon would make him cry out in his sleep at times. Johanna heard that Noah Schrock had also come down with the fever, but her concern for Andrew made her blind to anything else.

On Wednesday morning, Johanna sat on the stool next to Andrew's bed in the Bontragers' wagon while Nancy slept on her own pallet toward the front. Andrew's mamm had kept watch over him through the long nights, while Johanna spent her days with him. His fever had just broken for the third time, and she was wiping the sweat off his face with a cool cloth when he opened his eyes. They were clear, seeing her for the first time since the fever had taken him to his bed.

"Johanna?" His voice was a hoarse whisper. "Am I dreaming again?"

"You're awake." Johanna couldn't keep from smiling in relief as she sat back and rinsed the cloth in the pail of water at her side. "How do you feel?"

"Like a drowned kitten." He scratched his chin, thick with whiskers. "How long have I been sleeping?"

"More than two days."

"Two days," Andrew echoed. His eyes drifted closed again.

Johanna picked up her knitting and continued on a stocking as Andrew slept. The wagon rocked with an even rhythm and she yawned. It wouldn't do for her to fall asleep too. Andrew's even breathing mingled with Nancy's slight snores, and the air inside the wagon was heavy and close. Her knitting had fallen into her lap and her head was nodding, when from outside the wagon came the calls up and down the line. Johanna stood to look out the front of the wagon. They had reached an open area in the thick woods, and the road was climbing to a rise ahead. From here she could hear the voices. They had reached Indiana and would be stopping for the noon meal when they found a likely spot.

Andrew's eyes opened again when she made her way back to her seat. "Jo, have you been here the whole time?"

"During the day, while your mamm slept. We've taken turns watching over you."

Nancy rose from her bed and made her way toward Andrew. "Is he awake?" She laid her hand on his forehead. "His fever is gone."

"He woke just a few minutes ago."

Johanna rose to give Nancy her place, but Andrew's mamm pushed her back on the stool.

"I'll go tell Yost that Andrew is better." She squeezed Andrew's shoulder. "We've been so worried about both you and Noah, but it looks like you're on the mend." She turned to Johanna. "Keep him in bed. Even if he feels better, he shouldn't try to get up yet. Once we stop for dinner, I'll bring some broth for him to eat."

After Nancy climbed out of the wagon to sit on the front bench where she could talk to Yost, Andrew took Johanna's hand in his, his eyes already closing again. "Stay with me, won't you?"

"Of course I will. But you should keep awake long enough to eat."

He turned his head on the pillow. "You can wake me when Ma brings my food."

His eyes were closed, but his face was peaceful. Johanna pushed his hair back from his forehead and smoothed the line over his left eyebrow. His face had become as familiar as her own through the hours she had spent watching him. She laid her hand on his cheek, now cool and dry.

Andrew mumbled, and Johanna leaned closer. "What did you say?"

The corners of his mouth turned up, even though his eyes were still closed. "I love you, Jo."

256

20

The wagon lurched, throwing Jacob to the edge of his pallet and nearly onto the floor of packing boxes that lined the bottom of the wagon. Sunshine had warmed the canvas cover until the interior of the wagon was bright and hot. He stood on the unsteady floor, pulling his suspenders over his shoulders. It must be nearly noon.

He poked his head out the front of the wagon just as Josef urged the team up and over a rise and onto flat land. Their wagon was in the lead, and Jacob could hear the team behind them start up the same slope.

"Where are we?"

Josef answered from the saddle on the near wheel horse. "Eli and Yost say that we crossed into Indiana this morning. We'll stop for the noon hour just ahead." He pointed to a grassy meadow surrounded by trees.

"The ground looks drier than we've had the last week."

"We've been climbing all morning. Yost said that we'll be traveling through scattered prairies and forests until we reach our destination. The road follows the higher land between the lakes."

Jacob looked into the northwest sky where gray clouds had gathered. "It looks like we might run into that rain Yost predicted last night. The air feels heavy enough for a thunderstorm."

Josef eyed the clouds. "Ja, and it will be here soon." He clucked to the horses to pick up their pace.

Jacob put his boots on, then swung down to the ground from the rear of the wagon. He jogged to the side of the road as the other wagons went by, then fell in beside Henry and the girls. They were walking with Mattie's nephews behind the last wagon and the boys were soaked from head to toe.

"What happened to them?"

Hannah and Mattie laughed while Naomi smiled. "They were trying to catch crayfish in the last creek we crossed and fell in."

"We didn't fall in," Mose said from behind them. "We were trying to catch a big old crayfish and he went under a rock in the deepest part."

"We didn't fall in," Menno echoed.

"If Peter was here, he would have caught him." Mose caught up to Jacob, looking up at him. "Why did Peter have to stay in Ohio?"

Jacob patted the boy's wet shoulder. "He wanted to come, but Daed needed him to help out there. They'll be coming to Indiana in the fall."

"You'll be our neighbors, won't you? Peter and I are going to build a house in the woods and live with the Indians."

"And hunt bears," Menno added.

"Look, we're stopping!" Mose and Menno ran ahead to where Josef had pulled the team off the road and into the meadow.

Jacob watched them run. Years ago, that would have been him and Hansli, running to find whatever mischief they could get into.

"What are you smiling about?"

He turned to the others, all staring at him. "Boys. They make a game out of everything, don't they?"

"Girls do too. Come on, Naomi!" Hannah grabbed Naomi's hand and they ran after the two boys. Henry followed, whooping as he ran, leaving Mattie laughing as she walked next to Jacob.

"You're not going to run with them?"

She smiled at him. "And leave you here alone? That wouldn't be kind."

Cole's words echoed in Jacob's mind. Mattie had said she wouldn't go to Oregon with the thief, but Bates had sounded so sure. And how could he tell what Mattie was thinking?

"You wouldn't leave me alone, would you?"

Her smile disappeared. "You're not talking about me following Naomi and Hannah."

He stopped in the road, reaching for her hand. When he tugged at it, she turned toward him.

"What Cole Bates said last night . . ." Jacob looked into Mattie's brown eyes. As soon as he had mentioned Cole's name, they had widened like a startled deer's.

"I told you. That Cole is a thief and a liar." But her eyes shifted away from his.

"You wouldn't go west with him?"

"Of course not."

He waited for her to raise her eyes. To look at him. But she looked at his knees, and past his shoulder. Anywhere but his face.

"I want your promise, Mattie."

She looked at him then. "You asked for my pledge to marry you, but I'm not ready to give you my answer yet."

"Then at least promise that you won't go with that Cole Bates or anyone like him. Pledge your word that you won't leave your family and . . . and me." Jacob's throat closed on the last words.

The corners of her eyes crinkled a little as she smiled. "I can promise that. I won't run away to go west with Cole Bates or anyone like him."

A tight band around Jacob's chest loosened at her words. "That's enough, then. I have your pledge." He stroked her arm, longing to hold her. "And perhaps someday you'll promise—"

She laughed. "You'll never give up asking me, will you?"

He pulled her to him then, hugging her the way he would hug Hannah, even though he would rather encircle her with both arms and never let her go. "Never." He whispered the word into her hair.

He released her before she pulled away. Before he kissed her.

Suddenly aware of the silence around him, he looked for the wagons. "They've already unhitched the horses."

"We need to hurry, then." Mattie tugged at his hand. "A storm is coming, and we'll want to get dinner finished and cleared up before it starts raining."

Jacob glanced at the clouds again. They hadn't drifted any closer but were building into thunderheads that towered in the sky.

Soon the camp had settled down to eat a quick dinner of leftover biscuits and bacon from breakfast. They had decided against building a cooking fire because of the approaching storm. Noah and Andrew, both shaky from the fever, joined the rest of the group for the meal, and Jacob found a seat near them.

"How are you feeling?" Jacob didn't want to look too closely at Andrew's pale face.

"Better." Andrew held his biscuit with a shaky hand. His normal teasing tone was gone, but he forced a grin even though the corners of his mouth quivered. "I'm so weak, though. It took all my strength to move two steps from the wagon to this bench. And now I don't even think I can get this biscuit to my mouth."

"Take it slow."

Andrew took a bite, then swallowed. "So, while I've been sick, you haven't been horning in on my favorite girl, have you?"

"Mattie?"

The grin came back, but disappeared. "I can't even joke like I used to." Andrew leaned down, his forearms on his knees. "The only one I think about anymore is Jo." He shook his head. "Jacob, I've got it bad. I even thought about asking her to marry me."

"You want to marry Johanna?" Jacob shot a glance at Andrew. No, he wasn't teasing.

"As soon as I can be baptized. I never thought I'd get married. No girl has ever made me feel like this, like I would clear forests for her, and fight bears, and . . . and . . ." He sniffed. "All the time I was sick, she was there. I can't imagine what my life would be like if I woke up someday and she wasn't by my side." He sat up and laid a heavy hand on Jacob's shoulder. "I'd do anything for her."

"Even join church?"

When Andrew smiled, all traces of the old mocking grin were gone. "How could I not obey the Good Lord when he has given me such a gift? Of course I'm going to join church, but not for her. Because of her."

Andrew tried to stand. Jacob helped him up and then supported him as he made his way back into the Bontrager wagon and his pallet.

Once he was settled in his bed, Andrew grasped Jacob's hand. "I'll be up and around again, and soon. I might never be so maudlin again, so I'm only going to say this once. I hope you find what I've found, Jacob. I know you like Mattie—keep after her until she surrenders to you. She can be pretty stubborn."

Jacob patted Andrew's shoulder. His friend's eyes closed in sleep before he could turn to go.

While he had been in the Bontragers' wagon, an eerie stillness had descended over the camp. The storm clouds had moved in and were churning in a greenish-gray mass, but only fitful gusts of wind disturbed the tree branches. A rumble of thunder bore down on the little meadow.

"Jacob!" Josef called. "Help me get the canvas tied down."

Jacob started across the circle as mothers gathered their little ones together and crowded them into the shelter of the wagons. The horses had been brought in from their pickets and tied to the wagon wheels, and Isaac and Eli were stowing the harnesses under the wagons. Jacob cast an eye upward again. They were in for a big storm.

As he and Josef tied down the canvas, the wind bore down on them in a strong gust, tearing at the tree branches and anything else that wasn't fastened down. Eli Schrock came running over to their wagon.

"Have you seen Mattie?"

"Not since before dinner." Jacob had to shout as another gust ripped the words away. "Is she missing?"

"She isn't in our wagon. I hoped she had decided to take shelter in someone else's, but yours is the last one I've checked." Eli held his hat against another gust and peered toward the line of trees at the edge of the meadow. "Lydia said someone had mentioned seeing early strawberries near the woods, but I don't see her there, either."

"I'll look for her." Jacob looked up just in time to see a lightning bolt jump from one cloud to another. A crack of thunder followed close behind. "I'll head over to the woods to see if she's there."

"Be careful."

Jacob nodded, and took off running for the line of trees. Just as he reached it, hail burst from the sky, pelting his back. "Mattie!"

The impact of the hailstones against the canopy of leaves overhead was deafening. If she answered him, he wouldn't hear her.

He turned the other way. "Mattie!"

Was that a shout in answer? He ducked under a low-hanging branch and peered through the twilight of the woods. The hail ended as quickly as it had begun, but now sheets of rain poured down accompanied by a loud crash of thunder. The center of the storm must be directly overhead.

There—a hand waved from under a shrub. He ran to it, ducked down, and found Mattie huddled under the roots of a tree that had fallen years before. The hollow gave some shelter, and he crouched there with her.

"Your daed is worried about you." Jacob shouted over the noise of the rushing wind that accompanied the rain.

"I'm sorry. I was picking strawberries and then the hail started."

Jacob saw no strawberries. Something churned in the cold pit that had become his stomach, and he heard Cole's words again. She wouldn't meet him in the woods . . . A vision of Cole and Mattie together burned into his mind. But she had given her pledge . . .

"Where are the strawberries?" He spoke carefully, as if it didn't matter.

"I dropped them." She waved toward the forest floor outside their shelter. "When the hail started, I just ran for shelter and dropped them all. There weren't many. Not even enough for one person. I guess it's too early."

Jacob pushed his suspicions down. Mattie wouldn't lie to him. When the next lightning bolt brightened the sky, he saw them. Three bright red berries, no bigger than cherry pits, lying among the grass blades just outside their shelter. He crawled forward and gathered them up.

"Are these all you found?"

"Oh, no. There were a few more," she stopped, looking at him sideways, "but I ate them. You can have those."

He held one up between his thumb and forefinger. "This won't put a dent in my appetite."

She giggled. "They were pretty sour, anyway. It's too early for strawberries."

The next rumble of thunder came from the northeast. The storm was moving on, but the rain still fell in buckets.

"We should go back to camp as soon as the rain lets up."

Mattie leaned close to him. "Ja, for sure. My family will be worried."

They sat in silence for a few minutes, listening to the rain.

A few drops made it into their shelter and Jacob drew Mattie close. He understood what Andrew meant, when he said he would do anything for Johanna. Right now, he had a wild wish that he was all alone in the world with Mattie and that they would live in this woods forever.

Mattie leaned forward to look out into the woods. "Is it getting lighter?"

Jacob pulled her back. She looked toward him and he couldn't resist. He kissed her, then kissed her again when she responded with a happy sigh.

"What has gotten into you?" Naomi spread a shirt over the branches of a shrub.

Mattie smiled, spreading a dress over the next shrub. Between the wind and downpour of rain in the storm, much of the bedding and clothes in the wagons had gotten soaked, so the group had decided to rest for the afternoon and dry their supplies out as much as possible. "I don't know what you mean."

Naomi came closer, lowering her voice. "Ever since you and Jacob came out of the woods after the storm, you've had that look on your face."

"What look?"

"That look that says you have a secret."

Mattie smiled again.

"There it is! So tell me, what is it?"

"If I have a secret, then I shouldn't tell, should I?"

Naomi raised her eyebrows, then moved to the next bush with another shirt while Mattie picked up a sodden blanket and shook it. Jacob's kisses had been too sweet to share them with Naomi yet. Kissing Andrew, when she allowed him to kiss her, had been awkward and funny. Cole . . . she swallowed. She didn't want to think about Cole.

But kissing Jacob had seemed so right. Something she could do for the rest of her life.

She spread the blanket out in a sunny space where the grass was drying in the sunshine. The storm had passed quickly, and the skies behind it were blue and clear. Yost Bontrager, with Daed and Henry, had gone down the road to see if anyone had suffered any more damage than they had, and the rest of the group were trying to dry out. Nothing had been lost, but a couple of the wagon covers had blown off, exposing the wagons and their contents to the downpour.

As Mattie shook out another blanket, sounds of the children playing a game of tag reached her. After the oppressive heat this morning, the cooler sunshine was a welcome treat, and the children were making a holiday out of it. She paused to watch them. Mose was "it" and the younger children ran from him with shrieks of delight. She counted eight children, including the three-year-olds, Leah and Mary. Mose was careful to run slowly so the younger ones had a chance to get away from him. When he did tag someone, it was seven-year-old Barbli Hertzler, Johanna's sister. The group of children had grown close on this journey, just as close as she had ever been with Johanna, Jacob, Hannah, and the others along the Conestoga Creek when they had been the same age.

Andrew must be feeling better. She had seen him at noon, sitting with Jacob. Noah was up and out of his bed this afternoon, too, sitting in the sunshine with Andrew, visiting while they watched the children play. She couldn't see Jacob from where she was, but earlier she had seen him with Josef, taking the horses out to graze farther away from the wagons.

Jacob. She smiled again as she reached for the next soggy item, a linen sheet. His kisses had reached deep into her, tugging at the desires that warred with the longing to see what was beyond this small meadow. Desires for the home Jacob planned, a farm built for future generations. When Jacob had held her in his arms, she felt that she could be content with him, anywhere he was.

Mattie pulled the sheet across three bushes, easing out the wrinkles as well as she could. She straightened the hem and looked at the expanse of the sheet. Even with her pulling and tugging, the wrinkles remained a nearly permanent reminder of being wet and crumpled, and stains where the sheet had pressed against the wet edge of the wagon streaked across the white sheet. It needed to be washed and ironed. Nothing else would bring back the snowy whiteness.

Like her sin. Hadn't Daed said something like that during evening prayers a few nights ago? Sin was a stain impossible to remove on our own. Only through Jesus Christ could one become pure and unblemished. At the time, she had taken comfort in the fact that her sins were nothing. A small lie here and there, perhaps. But not anything that would make her as stained and wrinkled as this sheet, right?

A sudden memory of Cole's dark eyes assailed her. She dropped the edge of the sheet and backed away.

"Mattie, help me with this blanket. It's too heavy for one person."

Naomi's call pulled her thoughts back to the task at hand. "Ja, for sure."

After they had spread the blanket across a grassy spot

in the sun, Mattie straightened to ease her aching back. "Is that the last?"

"I think so. Mamm was going to check the barrels to make sure they had stayed dry, but she would have let us know if she needed our help."

She caught sight of Jacob coming toward the wagons from where he and Josef had taken the horses. "I'll be back in time to help with supper."

Naomi glanced in Jacob's direction, then back at Mattie. "If you aren't back in time, I'll know where to find you."

Mattie grinned at Naomi's joke, but her sister had already turned to go back to the wagon. Ever since Johanna and Andrew had become a couple, Naomi spent more time by herself or with Mamm than with the group of young people.

Jacob watched her as she made her way toward him through the drying clothes and bedding. He met her at the edge of the meadow, and taking her hand, pulled her toward the cover of the trees at the edge of the woods.

"There is a lot to clean up after that storm." He pulled at her hand until she took a step closer to him. His smile pushed every other thought out of her mind. "Did anything get ruined?"

She tried to focus on his question. His warm brown eyes were very distracting. "I don't think so. The food barrels are tightly sealed, and a little rain won't hurt the clothes and bedding."

He leaned toward her and she met his kiss. She settled into his embrace.

"We can be married as soon as I have my land and build us a house. Maybe as soon as this fall."

Mattie backed away. "This fall? Isn't that too soon?"

"Why? That's half a year away." He smiled and pulled her close again. "I don't want to wait any longer, Mattie."

"But . . ." A sudden vision of a long winter trapped in a small cabin made Mattie's throat close in suffocating dryness. "I don't know if I'm ready to set up housekeeping yet."

Jacob's arms tightened around her. "What else would you do besides marry me?"

"I've told you." She motioned up and around them. "I want to see more than this world of trees and snatches of blue sky. Daed said that out in Iowa there are huge areas where no trees grow, and the sky is so big you can't see the end of it—" She stopped as Jacob released his hold on her and backed away.

"Nothing will make you content until you see the West, is that it?"

A twisting spiral of regret churned in her stomach when she saw his smoldering eyes, his lips pressed into a thin line.

"Why couldn't you come with me?" Her face flushed as the idea took hold. "We could marry, and then go west together. We could go all the way to Oregon and settle there."

He took another step back. "You would want to leave your family and the community, just to see a new country, when we have everything we need in Indiana?"

Mattie clenched her fists at his stubbornness. "You don't understand at all, Jacob Yoder. Trying to talk to you is like beating my head against a stone wall." She jerked away from him and stumbled toward the wagons.

His hand grabbed her elbow and spun her around. He gripped both of her arms in his hands. "You're right, Mattie. I don't understand." He dropped his hands. "I don't understand why you can't be content with what I have to offer you. Why you don't want to live the way we've been raised and taught." He turned away, his hands on his hips, then spun toward her again. "I don't understand why you are willing to throw away everything to chase some dream, especially after you gave me your pledge."

Mattie bit her lip. She didn't have an answer. Jacob's eyes were wet with unshed tears.

"And more than anything, Mattie, I don't understand how you could consider leaving me to go with that outsider, Cole Bates."

The spiral of pain and regret stopped its downward motion in her stomach and grew hard and hot. "I gave you my promise."

Jacob's face turned rigid. "But can I trust you?"

"Maybe I will go with him, Jacob Yoder, if only to get away from your pig-headed, self-centered, overbearing . . ." Mattie stopped, aghast at the words that crossed her mind. She pressed her lips together, staring at his glowering face. "Leave me alone, Jacob. Just go away and leave me alone."

He pushed past her and she collapsed onto a wet log, not caring about her skirt or anything else, and buried her face in her hands.

Mattie sat among the trees until the tears stopped. She slapped at mosquitoes and gnats, but nothing—nothing— could make her go back to the camp where she would have to face Jacob again.

"Mattie!" Henry's voice called.

"I'm here."

She could talk to Henry. He would understand why she couldn't tie herself down to a farm, and children, and all the work and responsibilities that would keep her imprisoned until she was an old woman. Her eyes grew hot as she remembered the worst part. Jacob didn't think she was worthy of his trust.

Henry came crashing through the bushes, red-faced and out of breath.

"Come quick. We need help."

Mattie jumped to her feet, her argument with Jacob forgotten. Something was terribly wrong. Each of her nieces' and nephews' faces flashed through her mind. "What happened?"

Henry stopped, gasping. He pointed toward the road with one hand. "We found a house . . . destroyed by a twister, Daed said." He stopped to breathe, then went on. "The family is trapped. Daed sent me back to get anyone who can help move logs. Mamm said you and Naomi are to come too, in case anyone is hurt."

"Ja, ja, ja. I'll get the bandages and medicines."

The farm was more than a mile up the road, and Mattie's side hurt by the time they got there. Naomi stopped short at the sight of the disaster. What had been a log cabin was now a pile of rubble. The roof had been plucked up by the storm and thrown to the side as if a giant child had grown tired of his playthings. A cow lay under the collapsed end of the barn, its head buried in the rubble and hind legs protruding like the twisted roots of a tree.

"This way," Daed called to the men.

Jacob was among those who lifted the heavy logs and threw them to the side. With each log they removed, two more had to be shifted aside to untangle it from the others. Mattie and Naomi held each other, waiting until they were needed, but could anyone be alive under that pile of wood?

A shout went up and before Mattie could move, Jacob had

jumped into an opening between the logs. She and Naomi stepped closer, and as the men bent to lift the bundle Jacob handed up, Yost Bontrager passed it to Naomi with a sorrowful look. Naomi's arms shook as she held the tiny baby, then laid it on the ground away from the commotion at the cabin.

"Naomi," Mattie said, knowing the answer. "The babe is dead?"

"It's an awful thing. Horrible." She grabbed Mattie's arm as she bent to look. "Don't. The wee child was crushed. You don't want to see it."

Another call came from Jacob in the depths of the house. This time Isaac jumped down to help him, and they passed up a man.

"He's alive," Daed said. "Carry him carefully to Naomi and Mattie."

Elias and Yost brought the man and laid him beside the small bundle of his child. Naomi knelt beside him.

"His breathing is so shallow."

Mattie knelt on the other side. "He has a gash on his head." She reached into Mamm's supply of clean cloths. "We can try to stop the bleeding, but we'll need to clean it and put a bandage on it."

Naomi helped her bind a cloth to the wound, but as they did so, Mattie felt the man's skull give way under their fingers. They caught each other's eyes.

The men brought another body to lay beside the first bundle. It was the man's wife. Without a word, Naomi took the woman's apron and covered her head and upper body.

"So sad." Mattie slumped on the ground. "The whole family, gone like this."

Naomi checked the man once more, then joined Mattie

on the grass. "Thankfully, he never woke to face the loss of his wife and child."

Mattie watched the men. "Jacob and Isaac are still inside. Do you think they'll find more of the family?"

There was sudden movement, and Daed looked toward them. "Mattie, Naomi, we need you."

Mattie ran to the destroyed house, Naomi right behind her. Daed wouldn't call them unless they had found someone alive.

Jacob lifted himself out of the hole, then reached behind him for a small child that Isaac handed up. Jacob carried the boy in his arms and made his way toward Mattie, his face black with dust and soot, streaked where tears had flowed. When he reached Mattie, he turned the boy toward her. He was about four years old, covered in ashes and soot. The sleeves of his shirt were singed, and he had a blistering burn on one hand.

"He was in the fireplace." Jacob's voice was hollow and strained. "Crouched against the stone of the chimney."

Mattie took the boy into her arms and wiped his face with the corner of her apron. "He needs water and food. And we need to take care of his burns. We'll have to take him back to the camp." She looked at Jacob. "There's no one else?"

He shook his head. "Isaac and I looked everywhere. We would have missed the boy if we hadn't heard him crying."

"Has he said anything?"

"Ne. Nothing at all."

Naomi handed Mattie a clean cloth. "He probably only speaks English, and we're speaking Deitsch." She lifted the boy's hand, examining his burns. "What is your name?" she asked in English.

"Davey." The boy started crying and reached for her.

Naomi took him in her arms. "Davey is a good name for

a big, strong boy like you. Can you tell me who else is in your family?"

"Ma, Pa, and baby Pru." Davey looked up into Naomi's face. "I hid, like Pa said. I hid."

"You did right to obey your pa. He would be very proud of you."

Davey laid his head on Naomi's shoulder and closed his eyes, the tears making him snuffle. "I was scared."

"Of course you were."

Naomi bent her head over his, holding him as securely as any mother with her frightened child.

Daed laid his hand on Mattie's shoulder. "How is the father?"

They stepped away from Naomi and Davey. "He died not long after you brought him out of the house. He was injured very badly."

Daed turned to the silent group of men who had gathered. "We need to dig graves. We can't leave them like this."

"What about the boy?" Isaac asked.

Several of the men looked toward Davey then, but he had fallen asleep in Naomi's arms.

Daed shrugged. "We'll have to take care of him until we find someone."

Davey stayed asleep as they lowered his parents and little sister into the graves, the baby in the arms of her mother. Daed prayed as they stood silently around the mounded piles of earth, and Jacob moved close to Mattie. She leaned into his strength, thankful for his presence even though the angry words from their earlier argument still pounded in her ears. In the face of this tragedy, whatever they had argued about seemed insignificant.

21

Jacob wandered around the destroyed cabin, looking for anything that might remain of the young family's lives. The little farm, set back from the road and surrounded by trees and swamp, was isolated. He and Isaac had stayed behind as the rest of the rescue party started back to camp, the little boy still in Naomi's arms. Jacob could see the path the storm had taken from the southwest before hitting the cabin. Northeast of the small clearing in the woods, the storm left a path of downed and broken trees in its wake, but then the trail of destruction disappeared. The storm had either dissipated or taken to the air.

"I want one more look inside the cabin." Jacob lowered himself into the hollow space near the chimney where they had found Davey.

"You don't think you'll find another child, do you?"

Jacob looked up at Isaac, silhouetted against the late afternoon sky. "There might be something left. Something Davey could keep to remind him of his family."

A table had been placed near the fire. Now crushed under

the end of a log, it had held a bowl of bread dough. The cracked bowl came apart in Jacob's hands as he tried to lift it, so he dropped it again. The cradle where they had found the baby listed to one side, and beyond it a chest of some kind lay under the end of another log. He pulled on the logs, but everything shifted and dust filled the streams of sunlight with sparkling motes.

"Are you all right?" Isaac's voice sounded far away.

"Ja, ja, ja." Jacob grunted as he pulled the broken chest into the only open space left. "I've found something."

Isaac dropped down into the cabin beside him and they pulled the broken pieces of the lid off the top. Isaac sorted through the objects in the chest. It was small, only about twenty-four inches long and eighteen high, but it was packed with embroidered linens and clothes. Along one edge was a sheaf of papers.

"These might give some clues to find the boy's family." Isaac packed the papers away again, laid the pieces of the broken lid on top, and lifted the box. "We can take the chest back to camp with us and look through it there."

Once they were out of the cabin again, Jacob hefted the box onto his shoulder. Before leaving, he took a last look at the destroyed house and barn.

"Why do you think this family settled here?"

"I don't know. They should have settled near neighbors." Isaac started toward the road. "Back away from the road like they were, and with no other farm around, it was almost like they were trying to hide. But for a man to try to make a home out of the wilderness without a community to help . . ." He shook his head.

"Do you think Naomi will be able to take care of that

little boy?" Jacob hadn't missed how much Davey looked like Hansli, with his straight white-blond hair. He was the same age as Hansli had been too.

"My sister has a soft heart for any creature that is injured." Isaac pulled a fallen branch to the side of the road. "She'll nurse him back to health." He grinned at Jacob. "Now my baby sister, Mattie, she's the one you seem to be more concerned with."

Jacob felt his face heat and he shifted the chest to his other shoulder, the one near Isaac, but the other man refused to take the hint.

"Mattie's a fine girl," Isaac went on. "Not as tenderhearted as Naomi, but a lot of fun."

Isaac continued, listing Mattie's good qualities. A list Jacob could have written himself.

"There's only one thing." As Jacob spoke, Isaac came up on his other side, the one without his burden. "Your little sister doesn't seem to like me very much right now."

"Don't let that worry you. Mattie is as flighty as a bird sometimes. But when she wants something, she won't give up."

Jacob shifted the box on his shoulder. Mattie had made what she wanted very clear, but following her into the West would be foolishness.

By the time they reached the camp, supper was ready. The blue sky filled with a clear light as the sun lowered behind the surrounding trees, and the air held the sweet freshness that often followed a storm. Jacob glanced at the boy, Davey, sitting on Naomi's lap with a thumb in his mouth and his other hand, the one with the burn, bandaged. The boy's storm had brought him such pain.

After the prayer was said, Jacob took the plate one of the

women handed him and made his way to a bench. He sat next to the chest on the ground and started in on the bean and ham stew. Too many hours had passed since dinnertime.

Johanna and Mattie walked by and Mattie paused, her attention captured by the wooden box sitting at his feet.

"What is that?"

"Isaac and I found it inside the cabin after you left. There are some papers in it that might give a clue to the boy's identity."

Mattie's gaze followed Johanna as her friend continued toward Andrew's seat near the fire, but her feet didn't move.

"You can sit with me." Jacob kept his voice neutral. Their argument still hung in the air between them. "After we eat, we can look through the box."

She sat down, but kept a distance away. "Naomi was hoping you wouldn't find anything."

Jacob followed the direction of her gaze. Naomi sat with her parents, trying to tempt Davey with a piece of cornbread.

"You don't think she wants to keep him, do you?"

"I know she does." Mattie stirred her stew. "I've seen her with hurt kittens or birds, but I've never seen her like this. She wants to be the mother he needs so badly right now."

Jacob watched Davey. The little boy pulled at the bandage on his arm, fussed, and turned away from the offered food. That burn had looked ugly from the glimpse Jacob had gotten of it. A person could die of a burn like that if it became infected.

"She shouldn't get too attached to the boy." Jacob watched the worried frown deepen on Mattie's forehead. "Little ones are fragile. You never know when they're going to take a turn for the worse and die."

Mattie turned to stare at him. "You're awfully callous about it."

He shrugged. "It's the way it is. Children die. They do it all the time." A sharp pain inside made him wince, like picking at a nearly healed scab. He knew too well how quickly a child like Hans—like Davey—could go from playing to dying from an illness in a matter of hours. He shoved at the hurt place, burying it deep.

Mattie's soft hand caressed his arm. "They don't all die." The warmth of her hand penetrated through his shirtsleeve. "I know what you're thinking, but Davey isn't Hansli."

Staring at the little boy on Naomi's lap, Jacob flexed his shoulders, working the tension out of them. Mattie could be right. He nudged the chest with his toe.

"These are Davey's things. Your daed should look through them."

"All right." Mattie took the box and started back to the other side of the camp and her family.

Jacob picked up the pieces of the broken lid and laid them on the bench next to him, arranging them in order like a puzzle. The lid had been made of three boards glued together into one piece, but the damage in the storm had split it along the seams. The top had been carved and painted with flowers and other designs, and German words circled the design. He turned his head, deciphering the words on the cracked surface. "Muller." He traced the letters with his finger. And the date, "17 Juli 1837." A wedding chest. Davey's last name was Muller, and his parents had been married nearly six years ago. He picked up the pieces again. Once the wagons reached Indiana and they were settled, he could glue them back together and repair the chest.

Jacob let his gaze drift across the camp to Mattie. Eli had the papers in his hand and was reading them one by one, but Mattie had lifted a white shawl from the chest and held it up. She stood and swirled it around her shoulders, the fine lace draping like spun gossamer over her Plain dress, transforming her into an English girl before his eyes. She lifted the edge of the shawl with her hand, fingers spread to admire the fine work. But when Eli gave her a frowning shake of his head, she folded the shawl and returned it to the chest.

Mattie. Pledged neither to the church nor to him, she was vulnerable to the world's ways. She had promised she wouldn't leave, but was it enough? Would she keep her promise? He had to keep her safe, whether she thought so or not.

Cole rubbed at his legs, sore from walking for the last two days.

The matched team of black horses he had stolen in Fremont had been too showy. Too distinct. He hadn't been in Perrysburg, on the north end of the Black Swamp, for more than an hour before they had been recognized. He had been in a tavern, sounding out the locals for a horse buyer who wouldn't ask questions, when some boy had raised the alarm. He had been lucky to escape with his own horse and his freedom, but lost the blacks.

That was three days ago, just before that disastrous attempt to make off with the Amish horses. He swore at the memory, making his bay shy. He'd like to know what kind of trick they thought they were playing. But time was getting short. He had to get those horses soon or give up on them.

He wiped his forearm across his brow, the sweat staining

his jacket sleeve. If Darrell hadn't gone and gotten himself killed, he could have left the blacks with him while he routed out the information he needed in Perrysburg. And between the two of them they could have gotten away with the Amish horses that night. But the fool was gone.

And then yesterday his own horse had thrown a shoe, so he was walking to the next town. Except there didn't seem to be any. Miles of wilderness interrupted by a farm or an inn, but no one who could re-shoe his horse.

The road was blocked ahead by a fallen tree. Cole had been walking over small trees and broken branches for the last quarter mile, but a tree this large could only have been toppled by a powerful wind. As he approached it, he looked for a way around. On the north side of the road, the trunk was supported by the crown of branches and the space beneath was high enough for a man to crawl under, but not a horse.

Leading his horse around the twisted roots of the tree took him off the trail and into some marshy ground, but he made it back to the road with little trouble. The horse balked at the edge of the verge, but he pulled at the reins until it was back on the road. The big bay limped behind him until Cole stopped.

"What is the matter with you?"

The horse tossed its head. He was a good horse, the best Cole had ever owned. But a lame horse was useless to him.

He went to the horse's left front hoof and lifted it. The bare hoof was beginning to split along the edge, but a stone caught in the frog was what was causing the limp. Cole pulled out his knife and pried at the stone until it fell out.

"There you go, boy. You'll be good for some more miles, won't you?"

Patting the horse's shoulder, Cole eyed the useless saddle perched on the gelding's back. It was tempting to ride, even for only a few miles. But if he did, the horse would become even lamer, and then where would he be? No. He'd have to find a farrier.

After another half mile, Cole caught the scent of wood smoke on the breeze. Another small farm, perhaps. Or a town. He picked up his pace until he caught sight of the canvas tops from a group of wagons. Keeping to the edge of the road where he could take advantage of the cover the underbrush provided, he drew closer until he could hear voices. He had caught up to those Amish movers again.

Tying the horse to a sapling, he crept forward until he could see the camp and watch the activity. Children played games near the wagons, while a group of women gathered clothing from where they were hung over bushes on the other side of the camp. A couple of the younger men sat near the fire, but both looked pale and weak.

Cole watched until he was sure Mattie wasn't in the group at the campsite. In fact, several of the movers seemed to be missing, including that Jacob Yoder, the one who had confronted him the last time he had run into them. He fished his tobacco out of his pocket and bit off a chaw. The Conestoga horses were picketed at the far edge of the camp, away from the road. If the rest of the group stayed away, tonight would be the perfect time for him to claim his prize. None of the people left in the campsite would oppose him, even if they were aware of what he was doing. He'd have to take the horses through the camp to get them to the road, but if everyone was asleep, that shouldn't be too much of an obstacle.

There was only one problem. Mattie was supposed to be part of that prize.

He hated that he couldn't forget about her. There was no reason in the world that he had to have her, but no other girl had captured him like she had. If he was going to Oregon, she had the spirit and fire to make it there with him. And the journey wouldn't get boring with her along. He flexed his fingers, remembering the feeling of her soft form caught in them.

Voices raised as a kid came running into the camp from the road beyond. Behind him came the rest of the group. Cole spit a stream of tobacco juice toward a nearby tree trunk and wiped his sweaty hands on his britches. Mattie was in the middle of them. No telling where they had been, but they were back, and they seemed excited about something. Mattie fell to the back of the group as everyone else gathered around a small boy with a hurt hand.

Cole dismissed the injured boy from his mind and watched Mattie. If she went into the woods alone, or back along the road, he might be able to head her off. But no. She was watching someone else up the road. That blasted Jacob and another man. Soon they would all be in camp and there would be no chance to go for the horses tonight.

Pulling back into the woods and his horse, Cole turned possibilities over in his mind. These movers were going west, and they'd stick to this road. But how far were they going?

Cursing under his breath, Cole shot a look at his horse as he untied him and started back toward the road. If the gelding hadn't thrown a shoe, he'd be able to follow the Amish movers until they stopped in a good place where he could take the horses. But with a lame horse, Cole himself might as well be crippled. He needed to find a farrier, or another horse. He'd have to go on up the road to the next town. There would be a town up ahead somewhere, and then he'd come back. He could even scout out the best place to waylay them.

He grinned at his own cleverness. He didn't need Hiram and Darrell. He'd do this job on his own, and then head west.

Crossing the road, he circled the campsite through the underbrush. He kept watch, but no one raised an alarm. Once past the Amish, he went back to the road, pulling the horse to a pace faster than they had been going before. He had a plan and itched to put it into action.

22

As Mattie climbed out of the wagon the next morning, the sky was dotted with wispy pink clouds, borne on a light breeze that fluttered the leaves in the tallest treetops. Birds sang in the branches, their music denying the violence of yesterday's storm, but broken tree limbs and scattered leaves were a remaining testimony.

Mattie had awakened often during the night. Davey slept, but his rest was interrupted by dreams or the pain in his burned hand. He would sit up on the pallet between Naomi and Mattie, not quite awake and disoriented in the dark and strange wagon. Eventually Naomi's voice would calm him, singing a nursery song or telling a story to distract him, and he would sleep again until the next nightmare startled him into wakefulness once more. His wounds, both his hand and his heart, would take a long time to heal.

Breakfast was quick and simple. The supplies were running low and they had decided that they needed to save at least half of what they had brought to sustain them for the first months in Indiana, until their first harvest. So dried apples, soaked and stewed, were the only food for the morning meal.

Mattie tied their milk cow, Pet, to the back of the wagon while Daed and Henry hitched up the team. The entire group was subdued this morning. Tired of traveling, Mattie thought. They must be close to their destination, but Yost had said their journey would take at least four more days.

The string of wagons made their way to the road and had started west by the time the sun touched the tops of the trees on the eastern side of the clearing. Mattie looked back at the small meadow at the side of the road. She should remember that place, where Jacob had kissed her for the first time. With the now-familiar sour turning of her stomach, she faced the truth again. Their first, and probably their last kiss. Since their argument, he had been friendly enough, but nothing more than that. No more long looks with their eyes meeting. No more tender touches on her hand or back. The last conversation they had was stilted and formal, with none of the close camaraderie they had shared before. Those few minutes during the storm had been an island of peace in the swirl of their lives. Lives where a kiss didn't make a bit of difference—at least, not to Jacob.

She faced the western road again and looked past the wagon in front of them to the road disappearing in the trees ahead. That view looked no different than the view to the east behind them. They were traveling through an endless forest, hemmed in by trees, the sky a narrow stripe above.

When they passed the ruined cabin, Mattie looked away. If Davey was awake, Naomi was keeping him inside the wagon. He didn't need to see the reminders of the tragedy that had changed his young life so abruptly.

Only a few hundred yards beyond the farm, the signs of storm damage lessened. Soon only a few wilted green leaves lay on the ground where the wind had tossed them. The storm had broken a narrow path through the woods, but a deadly one. Mattie shivered. If the storm had hit their camp with as much force as it had hit the Mullers' farm, would any of them have survived?

Mattie looked up and down the wagon train. She wished for someone to walk with and talk to, but her friends all had others to spend their time with. Johanna rode in the Bontragers' wagon with Andrew, and Naomi was keeping Davey occupied in their wagon. Even Mamm was busy entertaining her young grandchildren in the spring wagon. Jacob . . .

She wouldn't think about Jacob. Mattie kicked at a rock in her way. She liked Jacob. Of course she did. She probably even loved him. But . . . The memory of her dream still haunted her. The pull of what she might find behind that rock wall. The need to find a way through to the other side.

How could he expect her to become his wife when she didn't even know what she wanted yet?

"Mattie, slow down."

Johanna's call came from behind, and she stepped out of the path of the wagons to let her friend catch up.

"Can I walk with you?"

"I thought you were riding with Andrew."

"He needs to rest, and I'm ready to walk for a while anyway. I get so tired of riding all the time."

They fell in behind the Bontragers' wagon, the last one in line.

Mattie looked sideways at Johanna. "Are you thinking of marrying Andrew?"

Johanna blushed. "Why wouldn't I? I can't imagine not

spending the rest of my life with him." She leaned closer to Mattie and spoke with a lowered voice. "I worried when he was so ill. What if he never recovered? What if the illness left him so weak he wouldn't be able to support a family? Then where would we be?"

"But he is recovering, isn't he? You don't have to worry."

"But I still think about it. What would I do without him?"

Mattie tried to imagine her life without Jacob. Now that he was part of her world again, she wasn't ready to change that. But the plans he had . . . he didn't understand how they made her feel like her feet were mired in the mud.

"What about you?" Johanna continued. "You and Jacob have gotten quite close, haven't you? Has he talked about marriage?"

"We were always friends, even as children."

"He doesn't look like he's thinking of you as a child." Johanna hid her mouth in her hand. "I think he's smitten with you."

"I don't think I'm ready to set up housekeeping, though."

"Why not?" Johanna stopped walking, her eyes round. "What else would you do?"

"Don't you feel like there's more to life?"

Mattie walked on for a few steps and Johanna hurried to catch up with her. "What can be more important than building a home with the man you love?"

"I know that's what you want, and what Naomi wants, but I'm not sure I do. What if there's something better out there?" Mattie waved her hand toward the west. She stopped walking and faced Johanna. "Don't you worry that once you marry Andrew, one of you might discover that you've made the wrong choice? What would you do then?"

Johanna took Mattie's hand in hers. "I'll tell you what my mamm always said: 'Choose your love and love your choice.'"

"What does that mean?"

Johanna kept walking. "You choose to marry because you fall in love with someone. But then hard times might come, or troubles of other kinds, and you might feel that the love is disappearing. That's when you have to choose to love your husband because you are married to him." She smiled. "I don't quite understand what she meant, because I can't imagine my love for Andrew being threatened. But I will remember that we need to choose to love, even when we don't feel like it."

"Like we choose to love our brothers when they tease us too much."

Johanna laughed. "Ja, like that."

"But . . ." Mattie felt the thread of her dreams slipping from her fingers.

"But what?"

"What if there is something more?"

Johanna shrugged. "You decide to be content with the life God has given you. Why would you want more than that?"

Andrew peered out the back of the Bontrager wagon and waved to them. Johanna ran ahead to talk to him, but Mattie stayed in her place, trailing behind the wagons. Decide to be content with what God has given her? But what if he was the one who had placed this desire in her for the wide spaces and open skies of the west? She wouldn't want to disobey God.

Mattie watched Andrew's face as he talked with Johanna. He must have shared some joke with her, because his face broke into that carefree grin she knew so well. He and Johanna would be happy together.

The line of wagons slowed, then stopped. Mattie went to the side of the road to look ahead and saw the reason. A freight wagon was stopped at the edge of the gravel and dirt road. She walked ahead to hear the conversation between Daed and the freighter.

"Are you having troubles?"

Daed spoke in English to a short, round man standing next to the road. The wagon was the kind Mattie had seen several times on their journey. Made for hauling freight on smooth roads, it was shaped like an oblong box. A canvas cover was pulled tight over the load inside, and another man was lying on top of the load. He was still. Too still.

"Troubles and then some, neighbor." The man's face was red and angry. "Horse thieves struck us in the night. Shot my partner." He pointed toward the body on the wagon with a jab of his finger. "Stole the team. Left me here to rot."

The other men gathered around Daed, listening to the conversation.

"Your partner is—"

"Dead. Dead and gone." The man spit brown juice onto the ground. "Horse thieves and murderers. They should be hanged. Every one of them."

"How many were there?" That was Jacob's voice asking the question.

"I don't know. Took us by surprise. Bill here shot at them, but he was in the firelight, and they shot back. Then they were gone with the horses and Bill was bleeding out on the ground." The round man spit again.

Mattie backed away from the men as they continued talking. The man had said it was horse thieves, and that might mean Cole. But murder?

She turned over the memory of his threats to kill Jacob the first night after they left the Swamp. He had been forceful, and she had believed him then. But to go beyond the threats and actually kill someone? It couldn't have been Cole.

They took their leave of the man after promising to stop by the freight company office in Angola and send help back for him.

"You watch out for them thieves too," the man called after them as they pulled away. "Those horses of yours will be prime targets. Watch your backs!"

Mattie joined Johanna again, and as they passed by him at the rear of the line, the short little man winked at them, then sent a stream of brown tobacco juice off to the side.

"He doesn't seem to be too upset about his friend." Johanna moved to the side of the road, as far from the freighter's camp as she could get.

"Losing the horses made him angry, though. Maybe he didn't like his partner very much."

"Do you think we're in danger from the horse thieves, like he said?"

Mattie shook her head. "They were only two men and ready for a fight. We'll be safe with our daeds and the other men. And we won't resist the thieves, so no one should get hurt."

"The thieves had to be those Bates brothers, don't you think? Who else would be around here?" Johanna shuddered. "I don't want to think about it anymore. Let's hurry and catch up with Naomi. I want to see how Davey is doing."

Mattie stopped as Johanna ran ahead, and turned to peer back down the road. A man had been killed there last night. Killed by horse thieves. Cole couldn't be that evil.

∞

When they stopped for the noon meal, Jacob unharnessed the horses while Josef rubbed them down and gave them each a drink from the canvas bucket.

They had reached Angola midmorning. On the way through the town, Yost and Eli had found the freight office and sent help back to the man stranded along the road.

"Do you really think they'd hang those horse thieves if they find them?" Jacob asked as he pulled the harness off the last horse of the team.

"Ja, I'm thinking so, since a man was killed." Josef hung the bucket on its hook on the side of the wagon. "Do you think they will find them, though?"

Jacob shrugged. "I didn't see any sign of the stolen horses along the road. And the freighter didn't know how many men there were. What if there was only one?"

"You are talking of that Cole Bates?"

"We know he's still around, and he is a horse thief."

Josef gathered the picket ropes in his hand. "Ja, ja, ja. But is he a murderer?"

Jacob couldn't shake off the feeling of evil that came over him every time Bates's name came up. "I think he could be."

After the horses had been cared for, Jacob took his dinner plate to a shady spot next to the wagon. From here he could watch the rest of the group. Mattie caught his attention more than anyone else. She prepared a plate of food for Naomi, and then held it while Naomi tried to get Davey to eat. The little boy sat on her lap like a half-empty sack of cornmeal, turning his head away every time she brought a spoonful of mush to his mouth. Jacob looked away and took a bite of his own plate of mush sweetened with syrup. Hot and filling, it satisfied his empty stomach.

When he had scraped his plate clean, he took it to the women washing dishes, and then glanced at Mattie again. She was holding Davey while Naomi ate her own dinner, but the boy cried and fussed in her arms. He looked hot and feverish, and Jacob's stomach turned. The white-blond hair was wet and matted to the boy's forehead, just like Hansli's had been. His face was pale, with bright red blotches on his cheeks, just like Hansli.

Jacob went back to the wagon and stretched out on the grass to rest, covering his face with his hat. But he couldn't erase the memory of Hansli's face the last time he had seen him alive. Naomi and Mattie were both doting over the little English boy, but what would happen when he died? And he was going to die. It didn't matter how strong and sturdy he was, he was going to die just like Hansli did. No amount of loving care could prevent the inevitable.

He mentally shook himself and pushed away that black tide. There was no reason to think what happened to Hansli would be Davey's fate too. He tried to turn his thoughts away, but it was Cole Bates who intruded next, with the echo of his confident tone when he told Jacob that Mattie would go west with him.

Jacob's eyes popped open and he sat up, pushing his hat into place. He clasped his arms around his knees and leaned his forehead on them. He swallowed, his throat dry. As sure as the sun rose in the east, his Mattie was in danger in spite of her pledge. Her own desire to go west was just the enticement a man like Bates needed to lure her away.

He lifted his head again, swiping his hand across his face,

trying to erase the images that kept his mind reeling. He wouldn't get any rest this way.

Leaving the quiet noon camp, he walked to the grassy spot where Josef had picketed their horses with the others. A few of the big horses grazed, but most of them stood sideways to the sun, one hip cocked and their heads hanging. Tails swished at flies, but other than that, every horse was relaxed and calm. There was no danger that they were aware of.

He passed the horses and wandered toward the road. Except for the croaking of frogs deep in the woods and an occasional fly, all was quiet in the early afternoon sun. Nothing moved on the road except a garter snake flicking its way through the dust in the wheel track. With trees rising on both sides of the road, shadows dappled its grassy edges, rippling in the slight breeze.

Jacob stared at a dimple in the grass at the edge of the dusty road, now in sunshine, now in shadow. Kneeling close, he traced the mark with his finger. A hoofprint. And another. What he had thought was grass beaten down by wind or rain was a trail of hoofprints in the grass, off the road where they wouldn't be noticed by the normal traveler. Crouched close to the ground as he was, he could see the pattern leading to the west.

Glancing back toward the camp, he saw no one moving about yet, so he followed the trail along the road. There had been several horses, and one without a shoe. That horse must have been following the rest, since its prints overlaid the others. Every few yards, one of that horse's other hooves came down heavy, leaving a divot. The horse was lame, then, and either the owner didn't notice or didn't care.

At a sudden thought, Jacob straightened. A horse thief

wouldn't care. He could almost see Bates riding one of the stolen horses, leading the others behind in a string with the lame one following at the end. He peered into the distance where the road disappeared into the trees. His throat constricted, as the sure thought came to him. Somewhere ahead was the horse thief, Cole Bates, waiting for them.

When Davey finally drifted off to sleep, Mattie spread a blanket in the shade of the wagon for Naomi to lay him on.

"It seems his fever has lessened some, don't you think?" Naomi smoothed the fine light blond hair off the little boy's brow.

"He feels cooler." Mattie sat on the other side of Davey. She had retrieved the quilt block she was sewing when she got the blanket from the wagon and now she turned it over in her hands. Where had she left the needle? She found it in a seam and then fished in her bag for the spool of thread.

Naomi hadn't moved, but still stroked Davey's forehead. She had a look in her eyes that Mattie had seen before, when a stray cat with a broken tail had shown up at their farm back in Brothers Valley.

"You want to keep him, don't you?"

"Well, don't you?" Naomi bit her lip and looked down at the ground. Whenever Naomi was worried or upset about something, she had trouble making both of her eyes focus on the same thing.

"What is it?"

Naomi straightened the lock of white-blond hair one more time, then clasped her arms around her knees. "He needs us, Mattie. He needs me."

"He isn't Amish. He doesn't even understand when we talk."

"He can learn."

"And he needs a mother. A family."

Naomi met Mattie's gaze with her right eye. "I can be his mother. We can be his family."

"Think about what you're saying. He isn't a lost kitten or a bird with a broken wing. He's a little boy."

"I can't explain how I feel, but I know it is right."

Mattie sighed.

The corners of Naomi's mouth quivered. "Why don't you say what you're thinking?"

"What is that?"

Naomi laid her hand on Davey's chest, her fingers rising and falling with his soft breathing. "You're thinking that no man will marry a girl who has a son, and an English son, at that." Tears filled her eyes. "I wouldn't want to marry a man who couldn't understand why I'm doing this, so maybe you're right. Maybe I won't ever get married." She straightened Davey's curled legs and he sighed in his sleep. "But I think the exchange is worth it."

"Have you talked with Mamm and Daed about this?"

"They think it will be good for Davey to have a family adopt him."

"A family, Naomi, not a single woman."

"We talked about that too. But they still gave me their blessing, and said they would help." Naomi looked into Mattie's eyes. "More than anything, Davey needs a mother."

"What if . . ." Mattie stopped, not sure if she should mention her fears, but Naomi watched her face, waiting. "What if he doesn't get better?"

296

Naomi sighed. "His burned hand is healing, but he still doesn't take any interest in the other children. I think he will get better, but he needs to learn our language."

"That will come with time." Mattie threaded her needle and found the next patch to sew onto the block. "He's been through quite an ordeal." She looked at Naomi. Her sister hadn't slept more than a couple of hours at a time since they had found Davey.

"Why don't you lie down while he's sleeping? I'll be here to watch him."

Naomi stifled a yawn. "I could take a nap until it's time to start moving again."

"Shh." Mattie put a finger to her lips. "Get some sleep."

While Davey and Naomi slept, Mattie pushed her needle in and out of the short seam. Naomi's marriage quilt was taking shape, but would she ever get to use it?

She finished the seam and laid the quilt block in her lap. Davey was dreaming, his fingers twitching, and his knees jerking in his sleep. She reached to soothe him, but his face screwed up into a cry.

"Mama!"

Naomi sat up, turning to gather him in her arms. "It's all right, little one. I'm here."

"No, no." Davey pushed at her, his eyes wide with fright. "You're not my mama. Where is she? I want my mama."

With those words, he broke into sobs, but he wouldn't let Naomi comfort him. The more she tried to capture his flailing arms in hers, the harder he struck at her. She sat back, letting him cry.

Mattie reached out again to try to soothe him, but he struck at her too. By then Mamm had knelt on the blanket with them. Davey's sobs had subsided into soft cries, but he still refused to let any of them touch him. He turned face-down on the blanket, burying his head in his arms.

"What do I do, Mamm?" Naomi asked. "How can I get him to stop?"

"You'll just have to let him cry it out."

"But what do I tell him when he stops? If he's like this now, how will he react when he finds out what happened?"

Mamm gazed at the little boy, his hoarse sobs slowing into deep coughs. "Poor boy. I think he already knows, but it is becoming real for him and he doesn't know how to face it." She took Naomi's hand in her own. "Now is the time when he needs you the most."

Naomi shook her head. "Didn't you hear him? Didn't you see him?" Tears trickled down her cheeks. "He doesn't want me. Maybe someone else would be better for him."

Mattie's own eyes itched as tears threatened. Naomi loved Davey with that same fierce protective love she had seen in other mothers, but if he rejected her, what could she do?

Mamm frowned. "Will you give up so easily? We don't love our children only when they want us to. If you're going to be his mother, you need to love him more at times like this."

Davey still had his head buried in his arms, wet snuffles making his shoulders shake.

"You need to tell him the truth about his parents. And you need to assure him that he has a home here." Mamm reached up to caress Naomi's cheek. "You need to decide what is best for the two of you, if you're going to take on this responsibility."

Davey lifted his head, his face red and splotchy.

"Are you feeling better?" Naomi said to him in English, and then repeated the question in Deitsch.

He nodded and crawled into her lap. Naomi wrapped her arms around him, rocking him as she sat on the blanket. She laid her cheek on his head.

"I will tell you a story."

Mamm stood and grasped Mattie's hand, leading her away from the two of them.

"We need to let Naomi do this alone."

"Will she be all right?" Mattie turned Mamm to look into her face. "I mean, you're sure she'll be a good mother for Davey?"

Mamm smiled. "I think the Lord brought the two of them together. They need each other, don't you think?"

"But shouldn't he be in a family?"

"You're right. When we adopt children, we would normally seek a family to take them in. But this little boy needs so much love and attention right now. If Isaac or Noah took him as part of their families, he wouldn't get the same devotion that Naomi can give him." She took Mattie's hand and squeezed it. "Your daed and I believe this is what the Lord is telling us to do. Davey will have a home with Naomi as long as he needs it."

"But"—Mattie looked back at Naomi, holding Davey close as she told him of his parents' death—"what about Naomi's future? What man will want to raise a son that isn't his?"

"We leave that in the Lord's hands. After all, he chose Joseph to raise Jesus, didn't he?"

Mamm went to help Miriam with her little ones as the camp started to prepare for the afternoon's travel, and Mattie watched as Davey flung his arms around Naomi's neck, hugging her with all his might.

Naomi knew what God was calling her to do with her life. Mattie looked up at the overhanging treetops. Would he ever speak to her in the same way?

23

Cole woke to late afternoon sunlight piercing the canopy above him. He grabbed at the deerfly circling his nose, but missed. The pesky things would eat a man alive.

Scratching at the welts on his neck, Cole pushed away from the tree root he had used as a pillow. Living in the open wasn't his idea of luxury, but it would be temporary. He let his eyes rest on the four draft horses picketed next to the stream, cropping at the sparse grass. A good catch, these were. Nearly as good as those Conestoga horses the Amish movers had. They'd bring a good price in Independence.

He went to the stream and cupped the cold water in his hand, drinking before splashing the back of his neck and his face. He bent to submerge his hair in the stream and came up shaking like a dog, causing the horses to startle.

"Whoa, horses. Whoa." His voice calmed them.

He walked to the closest one and patted its shoulder. The matched team of Clydesdales all stood between seventeen and eighteen hands at the withers, towering over him as he walked between them. But they were well trained and gentle. They had followed him willingly since he had taken them from the freighters last night, even while he made the large circle around the town of Angola, following deer trails through the thick woods in the moonlight.

Pulling their picket pins, he moved each horse to a different grazing area. He needed to be sure they could reach both the grass and the stream before he left them. Cole patted the final horse.

"You're a beauty." He stroked the powerful neck, then ran his hand over the chest and down the front leg.

The best team he had seen in a long time, and worth the time and trouble to keep them in good shape.

Standing to the side with its head down was the bay gelding. It balanced on three legs, holding the left front one up with the hoof just touching the ground. It had finally gone lame during their escape from the freighters, holding them back all night long. Cole had fumed at the drag on the end of the line of horses, but he couldn't leave it behind on the road as a beacon to any lawmen who might be following.

He hated to give the horse up, but it was no use to him like this. He cursed his bad luck. With rest the beast would recover, but he didn't have time to rest. The Amish were coming along behind him, and he needed to choose his ground, be in control. Take them off guard and claim his prize.

The gelding shied as he approached it, but then stood quietly as he removed the halter and picket rope. The bay might follow the other horses for a mile or so when they headed south to Missouri, but eventually it would lag behind. Someone would run across it and think themselves lucky to find such a fine animal.

Leaving the horses in camp, he threaded his way through the underbrush toward the road a quarter mile north. When he heard the sound of teams and wagons on the highway, he halted in the shadows well away from the road. A string of freight wagons passed by, each of the five wagons with a four-horse team. The teams glistened with sweat, white foam marking the line of the harnesses. The afternoon was warm, but not that hot. The freighters were pushing their teams hard. He eyed the men on the wagon seat next to each of the drivers. They were armed and watchful. Whatever they were hauling in those wagons, it was valuable.

Cole licked his lips and tasted salt from his own sweat beaded on his skin. He itched to follow those freighters and capture the booty, but Pa had been adamant in his instructions. They were to take only the horses, not the wagons. Wagons couldn't travel as fast as a man on horseback, and they were too easy to track. A man could disappear with horses, especially if he had gotten them from greenhorns.

The men guarding those wagons were no greenhorns. Cole slid behind a tree as one of them peered into the underbrush, nearly meeting his eyes. When this bunch stopped for the night, they'd post a watchman. Probably hobble the horses too. No, this job was too risky. Pa wouldn't even try it. Cole could hear his voice in his head: "The wily fox takes the easy pickin's."

These weren't easy pickings.

The wagons passed on down the road and out of sight. Cole made his way to the edge of the gravel and dirt expanse, listening and watching. Other than the receding jingle of harnesses from the freighters' wagons, he didn't hear anyone on the road.

He set up a broken branch, making it look as if it had fallen to this spot, leaning against an old log covered in shelf fungus. It had to look natural, and he needed to be able to spot it when he came back this way. Otherwise he'd never find those horses hidden by the stream again. He stepped back. Yeah, he'd be able to spot it.

Sure of his bearings, Cole headed east. He had to locate those Amish movers before he could work out a plan to get the horses and that girl.

"By tomorrow night, we'll reach LaGrange," Yost Bontrager announced as they set up camp that evening. "We'll head west from there toward the area where last year's settlers purchased land. We've almost reached our destination."

Mattie had expected to feel some relief when the news came, or elation like the rest of the group, but she turned away from Naomi and Mamm and hid herself behind the wagon. In two days, three at the most, they would be finished traveling. Nearly a month on the road, and nothing had changed. Still hemmed in by trees all around, trapped by the narrow road. Indiana was no different than Brothers Valley, except the rolling hills weren't as steep. Her eyes burned. When Daed had said they were moving west, she had expected . . . what? She took a few more steps away from the others. Whatever she had expected, it wasn't this smothering forest.

She fumbled for the water bucket hanging on the side of the wagon.

"I'm going to find some water," she called out, not caring if anyone heard or not.

The woods reached out to her with eager fingers, pulling her in. She followed a slope downhill, hopefully toward a stream. The beeches and maples gave way to a stand of white pine trees. Their soft needles brushed her arms as she passed through, her footsteps soundless on the carpet of pine needles. Slowing her steps, she held her hand open to the long pine needles that swept over her palm with graceful strokes. Looming above the seedlings and young trees were straight, bare trunks with crowns far above that sheltered their pine tree children below, dancing in the light breeze. As she entered the stand of mature trees, the seedlings disappeared. Brown pine needles carpeted the ground between the trunks, dampening any noise from the outside world.

The slope grew steeper and Mattie let it lead her to the bottom of a dell. The small depression was dry. Mattie shifted the bucket to her other hand and turned in a circle to get her bearings. Pines surrounded her, marching up the shallow slopes. Heading back the way she had come wouldn't help her find water, so she went in a different direction. There must be a stream or spring nearby.

When she reached the top of this slope, she was still surrounded by the soft pine trees. Checking the direction of the sun so she wouldn't get lost, she started down the far side of the slope. Partway down, the pines ended in an open meadow with willows here and there. On the far side, beyond a band of reeds and other shore plants, water shone in the sunlight. A lake. It was too far from the camp for carrying water, but perhaps they could catch some fresh fish for supper.

She started across the meadow. Halfway across her foot suddenly sank into a muddy hole up to her ankle. Mattie pulled it out, then stepped back into another soggy spot covered with grass. Between here and the lake, fifty yards away, the ground grew wetter. Standing pools of water glistened in the late afternoon sun, narrow mounds of weeds and grass twisting between them. Cattails grew everywhere, their grasslike leaves still short and barely showing among the other plants. Here in the open the sun shone hot. Deerflies circled her head in their whining hunt for bare skin, and delicate damselflies lowered their needlelike bodies toward the surface of the oily, rank water.

There was nothing else to do but to go back. She turned around and retraced her steps, but somehow, when she reached the trees she was in a stand of cottonwoods, not the tall pines.

She fingered the pail's handle and looked around. The lake was still there, across the marshy meadow, and the slope still rose above her. She should go back to the camp, then she could tell the others about the lake. When Henry came back with her, they could get some water and maybe even catch a few fish. All she needed to do was go to her left to the pine trees, and then she'd be on her way back to camp.

Once in the pines, she walked up the slope, away from the lake. At the top of the rise, she checked the sun. It was behind her . . . but it should be on her left. Her stomach sank with a twisting wrench. She couldn't be lost. She turned toward the north, keeping the sun firmly on her left, and started down the slope. She came to a stand of black raspberries and stopped. The canes were thick to her right, following a clearing down the slope and toward the east. She turned left to go around the prickly plants, back up another slope.

At the top, she stopped again, out of breath. The sun was below the top branches of the trees directly in front of her.

"I won't panic."

As she watched the sun, it seemed to sink even farther.

"I can't panic." She took a deep breath. "When I left the camp, I went south. So if I go north, I'll eventually come to the road, even if I don't come to the camp first. And once I'm on the road, I'll be able to find the camp."

Mattie grasped the pail's handle to keep her fingers from trembling. She had a plan, but she must find the road before the sun set.

She turned to the right, keeping the sun on her left once more, and walked. No matter what, she must keep the sun on her left.

The air around her turned dusky, even though the sky through the branches above her was still a bright blue. Mattie hurried, stumbling over sticks and the uneven ground. Finally, just when she thought she would have to spend the night in the woods, she stepped into an open place. The road.

Mattie sank onto the grass at the edge of the dirt highway, trying to catch her breath. She could cry from the relief of the sight of the narrow dirt ribbon through the trees, but she had to keep going. It would be dark soon, and she needed to get back to camp before then. Her family was probably already worried about her.

She had walked down the road for nearly a mile before remembering that she had left the pail behind where she had rested.

"I'll go back for it in the morning."

Her voice sounded thin in the growing darkness. Once she reached the camp, she would never be so foolish as to go on an errand by herself in a strange place. She spoke louder, letting her words push against the dusk.

"Keep walking, and don't worry. You'll be back in the camp before you know it."

A shadow moved in the trees at the side of the road.

"You won't find it that way, Mattie-girl." Cole stepped into the road, his teeth gleaming in the dusky shadows of his face. "Your folks are camping a couple miles back. I knew you would be willing to come with me, but I didn't know you'd be so eager that you'd come to find me."

"No." She shook her head, taking another step back. "I got lost."

He moved close enough to grasp her arm, but she jerked it out of his reach.

"You know that isn't true. You saw me scouting out your camp this afternoon, didn't you?"

"I don't know what you're talking about."

He grinned at her. "I'm going to take the horses tonight, then we'll be off to the west. Just you and me. You coming to find me like this makes things so much easier."

Mattie clasped her shaking hands together. "Why do you think I'd go west with you? I won't leave my family."

Cole chuckled, low in his throat, and took a slow step closer. "I've seen it in your eyes, love." He lifted her chin with his finger. "Every time I mention Oregon, your face lights up."

His eyes seemed to glow in the growing darkness. Every star that strained to shine in the deepening blue sky was reflected in the obsidian flecks. Mattie spun to flee back down the road, but tripped and fell headlong in the dirt and gravel. Cole was standing over her before she could move.

"Oh, Mattie-girl." His voice was tender, crooning, but the hand that grasped her arm was as hard as flint. "It's too dark to be wandering down the road alone. You can stay with me tonight. I'll take good care of you."

He lifted her close to him in the dark, and Mattie flinched

as he pulled her kapp from her hair and loosened the long strands. "I need to wait a few hours before I fetch that lovely string of horses from your folks. We can have some fun while we wait, don't you think?"

She tried to tear her arm out of his grasp, but his fingers only dug in tighter.

"Don't fight me." He knotted her hair in his other hand and forced her close to him. His breath singed her cheek. "We both know you came to look for me. Do you think your friends will believe anything different?" Cole tugged her closer and whispered in her ear. "You're mine, Mattie-girl. You've been mine since the first time we met."

"No." Mattie struggled, but his hold was too tight.

"We're going west together, just like you wanted. I need those Conestoga horses for a stake, and then we'll head off to Oregon. Just you and me."

"I don't want to go with you."

His confident chuckle raised the hair on the back of Mattie's neck. "You will. You don't have any choice." His breath in her ear chilled her skin. "Your reputation is ruined now. No matter what you tell that Amish sweetheart of yours, he'll never believe you didn't come looking for me." He leaned away from her, stroking her cheek as he watched her face. "And I'll swear to him that you came of your own free will. Even if he found you and took you back, he'd always doubt you, wouldn't he? That smug face of his would never smile at you. Every time he looked at you, he'd think of me kissing you, and he'd always wonder whose kisses you liked better."

Mattie shuddered as his fingers slid to her neck. He leaned closer, his eyes gleaming in the faint starlight. Bile rose in her throat as she realized he was going to kiss her. She turned her head, grasping his fingers between her teeth, and bit down as hard as she could.

He screamed, then cut it short in a grunt as he caught her jaw in a swing from the bitten hand. He didn't let go of her hair, but dragged her to a tree and threw her against it. The rising moon, nearly full, shone on him as he stood above her, cradling his hand and swearing at her. He grabbed her kapp from the ground and wrapped his hand, holding the makeshift compress against his bleeding fingers with his good hand.

Mattie pulled her knees up, getting her feet under her so that she could try to run, but he kicked at her legs, jerking them out straight.

"Don't you think about trying to get away." His voice shook as he tried to control it. "This doesn't change anything, except that the trip to Oregon isn't going to be as comfortable for you as it could have been." He leaned down and pulled her toward him with his good hand. "I need to put you somewhere safe until I get this job done. Come on."

He flicked her wrinkled and bloody kapp off his hand and picked up his hat. He started into the woods, pulling Mattie by the arm, dragging her when she stumbled on her stiff, cold feet. When she tried to pull out of his grasp once, he whirled around and caught her again with the back of his hand.

"My pa might be a lousy father, but he taught me the right way to treat women. You try to get away again, and I'll kill you."

Terror gave way to rage, filling Mattie's breast with a white-hot, reckless sword. "You murdered that freighter."

He pulled her toward him, his face distorted. "Who told you that?"

"No one. I knew as soon as I saw the man's body, even though I didn't want to believe it."

Cole's face turned calm, his eyes as cold as ever. "No one can prove it, and if you think I'll be easier on you to keep you quiet, you've got another think coming."

Cole grabbed her hair and pushed her along in front of him. The moon was nearly overhead when they came to a clearing and the light shone bright, revealing four horses picketed near a stream. Cole's saddle lay on the ground at the base of the tree he thrust her against. He pulled a rope out of his saddlebag and tugged her arms around the tree, tying them behind her. She tested her bonds, struggling to get free, but his knots were tight. She was helpless.

Cole caught her chin in one hand and turned her face to the moonlight, grinning when she winced. "I'm not sure which of us got the worst of your first lesson, Mattie-girl. You got me good with that bite, but I gave you some bruises that will last for a while." He squeezed the sore jaw tighter. "Just remember that the next time you want to show me some sass. I give back as good as I get, and I always win."

He bent toward her then and caught her mouth in a kiss, rough and possessive. He pulled away, breathing hard and fast, and ran a finger along her sore mouth. "I'll be back with those Conestogas, Mattie-girl, and then we'll ride for Missouri."

24

Jacob and Josef took charge of the teams of horses as the group made camp. With thieves around, they needed to take care with them, whether Cole Bates was involved or not.

Josef fashioned hobbles from a length of soft cotton rope Yost had in the Bontrager wagon, and they used them to restrain each of the horses. Hobbling made it difficult for the horses to walk quickly, and trotting or running was out of the question, ensuring that the horses wouldn't be easy to steal. By the time Jacob had helped Josef hobble the last horse, stars had begun to appear in the sky and supper was ready.

It wasn't until he was seated with Josef and Andrew that Jacob realized he hadn't seen Mattie. He took a bite of the stewed beans. Naomi and little Davey weren't around either. The boy's hand must have gotten worse, and Mattie was helping to care for him.

After supper, though, when he took his plate to the dishpan to be washed, Naomi was there, drying and stacking the plates as Johanna washed them.

"Mattie must be with the boy?"

Naomi's towel stopped circling the plate in her hand. "Ne. Davey is sleeping. I haven't seen Mattie since we made camp. I thought she was helping you with the horses."

Jacob ignored the sinking feeling in his stomach.

He found Henry sitting near the Schrock wagon, finishing his own supper.

"Have you seen Mattie?"

Henry shook his head. "I heard her say something about getting water when we made camp. Isn't she here?"

"I don't know yet." Jacob gazed at the faces around the camp. Beyond the circle of the campfire, darkness reigned, but here in the shelter of the wagons, each familiar face glowed with the dancing light from the fire. He patted Henry on the shoulder. "She's probably in one of the wagons. I'll look around for her."

Jacob circled behind the wagons, but there was no sign of Mattie. He peered into the black underbrush at the edge of the clearing and the thick trees that towered above him. He didn't want to raise an alarm unless it was necessary, but where was she?

He made his way to Eli Schrock as he sat with the other men, discussing the trail ahead. Eli looked up as Jacob approached.

"Is something wrong? You look worried."

Jacob tried to clear his brow. "I don't know if there's anything wrong or not, but I haven't seen Mattie since we made camp."

Eli stood and called for everyone's attention. "Has anyone seen Mattie this evening?"

Mose stepped forward. "I saw her take a pail and go that

way." He pointed into the woods. "She said she was going to find water."

"Did anyone see her come back?"

Silence met his question, and Jacob's stomach turned over. Mattie was missing. Lost in the woods? Or did she break her pledge to him and disappear to the west?

Eli turned to the men around him. "We need to search for her."

"It is dark already." Josef stood next to Eli. "We should make torches, and go out to search in pairs. We know she went into the woods, but she may have come out to the road either east or west of us. I suggest that we search all three areas."

The men agreed with Josef's plan. With Andrew and Noah staying behind to watch for her return to the camp, the rest of the men split into three pairs. Eli headed for the woods as soon as his torch was lit, followed by Henry. Mattie's brother Isaac, along with Yost Bontrager, started down the road, heading east. Jacob picked up his torch and glanced at Josef. At his nod, they started down the road toward the west.

"Do you think she could have made it to the road?" Jacob slowed his pace, letting Josef catch up with him.

"Unless she got turned around in the woods. But if Mattie realized she was lost, I think she would have thought clearly enough to head north, knowing she would find the road."

Not if she had planned to run away the entire time. Jacob shook his head, trying to clear out the thoughts that crowded in. He couldn't have been so wrong about Mattie. Not his Mattie.

Stars shone in the sky ahead of them. The moon wasn't up yet, and at the pace he was walking, Jacob would miss any sign she might have left when she came out of the woods.

He slowed and held the torch in front of him, lighting the ground along the road.

"Look!" Josef ran ahead and picked up something from the grass. "Bring the light. I think it is the pail from the Schrock wagon."

Jacob held the torch near the wooden bucket. "There is the plugged knothole in the side. Ja, for sure this is the Schrocks' water pail."

He lifted the torch high and looked up and down the road. "Mattie!" As loud as he called, it seemed his voice was swallowed by the crowding trees.

"If she had gone east from this point, she would have arrived back at the camp." Josef started walking west. "So she went this way."

"Wait." Jacob stood in the grass where they had found the pail. Mattie had been here, and had gone west. Why had she dropped the bucket? Why hadn't she come back to the camp? He shook down the suspicions that crowded his mind. "We need to tell the others we found this clue. One of us needs to go back."

Josef turned around. "You are right. I will go back to the camp while you go on. I'll give the message and then catch up to you as soon as I can."

Jacob watched until Josef was beyond the circle of light from the torch. Overhead, the sky had turned black, with stars shining in a ribbon above the gap in the trees.

He had taken a dozen steps to the west before he had the thought that she could have gone back into the trees at some point. She wouldn't if she was looking for their camp, but if she had come to meet Cole—

Breaking that thought off with a groan, he continued

walking, but kept the torch raised in his left hand so that he could see the grassy edge of the road. After more than a mile, he saw a gap in the trees. Jacob stood in the spot, holding his torch close to the ground and the trampled grass. Someone had been here this evening, but where were they now?

Casting the torch in a wider circle, he spied a white cloth on the ground. His stomach clenched when he recognized Mattie's kapp. He picked it up and sank onto a fallen log. The torch dangled, forgotten in his hand as he buried his face in the white cloth. Mattie's fragrance of mingled soap and wood smoke filled his senses. Leaving her kapp behind was something she would never do . . . unless she had turned her back on her family and the Amish community.

He turned it over in his fingers, pushing at the wave of anger that crested and broke over his head. His Mattie, stolen by an Englisher, just as Liesbet had been. He had known she was in danger, but she had given him her pledge. She had promised she wouldn't go west with Cole or anyone like him. She had lied to him. Lied. And he had been fool enough to believe her.

The flickering light from the torch caught a dark spot on the kapp, and he held it closer to the light. Dark red, and still wet. Blood.

His fingers grew cold, but at the same time a bubble of hope rose. Perhaps Mattie had fought back. Maybe she hadn't left her kapp behind by choice.

Jacob rose to his feet and paced the length of the opening and back. He didn't have to wonder who she had fought with. It had to be Bates. And it wasn't very long ago. Bates had taken her away from this spot . . . he must have been afraid that someone would look for her.

The flame of the torch forgotten in his hand guttered and he lifted it up, trying to preserve the light. Cole Bates was right to be worried. He should know that Jacob would follow Mattie until he found her and brought her home.

Mattie opened her eyes. The moon had moved toward the western treetops, but still filled the small clearing with its light. She must have slept.

Her shoulders ached from being stretched around the tree in this unnatural position. She tugged, testing the rope Cole had used to tie her once more, but her sore shoulders kept her from using any strength in the pull.

She let her chin drop forward. Her hair, loosened from its normal bonds, hung along the sides of her face. One of the horses shifted its feet and blew. Mattie lifted her head and stared at it. Four horses. A matched team. Something pounded at the fog that filled her head. The freighter. He had described the stolen horses. She let her head fall back against the tree trunk. She had been right. It was Cole who had stolen the horses. Cole who had shot that freighter and killed him.

Cole who had left her tied to this tree to steal Daed's horses, and the Bontragers', and the Yoders'. He wouldn't hesitate to shoot anyone who interfered.

With sudden clarity, Mattie knew Jacob would be his target. She struggled against the rope that tied her with frantic tugs, in spite of the pain in her arms. Jacob wasn't the only one in danger. None of them were safe from Cole. Daed, Noah, Isaac, Henry . . . What would keep him from killing them all?

She thrashed from side to side, her feet kicking, but it was no use. The rope was tight and strong, and the ground under her feet was wet. Slippery. The odor was overpowering. Cole had tied her behind two of the horses, and her kicking had brought her feet into contact with their droppings. She pushed at the ground with her heels, slipping and sliding, until she was upright against the tree once more. And then the tears came.

What had possessed her to leave the camp by herself? Was Cole right? Had she been searching for him?

She shook her head. "Ne," she sobbed. "Ne, it can't be true."

But when she left the camp to find water, she had been so miserable. She had left looking for more than just a pail of water. She had wanted solitude. To leave the crowded campsite behind and be alone for once. To look for . . . what?

Not Cole. Ne, not him.

Mattie leaned her head back against the tree again, staring up at the moon that drifted between the high branches. She tried to swallow the lump that had grown in her throat, but it didn't budge.

What would Mamm do?

Pray, of course.

God would hear Mamm's prayers, and Naomi's. They were good people who would never go off, leaving their family and the community behind.

But Mattie had gone her own way, in spite of her pledge to Jacob. She had turned her back on everything God had given her, and for what? A dream of something more?

God wouldn't listen to her prayers. She wasn't worthy to ask him for anything. She wasn't worthy to go back to the camp, even if she could be free of Cole's bonds. She could only sit in the dirt and filth, her head uncovered and her hair unbound, and wait for Cole's return. Then he would take her west.

A short laugh pushed its way past the lump in her throat. For as long as she could remember, she had wanted to travel to the West to see the high mountains, the vast prairies. Everything the poster in the store in Somerset had advertised. "The land of milk and honey," it had claimed. And now she would go with Cole.

It was as if God had opened his hand and let her fall into the pit of her own desires, out of his protecting grasp.

Tears trickled down her face and dropped from her chin, and she let them flow. She closed her eyes again. Everything she had ever thought she wanted lay before her. But at what cost?

"Please." She whispered the word. "Save Jacob from Cole. Save my family. Keep them safe. I'll do anything."

She stopped herself. Anything? Would she spend the rest of her life with Cole, if that would keep her family safe?

Mattie drew up her knees, making herself as small as possible. She was trying to bargain with God, but God didn't bargain. He bestowed his grace and mercy where he chose, and nothing she said or did would change his choice.

It was only by God's grace that Jacob and her family could be kept safe from Cole. It was only by his mercy that she could hope to see any of them again, but she didn't deserve any mercy from him. She deserved to be taken away by Cole, to whatever fate he had planned for her.

"Dear Lord," she whispered, "have mercy on me. I'm not worthy to be your daughter, not worthy of your notice. But please, have mercy."

Cole made his way east through the dark woods. It was best if he avoided the road. By the time daylight broke, he'd have a nice string of Conestoga horses to add to the four Clydesdales. Once he had come back for the team and the girl, they'd have to head cross-country, straight south until they hit the Wabash River.

When they got to the river, he'd use Pa's money to buy a barge big enough for all the horses. By then that Mattie-girl should be used to him. Very used to him.

He rubbed sweaty palms on his trouser legs.

The Wabash to the Ohio, then to the Mississippi and St. Louis.

He stopped in his litany. St. Louis. Once they got there, they'd have to go up the Missouri River to Independence, and that was work. He could leave the river there and travel the rest of the way on horseback, or maybe get a wagon.

His pace picked up as he found a deer trail, his feet pointed toward the Amish camp, but his head in Missouri. Missouri would be dangerous. If he ran into anyone who knew him, word could get back to Pa. But once they reached Independence, they'd be set until they were able to join up with a wagon train heading for Oregon. He'd be living high on the hog with the money from selling the horses, and he'd have the girl to keep his bed warm at night. Not a bad plan at all.

When he reached the Amish camp, he circled it, staying close enough to watch the movers. He only counted two men, but the women were busy, gathering up the children for bed. He had spent enough evenings watching them that he knew the routine as well as they did.

Why were there only two men? If he waited until the camp was quieter, he was in danger of the other men returning. But if he moved too soon, there were too many people around and awake who could spot him and raise an alarm.

He decided to wait. He found a log farther back from the road, within sight of the horses, and settled in. He fished his chaw of tobacco out of his pocket and wrenched off a piece with his teeth, keeping his eyes open. The horses grazed or stood quietly, close together. It seemed the movers had learned their lesson and were keeping a better watch on their horses. But as long as there were only two men in camp, he wouldn't have any problems.

The camp quieted as the women took the children into the wagons. Cole risked moving closer until he could see the two men sitting at the fire. He looked again. There were three now. The third one was talking, but Cole couldn't make out what he was saying. He held a bucket in his hand and was pointing down the road toward the west. Cole spit out his tobacco, all his senses alert. If all three of the men headed down the road, the horses would be easy pickings.

The third man left. Cole strained his eyes to see past the fire. It looked like he went back to the road heading east, while the first two men stayed in the camp.

He made his way toward the rear of the clearing so that when he came out of the woods, the horses would be between him and the fire. He reached the first animal, his exploring hand finding a bony hip. A cow. It moved away from him, then fell to grazing again. He reached for the next animal, its silhouette against the stars showing the horse's head clearly. He pulled the picket, then led the horse into the trees . . . except that the horse didn't follow. Going back to it, he saw the problem. White rope tied around the front legs gleamed in the moonlight. Each horse was hobbled with cotton ropes.

Cole cursed under his breath, then glanced toward the fire. The men hadn't moved. He pulled his knife out of its sheath at his belt and sawed through the hobbles. The gelding kicked at him and whinnied. Cole froze, his knife in one hand and the horse's picket rope in the other. He looked toward the fire again, but the men were gone.

Spilling curse words into the horse's ear, he went to the next horse, cut his hobble, and pulled the picket line out of the ground. Two down, but where were those movers? They couldn't just disappear.

He reached for the next horse, but a figure loomed out of the dark to his right. Cole lunged toward the man, stabbing him with the knife, and his target fell back with a cry. He pulled two more picket pins, slicing through the hobbles. His knife, slippery in his sweating hand, slid out of his grasp to the ground, but he couldn't take the time to look for it. Five horses were better than none. It was time to leave.

Starting for the road, Cole pulled the reluctant horses after him. Finally, one broke from a walk to a trot, and then they were all on the move. He led them past the fire and toward the road, running with the horses close behind. Once he was clear of the camp, he could mount one of them and ride. Taking the road would be risky, but it would give him the speed he needed.

Then a man appeared in front of him on the road, standing in his way. Without his knife, and with the horses' lead ropes wrapped around both hands, Cole had only one alternative.

"Out of the way, or I'll run you down," he yelled, his voice hoarse. He cursed when he heard his own fear floating into the night.

The horse at his right shoulder spooked, jumping to the side and pulling Cole's hand backward with a solid jerk. The pain in his shoulder was white-hot, with a sickening quiver that spread through his stomach as the horse tossed its head again. Cole sunk to his knees, black fog covering his vision.

He heard the figure step close to him and Cole shook his head. He had to see his enemy, he had to get away.

"Whoa, whoa," a gentle voice spoke in the dark, and the horses turned in a circle, toward the man, dragging Cole with them until he came to his senses enough to let go of the ropes.

Cole staggered to his feet, cradling his useless right arm with his left.

"Now, you would be having horses that are not yours?" The man's voice, heavily accented, held a note of amused interest.

"What is it to you?" Cole spat the words as another wave of nausea washed over him.

"We haf need of these horses, but you do not. If I understand good, then you already haf a team of horses, ja? The Clydesdales from the freight company." The Amish mover stepped closer to him. "You don't need more horses, but I think you are needing our help."

"Leave me alone." Cole twisted away and staggered, falling to one knee.

"Easy, Bates. Easy." It was a new voice. Now there were two of them. "Come back to the fire with us. My wife will see to your arm."

"No you don't. I have to get out of here, and I'm taking

the horses with me." The men lifted him to his feet and turned him toward the camp, but he jerked away, setting his teeth against another wave of pain. "I've already used my knife on one of you, and I'll do it again if you don't listen to me."

"Andrew is fine. Your knife only cut his arm a bit, but you left a hole in his shirtsleeve. We have some supper left, and we will take care of your arm."

Cole backed away. The first mover had gathered the horses together and was leading them back toward the camp. What was wrong with these people? If he had caught someone stealing his horses, one of them would be dead.

"I am Isaac Schrock," the man said. He grasped Cole's left elbow and started toward the camp again. "We have been running into each other ever since you stopped by my father's farm in Brothers Valley. We know you, and you know us. We will show you the hospitality we can."

Cole pulled his arm out of Isaac's grip. He reached for the pistol in his coat pocket, but his left hand was clumsy and he dropped the gun on the ground. Isaac picked it up, emptied the ball and wadding out of the barrel, and handed it back to him. Cole threw the useless piece away from them both.

"You don't know me. You don't know anything about me."

Moonlight gleamed on Isaac's teeth as he smiled. "For sure, we do. You are missing your brothers, though. Will you meet up with them again soon?"

Not if he could avoid it.

"Leave me alone." Cole stumbled back as Isaac reached for his left arm again. "Leave me alone and let me get on my way. I won't try to steal your horses again."

"If that is what you wish. Although it pains me for you to leave without aid or food."

When Cole swung back to the road, excruciating pain hit him again and he fell face-first onto the road. The last thing he knew was the grinding of stones into his cheek.

25

The moon had spanned the open sky above the road and was lowering near the western treetops by the time Jacob drew near the end of the trail he was following and caught the scent of horses. Someone was up ahead, most likely Bates. Jacob lowered the torch in his hand. Without its light, he would have a hard time following the trail, but the flame announced to anyone ahead that he was coming. He thrust it into the damp grass at his feet, extinguishing it, and went on.

As he came closer to the horses, he slowed. There was no sign of a campfire, and no noise or movement other than from the horses. If Bates was there, he was asleep. He stepped closer, placing each foot with care. Any noise could spook the horses and bring unwanted attention. He came to a tree where the first horse was tied and stroked its nose when it turned toward him. Using the horse as cover, he looked past it toward a narrow space between the trees. He counted three more horses in the moonlight, and from the strength of the odor rising from the ground at the horses' feet, they had been here for at least a day, maybe more.

Jacob circled around the small clearing. Going from the first horse to the second, he could tell they were the same size and color. The horses had matching white blazes on their faces and matching white feet. These were the horses that had been stolen from the freighter. They had to be.

As his eyes grew used to the darker shadows at the edge of the small clearing, he could see a mound next to another tree. He moved past the horses and bent over—Mattie!

He crouched next to her sleeping form.

"Mattie." He ran his hand from her shoulder to her elbow and found where her hands were tied together behind the tree. He cut the rope and said her name again, but there was no response.

Jacob looked around the space beneath the trees. No one else was there. Bates had left her here, helpless.

Lifting her hair, he pushed it behind her neck and tilted her chin toward him. The moonlight was bright enough to show a bruise on one side of her face, dark against her pale skin. Jacob clasped her in his arms and pulled her to his chest, bending down to lay his cheek on her head. His eyes stung as tears filled them. Mattie. His Mattie. He had failed her, and she paid the price.

She jerked as she came awake, pulling back from him, then reached toward him as she recognized him.

He pulled her close again. "It's all right. I'm here."

Mattie pushed her way free of his arms again and to her feet, leaning against the tree she had been tied to. "Cole. He went to steal our horses. He won't let anyone stop him." She gasped for breath as her tears turned to sobs. "I'm afraid he'll hurt someone like he killed that freight wagon driver."

"We'll go back to the camp to warn them."

"Ne, it's too late. Cole has been gone long enough . . ."
She looked over his shoulder toward the west. The moon
had disappeared behind the trees, but the sky was turning
pale with the coming dawn. "He'll be back here soon." She
pushed at him. "You must go before he comes. Go!"

Jacob shook his head. "Not without you. Even if you think
you want to go with him, I'm not going to let you turn your
back on everyone who loves you to go with a man who would
do this to you." With one helpless gesture, Jacob included
her bruise, her muddy dress, and the cut rope.

"It's too late. If you take me with you, he'll just come
after us and kill you." Mattie hung her head so low, he had
to lean toward her to hear the next words. "I'm not worth
you getting killed over."

He pulled her toward him, ignoring her struggles to free
herself until she was finally quiet in his arms. "It doesn't matter what he's done to you, Mattie." She struggled again, but
he held on tight. "It doesn't matter. Your worth is far above
rubies, and I would gladly die to keep you safe."

She sagged in his arms at these words, then clung to him,
clenching her fingers in his shirt. He let her cry until her sobs
subsided into shuddering breaths.

"I don't want to go with Cole." She pressed her face into
his chest and he held her tight. "But I don't want to lose you,
either. He's a dangerous man. A murderer."

"I know." Jacob looked at the team of horses tied to the
trees. Bates had paid a terrible price for them. "You and I will
take these horses, and then we'll start back toward the camp."

"If we run into Cole, he won't hesitate to shoot you."

Jacob released her and smoothed her tangled hair back
from her face. "We'll pray that he doesn't get the chance."

By the time Mattie helped Jacob untie the draft horses and lead them to the stream to drink, the night had turned to pale dawn. The team was docile and well trained, and they followed Jacob willingly as he tied them in a line.

"Now it's your turn." Jacob stood next to the lead horse and laced his fingers into a makeshift stirrup.

"You want me to ride?"

"You're hungry and exhausted, even more than I am. I'll feel better if you ride back to the camp."

"But I've never ridden a horse before."

Jacob straightened up. "With all the things you've dreamed of doing, all the places you've dreamed of going, and you've never ridden a horse?"

Mattie felt a bubble of laughter rise in her throat, and she smiled, the pain and fear draining away as she looked into his eyes. Eyes that held the promise of home. "I'll ride."

He leaned over again and she put her foot in his hands. He boosted her onto the horse and she grabbed the golden mane. The horse's back seemed as wide as her bed in the wagon, and her fingers clenched the coarse hair as the animal shifted under her.

"Don't worry. All you need to do is hold on."

A crackling sound came from the underbrush and Mattie froze. Jacob reached for her hand and held it as the noise came closer. Mattie sighed with relief when she saw a horse's head poke through some leafy branches. It limped toward them with a rumbling nicker.

"That's Cole's horse, but it's lame," Mattie said. "Cole must have set him loose."

Jacob squeezed her hand, then let go to take the lead rope. "He can follow us back to camp if he wants to. Josef will know how to help him."

He clucked to the team of draft horses and led them down the trail toward the road. Mattie turned around to watch the bay fall into line behind the bigger horses.

When they came to the road, the sky had already turned to the golden blue of sunrise. Mattie closed her eyes and let the sunshine bathe her with its light. As the horses settled into the rhythm of their steps, Jacob fell back to walk next to Mattie's knee.

"We need to be alert. If Bates was successful and stole the horses, he'll be coming this way."

"He would have come back for these other horses—and me—by now, wouldn't he? Something must have happened to delay him."

Jacob's mouth was set in a grim line, but he continued walking.

Mattie held tightly to the horse's mane as they went along, every step becoming a jarring bump. Her seat would be sore by the time they reached the camp, but she put that thought in the back of her mind. Her biggest concern was what had happened in the camp overnight.

Henry was the first to see them coming. Mattie stretched as tall as she could to answer the wave of his hat by flinging her arm back and forth in the air. As he turned back to shout the news to the others, she sagged down again and started crying with hiccuping sobs.

"I don't know why I'm crying now," she answered Jacob's glance. "I'm so relieved to be back." She hiccuped again.

"It's all right." He patted her hand, tangled in the golden mane. "You go ahead and cry."

When they reached the camp, they were surrounded by Mattie's family and friends. All Mattie saw after she slid down from the horse's back was a blur of faces until Mamm held her tight.

"I'm so glad you're home and safe," Mamm murmured in her ear. "So thankful." She held Mattie at arm's length, tears glistening in her eyelashes, then hugged her again.

Jacob was surrounded by her brothers and the other men.

His voice rose above the others. "What happened? Did Bates come here last night?"

Elias Hertzler nodded as everyone became quiet at Jacob's question. "Ja, he did. He tried to steal the horses, but Andrew, Isaac, and Josef stopped him."

"What did you do?"

The men exchanged glances. "He got himself into a real mess. In his hurry to untie the horses, he got tangled in the lines and was injured. We fed him breakfast, but he won't accept any other help from us."

Mattie looked from the men to Mamm, who nodded toward the man hunched on a log near the fire, with one of Mamm's quilts around his shoulders. His head hung between his knees. Cole was a pitiful sight, but Mattie's stomach twisted with fear in spite of it. She turned her back on him and listened to the men's conversation.

"What will we do with him?" Jacob asked.

"Isaac and Andrew took two of the horses and started back toward Angola. They'll tell the sheriff there about him." Daed stepped closer to Mattie, putting his arm around her shoulders. "I'm glad you're safe, daughter. I'm thankful Jacob found you."

Mattie's eyes filled with tears again. Mamm, Daed . . . they were all treating her so kindly, and she didn't deserve it. She glanced again at Cole, still sitting on the log, seeming to take no notice of the people around him.

"I'm sorry I caused such trouble."

Daed squeezed her shoulders. "You go with your mamm. She'll take care of you."

Mattie obeyed Daed, glancing at Cole again as she passed by him. This time she felt a wrench of pity for him, but shuddered. She would never forget how it felt to be at his mercy.

By noon, the sheriff from Angola still hadn't arrived. Dinner was stew, made from some rabbits the boys had trapped, and noodles made from the dwindling store of flour.

"I'll take some to Cole." Mattie held out a bowl for Magdalena Hertzler to fill.

Johanna's stepmother hesitated. "Are you sure? He isn't a very friendly man."

Mattie's chin tilted up. "I know. But I need to do this for him, after everything that happened last night." She swallowed, her confidence wavering. "I'll be fine here in the daylight, in the middle of our camp." She smiled at Magdalena and took the bowl to the bench by the fire where Cole still sat.

He didn't look up as she approached. She sat next to him and held out the bowl.

"Here."

"What?"

"Have some stew. You must be hungry."

He sat up, letting the quilt fall off his shoulders. His right arm was bound against his body with strips of cloth. He reached for the bowl with his left hand, then drew it back.

"Never mind. I can't eat it anyway."

"Do you want me to feed you?"

He met her eyes then, the black lights gleaming under his brow. "You would do that for me?"

Misgivings made her stomach swirl, but she lifted the spoon. After all, he was only a man in need. He opened his mouth and she stuck the spoon in, feeding him as she would one of her baby nieces or nephews.

His eyes didn't leave hers until the bowl was empty.

"Thank you, Mattie-girl."

His voice was low and intimate, and he gave her a slow smile. Mattie looked around the camp. Everyone was busy except Jacob. He watched them with a frown.

"I wouldn't want you to go hungry." She stood. "The sheriff will be here soon. Maybe you should get some rest."

"You could do something else to help me."

"What?"

He beckoned her closer and she leaned toward him slightly. "Talk with me. Don't make me sit here alone."

She almost laughed at that. "You are surrounded by the whole camp. You aren't alone."

"Nobody talks to me, though. They act like I'm invisible, except for the stares."

"All right." She started to sit next to him again.

"Not here. Can't we walk or something? I need to be on my feet. I'm not used to just sitting like this."

Mattie wavered. Once the sheriff took him, he would probably never be free again. He would be punished for the murder of the freighter and spend the rest of his life in a jail cell.

"I'll walk with you, as long as we don't leave the camp."

He stood and she led the way toward the meadow where the horses and cows grazed. Jacob watched them. When he moved to follow them at a little distance, the twirling in her stomach slowed. She would be safe, even this close to Cole, as long as Jacob was watching out for her.

In the middle of the meadow, Cole stopped next to one of the horses.

"It's too bad."

"What is?"

Cole glanced at her, then turned back to the horse. "These really are the finest horses I've seen. It's too bad I won't be able to use them to give me a start in Oregon."

"But they aren't your horses. You are very quick to forget that."

He smiled. "But they could be mine, if luck had been with me." He turned to her again, keeping his voice low so the words wouldn't carry to Jacob. "You could be mine too. It isn't too late."

Mattie felt her cheeks heat, and the clenching swirl was back. "I'm not yours, and I never will be."

"Mattie-girl, think what you're giving up." He took a step toward her. "Oregon, the mountains, the ocean. Think of the adventures we could have."

She pulled her lip between her teeth. The old dream. She turned it over in her mind, but it held no allure for her anymore.

Cole continued. "All we would need to do is walk a little farther, a little faster, and leave all these Amish behind."

His voice was silky, pulling her into his gaze. "You and I, Mattie-girl, off to the west, as free as birds."

In the high branches of the trees, a mockingbird started singing, its musical repertoire catching her soul, tugging at her. But she stepped back from Cole, shaking her head.

"No. I won't help you escape, and I won't go with you." Like a perfect stitch sewn in a seam, her words fell true. "I don't want to go west." The seam strengthened. "I know what God is calling me to do. I'm going to stay with my family and my faith. I'll never see the mountains, but my life will be so much better than you could imagine."

A twisting darkness passed over Cole's face, but she was no longer held captive by his gaze. His eyes narrowed. "You'll regret this. You'll always be sorry you settled for the safe route and didn't take this chance with me."

He turned with a jump and started running toward the edge of the meadow. But Jacob had been watching, and he was after him, tackling him like a greased pig just before he reached the trees. The two tumbled over in the grass and weeds, startling the horses. More men rushed past Mattie, and soon Cole was standing upright again, his face pale as he clutched his right arm. Strangers stood on each side of him. The sheriff and his deputy had arrived from Angola.

They shoved the struggling horse thief between them toward the road. As they passed her, Cole twisted around.

"You'll regret this until the day you die. You'll always wish you had taken your chance."

Mattie watched him go. Jacob walked up behind her, laying his hand on her shoulder. She reached to grasp it as she watched the sheriff direct Cole to mount a horse and then tie his hands to the saddle horn. Cole didn't look back as they headed down the road toward Angola.

Jacob squeezed her shoulder and she turned around. "Will you regret not taking the chance, Mattie?"

Mattie took a deep breath and smiled as she let it out. "Ne, I won't. I'm just thankful I don't have to regret making a terrible mistake."

He glanced beyond her toward the busy camp, then tugged her behind a couple of the horses, smiling as he pulled her close.

"One thing I know is that this isn't a mistake."

As Jacob folded her close to him and kissed her, she melted into his arms, thankful to be home.

26

E ven after the wakeful night they had, the whole group agreed that they were anxious to get to their destination. So although Mattie wished she could sleep the day away under a shady tree, she helped Mamm get the wagon ready for the day's journey before she made a pallet for herself on top of some packing crates and slept.

It was noon before she woke, groggy and hungry. She brushed the wrinkles out of her clothes as best she could, then combed and twisted her hair before putting on the extra kapp she had brought. She would have to make a new one to replace the one she had lost.

When Mattie poked her head out of the wagon, she saw they had stopped in the middle of a town. The shady town square had become their noon camp. Mamm had gathered the little ones on a blanket spread on the grass, and Naomi sat there with Davey, the boy's head lying in her lap.

She turned to climb out of the wagon, and Jacob was by her side, his hand supporting her elbow as she jumped from the wheel spokes.

"How are you?" He didn't smile as he spoke, and his mouth was pinched with worry.

Mattie smiled to reassure him. "I could have slept longer, and I'm a little sore, but I'm fine." She looked across the street at a collection of buildings, including a bank and a general store. "Where are we?"

"Springfield, Yost said. He expects we'll reach the Amish settlement in Newbury Township early tomorrow."

Mattie bit her lip. Yesterday she had hated the thought of settling here, but after her experience with Cole, she had no desire to be anywhere but with her family. She looked up at Jacob, who was watching her closely.

"It will be good to stop traveling."

"You think so?" His eyebrows lifted in surprise. "What changed your mind?"

Mattie hugged her arms close. "Can we walk a bit? I don't want the others to hear us talking."

"Ja, for sure." He led her across the street to the board sidewalk that ran in front of the buildings.

They walked in silence past the general store and the milliner's. Then the sidewalk ended, and they stepped down into a dusty trail in the grass at the side of the street. Jacob stopped in the shade of a tree in front of a white frame house surrounded by a picket fence. Mattie touched the top of one picket, then the next.

"Last night, you said . . ." She stopped with a sigh. How could she get Jacob to understand they could never marry? "You said that you would die for me."

He took her hand. "I would, Mattie. I would do anything for you."

She shook her head, pulling her hand away. "I'm not worthy

of that. I'm not the right girl for you." She turned away from him and rubbed the top of the picket with her thumb.

"What do you mean? Is this about wanting to go west to Oregon or someplace? We can work that out." He kicked the dusty path behind her. "When you were lost—when I thought you had gone with Bates—it about killed me. The thought that you would leave me, your family . . . I had to try to get you back." He pulled her elbow around so she faced him. "I knew then that I would do anything for you. I would even go west, if that's what you want."

Mattie's throat closed. "All I want to do is crawl in a hole and hide." She swallowed her tears down through the choking pressure. "I'm nothing, don't you see? If you hadn't come to find me, Cole would have taken me away. Maybe that is what I deserved." She pulled away from him again, turning her back so he couldn't see the tears. "I'm not worthy of being part of my family, or part of the church, and certainly not your wife. I've thought and done terrible things."

He jerked at her, pulling her around to face him again. "Mattie, tell me. Did Cole . . . did he hurt you?" She shook her head and the hands gripping her arms relaxed. "Then what have you done that is so terrible?"

"I wanted to go to Oregon. I wanted it so badly that I even thought about what it would be like to go with Cole. I was tempted, don't you see? I . . . he said I came to find him last night, and that's why I stumbled into him." She hiccuped. The tightness in her throat loosened as her confession spilled out. "And perhaps he was right. I was so angry when I left the camp to find water that maybe I did go to try to find him. All I could think about was what I wanted, not about my family, or you . . . or the promise I made to you." She looked into his eyes. "I was wayward and prideful. I'll never be a good wife or church member."

"But you didn't go with him." Jacob's eyes brimmed with his own tears. "You've learned something, haven't you?"

Mattie twisted the edges of her apron between her fingers. "I've learned how dreadfully sinful I am." She wiped at her eyes. "I know I'm only here today because of God's mercy. I don't deserve to be safe, at home with you and my family."

"Anything else?" His voice, soft and tender, tugged at her heart.

"I learned just how foolish my dreams have been. I've been fighting against God and his will, but this—" She searched for the right word. "This surrender to him . . ." She sighed, her spirit as sore as a healing burn. "I finally understand what it means to face your own emptiness."

"And once we see how unworthy we all are, then the only place to turn is to God."

A tear trickled to the end of her nose and she wiped it away with the hem of her apron. Jacob was right. "He's all I have left."

"Not all." Jacob rubbed her arms with his thumbs.

Finally he asked, "Do you still want to go to Oregon?"

She shuddered, her throat full again. "Don't speak of Oregon. It makes me think of *him*, and I don't want to think of him ever again."

He smiled, and lifted her chin with one finger. "Do you think you might learn to be content with me?" He lifted one eyebrow. "I'll try to make life interesting for you, even here in Indiana."

Mattie smiled at the comical look on his face. "How would you do that?"

Encircling her with his arms, he pulled her closer, and the soreness eased. "For one, I can make you laugh." She had to nod at that. "And I'll keep you busy chasing after little ones all day."

"Whose little ones?" She relaxed in his arms.

"Our little ones." He gave her a quick kiss. "Dozens of little Yoders with socks to darn and britches to patch. You'll be too busy to get bored with your life."

She melted into his next kiss, one that banished all other thoughts from her mind.

The next day, Mattie walked with Jacob behind the green wagon. Even though their hands never touched, Jacob felt like he could have been walking arm in arm with her. The camaraderie he had missed was back, along with something else. When he looked into Mattie's eyes, he saw a peace that had been absent before.

Farms lined the road, with rough cabins and split rail fences, but some of the settlers had already built barns of sawn lumber. In the afternoon, one of the farmers hailed the lead wagon in the group.

"Yost Bontrager!"

Yost's return greeting told Jacob that the two men were old friends.

"More than old friends," Mattie said when he asked her. "That's Solomon Plank, one of our neighbors from Brothers Valley who immigrated here last year."

Andrew jogged down the line of wagons. "We're camping here tonight. Solomon said to settle in the meadow there behind the house." He waved toward the spot with his hand, then went on to the rest of the wagons.

"We're here." Mattie caught Jacob's hand in hers. "We're home."

She went to help her family set up their camp while Jacob and Josef unhitched the wagon and picketed the horses. No need to worry about horse thieves, now that Bates was in jail and they were in settled country again. Jacob rolled his shoulders, glad to be relieved of that burden of worry.

The Plank family joined the emigrants around their campfire for supper that night, Solomon contributing a young pig for roasting. After the meal, the entire group gathered around him, eager to hear every detail about their new home.

"Several new families have moved into the settlement since you were here last summer," Solomon began, nodding toward Yost and Eli. "After we arrived in the spring, another group from Holmes County came in the fall. There were several families, and they almost doubled the size of the community here. They settled in Elkhart County, after we had decided to settle here in LaGrange County."

"Does that make a division in the community?" Elias Hertzler asked.

"It's only natural that folks want to live near people they know, their friends and family. But there is a difference between us and the Holmes County families. They seem to be more change minded, settling near the Mennonites and such, but nothing will come of it, I'm sure. We worship together and support each other as a church should."

"We've seen quite a few farms along the way," Yost said, "many more than there were last year. Is there still land available to buy?"

"There is plenty, but of course, the choicest lots have already been sold. Some of the holders of the original land grants from ten years ago are ready to make a profit from their investment and move on farther west. Between here and Elkhart County, south a few miles in Eden Township, there is some nice farmland for sale. A little to the west of there, along the Little Elkhart River, the land tends to be marshy, but it could be drained to make fields that will be more fertile than you can imagine." Solomon unrolled a map on his knees and all the men leaned closer to look at it. "I got this from the land office in Ft. Wayne last spring, and I've marked off the parcels that have sold since then." He pointed to several areas with his finger.

As Solomon talked, Jacob's mind was filled with the plans for his farm that had kept him occupied through the long winter. Solomon Plank's farm looked nothing like the settled farmland back in the Conestoga Valley, or even in Holmes County. But Solomon and his family had only been here since last spring. The small log cabin and lean-to barn were enough to house the family and animals while Solomon had worked to clear the fields. The spot where they were camping had been cleared in the last month, from the fresh-cut look of the stumps that dotted the space. Jacob noticed the corded muscles of Solomon's forearms in the firelight. Clearing his own farmland wouldn't be easy, and he had promised to clear Daed's land first. He had a lot of work ahead.

Mattie stood with Johanna and Naomi across the way, listening to the conversation. It didn't matter how hard he needed to toil, it would be worth the work to make a home for Mattie and their family. She lifted her eyes and met his, then a smile spread, starting at the corners of her mouth.

It would all be worth it.

The next morning, Jacob, Josef, and Andrew left the camp

in the Bontragers' spring wagon. While the rest of the families were content to lay by for a day after their long journey, Jacob was anxious to start hunting for his land, and so were the others.

"Remember," Josef said as they started out, "Christian wants our farms to be close together."

"Ja, I remember." Jacob, sitting in the front seat of the open buggy, scanned the land on either side of the road as the horse walked south on the rutted wagon trail, winding between huge tree stumps. Lower stumps, cut close to the ground to allow wagons to pass over them, dotted the trail. The woods were dense, and the early summer morning was filled with birdsong. Mattie had longed for open prairies. "I'd like to find some land where the trees aren't so thick."

"You'll only find that in marshy meadows." Andrew snorted from the backseat. "It's either drain the swampland, or cut down the trees as you go. I'm not sure which one means more work."

"Which would you rather do?" Jacob twisted around in his seat to look at his friend. Andrew had Solomon Plank's map unrolled across his knees.

"I'd rather take the trees. A man can use the timber to build a house, or a barn, or whatever he needs. When you drain the swamp, all you do is dig ditches."

Jacob settled back into his seat. "Didn't Solomon say there was higher ground somewhere? Toward Clinton Township?"

"I think he said something about the Elkhart Prairie, but that land was too expensive for him." Andrew studied the map. "It's farther west too. Quite a distance from the settlement."

A whiff of wood smoke signaled that they were approaching another farm. It was on a corner, and Josef turned right, heading southwest. This road was well traveled and he urged the horse to a trot.

Andrew leaned forward and tapped Josef on the shoulder. "Do you have any idea where you're going?"

Josef shrugged. "Solomon said most of the land near his farm was already purchased. I thought if we went south a bit, toward Hawpatch, we'd find those unsold parcels that Solomon pointed out to us last night."

"I think I'd like to look at Elkhart County." Andrew sat back and lifted the map to examine it more closely. "Solomon said the folks over that way were more progressive."

"You'd want to live among the change-minded group?"

"Why not? Their ideas might be worth listening to."

Jacob exchanged glances with Josef, but didn't say anything. He saw nothing good out of taking new ideas seriously, especially not after the church leaders had already discussed and rejected them. Their decisions had been final, and the Amish held a firm stance against the ideas that had been proposed. But it appeared that Andrew was sympathetic to the change-minded faction back in Pennsylvania. Or perhaps all of the Bontragers felt this way.

As they went farther south, the trees thinned, until there were open acres along the roadside. Josef slowed the horse.

"This area looks like what your daed was looking for, Jacob."

Jacob twisted around in the seat. Andrew had his finger following a line on Solomon's map. "Can you find where we are?"

"I think we're about here." Andrew's finger stopped. "Some of the land that Solomon marked as being for sale is to our west about a half mile."

Ahead was another wagon road, and Josef turned west. Before they had gone very far, they came to a house along the roadside. A middle-aged man came out of it as they stopped.

"Step down, boys, and help yourselves to the well. I don't get many visitors."

Jacob leaned forward. "We heard that you might have some land for sale."

"I sure do." With that, Jacob stepped out of the spring wagon. The man reached out to shake his hand. "I'm Slayton."

After introductions were made, and Josef explained the kind of land they were looking for, Mr. Slayton led them farther down the lane, pointing out the features of the land. He owned an entire section, having received the land grant twelve years earlier.

"I'm ready to move on, though." Mr. Slayton ran his thumbs along his suspenders. Jacob had already discovered that the man always had a smile on his face, and his jovial manner was infectious. "Too many people settling in this part of the country, and I'm not a farmer. It's time for me to move on west where the game is still plentiful and a man has room to stretch."

They spent the rest of the morning exploring the land, then stopped with Mr. Slayton for a simple meal of dried meat and sourdough bread. Over lunch outside the cabin, they came to an agreement over the terms of the sale.

"My neighbor to the west has a half-section to sell, as well, if the others in your party are interested." Mr. Slayton eased back on his stool and leaned against the wall of the log house. "And meanwhile, I'll meet you in LaGrange tomorrow morning to transfer the deeds."

As they took their leave, Jacob couldn't keep the grin off his face. He had found the perfect piece of land, and he couldn't wait to show it to Mattie.

The next morning, Mattie busied herself helping Mamm with the laundry. Daed and the other men had gone with Solomon to look at land for sale, while Jacob, Josef, and Andrew had gone the other direction in the second spring wagon. They hadn't said what errand they were running, though.

"I will be glad when we're finally settled again, and we can get back into our routine," Mamm said. She lifted one of Henry's white shirts and clucked her tongue at the stains on it. "This doing laundry whenever we're stopped for more than a day doesn't keep the clothes very clean."

"As soon as Daed finds the farm to buy, at least we'll be camping in one spot until he builds the cabin."

Mamm sighed. "When we moved to the Conestoga Creek, we bought a house and farm from a family that was moving out. We did the same when we moved to Brothers Valley. But here we'll have to start from scratch." She dropped some trousers onto a pile with the other dark clothes.

"We're building something out of the untamed wilderness. Don't you think that's exciting?"

"Exciting, maybe. But it's also a lot of work. I'm glad your daed still has Henry at home to help him."

"Isaac and Noah will buy farms near ours, won't they?"

"I hope so." Mamm dropped the last pair of socks onto the pile of dark clothes. "Would you see if Naomi has the water hot yet? I'll check on Henry. He was supposed to be getting the washtub out for us."

Naomi stood next to the fire where a full pot of water was heating. When Mattie joined her, she smiled and pointed toward the children playing a game between the tree stumps. "Look at that Davey. He's fitting in well, now that he feels better."

The little boy followed Mose and Menno as they jumped from one stump to another. "He is, for sure."

"And he's learning to speak Deitsch so quickly. The other children are helping him."

"Mamm wants to know if the water is hot enough yet."

Naomi turned toward the fire. "You probably thought I had forgotten all about it." She lifted the lid of the pot slightly and steam escaped into the air.

"You did seem preoccupied with Davey."

"You're right." Naomi glanced over her shoulder at the children again. "I know he's only been with us for a few days, but already I can't imagine what my life would be like if I didn't have him to care for."

Mattie saw a familiar look in her sister's eyes. "I think you've fallen in love with him." Naomi raised her eyebrows, and Mattie went on. "You look like Annie did when her little Levi was born. Like you see the future in his face."

"Ja," Naomi said, drawing the word. "Ja, I think you're right. I heard Mamm say once that children are God's promise for the future. Davey is all that and more."

Mamm, Lydia Schrock, and the others set up their washtubs on the benches near the fire, and while Henry hauled water from the nearby stream, Mattie helped pour water from the big pot over the fire into each tub. Mamm started soaking her white pieces first, using her washing bat to agitate the water and the clothes.

Hannah had set up her tub near Mamm's but was soon done with the few clothes that she and Josef needed.

"If you give me some of your dark clothes, I'll wash them for you."

Mamm smiled at her. "That is kind of you, Hannah." She nodded toward the pile at her feet. "Take as many as you wish." She swirled the clothes again and bent to scrub Henry's shirt with the soap. "I've wondered how your mamm is doing. You'll be anxious to see them at the end of the summer, won't you?"

"Ja, for sure." Hannah lifted a pair of trousers with her bat and plunged them into the water again. "I try to trust in the Lord for her safety, but I can't help worrying."

"Will you and Josef go back to Ohio at the end of the summer to help them move?"

Hannah shook her head. "Only Jacob will, after we're settled on the farms and get the garden planted. Josef and I will stay here to continue getting things ready for them."

Mattie listened to the conversation with her heart sinking. She had forgotten that Jacob would be leaving in the autumn, but he had promised he would go back to Ohio. His family needed him to help continue their journey to Indiana.

At noon the women and children ate a cold dinner. Afterward, Mattie and Hannah were taking clothes from where they had been spread to dry on the bushes and folding them when the young men returned.

Jacob met Mattie's gaze. "We thought we'd take you girls for a ride this afternoon."

His face became bright red, but Andrew finished for him.

"We'd like to take Johanna and Hannah too, of course. We'll be back before dark."

"There's so much work to do—"

Mamm laid her hand on Mattie's arm. "You girls have been working hard," she said in her quiet voice. "You should go for a ride. Naomi and I will have our turns when your daed comes back."

With that decided, they were off. Josef kept the horse walking down the narrow dirt road as they headed south.

"What is the mystery? Have you found farms to buy?" Johanna asked. The girls sat in the backseat together while the men were in the front.

"Nothing doing," Andrew said. "We want to surprise you."

They had traveled several miles, the last few on an improved road, when Josef turned into a narrow lane. Before they had gone very far, Josef pulled the wagon to a halt. "This is your stop, Andrew."

Andrew jumped down from the wagon and gave Johanna his hand to help her out of the open wagon.

"We'll be back in a little while." Josef clucked to the horse and they sped away.

"We're going to leave them there in the woods?" Mattie turned in her seat, but Andrew and Johanna had already left the road.

"Andrew is showing her the parcel he found." Jacob turned in his seat to watch her. "Our turn is next."

Josef continued down the lane, past a log house on the right, then drew to a halt at the side of the road. Ahead of them a hundred yards or so, a stream crossed the lane.

Jacob jumped down from the wagon and reached for Mattie's hand while Josef tied the horse to a small tree.

"Are we here?" Mattie saw only trees and more trees, until the canopy thinned out near the stream in the distance. She saw nothing that made this piece of land any different from the surrounding area.

"This is it." Jacob didn't release her hand, but pulled her close to him. "There are three lots here, each of them one hundred sixty acres." He pointed across the road and behind them. "That's the best one, the one with the log house. The land is more level, and we thought that would be good for the folks." He turned to the trees at their left, along the south side of the road. "This one will be ours." He squeezed her hand and she felt her face heat up. Hannah smiled at her as Josef helped her down from the spring wagon.

"And over here is ours." Josef walked with Hannah toward the stream, pulling her hand into the crook of his arm.

Jacob tugged at Mattie's hand. "Come on, I want to show you what I found."

Threading their way through the trees, Jacob led her into the woods a short distance until he came to a steep bank. "This is one of the best features of our land. With this spring, we'll have fresh water without having to dig a well."

Mattie stepped closer to the circle of green at the base of the bank with the pool of water in the center. Moss-covered rocks surrounded the spring and followed the water as it formed a small runlet flowing downhill toward the larger stream she had seen earlier.

"We can build our cabin here." Jacob walked to a small rise a short distance from the spring.

"And someday a house?" Mattie closed her eyes and again saw the farm in Ohio, with the wife standing at the Dutch door and the little girl feeding the chickens. "A white frame house with a Dutch door?"

Her eyes still closed, she felt Jacob's arms encircle her

waist from behind as he laid his chin on her shoulder. "And a springhouse made of limestone to keep the milk cool in the summer."

Mattie could feel his breath on her ear as he spoke, sending goose bumps down her spine.

"But I haven't shown you the best part." He took her hand. "Come with me."

He led her up a slope, into the trees.

"You're sure we won't get lost?"

"Trust me."

As they climbed, the trees thinned, then suddenly they stepped out into an open meadow.

"This is a knob, rising a bit above the surrounding land." He took her shoulders and turned her so that she was looking southwest. Prairie land fell away below their feet, a vast open meadow.

"But how—"

"It's a natural prairie. It's yours, Mattie, as if the Good Lord knew we would find this land and had planned it as a special gift for you."

She drank in the open sky above her, the woods around, and the hazy blue horizon to her west, her heart nearly bursting with thankfulness.

"What do you think?" he asked. "Could you be content here with me in this pleasant prairie?"

She turned in his arms and clasped her hands behind his neck. "Always, Jacob. Always and forever."

Epilogue

September brought bright blue mornings that turned crisp as the month waned toward October. Mattie straightened her back, stiff from bending to pick the last of the summer's cabbages from the garden. The trees at the edge of the clearing glowed, as if the yellow, red, and orange leaves were drawing the last of the summer sun into the roots.

Jacob had been gone for a month. At the end of August, when the leaves were still green and the days were sultry hot, he had saddled the bay gelding and headed back to Ohio. The time since then had been busy with harvesting and drying the vegetables to get the settlement through the winter. Mattie had spent as much time helping Mamm prepare as she had at Hannah and Josef's, putting up the produce from the garden they had planted for themselves and Jacob's family.

Mattie cut three more cabbages loose from their stalks before Henry returned with the stone boat. They had used the sledge to pick rocks from the garden after they cleared and plowed it, and now it worked even better to carry the produce to the cabin and the root cellar Daed had built below it.

"You're almost to the end of the row." Henry pulled the stone boat to the pile and started transferring the cabbages over.

"We have plenty of heads. They did well this summer, even though some of them split in the heat last month."

"More sauerkraut for me." Henry grinned and rubbed his stomach.

"I've never seen anyone who loves sauerkraut as much as you do."

"Does Jacob like it?"

Mattie felt her face heating. She turned away so Henry wouldn't see and tease her for it. "I have no idea. We've never talked about things like sauerkraut."

"Then what did you talk about every evening this summer when he came over?"

"Things." Mattie couldn't keep a smile from spreading. The long summer evenings were just a taste of the sweet companionship they would enjoy for the rest of their lives.

"Shouldn't he be getting back from Ohio soon? He's been gone forever."

Mattie sighed. "He should be here any day. Don't forget, they have the sheep to bring with them, and the little children might not travel well." She continued the list of reasons for his delay in her mind: the rivers might have been too high to cross, or they might have been delayed by rain. She refused to consider that anything might have gone wrong.

After Henry filled the stone boat, he dragged it back to the cabin. Daed, with Henry's help, had cleared an acre of ground before helping Noah, and then Isaac. Davey had worked as hard as any of the men, even though Naomi had protested.

"Let him be," Mamm had said. "He's old enough to be a good helper, and he wants to fit in."

Mattie smiled as she cut the last cabbage. She stood, looking around the small farm for Davey. She spied him at the edge of the clearing, cutting away the underbrush. Always busy, that one. At least he stayed out of mischief. She remembered Henry at that age. Isaac and Noah had called him a pest because he was always underfoot.

"Shouldn't you be working?"

Mattie whirled around at the sound of Jacob's voice. He stood at the edge of the garden, his clothes dusty from travel, but the smile on his face was as wide as hers.

"I am working, can't you see?"

He took a step closer. "I saw you staring off into the distance. Were you dreaming again?"

"If I was dreaming, it was only about you."

They met in the middle of the garden and Jacob gathered her in his arms. "I missed this."

She wiggled closer and tucked her head under his chin. "I did too. When did you get home?"

"Just now. I put the sheep in their pen and came straight here."

Mattie stepped back to look at his face. "Is everyone all right? Your mamm and daed? The children?"

"All of them." He tweaked her nose. "Even the babies."

A pinching worry eased. "What are their names?"

"The squirmy one with the red face is Rachael, and the one who cries all the time is Gideon."

Mattie laughed at the face he made. "You won't talk about your own children that way, will you?"

Jacob's expression softened as he held her cheek in his palm. "Not with you as their mamm. They will be the prettiest babies who were ever born."

"Or the handsomest."

Jacob held her eyes with his own as the moments stretched out. Davey's hacking at the underbrush was the only sound Mattie heard.

"When can we be married?" Jacob's brow puckered. "The cabin is ready. Daed said he'll give us half of the flock of sheep, so we'll have mutton and wool. We'll have to wait for a cow, since he promised the spring calf to Hannah and Josef."

Mattie took his hand. "My daed said we can have our calf. And I've been working all summer to be ready. I finished my quilt, and Mamm has some coverlets for me. I've been spending my sewing time making sheets for our bed." She felt her face redden at that. It was one thing to prepare the bedding, but another to think about actually using it.

"In a month? Can we be married the first of November? The farmwork will be done by then."

Mattie thought of the little cabin Jacob had built on his farm, the springhouse, and the small clearing, nearly identical to Daed's, where they had planted a garden. It was an island in trees so thick she risked losing her way if she wandered out of sight of the cabin, but she could always find her way to the knob rising from the forest and the prairie land. What had once appeared closed in and stifling was now cozy and homelike. With Jacob, she would be as snug and content as she could wish.

"The first of November will be fine. I'll be ready to set up housekeeping by then."

Jacob tucked her head under his chin again. "And I'll make sure the farm is ready for winter." He squeezed her tighter. "I'm ready to start on our great adventure together."

Acknowledgments

A book is never written by only one person.

I'd like to thank my dear husband and my children. I'm sorry I seem to spend more time talking to my characters than I do to you.

And a big thank-you to my agent, Sarah Joy Freese of WordServe Literary Agency. Knowing that you are "in the loop" in marketing and publishing decisions keeps me from second-guessing myself too much.

Most of all, without the great editors and other staff at Revell, this book would never have become a reality. Thank you for all of your hard work!

Author's Note

The research for this story took me from the mountains of Pennsylvania, to the rolling brown waters of the Ohio River, to the swampy marshland of the Ohio-Michigan-Indiana borders, and finally to the prairie lands of LaGrange County, Indiana.

In the midst of my research, my eighty-six-year-old father and I traveled along the backroads of Amish country, following my characters' route from Somerset County, Pennsylvania, through rural Ohio. We finished the trip by traveling up the ancient route along the Indiana/Ohio border to Dad's home in Goshen, Indiana.

Our first stop was in Pittsburgh to visit my aunt Ruth and my cousin and her husband, Carol and Grady. They live near the Allegheny River, close to the location where our fictional Amish travelers crossed that river.

We stayed with an Amish family in Holmes County, Ohio, sharing the joy of their children's last day of school and learning how the modern Amish families cope in their changing world.

We also traveled through the flatlands of northern Ohio, once the home of the Great Black Swamp. For a fan of Gene Stratton Porter's books like me, learning about the history of this fertile farmland was fascinating. Miles of impenetrable forest and swamp once stood where barns and fields of corn now hold sway.

Another spot where we stopped was Greenville, Ohio, to visit my very special "aunt" Wavelene—my mother's dearest friend since their college days. This was the site of the signing of the famous Treaty of Greenville in 1814. It was called "a treaty of peace and friendship" between the United States and the Native tribes in central Ohio and Indiana.

Each stop along the way brought the settings of Mattie's and Jacob's story to life in my mind, and I hope I was able to translate what I learned into a satisfying reading experience for you. Words are often inadequate.

But the problem—or I should say, the blessing—of my research trip is that for every question I answered, three more took its place. Each of the three states we visited has its own fascinating history. Many more stories will grow out of the details I learned on that trip! I hope you'll be along for the journey.

I would love to hear from you! Visit my website, www.JanDrexler.com, or my Facebook page, www.facebook.com/JanDrexlerAuthor.

Read a Sneak Peak
Book 3 in the
JOURNEY TO
PLEASANT PRAIRIE
series

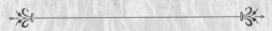

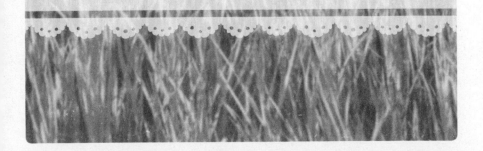

1

"Davey!"

Only the echoing chop of a felling ax answered Naomi Schrock's call. It must be the new neighbor to their north. Daed had said someone had bought the last quarter-section still remaining between their land at the edge of the Hawpatch and the marshes that surrounded the Little Elkhart River.

Naomi shaded her eyes against the setting sun. The late afternoon light was bright, a last burning gasp before night fell. Where was that boy?

"Davey!"

He must be out of hearing distance again, but which direction had he gone this time? The regular *chop-chop* of the ax drew her attention again . . . just as it would have drawn Davey's curious mind. With a sigh, Naomi gathered her skirts in her hands and plunged into the forest at the north edge of the clearing. The path was easy enough to follow. Davey liked to stick to the narrow deer trails through the underbrush.

In the three years since her family had arrived in the Haw Patch in northern Indiana, Daed had made some progress in clearing the trees. The log home he had built that first summer was comfortable, although Mamm still missed the white frame house in Somerset County, Pennsylvania, that they had left behind when they made this move.

But Daed's dream of being part of a new Amish settlement had been realized. More than thirty families had bought land in the northern Indiana forests, and additional settlers still appeared each spring and summer.

Like this unknown owner of the felling ax. The faint trail Naomi followed was leading directly toward the sound. She could only hope that Davey wasn't making a pest of himself with their new neighbor.

Naomi emerged from the forest into a small clearing. Twenty feet away, on the opposite side, was the wood chopper. His back was toward her, his legs braced for the shock of each blow of his ax as it took decisive chunks out of the trunk of a tall maple tree. Standing on a stump, off to the side, was seven-year-old Davey, his hands covering his ears. The edges of his blond hair swung below the brim of his hat as he flinched with each ringing chop of the ax.

A wagon to Naomi's right was the man's home. A cooking fire ringed with stones was nearby, and a dozen tree stumps filled the clearing floor, with the felled trees stacked in the center, stripped of their branches. A pile of brush rose in the center of the space, and a stack of firewood lined the edge of the woods near the wagon, testifying to the new neighbor's industry with a saw as well as the felling ax. There was no sign of a family, though, just as Daed had said. He must have come ahead to build a cabin before bringing the rest of the family along.

Just then a loud crack boomed through the afternoon air and the tree swayed, twisted, and tilted—right in the direction of the stump where Davey was standing. Naomi's feet started moving toward her son without any thought beyond snatching him out of the path of the tree that rushed downward with increasing speed. But the stranger was faster than her, and grabbed the boy off the stump as he leaped out of the path of disaster.

Man and boy rolled to a halt at Naomi's feet, Davey's gleeful laugh showing that he had never realized the danger he had been in. The panic drained from her body, leaving her sore and irritated.

"Davey Schrock." Naomi balled her fists on her hips for emphasis. "Didn't you hear me calling? You know you're not to wander off in the woods without telling someone."

Her voice startled both of them, and two pairs of eyes looked at her. Davey's blue gaze met hers briefly, then lowered as he blushed, embarrassed that he had been caught misbehaving again. But the man's brown eyes changed from a startled flash to a crinkling smile. He rose from the ground, setting Davey on his feet. He retrieved his hat from where it had rolled and brushed it off with a practiced sweep of his hand.

"You must be Davey's mamm." As he settled his hat on his head, he shifted his gaze from her cast eye to her good one, and she felt her cheeks heat. "I'm Cap Stoltzfus, just arrived from Holmes County."

Naomi grasped Davey's hand and pulled him close. "Ja. I'm Naomi. I'm thankful you snatched my boy from the path of the falling tree."

She glanced at the man again. He was still looking at her, standing a good six inches taller than her. His beard touched his chest, indicating his married status.

"I met your husband yesterday. He came by to welcome me, since we're close neighbors."

Naomi's face heated again. "You met my father, Eli Schrock. He told us about you at supper last night."

"Then I look forward to meeting more of your family tomorrow. Your daed told me where the Sabbath meeting is to be held." He reached out to brush some leaves and twigs from the back of Davey's shirt. "You have a fine son here."

"Will we meet your family soon?"

Cap took a step back, his face as closed as if he had slammed a shutter tight. "My family is . . . is lost."

Naomi was suddenly aware of the shadowed twilight under the surrounding trees. She hugged her elbows as the cooling air reminded her it was still early spring. "Davey and I must be getting home. No one knows where we are."

"Ja, for sure." He took another step back, half turning from her.

Davey pulled his hand out of Naomi's grasp and tugged at Cap's sleeve. "Will we see you at meeting?"

He squatted on the ground, his face level with the boy's. "I'll be there."

Davey grinned and threw his arms around the man, giving him one of his impetuous hugs. Before Cap could respond, Davey was off, running toward the deer trail and home.

The man hadn't moved, even when Naomi looked back

as she followed Davey into the woods. He still knelt on the ground, his head bowed.

∞

The damp seeped through the knees of Cap's trousers, bringing him back to the present. The clearing full of stumps. His wagon home. His new life . . . without reminders of Martha at every turn.

He retrieved the felling ax from where he had dropped it when he had heard that sickening, twisting crack of the maple tree and realized Davey was in its path. His knees still trembled at the thought of how close disaster lurked on every side of this life in the wilderness.

Cap found a rag in his toolbox and wiped the head of the ax until it was clean and dry. Winding his way between the stumps, he spanned the short distance across the clearing to his wagon, stowed the toolbox on the shelf in front of the rear wheels, and hung the ax from its hooks inside the wagon bed.

Silence rose all around him as he brought the coals of his fire back to life and rummaged through his food box for something to eat for supper. Some smoked beef and schnitz, the sack of dried apple slices his sister had sent with him, were all that he had left of his supplies. Come Monday, he would have to take some precious time to go fishing or hunting, unless he chose to starve to death here in the forest.

He set a pot near the fire with some water and the schnitz in it, wishing he had some ham. The smoked beef was food, but after almost three weeks of nothing else, he was getting hungry for something different. But he wasn't one to complain. He was thankful for what he had. Sticking a bit of the beef in his mouth, he savored the smoky, salty flavor as he waited for the water to boil.

That Davey. A grin spread over his face in spite of himself. The boy was bright and lively, a curious lad. When he had emerged from the woods during Cap's noon meal, he had changed everything. Not only did he keep the conversation going with his persistent questions, he was never still. Cap had finally told him he had to stay on the stump, out of the way, while he worked to fell the maple tree.

And those questions! Davey never stopped with his why-this and why-that until Cap was out of answers.

Staring into the flames, Cap chewed the beef, softening the tough fibers. He knew why he had enjoyed Davey's visit so much. The boy was the same age as his son would be. The son he had never known.

He put another stick on the fire, turning his thoughts in another direction, and Davey's mother came to mind. Naomi. She looked too young to be the mother of a seven-year-old, but some women looked young for their age. She hadn't mentioned a husband, beyond correcting his assumption that Eli was Davey's father, and Davey hadn't mentioned a father in his nonstop talking. Could it be that she was also widowed?

He might find out tomorrow, if he could follow the directions Eli gave him. The meeting was at one of the Yoder farms, two miles south and a half mile east. He was looking forward to meeting more of his new neighbors, here in the northern Indiana settlement. After enduring his sister Ruth's nagging for years, a new beginning in a settlement where no one knew his past was a welcome idea. Perhaps he could hope that no one would be trying to set him up with one of their daughters or offering farmland in exchange for marrying their sisters. He'd had enough of that back in Ohio.

He didn't intend to marry again just because he was lonely, or because he settled for some likely girl he could never love. When Martha had made him promise to marry again, on that horrible day when her life was draining from her, he had intended to keep that promise. But as the years passed, he hadn't met anyone who appealed to him. Now, nearly seven years after Martha's death, the sting of losing her had faded, but not the memory of the joy of being her husband. He didn't intend to settle for anything less if he married again.

Sunday morning dawned with the promise of rain. The sky above Cap's clearing was overcast with a cover of light gray clouds, a chill breeze blowing in from the northwest. Even the birds were subdued, their usual morning cacophony reduced to a few chirps from the surrounding trees. To the west, where the forest sloped toward the marshy ground along the Little Elkhart River, wisps of morning mist floated between the tree trunks. Not quite fog, but not rain either.

After grabbing a handful of the dried apples to eat as he walked, he started for the trail that ran north and south along the edge of his property line. The rain held off until he reached the crossroads where Eli had said to turn east, and he hurried to reach the meeting before the drizzle turned into the heavy rain he knew would follow it.

Once he turned east, the road was crowded with families heading to the Sabbath meeting. He caught up to a young couple and exchanged nods with the husband as they reached the yard of a two-story house. The board siding was new, covering the bare logs of the original cabin. Cap took his place in the line of men and followed them into the house for worship. He found a seat on a bench near the back of the rows.

The room filled quickly with families, young couples, and single men. Just like at home in Ohio, the young people filled the front benches, directly behind the ministers. Cap glanced at the benches on the other side of the room where the women and children sat, and sure enough, there was Davey sitting with Naomi and an older woman. Davey stood next to his mother, craning his neck to search through the rows of men until he spotted Cap and waved. Naomi shushed the boy, sitting him on the bench beside her, but not before she glanced his way and he saw a telltale blush creep into her cheeks.

As the crowded room grew quiet, Cap waited. He slid his glance to the face of the man beside him, an older man with a graying beard halfway down his chest. Bushy eyebrows knitted in concentration as the man studied his clasped hands. A stray fly circling and then landing on the man's thumb didn't distract him from his meditation. Finally, one of the ministers started the first hymn. The long, low note gained strength and volume as other members of the congregation joined in. Copies of the Ausbund were scattered among the congregation so that everyone was able to follow the words.

The familiar sense of unease tugged at Cap. He knew the hymn they were singing, understood the words of praise to the Lord, and he knew what to expect next as another one of the ministers called them to prayer. A kneeling prayer, long enough to make his knees ache in agony, followed by more singing, and then sermons until noon. A simple meal, fellowship with the community, and the long walk home to his empty clearing.

He let his gaze wander around the crowded room, finally stopping when he saw Naomi's face. Davey's mother held a copy of the Ausbund, sharing it with the women sitting near her. Her face was peaceful as she sang, as if she really was singing to a God who was with them in this room.

Cap glanced up at the ceiling of painted boards and mentally shook off the thought. The Lord was in his place, and Cap was in his. That was the way it should be.

Naomi had been painfully aware of her new neighbor sitting to her left and slightly behind her all through the morning. She hadn't planned to look for him until the noon meal after the service, but when Davey had erupted with delight and she had looked to see what he wanted to show her, she had met his smiling gaze in spite of herself. For the rest of the morning, no matter how hard she tried to concentrate on the worship, his dark brown eyes were all she saw.

But now, with the service ended, she had tasks to do that would keep her mind off of Cap Stoltzfus. While Davey ran off to play with the other children, Naomi threw herself into the final preparations for the noon meal. Annalise Yoder had prepared a huge kettle of bean soup the day before, and Naomi ladled the steaming, savory stew into bowls and handed them to others, who set them on the long tables for the first sitting.

The ministers and older men ate first, and as soon as they were done, the bowls were washed and filled again. Naomi ladled soup until the kettle was nearly empty, and then it was finally her turn to sit at the table with the other young, unmarried women. Susan Gingerich took a seat on the bench beside her.

"Have you met the new man from Ohio?" Susan broke pieces of cornbread into her soup. "Isn't he the best-looking man you've ever seen?"

Naomi shifted slightly. "I met him yesterday. His farm joins ours on the north side."

Susan's brow lifted. "Is that right? He came by to visit with your daed?"

"I went to his clearing to fetch Davey."

Susan's brow lifted even higher. The Gingerich family had come to Indiana from Wayne County, Ohio, at the end of the winter, and Naomi hadn't been able to get to know Susan very well yet. Her family had settled in the western part of the community, near Rock Creek, in Elkhart County. Naomi felt her cheeks heat as Susan prepared to ask the question that new folks always posed whenever Davey was mentioned.

"I've been wanting to ask you." Susan's voice dropped to a whisper. "What happened to Davey's father?"

Naomi stifled a sigh and covered it with a spoonful of soup. As she ate that spoonful, and the next, she wondered what would happen if she told Susan something that would send gossiping tongues wagging. But she couldn't lie. Davey's story wasn't anything she was ashamed of.

"Davey's parents were killed in a storm when he was little. Our family took him in, and I became his mother."

As she blew on her next spoonful of the thick bean soup, she glanced at Susan's face. A frown passed quickly before the other girl recovered.

"That's a terrible thing for him. It must be hard for you, though, to have to care for such an active boy. Were you and his real mother close friends?"

Naomi ignored the slight. As far as she was concerned,

her adoption of Davey made her his real mother, even if she hadn't given birth to him. "They were strangers to us. We found Davey hiding in his family's cabin after it had been destroyed by a twister." Naomi's stomach wrenched as it always did when the memories of that day surfaced. How they had found Davey's parents and baby sister in the wrecked cabin, and Davey hiding in the fireplace. From the moment she had taken him into her arms and her heart, Davey had been her son. It was a feeling she had never been able to explain.

"How long have you and your family lived in Indiana?" Susan smiled at her, friendly now that Davey's background had passed inspection.

"We moved from Somerset County three years ago."

"Somerset County? In Pennsylvania? Most of the folks who live in our part of the district are from Ohio."

Naomi took a piece of cornbread from the plate that was being passed down the table. "And most of this part of the district was settled by families from Pennsylvania. Folks like to settle near their friends and family."

"I suppose so." Susan looked toward the barnyard where the men had gathered to talk. "I wonder why Cap Stoltzfus chose to buy land in this part of the district. After all, he's from Ohio too."

"Did you know him when you lived there?"

Susan shook her head. "He must be from Holmes County. There are some pretty tradition-minded folks down by Walnut Creek, and we never had much to do with them."

When Susan turned to say something to the woman sitting on the other side of her, Naomi stood, taking her empty soup bowl and Susan's to be washed. This wasn't the first time someone had spoken openly about the distance between the two parts of the Indiana church district, but she didn't want to hear it. The folks in Holmes and Wayne Counties in Ohio were different districts, but they were still Amish. Susan wasn't the first person she had heard who talked as if there was some kind of wall between the two counties. If they weren't careful, the same kind of division could happen here.

After the dishes were clean, Naomi found her sister, Mattie Yoder, and their friend, Hannah Bender. Hannah scooted over on their bench so that Naomi could sit between them and threaded her arm through hers.

"We don't get to see each other as much as we did in the winter, since we've been so busy planting the gardens and all." Hannah squeezed Naomi's arm. "What have you been doing lately?"

"The same things you have been, for sure. Getting the garden ready, cleaning out the potato hole—"

"Now you sound like Jenny Smith." Mattie laughed as she said it. Jenny lived on the farm south of Mattie and Jacob. Her father had been one of the first pioneers in the area fifteen years before and was one of their few non-Amish neighbors. "She always calls their root cellar a potato hole."

Naomi laughed with her. "Jenny's way of talking is so funny, I find myself using her phrases instead of our own. Besides, when the only vegetables in the root cellar are potatoes, we may as well call it a potato hole."

Hannah turned to Mattie. "Did Jacob give you the carrot seeds I sent over? They will be a fine addition to our gardens this spring."

As Mattie and Hannah continued discussing their gardens, Naomi's attention was drawn to her mamm, sitting on a bench across the room with Annalise Yoder, Hannah's mother. Annalise was holding her granddaughter, Hannah's new baby, born just a month earlier. The baby lay in her grandmother's arms with her face turned slightly, fast asleep. Mamm held her four-month-old granddaughter, Isaac and Emma's Dorcas, while she slept. The two grandmothers chatted quietly, content to let the babies sleep. Annalise kept one eye on the group of children playing in the yard, where her daughter, Margli, and some of the other girls were playing with the little children. Annalise's three-year-old twins, Gideon and Rachael, were among them.

If Mattie felt left out when the young mothers of the community discussed diapers and feedings, she never showed it. She and Jacob had been married for more than two years now, but hadn't been blessed with any little ones yet. But Naomi felt the pain of her own empty arms as she grew older and no man considered her a good companion for marriage, or even friendship. Even with Davey to care for, she still couldn't resign herself to never giving him a father, or brothers and sisters. If she felt this way, how must Mattie feel as the months and years passed by?

Jan Drexler brings a unique understanding of Amish traditions and beliefs to her writing. Her ancestors were among the first Amish, Mennonite, and Brethren immigrants to Pennsylvania in the 1700s. Their experiences are the basis for her stories. Jan lives in South Dakota with her husband, their four adult children, two active dogs, and a cat. When she isn't writing, she enjoys hiking the Black Hills and the Badlands. She is the author of *Hannah's Choice* and the Love Inspired novels *The Prodigal Son Returns*, *A Mother for His Children*, and *A Home for His Family*.

Meet
Jan Drexler

www.jandrexler.com

Learn about the Amish

Find recipes, sewing, and quilting patterns

And more!

"A great read for anyone who enjoys a page-turning mix of appealing characters, exciting story action, sweet romance, and interesting history."

—Ann H. Gabhart, bestselling author of *The Innocent*

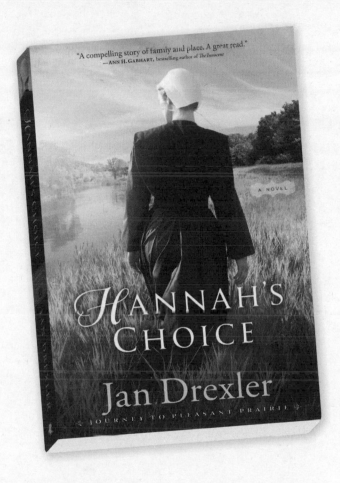

"A compelling story of family and place. A great read."
—ANN H. GABHART, bestselling author of *The Innocent*

A NOVEL

*H*ANNAH'S CHOICE

Jan Drexler

JOURNEY TO PLEASANT PRAIRIE

When two young men seek her hand in marriage—one offering the home she craves and the other promising the adventure of following God's call west—Hannah Yoder must discover what her heart desires.

Я Revell

a division of Baker Publishing Group
Grand Rapids, Michigan

Available wherever books and ebooks are sold.